BLAKE FRIEDMANN
Literary, T.V. & Film Agency
37-41 Gower Street
London WC1E 6HH
Telephone : 071 631 4331
Fax: 071 323 1274
Tlx: 262433 Ref: W6867

SO FAR FROM HOME

SO FAR
FROM HOME

James Mitchell

HEADLINE

First published in Great Britain in 1995
by HEADLINE BOOK PUBLISHING

10 9 8 7 6 5 4 3 2 1

British Library Cataloguing in Publication Data

Mitchell, James
So Far from Home
I.   Title
823.914 [F]

ISBN 0-7472-1197-3

Typeset by Keyboard Services, Luton, Beds

Printed and bound in Great Britain by
Mackays of Chatham PLC, Chatham, Kent

HEADLINE BOOK PUBLISHING
A division of Hodder Headline PLC
338 Euston Road
London NW1 3BH

For Simon and Janice

NATASHA

1

The Reverend Matthew Tyrrwhitt opened the anthology at his favourite poem, Gray's *Elegy written in a Country Churchyard*, and his eyes went at once to his favourite line: *And Melancholy marked him for her own*. The parson considered it and found it perfect, as he always did, for Melancholy had marked him, too: he had so much to endure, and for so many reasons. But the thing was that Melancholy could be, if approached in the right spirit, a soothing, perhaps even a pleasurable experience. Certainly the poet Gray had made it seem so. A country churchyard was essential, to be sure, but then he had a country churchyard within twenty yards of his front door. Music, too, would have been a help, to evoke a mood at once sombre and beautiful, and unreal. That tune Pavlova danced to, that would be perfect. *The Dying Swan* – yes, that was it. Next time he was in Newcastle he would buy the record, and persuade Oliver to let him use the gramophone. After all, he thought, it's my gramophone.

In the meantime he could sit in the comfortable silence of his study, and ponder the reasons why Melancholy had marked him. There was, after all, nothing else to do till tea-time. Without doubt his late wife was the most important reason, and yet this on the face of it was strange: she was his *late* wife after all. However, without Augusta there would have been no Oliver, no George. Plenty of cause for Melancholy there . . .

Moreover, she had not been nearly so rich as he had been led to believe, and he was a Tyrrwhitt and second cousin to an earl, a man who should have been entitled, predestined even, to preferment in the Church of England. His kinsman was on familiar terms with the Archbishop. *They played golf together*. But it wasn't enough. Preferment entailed a certain display of worldliness, and that meant money – and Augusta had brought him far, far less than was needed. Then, as a sort of negative bonus, she had presented him with sons instead, Oliver and George. His Jacob and his Esau. With those two additions to his woes, a bishopric was out of the question.

The parson contemplated his offspring in his mind's eye. Oliver (Esau) had been a good soldier and a good horseman, with a good war

3

record and a promising career ahead of him – until some fool of an Irish peasant had shot him in the leg. Oliver had come home instead to the rectory at Haydon Priors, where indeed there was room enough. Far too much room. 'Don't worry, Dad,' he would say, all too often he would say, as he limped towards the decanters. 'I'll never leave you.' His father was quite sure he meant it. In Ireland Oliver had learned a great deal about inflicting pain.

Then there was George (Jacob), the smooth man. Goodness how smooth. Successful, too. A first-rate solicitor with an assured income, he was already a partner, and if he too lived at the vicarage at least he was out during the day. The trouble was that he was so clumsy. Incapable of crossing a room without tripping on a rug or breaking a piece of china. And then there were his ludicrous war wounds. Even in the privacy of his own mind the Reverend Matthew Tyrrwhitt thought it best not to dwell on them. Instead he tried to remember the tune of *The Dying Swan*. He had heard it only once, shortly after that conference in Canterbury, when he'd slipped across to Paris for the weekend and watched Pavlova dance. Melancholy had marked her all right, but the tune would not come . . . Coal popped in the fire and he opened his eyes. Mrs Greenhalgh stood beside him. His housekeeper. More Melancholy, he thought. A bishop would have had a butler. True, Mrs Greenhalgh was very pretty, if mature, but what was that to him?

Mrs Greenhalgh said, 'There's a Young Person to see you.'

This wasn't Melancholy. This was a damn nuisance. 'Young Person' from Mrs Greenhalgh meant young woman, and almost certainly what Mrs Greenhalgh would call 'in trouble'. Young persons were the concern of his curate in charge at the nearby pit village of Slagsby, which was where they got into trouble. They had no business pestering him at Haydon Priors.

'I hardly think—' he began.

Behind Mrs Greenhalgh the young person spoke. 'If you have not finished sleeping I can wait,' she said, 'provided that your woman brings me an ashtray.' It was a pretty voice, low-pitched and with the hint of an accent, but by the end of the sentence the parson knew that the days of tranquil Melancholy were over. He turned, and stared. Normally his manners were polished, his control good, but this time he gawped like a hobbledehoy. He couldn't help it.

She was quite short, but with a grace that made her seem taller than she was. Neat figure, a very pale complexion – and what he could see of her hair beneath the cloche hat was a gleaming black that glowed like the coals in the scuttle: but it was the clothes that made him stare.

4

Somehow he knew at once that they had been made in Paris: a suit of a blue he had thought belonged only on peacocks, with a skirt indecorously short but cut by a master, and shoes of glacé kid that were precisely the colour of the suit. In her hand she carried a handbag of embroidered silk, with colours enough for a sunburst. There were no visible signs that she was in trouble, but that was his only consolation.

'Forgive me,' he said, 'but I do not think we've met. I feel sure that I would remember if we had.'

She chuckled, and he thought of a cat that purrs just before it leaps.

'We have not met,' she said. 'How could we? This is my first visit to England. But we are relatives, I'm told.'

'Indeed?'

'Yes. My mother was Diana Tyrrwhitt. She had a sister called Clemency, who married a Frenchman called Jacquard.'

The parson felt like a prisoner who hears the last bolt rammed home. There could be no escape.

'They were my cousins,' he said.

'So the Jacquards told me. I have been staying with them.'

'In Paris?'

'Yes. It was interesting. Delightful too, sometimes.'

The parson tried not to look at her legs. They were pretty legs, and sheathed in silk, but no concern of a parson, especially in his own parsonage.

'Forgive me,' the young person said, 'but is it not the custom in England to ask a lady to be seated?'

'Oh, good lord,' Tyrrwhitt said. 'Forgive me, please.'

Mrs Greenhalgh cleared her throat, a painstaking business. 'Excuse me, sir,' she said, 'but Miss has brought luggage. Rather a lot of luggage.' The thought seemed to please her for some reason.

Miss at this point was opening her handbag, and taking from it a cigarette case, cigarette holder and lighter. Parson and housekeeper alike stared as if she had produced a loaded revolver.

'We'll talk about that later,' said Tyrrwhitt at last. 'Bring tea for now.' He turned to the Young Person. 'You like tea?'

'You have a samovar?'

'Certainly not,' said Tyrrwhitt. He had no idea what it was, but it sounded exotic.

'You have no vodka?'

'No.' Tyrrwhitt knew what that was, but it was not the time for a homily.

'I'm told it is possible to acquire good vodka here but it takes time,' the Young Person said. 'Tea will do.' She turned to Mrs Greenhalgh.

'Bring me an ashtray at once.' To her own amazement, and Tyrrwhitt's, Mrs Greenhalgh rushed off to find one. Miss chose a seat near the fire and lit a cigarette. Tyrrwhitt felt that she should at least have asked permission first, but found it impossible to say so.

'Is she yours?' the girl asked him.

'I beg your pardon?' said Tyrrwhitt.

'The *služanka* – the servant. In my grandfather's day one owned one's servants, rather as one owned one's horses and dogs. Later they were freed, but they stayed on with their masters. It was a great nuisance.'

'How a nuisance?'

'They ate rather a lot and worked very little. But then Lenin came along in 1917 and set us free from them.'

'Quite so,' said Tyrrwhitt, and then: 'Forgive me, but I do not know your name.'

'Natalya,' she said. 'The Countess Natalya Krilova. But Léonide Jacquard thought it would be best if I became Natasha Tyrrwhitt, though it is not easy for me to say.' She flicked ash towards the fire, more a ritual gesture than deliberate aim. It landed just short of the carpet. 'I have a letter,' she said.

'For me?'

'As much as anyone.' Tyrrwhitt flinched, but took the envelope she gave him. *To Whom It May Concern*, it began.

Mrs Greenhalgh scurried in with an ashtray as Tyrrwhitt read the letter, looking first for the signature: *Jean-Claude Jacquard*.

Natasha, Jean-Claude informed him, was a delightful girl who had many stories about life in Russia – some droll, some heart-rending. To have entertained her was not merely a privilege, it was a duty. She was a relative by marriage after all, and a member of the old and so distinguished Krilov family. But now it was felt that Natasha would be best among those of her own blood. Perhaps Lord Kielder himself might be the one to decide who should be the mentor for such a charming young woman? Her clothes and jewelry were the gift of the Jacquards, and there was also an allowance until more suitable arrangements could be made, as well as a legacy, but that was conditional on her staying away from the Jacquard family. They had enjoyed the pleasure of her company for ten months. To see her again soon might well impede the process of her assimilation by the Tyrrwhitt family . . .

'Monsieur Jacquard writes that your family was distinguished.'

'The Tyrrwhitts?' The news seemed to surprise her.

'The Krilovs.'

'Distinguished? Yes, I suppose they were. One was shaved

6

personally by Peter the Great – he disliked beards, you know – and one was the lover of Catherine the Great, though I do not think that that is a claim to distinction—'

'Certainly not,' said Tyrrwhitt.

'—So was every other officer in his regiment. But there were also a poet Krilov, several ambassadors, and a general who won a skirmish at the time of Napoleon. I suppose they were distinguished, in a small way.'

'Why do you say were?'

'Because they are all dead. Every one. Except me – and I have become a Tyrrwhitt.'

'Forgive me,' the Reverend said cautiously, 'but are you quite sure?'

'Oh yes,' she said. 'Dimitri saw the records.'

'Dimitri?'

'Forgive *me*,' said Natasha, 'but we do not talk about Dimitri. Not yet.'

She threw her cigarette stub into the fire and immediately lit another, inserting it into her holder which was made, the parson guessed, of jade.

'This Lord Kielder,' she said. 'He is also a count? No. You do not use the word. A *Graf*?'

'An earl,' Tyrrwhitt said. 'The Earl of Kielder. The word is different but the rank is the same.'

'In London I was told that he was in Africa, slaughtering animals.'

Tyrrwhitt did not wish to know who had told her. He wasn't strong enough to know. Not yet.

'We call it hunting big game,' he said.

'They used to do that in Russia, too. There are those who say we still do. Are you not wondering how I got here?'

'Train and ferry, I should suppose,' said Tyrrwhitt. 'Unless you came by aeroplane.' She looked the sort who might. 'I can think of no other way.'

'Léonide brought me,' she said, and smiled. 'When she found out that Lord Kielder was away, she said I must come here. In London we stayed at the Ritz – which is not so nice as the one in Paris, though with not nearly so many Americans. But I did not mean that.'

'What, then?' Tyrrwhitt looked at the clock. It was almost four. Mrs Greenhalgh always brought tea at four, and he very much wanted his tea. Needed it.

'She brought me out of Russia,' said Natasha. 'Until I met her I thought it would be impossible to leave Russia. Did they love me so

7

much, those comrades, that they could not bear to let me go? I doubt it very much. After all, they sent my father to Siberia to die, and they shot my mother before my eyes so that I could be quite sure she was dead.'

Tyrrwhitt said desperately, 'How did she get you out?'

'She is a Communist,' Natasha said, 'and a poet. Silly poems about the Revolution. She had also met Comrade Lenin. He was the one who gave permission for me to leave. She still has the paper. When she thinks I'm not watching she kisses it. Like a relic. But I always watch. Quite soon you will find that is true.'

Inside his mind Tyrrwhitt screamed: 'Tea. I must have *tea*!'

From the hallway he could hear the voice of his son Oliver, declaiming verse like a bad actor. That meant he was drunk, and *that* meant he had been to his club in Newcastle. Today it was Rupert Brooke. Oliver despised Rupert Brooke, even if he was dead.

> *'God,* (Oliver bawled) *I will pack, and take a train,*
> *And get me to England once again!*
> *For England's the one land I know,*
> *Where men with Splendid Parts may go.'*

There was a sudden, tremendous crash. Oliver, it seemed, had tripped over Natasha's luggage. Definitely not a day for quiet Melancholy, Tyrrwhitt thought, but at least Oliver was silent now.

He looked at Natasha, whose face remained impassive. Her colloquial English was by no means perfect, he thought, but she seemed intelligent and perceptive. She obviously knew that what she had just heard was improper.

'My son Oliver,' he explained. 'My elder son. He fought for three years on the Western Front.' She said nothing. 'He was wounded but recovered, and won medals. He was a good soldier – with the prospect of a fine career in the Army after the war – until he was shot in the leg by a Fenian hooligan. His leg was irreparably damaged, and his career in the Army was finished.'

'What happened to the hooligan?' Natasha asked. It was not the question he had expected, but she seemed to consider it important.

'He was shot dead.'

'They never believe it will happen,' she said. 'Till it does.'

Stick to the point, Tyrrwhitt told himself. 'The thing is,' he said, 'that when he had to leave the Army, Oliver knew his life was over.'

Fool, she thought. Life is never over until you are dead. Dimitri would never—

'And so poor Oliver is a little weak sometimes,' Tyrrwhitt said,

8

'and drinks rather too much – and makes up rather rude parodies of poems and songs.'

'Parodies?'

She had lived in Paris, he remembered, and in any case, all aristocratic Russians spoke French rather better than they spoke English.

'Pastiches,' he said, and she nodded.

The fat priest is upset, she thought, not for this Oliver but for himself, because his son has disturbed his repose and so have I. She wondered why it was that priests were so often fat as Mrs Greenhalgh brought in tea, and then she knew. Sandwiches, and three different kinds of cakes – two of them made with cream – *and* chocolate biscuits. The wonder would have been if the fat priest had been thin.

Tyrrwhitt began to question her about the Tsar and Tsarina, and their children too – the four pretty daughters and Alexei, the even prettier son. Yes, of course, she said. Of course she had known them. In St Petersburg, at court, it was impossible not to know them – poor, bewildered Nicholas, who grew even more bewildered as the war was lost, and his wife who thought that all would be well, if only everyone would do what Rasputin wanted. Especially the ladies.

Natasha had no doubt that the Reverend Matthew Tyrrwhitt would have liked to ask her about Rasputin, perhaps even wondering if she had ever done it with him (though as Dimitri said, at twelve she would have been far too young. Rasputin liked his fruit ripe). He didn't, of course. He was the sort of priest who was far too shy to ask about such things, much as he might want to. Perhaps, she thought, if he ever deserves a treat, I shall tell him how Prince Yusupov and his gang murdered Rasputin. Just like the cinema. Only they were all as big fools as the Tsar, Dimitri had said. They left it much too late.

The study door opened and a young man came in. His hair was damp, water splashed on his face, and he had changed his shirt, of that she was sure. Pale, too. Perhaps he had made himself sick?

'Ah, Oliver,' Tyrrwhitt said. 'I've no doubt Mrs Greenhalgh told you we have a visitor? This is Natasha – a kinswoman of ours – just arrived from Paris, and Russia before that. Quite an Odyssey.'

'Yes indeed,' said Oliver, and limped towards her. 'How delightful to meet you.' She offered him her hand, and he took it and bowed. Not ungraceful, she thought, but well below the standards of St Petersburg.

Oliver sat and she poured tea for him as his father began to tell of her arrival. Not a good-looking face, she thought, but a strong one:

9

the face of a man who should be out doing things, not limping around a vicarage. The look of a People's Commissar perhaps? She did not think that she would ever like him.

'Very interesting,' Oliver said at last, 'but I'm sure your escape from Russia would be an even more exciting story.'

'Escape?' said Natasha, who seemed surprised. 'Léonide simply took me away.'

He grinned at her. The grin was at once mocking and attractive. 'No dangers?' he said. 'No adventures?'

'Perhaps a few.' To tell the truth would be to risk being branded a liar.

When the soldier shot her mother, she had fled. The soldier had fired at her, too, but missed. (The standard of marksmanship in the Tsar's army was dreadful, Dimitri had told her. Yet another example of the goodness of God.) She had roamed the streets alone for two nights, then one of Ivan's gang had found her and taken her to Ivan. Just as well, she thought. For two days and nights I hadn't eaten, nor did I wish to live. Ivan's gang changed all that. Like herself, their parents had all been wealthy, and like herself they were now destitute. But they were together – and that one fact gave them the will to live. Besides, if they did not stay together, if they were caught, they would be sent to some dreadful 'Rehabilitation Centre', perhaps in Siberia. It was better, much better, to stay with Ivan's gang and become a bandit.

Because she was pretty, she was taught how to be bait: the tasty morsel to entice the kind of fish who liked them young. She was just thirteen at the time. All the same she had learned to swing her hips and make the most of what breasts she had as she lured the fish down the alley to where her room was supposed to be . . . where the bigger boys waited with clubs and stones. (The younger boys and girls acted as lookouts, and very proficient they were.)

She had learned to spot the fish who might have money, or better still, something to trade, like a watch or a ring. It all went on food. Cigarettes, sometimes, for the ones who had done especially well, and vodka when the nights grew colder, but mostly they bought food. When there was none they talked about it. Remembered meals at birthday parties or in restaurants, from that fabulous time when they had all lived in palaces. Fabulous indeed, she thought. Like the Fables of Aesop.

'It must have been a difficult time, too,' said Oliver.

She smiled. 'Difficult' was such a silly word to use. Almost as silly as 'exciting'.

'Why, yes,' she agreed. 'It was difficult, sometimes.'

'And yet you smile,' he said.

'Because I am not there,' she said. 'I am here.'

'A sight for sore eyes,' said Oliver.

Hastily his father said, 'Would it be in order to ask how you met Mademoiselle Jacquard?'

Because Dimitri was dead, she thought, and I was on my own. Back in St Petersburg, which I now must call Leningrad. Before he died, Dimitri had given me papers – he was very good at papers – and I had a job in a cigarette factory, which was as good a job as you could get, unless you became greedy and stole too many and they put you in prison. The cigarette factory was extolled as a model, and visiting foreigners came there too. Like the French Communist, Marcel. But even if he were a Communist, he was French, too, and invited her out to dinner.

They went to a restaurant that had once been her parents' favourite, but which now only foreigners and important Party members could afford. Fortunately for her, the maître and waiters had all been sent away. Siberia again, no doubt, to learn about coal mining. But they had kept on the kitchen staff. The food was as good as ever. Marcel had been astonished, but then all Frenchmen were astonished when they ate a good meal outside France. He had asked her if she were a Communist, she remembered, but she hadn't laughed. She had cast down her eyes instead and said meekly that in Russia to be a Communist was not a right, it was a privilege – and that to earn that privilege was her most cherished hope. He had then invited her to be his mistress. Among the benefits this would bestow, apparently, were regular meals and her hope's fulfilment. It was the best offer she had had till then: better than luring 'fish', better than making and stealing cigarettes. And as she had no hope of leaving Russia she would be safest joining the Party. If she intrigued and got on, she might even eat in good restaurants and pay her own bills. It was definitely an offer, but before she could reply to it Léonide appeared – and just as well, she thought. Marcel would have been awful to sleep with. On the other hand, Léonide had instantly spotted her resemblance to the Tyrrwhitt who had married into the Jacquard family, which made it necessary to be rid of Marcel. This she had done by pretending to fall violently in love at first sight with Léonide, which in one way had not been a good idea.

She turned to Tyrrwhitt. 'I met Mademoiselle Jacquard in a restaurant,' she explained.

'I hope it was a good one,' Oliver said. An ironist?

'Extremely. I was taken there by a French Communist who was trying to seduce me.' Oliver snorted, and his father dropped his

11

cream cake. It had needed but that. 'Léonide also is a French Communist. She joined us, and the man left.'

'Hardly flattering,' said Oliver.

'She told him to go. She was a more important Communist than he was. She had dined with Lenin four times.'

'For a party so devoted to idealism they seem to attach a great deal of importance to food,' said Oliver.

'If you persist in interrupting me I cannot answer your father's question.'

Oliver glared, and when his father said, 'Yes, do be quiet, there's a good chap,' he glared even more, which pleased her. It showed how easy it was to make him angry.

'One of our family married into hers,' said Natasha.

'Your Aunt Clemency,' said Tyrrwhitt. Natasha looked at him. 'Sorry,' he said. 'I'm as bad as Oliver.'

Oliver glared again. Really, it was quite a pleasant afternoon.

'Léonide saw that I resembled Clemency Tyrrwhitt, and in the end I told her why. She was horrified.'

For once the parson became querulous. 'I don't see why,' he said. 'We're a perfectly respectable family.'

'But some of us are bourgeois, and some are aristos.'

'But dash it she's a bourgeois herself,' said Tyrrwhitt.

'Léonide has renounced the bourgeoisie,' Natasha said firmly. 'She is now a committed artist and intellectual.'

'Sounds more like a—' began Oliver, but this time it was his father who glared and he was silent.

'If you were about to use a coarse phrase for stupid person, then you are right,' Natasha said. 'She is that. But she is also clever.'

'*Clever?*' This time father and son spoke together.

'Do you think it is an easy matter to take a Russian out of Russia?'

'Forgive me,' Tyrrwhitt said, 'but from the way you speak you seem to consider your homeland a most unpleasant place.'

'It is.'

'And yet – forgive me again, my dear child, but I must ask you this – the Dean of Canterbury visited Russia not long ago. He went everywhere. Hospitals, factories, collective farms. Even the ballet. He was most impressed.' She waited. 'He is my superior in the Church, and an honest and dedicated Christian. I may not share his politics, but I would never question his regard for the truth. Would you ask me to believe that he lied about your country?'

My country died in October 1917, she thought, but I shall not tell you so.

'Of course not,' she said aloud. 'I am sure he said what he believed to be true. And he was not alone, was he? There was a duchess, and that Irish playwright, and so many of your Members of Parliament. Comrade Lenin had a phrase for them – "the useful fools".'

Oliver gave a yelp of laughter.

'Forgive me,' Tyrrwhitt said again, 'but I must ask you this. Who told you about Lenin's words?'

'A man who is dead,' said Natasha. 'A man whose word I believe as you believe your superior priest.'

Her body stirred in the vast leather chair. It was no more than reaction to comfort and the fire's warmth, but Oliver was watching her as if she had started to undress, and that would not do. Not yet anyway. She turned to the – inferior priest? Surely that couldn't be right?

'If you will excuse me,' she said. 'It is a long journey from London. I should like to lie down for a little, before you decide what to do with me.'

'Decide what to do with you?' said Oliver. 'You'll stay here, of course.'

'Until Lord Kielder returns from Africa,' said his father. 'He is the head of the family, after all. The decision must be his.'

'But he can't just send her away,' Oliver said. 'Any more than we can.'

'He may wish Natasha to live with him,' said his father.

What Oliver wants, she thought. What Lord Kielder wants. And no doubt what the still-unknown brother George wants, too. No mention of what Natasha wants.

And yet hers were the only wants that mattered ... must be fulfilled. It was apparent that she would have to be more than a little devious about how she achieved this, but for the Countess Natalya Krilova, deviousness had never been a problem.

2

The vicar rang for Mrs Greenhalgh, who took Natasha up to her room. Her luggage was already there. Nine pieces, including a trunk.

'I got the gardener to bring it up,' Mrs Greenhalgh said. 'And the boot boy.'

'Quite right,' said Natasha.

'Shall I unpack, miss?'

'Yes, please.' Natasha handed over her keys. It was a pretty room, light and airy, yet warm. Someone had lit a fire. The boot boy, perhaps? She sat by it in a neat little Victorian armchair, smoking a cigarette and watching Mrs Greenhalgh at work. The housekeeper didn't seem to mind a bit.

'You have lovely things, miss,' she said.

'Paris,' said Natasha.

'Yes indeed, miss,' said Mrs Greenhalgh, taking Paquin and Poiret and Chanel from the trunk.

'The Jacquard family were most generous,' said Natasha. 'Also, the Tyrrwhitt who married one of theirs left money for my mother. They gave it to me.'

'Lady Clemency, miss.' Natasha nodded. 'You reminded me of her, miss. She was a spirited lady, too.'

'You knew her?'

'Not for long, miss. I was lady's maid to the Countess – Lord Kielder's wife. Lady Clemency went off to Paris soon after I came to Kielder Hall.'

'What happened to the Countess?'

'She died in childbirth miss. The baby died, too. A boy it was.'

Natasha said something in Russian.

'It was sad, miss.'

'I am sure. Has the Earl other children?'

'No, miss.'

'Very sad,' said Natasha, and then: 'This is a nice room.'

'Not what you're used to though, miss,' said Mrs Greenhalgh.

The palace in St Petersburg? The hut in Siberia? The house in the VIIIth arrondissement?

15

'Not exactly, no,' she said.

'The Russian aristocracy always had high standards.' Mrs Greenhalgh's voice was approving. 'We had one or two up at the Hall. And my Herbert said the same.'

'What is a Herbert?' Natasha asked.

'He was my husband,' Mrs Greenhalgh said. 'Warrant Officer Class Two, Royal Northumbrians. Same regiment as Mr Oliver.'

'Is it a good regiment?'

'Pretty good, miss. Not the Guards or the Rifle Brigade, but better than most.'

'And your husband went to Russia?'

'Murmansk,' said Mrs Greenhalgh. '1919. He died there, miss. Pneumonia.'

There is altogether too much death, thought Natasha. She said aloud: 'Was Mr Oliver a good officer?'

'Herbert reckoned so, miss. A one for getting on, Mr Oliver.'

'Is that bad?'

'Oh no, miss. Only he volunteered to fight the Fenians and that was a mistake, even if he hadn't been shot.'

'Why is that?'

Mrs Greenhalgh said repressively, 'Fighting Irishmen is low, miss.'

'I should like to bathe,' Natasha said. 'Is that possible?'

'There's a geyser, miss,' the other woman told her, 'but you have to watch it. Better let me run your bath.'

'Of course,' Natasha said.

Serves you right, Mrs Greenhalgh admonished herself. You didn't suppose she'd run her own bath, did you? All the same, it's good to look after a proper toff again. The genuine article. You can always tell.

When she came back, Natasha had taken her clothes off and was hunting for a dressing gown. And very nice too, Mrs Greenhalgh thought. Very nice indeed. Proper woman's body. Out then in and out again, and all in proportion. Not like the flat-chested miseries you saw these days. Talk about famine relief ... All the same, she'd picked up a couple of scars somewhere. Not that they'd show, not even with the kind of evening dresses she'd bought in Paris. Natasha pulled a piece of translucent silk from the wardrobe, and Mrs Greenhalgh said firmly, 'No, miss.' Natasha turned to face her, undisturbed by the fact of her nakedness, perhaps even unaware that she was naked.

'I brought you this,' Mrs Greenhalgh said, and produced a woollen robe a nun would have thought discreet. 'Belonged to the vicar's

16

wife, miss. It can be very draughty down that passage, and Mr Oliver's on this floor.'

Natasha wallowed in her bath, and tolerated the scent of the late Mrs Tyrrwhitt's bath salts, then went back to her room. The parson's wife had been quite large: only Natasha's face was visible in the robe. One door across the corridor was slightly ajar. Was Oliver peeping to see Venus arise from the foam? she wondered. If so, there was a hell of a lot of dark-grey foam. All he would see of Venus was the face.

Mrs Greenhalgh helped her to dress, brushed her hair and manicured her nails. She had chosen the Paquin: a short evening dress of a lemon colour that glowed even in the dim light of the bedroom, and a diamond necklace that had once belonged to Lady Clemency Jacquard.

'Very nice, miss,' said Mrs Greenhalgh. 'Now, if there's nothing else I'd better see about the dinner.'

'You're the cook, too?' Natasha was startled.

'Oh no, miss. Housekeeper, that's me, and acting temporary lady's maid, as my Herbert would say. We do run to a cook. Only she needs watching.'

'I see,' said Natasha.

'I daresay you do, miss,' said Mrs Greenhalgh. It didn't sound like the VIIIth arrondissement at all.

'Before dinner,' said Natasha, 'will there be drinks?'

'Whisky for Mr Oliver,' said Mrs Greenhalgh. 'I don't think the Reverend's ever heard of cocktails.'

'And wine?'

'Christmas and birthdays, miss. Not otherwise.'

'But there *is* a cellar?'

'Oh yes, miss. Some of the claret's quite decent.'

'Would you tell Mr Tyrrwhitt that my doctor says I must drink wine – red wine – every day. Champagne also, whenever possible. I was very ill in Russia, you see, and wine is essential. The Jacquard family were most understanding about this.'

Mrs Greenhalgh took it without a blink. 'Yes of course, miss.'

'It is very strange,' said Natasha. 'I have never stayed at a priest's house before.'

'We call it the vicarage, miss.'

'Then I shall try to call it that too,' decided Natasha, 'so long as there is wine.'

Mrs Greenhalgh left, and Natasha opened the one case for which she had not handed over the key. Inside it, amongst other things, was a bottle of vodka. Just one, she thought. Priests were often unreliable. All that faith – it upset them so.

17

There was champagne before dinner. The priest explained that it was to welcome her to the Tyrrwhitts', and she smiled and was charming, and he smiled back, even though he obviously disapproved of her dress. But there was no point in worrying about that, she thought. He would disapprove of all her dresses. She drank her champagne instead, and really it was not at all bad. Oliver, she noticed, sipped cautiously, as if astounded that there was champagne at all, regardless of quality. His brother at least looked grateful. When the priest summoned his younger son to be introduced, George approached warily, yet managed to trip on the edge of the carpet, so that the champagne slopped in his glass. Oliver assumed the satisfied look of one whose prophecy has been fulfilled.

'This is my son George,' said the priest. Unlike Oliver he seemed relieved, perhaps because none of the champagne had reached the carpet. He led Natasha forward. 'This is your kinswoman Natasha,' he said to George. 'Some might find the relationship tenuous, but I assure you it is there. In happier times she was known as Natalya Krilova, but now she has adopted our family name, and we are honoured.'

'How do you do?' said George, and offered his hand, and she took it.

'How do you do?' said Natasha.

'How strange it is to find I have such a beautiful kinswoman,' said George, and Oliver looked startled, as if George had no right to speak so prettily. She smiled at him, and drank her champagne, but more slowly. There seemed to be only one bottle.

All three men were in evening dress: the brothers in dinner jackets, the priest in some garment longer than a jacket, and with white tabs instead of a black bow tie. The sort of evening dress the priests in England wear, she thought, and looked again at George.

He had none of Oliver's obvious recklessness, but on the other hand he was prettier. *Much* prettier. And he was clever, too. As the priest rambled on about the pleasure of having such a lady to grace their dinner table, Oliver was doing his best to tease his brother, without success. George didn't even bother to reply; he merely looked at Natasha as if having her to gaze upon was a more than adequate substitute for conversation. Oliver glared again. How easy it was to make him do so. A parlourmaid came in and announced dinner at last.

'How I do run on,' said the priest. 'Such garrulity. I've become a regular chatterbox. You must blame it on the champagne.'

A priest become garrulous on one glass of champagne? she marvelled, and wondered what Rasputin would have made of that.

18

'Come, my dear,' he said and offered his arm, then to his sons: 'You two chaps make your own way in. Quite soon we must invite some ladies – make up a proper party. We can't bore Natasha with our masculine meanderings every evening.'

The dinner was much as Mrs Greenhalgh had foretold. The cook did bear watching, and had been watched just enough. There would be no threat of indigestion, but no cries of rapture, either. The Burgundy, however, achieved excellence in everything except quantity.

As they began on the savoury Oliver said, 'Do we meander, Natasha?'

The casual use of her name annoyed her, but she did not let it show. 'You talk as men talk,' she said. 'Sometimes to the point. Sometimes not.'

The conversation had been mostly about hunting, and when the Earl would come back, and a miners' strike that had happened not long before. Of the three topics, the Earl's return seemed by far the most important.

'We talk as men talk.' Oliver repeated her words as though they required much thought. 'So women don't talk as we do?'

'Of course not,' she said.

'Then how do women talk?'

'Like me,' she said. George chuckled, and Oliver glared, his fifth – or was it sixth? – glare of the day, and easily his best so far. She wondered if quite soon he might try to hit her.

'We shall forego our glass of port,' said the priest. 'It would be unkind to indulge ourselves while Natasha sits alone. Let us go to the drawing room. There is a very good chance that coffee awaits us there.'

He smiled and led out Natasha. No grace was said at the end, but one at the beginning of course, delivered by the priest in his special priestly voice, and in Latin, too.

Coffee did await them, and very nasty it was. There was no sign, either of chocolates or *petits fours*, never mind brandy. The vicarage, like its inmates, had possibilities, but there was a great deal to be done. She turned to George.

'Your father tells me you are a lawyer?'

'A solicitor,' he said.

'There is more than one kind?'

'In England, yes. Here we have barristers, too. They're frightfully grand and wear wigs and gowns and make huge sums of money – or else nothing at all.'

19

'Ah,' said Natasha. '*A Tale of Two Cities*. Bardell versus Pickwick.'

'Solicitors don't do all that badly,' said Oliver. 'Remember Dodson and Fogg.'

'Also in *Pickwick Papers*,' she said.

'Just so. But barristers stand up in court and bully juries and harangue judges, whereas solicitors make their money sitting down.'

'Perfectly true,' said George, and smiled at his brother.

'And even if they don't make vast sums, it's not exactly a pittance,' said Oliver.

'No indeed.' George nodded.

'Sitting down can be tricky sometimes,' said Oliver.

'Oh agreed,' said George, 'but one must master the art, you know, if one aspires to more than a pittance.'

She was watching a fight, she knew, and so far George was winning, but when Oliver opened his mouth again the priest said, 'I think we'll leave it there, don't you?' in the hardest voice she had yet heard him use, and Oliver was silent. The priest, it would seem, had a weapon of which his son was afraid.

'Did I tell you that Lord Kielder was in the Diplomatic Corps before he succeeded?' the priest asked Natasha.

Succeeded in what? she wondered, then realised from the reverence in his voice that he must mean the title.

'No,' she said. 'How interesting.'

'I believe, in fact I am almost sure,' he went on, 'that he was stationed for a while in St Petersburg.'

Oliver looked up.

'Then he will almost certainly have met my parents,' Natasha said.

Oliver took his brother's empty cup from him, and put it on the table. 'Better safe than sorry, old chap,' he said.

'How very kind of you, old chap,' said George, but as Oliver turned away Natasha noticed that George's hands became fists, then opened again as Oliver turned back. How sensible not to let your brother know he hurts you, she thought, but it must be a dreadful strain. Night after night, and all day too at weekends.

She waited to see if there would be brandy, or even Benedictine, but there was none. Instead the priest asked her if she played the piano. She was about to deny it – after all, there had been nothing about her piano-playing in the Jacquard letter, which of course she had read – but then it occurred to her that if she played the piano she couldn't be expected to talk as well.

'Sometimes,' she said.

'Would you do so now?' he asked, and nodded to where the piano stood: well away from the fire, but out of draughts, too. 'It was my wife's,' he told her.

Then she knew something about pianos, Natasha thought, and wondered if the late Mrs Tyrrwhitt had played well. She took off her rings and opened the piano lid, then began to pick out chords. Not bad, she thought. Neglected but not bad. Suddenly she embarked on a Chopin prélude. For some reason Westerners always expected Russians to play Chopin, even though Poles and Russians detested each other. It was perhaps a little daring to choose Chopin, particularly as a first piece, but after all she hadn't had so *very* much to drink, and anyway God was good to her. She finished in triumph. The applause was tremendous.

'But that was marvellous,' said George.

'Such technique,' said Oliver. 'Like a professional.' The priest scowled at the use of such a word.

'*Maman* used to think that I had talent. She arranged that I should attend the Conservatoire. Quite privately, of course.'

'Of course,' said the priest, and ceased to scowl.

'*Maman?*' Oliver repeated. 'That's French, isn't it?'

'People of good family often spoke French at home,' she said. 'Shall I play some more?'

'Oh please,' said George. 'That piece about the moon. A German wrote it.'

Beethoven's Piano Sonata in C Sharp Minor, she thought. *The Moonlight*. She wondered if English people knew if Beethoven had written anything else, but they all knew he had written that . . .

George waved a hand more or less in time with the first movement, then seemed vaguely surprised that there were two more.

When she finished they applauded again, but she turned down the lid and put on her rings once again.

'No more?' said the priest. He seemed disappointed.

'It's such a rare treat for us,' said George.

'Forgive me,' said Natasha, 'but I am a little tired. And anyway, surely your mother played for you?'

'Before the war,' Oliver told her. 'When we were schoolboys. She would play for us in the holidays.'

'And afterwards?'

'The war kept me rather busy,' said Oliver, 'and George didn't exactly sit it out.'

'But when the war was over?'

'She died,' said the priest. 'Of influenza. In 1919.'

'How sad for you all three,' she said. 'A house with no lady.'

'We have one now,' said Oliver.

'Yes, indeed,' said George. 'Will you play for us tomorrow?'

'Early supper tomorrow,' the priest reminded them. 'Parochial Church Council meeting. You both promised to be there.'

'The day after, then,' said George.

'The day after is Sunday,' said the vicar. 'There is music appropriate to the Sabbath, but not in the drawing room. The servants might not understand. Which reminds me.' He turned to Natasha. 'On Sunday there is Morning Prayer at nine, then Sung Eucharist at ten thirty. Highish you may say, but not too High. No bells, and certainly no incense. And of course, Evensong at six. Which will you attend on Sunday?'

Natasha said firmly, 'It is difficult.'

'You may go to both if you wish.'

'I'm afraid not,' said Natasha, still firm. 'My nearest church is rather far from here.'

'My dear girl,' said the priest. 'It's the merest stroll.'

'I belong to the Russian Orthodox Church,' said Natasha. 'The only one I know outside Russia is in Paris. There too they have music appropriate to the Sabbath. It is very beautiful.'

'But how can you be Russian Orthodox?' The priest sounded appalled. 'Your mother was an Anglican. We all are.'

'She changed,' Natasha said. 'No doubt because she loved my father. Besides, it would have been impossible to be Church of England in Russia – and even more so now. Even if Lenin did allow your Dean in.'

'Useful fool,' said Oliver, but Tyrrwhitt didn't even frown: didn't even hear. Tyrrwhitt was thinking: 'Melancholy' is far too inadequate for this. A Roman Catholic would have been bad enough, but Russian Orthodox! And what will Lord Kielder say? *He plays golf with the Archbishop*.

Natasha rose. 'Excuse me,' she said, 'but I am so sleepy.' She shook hands with Oliver and George, then inexorably offered the priest her cheek to kiss. A Russian custom, he thought miserably – a Russian *Orthodox* custom – and he kissed it.

'Goodnight,' said Natasha, and George hurried to open the door for her, kicking over a small footstool as he did so – an event apparently so commonplace that his father and brother didn't even bother to react.

When George had shut the door behind her Oliver said; 'Well, well, well.'

'And what is that intended to convey?' said his father.

'Well, Dad,' said Oliver, 'she's hardly the most typical of English roses, is she?'

His father thought of Stravinsky's *Firebird*, seen in Paris. Nijinsky and Karsavina had danced it, and he had sat in the stalls. Bow tie and dinner jacket, of course. Clerical dress would have been unthinkable.

'Perhaps not,' he said.

'Something far more exotic,' said Oliver. 'An orchid in a heated room, warm and safe, while the snow outside falls like a curtain.'

Tyrrwhitt said severely, 'These excursions into poetry are unseemly. The young lady is our guest – and our kinswoman.'

'She wasn't all that safe, either,' said George, and his father looked at him suspiciously, but George was guileless enough. His look expressed sympathy, no more.

'Quite right, George,' he said. 'There can be no doubt that Natasha has suffered. We must all do our best to make her stay here a pleasant one.'

'Until Lord Kielder returns,' said Oliver.

'Until, as you say, Lord Kielder returns.'

Natasha came back from the bathroom. Really, that thick dressing gown had been an excellent idea. There were draughts everywhere . . . In her bedroom, Mrs Greenhalgh was hanging up her clothes.

'I trust you had a pleasant evening, miss?' she said.

'Pleasant enough.' Natasha smiled. 'Three gentlemen to choose from.'

You've had your pick from better than that, Mrs Greenhalgh thought.

'The music was lovely, miss,' she said.

'I'm glad,' said Natasha. 'Did the cook enjoy it too?'

'Her?' Mrs Greenhalgh sounded scornful. 'She thinks *Lily of Laguna* is highbrow. No class at all.'

'Not even at the cooking stove,' said Natasha.

'She's a trial all right,' said Mrs Greenhalgh. 'Even a cross to bear, when you consider whose house we're in, but we're miles from anywhere here, miss, and parsons – they never attract them that's used to good service.'

'You're here,' said Natasha, and Mrs Greenhalgh smiled.

'Thank you, miss,' she said, 'but then I owed Lord Kielder a favour, and he sees I don't lose by it.'

3

The next morning she went to Newcastle to go shopping. Saturday was a busy day according to Greenhalgh, and there were frequent trains. There were also three stores with definite possibilities. In each she began by buying trivia: combs, stockings, handkerchiefs, toothbrushes, and then the sort of fancy wrapping paper that was used for birthday presents.

After that she stole things: a watch in one store, a bracelet in the second, and in the third a brooch that would be just right for Mrs Greenhalgh, once they knew each other better. Also she bought some flowers, as Dimitri had taught her. Store detectives were rarely interested in young and well-dressed ladies with flowers and wrapping paper, which could only mean a party. Later she would visit the city called York, where they held horse-races, and take the watch and bracelet to a *mont de piété*, which for some reason was known in England as a pawnbroker's, according to her dictionary.

In the meantime she went to a hotel Mrs Greenhalgh had recommended, and ate a far better lunch than the priest's cook could ever hope to achieve. It was altogether a pleasant restaurant. One man dining on his own had even attempted to – what was the English expression? – pick her up, that was it: but the head waiter had dealt with him. Rather a pity, really. He seemed rich. On the other hand she was staying with a priest, and she must try to keep certain standards. Dimitri had been firm about that, too. And she could certainly afford to pay for her own lunch. The Jacquard allowance was really quite decent. All the same, why spend your own money when you could spend other people's? Her fingers explored the watch and bracelet inside her handbag. Why indeed? she thought.

She returned to Haydon Priors much too late for tea. The priest appeared agitated. Young ladies, it seemed, were allowed to go shopping, but not for such long periods of time. She must be starving, he fussed. That she should take lunch on her own didn't even occur to him.

'I look forward to my dinner,' she said, and gave him her flowers. 'I don't know if it is the custom here, but since I cannot go to your church I should like to give you these flowers instead.'

'How very kind,' he said. 'But are you sure you can't come to my church?'

'No, no.' She was adamant. 'My parents would have been most upset. So would my priest. But I do not forget my prayers.'

The Tyrrwhitts ate an early supper, and Natasha went up to her room to dawdle and drink vodka until the three men had gone off to the Parochial Church Council, whatever that might be. When the coast was clear, Mrs Greenhalgh called her, and she went down to cold salmon and cold beef and salad, none of which appeared to have been prepared by the vicarage cook. She said so to Mrs Greenhalgh.

'Her?' Mrs Greenhalgh snorted. 'Of course not. I telephoned the Hall.'

'The Hall?'

'Kielder Hall, miss. Where His Lordship lives. The cook there's a pal of mine.'

Natasha helped herself to more salmon.

'I'm delighted to hear it,' she said. 'And the wine – did that come from the Hall, too?' The wine was a claret that Jacquard himself would have approved.

'In a way, miss,' said Mrs Greenhalgh, and Natasha asked no more questions.

She was eating grapes from His Lordship's hothouse when Mrs Greenhalgh came in once more.

'Beg pardon, miss,' she said. 'It's Mrs Cantripp.'

What is? Natasha wondered. Aloud she said, 'Oh yes?'

'Lives in the village,' Mrs Greenhalgh explained. 'A widow. Husband killed in the war. She does good works.'

And there you had her, thought Natasha. Her whole life in four sentences, and hardly a word with more than one syllable.

'But she can't have asked for me?'

'Oh no, miss. It's the vicar she wants – about the Slagsby Shoeless Children's Fund. Only he's out, miss.'

'Parochial Church Council?' said Natasha.

'Just so, miss.'

'Bring her in here,' said Natasha. 'She can have some grapes. Better bring another glass, too.'

Quality, Mrs Greenhalgh thought. You can always tell. Never mind what you want – just concentrate on what *I* want. But nice with it, and willing to share. Not that there was much left in the bottle.

26

She went out and came back with another glass and a nervous but quite pretty woman. Cantripp, thought Natasha. And a widow. She is exactly what George needs.

The clothes, however, were *not* good. Brown is the wrong colour for a lady who is almost, though not quite, a blonde, and the shoes, though expensive, were not pretty. But her features were regular, and her eyes a surprisingly deep blue. The figure, too, was pleasing. Perhaps a little too full for fashion, but acceptable in a widow – what Dimitri used to call a 'good armful'. The stockings at least were correct: silk and unsagging.

'Your stockings are good,' said Natasha.

Mrs Cantripp jumped. 'I beg your pardon?' she said.

'Quite all right,' said Natasha. 'Please sit down.'

Mrs Cantripp sat, rather nervously. True, Mrs Greenhalgh had said something about a countess . . . but a *Russian* countess? Russians were notoriously eccentric: sometimes dangerously so. Natasha poured wine into the glass Mrs Greenhalgh had brought. There wasn't an awful lot left, but what there was she passed to her guest, then rang the bell on the table.

'Oh, I don't think—' Mrs Cantripp began.

'Please take it,' Natasha said. It might have been a bagful of rubies. 'Mrs Cantripp.'

Mrs Cantripp looked up obediently. 'Yes?' she asked.

'An unusual name,' said Natasha.

'Not common,' Mrs Cantripp agreed. 'By no means.' She took a cautious sip of wine. 'And you are the Countess Natasha?'

'Not any more,' Natasha said. 'Comrade Lenin did away with all that. And Comrade Stalin and Comrade Trotsky too, of course.'

'Of course.'

'Though Comrade Trotsky has been having a bad time just lately.' The thought was pleasing. 'Are you of the Left?'

'Oh no,' said Mrs Cantripp, shocked. 'My husband always voted Conservative.'

Mrs Greenhalgh came in, and Natasha gestured to the decanter. 'We need more,' she said.

'Very good, miss,' said Mrs Greenhalgh.

'Please,' said Mrs Cantripp, 'I honestly don't think—'

'I cannot possibly permit you to drink alone,' Natasha said, and Mrs Greenhalgh took away the decanter to be filled. And just as well, thought Natasha. I drank far too much vodka before dinner. Red wine is just what I need.

'There should be a parlourmaid to do that,' she said at last.

'Perhaps it's her night off,' said Mrs Cantripp.

27

Natasha said vaguely, 'Night off?' And then: 'Oh yes, of course. In France too they had such things. You are a widow?'

'My husband was killed in France in 1918. He was a major.'

'A good regiment?'

Mrs Cantripp looked first flustered, then annoyed, like an angry pigeon, thought Natasha, who said hurriedly, 'You must excuse me, but Oliver and George set great store by such things, as indeed we did in Russia – though we still lost.'

'We, on the other hand, won,' said Mrs Cantrip. A very angry pigeon. 'Though I do see what you mean,' she went on more calmly. 'Francis was in the Border Regiment. It was considered reasonably good.'

'Like the Royal Northumbrians?' said Natasha.

'Very possibly.'

Really, she thought. The woman isn't just brusque, she's downright rude; but then Mrs Greenhalgh returned with the decanter, poured more wine. Mrs Cantripp sipped. It was jolly good wine. It must be, Mrs Cantripp thought as she sipped again, because she's foreign. Natasha offered some grapes. They too were delicious, and really a little wine could do no harm. Not this wine.

'I came to see the vicar,' she said.

'He's at the—' Natasha looked at Mrs Greenhalgh.

'Parochial Church Council, miss,' said Mrs Greenhalgh, and left them.

'About shoes – that was why you came, and children. You have children?'

'No, no,' said Mrs Cantripp.

Perhaps George will give you some, Natasha thought. It would be good for both of you.

'The shoes are for the miners' children in Slagsby. It's a village near here. You haven't been to it?'

'Not yet,' said Natasha.

Mrs Cantripp lowered her voice. 'A terrible place. Really quite dreadful. It's full of miners, you see, and they either drink and fight or else they're on strike and the poor children have no shoes, and so I help with a charity to buy shoes for them.'

'I see,' said Natasha. 'Is the vicar their priest too?'

Mrs Cantripp looked shocked. 'Oh no,' she said. 'At one time the vicar of Haydon Priors was responsible for Slagsby, but now Mr Tyrrwhitt has a curate there. He pays him himself, I believe. Mr Tyrrwhitt, I mean. Mrs Tyrrwhitt was quite comfortably off, although Oliver thinks his father had hoped for more. As a matter of fact she was my aunt.' Really, she thought, besides being so good this wine is *strong*. Even so she took another sip.

'The thing is,' she said, 'that we need more money. For the shoes for the children.'

'You want me to give you money?' Natasha looked about for her handbag. After all, she could always steal it back in Newcastle.

'No no,' said Mrs Cantripp. 'I want to organise a whist drive – or perhaps a concert. And for that I need the church hall.'

'I don't play whist because it makes me angry, but if there is a concert and you need a pianist I shall do my best for you.'

'That is most kind,' Mrs Cantripp said, and wondered how accomplished a performer Natasha was. She should be good. So many of them were. Tchaikovsky, for instance. Chaliapin.

They gossiped a little while longer. Gossip was so useful, thought Natasha. You could learn so much. About Mrs Cantripp's not-quite-wealthy aunt, for instance, who had married the priest. It was most enjoyable. But then the Tyrrwhitt men returned and the parson was archly surprised to find two ladies in his dining room, drinking wine. Mrs Cantripp blushed, but Natasha gestured at the decanter.

'We saved you some,' she said. 'Shall I ring for glasses?'

Oliver said at once, 'No, I'll do that.'

'In the drawing room,' said the vicar.

In the drawing room they talked of Slagsby and shoeless children.

'Your *curé* must be a very busy man,' Natasha said. '*Curé*? Is that right?'

'Curate,' said Oliver. 'Father's deputy, so to speak. But why should he be busy?'

'So much fighting and drinking and strikes,' said Natasha. 'It sounds exciting.'

'It is disgraceful,' said Tyrrwhitt. 'Fortunately, many of them are Nonconformist, or even Catholic, so they don't bother him unduly.'

'Not when it comes to reading the marriage service, anyway,' said Oliver.

'That will do,' snapped his father.

How beastly men were, Mrs Cantripp thought. But that was probably in reaction to the dress she's wearing. What she could only describe as a very deep pink, and Paris written all over it and showing far too much skin. And leg. Not that she hasn't got good legs, Mrs Cantripp conceded, but then so have I. Perhaps I should show mine more ... Damn wine anyway.

Gently, inexorably, Tyrrwhitt reminded them that for him at least the next day was a working day. Mrs Cantripp rose at once.

'Must you go?' asked Natasha.

'Yes indeed,' said Mrs Cantripp.

'But we haven't decided about the concert,' Natasha objected. She turned to Tyrrwhitt. 'There is to be a concert and we need the church hall. I shall play the piano.'

Tyrrwhitt disliked concerts, but if he refused permission Lord Kielder might hear of it, and the Earl, like Natasha, was musical.

'What a treat for the village,' he said diplomatically.

Well, at least it seems that she can play, thought Mrs Cantripp.

Next day the priest laboured, and Natasha rested. It was easy enough to do, since both brothers spent quite a lot of time in church, and the servants took it in turns to go. She had discovered that besides Mrs Greenhalgh there was a parlourmaid, cook, kitchenmaid, gardener, and a boy who helped in the garden and cleaned the shoes. Apart from Mrs Greenhalgh, all of them had achieved an ineptitude that was almost Russian, but Mrs Greenhalgh was all she needed.

She breakfasted on tea and toast in bed. The English were quite good at certain things. This marmalade, for instance . . . The church bells ceased at last (really, it was distracting to have them *quite* so close to one's bedroom) and shortly afterwards the sound of singing began. Hymns, of course, but after the bells she found them soothing . . .

Haydon Priors was a good place. Dull, but good. She would have to do something about the cook, but the house was warm, and Mrs Greenhalgh was an excellent maid. It meant that she had to neglect her duties as housekeeper but that could not be helped. Newcastle was good, too. Pretty things to steal in the stores. Too few stores to steal in very often, but there was always York, and she could go to London now and again. In London Léonide had taken her to Harrod's and it was as if she had died and gone to Heaven. Even the rue de la Paix had nothing like it: not under one roof. The singing reminded her again that it was Sunday and she crossed herself, and tried to remember her chain of thought.

Haydon Priors was a good place. Well, so it was. But a dull place, and that was true too. Still, there was Mrs Cantripp to work on. Natasha contemplated her as a sculptor might contemplate a block of marble. Something could be done with Mrs Cantripp, of that she was sure. Moreover, she was malleable. There was no doubt that Natasha's first instinct had been right. She would be just the one for George.

So far, there had been no one right for Oliver. It was true that she had been in the vicarage for no more than a few days, but even so she already knew that it would not be easy to find anyone right for Oliver.

He had no such problems, however. He wanted *her*. And Mrs Cantripp wanted *him*. She had seen the signs, and knew she wasn't mistaken. It was very tiresome of the widow, Natasha thought, but no reason to give up in despair. Something could still be done. The first thing was to make her buy proper clothes.

She began to think of Lord Kielder, shooting beasts in Africa. The priest was afraid of him, but that might simply be because the lord had power, and the priest was afraid of power. So many priests were – in Russia, at any rate. Oliver had not seemed afraid of him. Respectful, certainly – but not afraid. That might be because the Earl gave Oliver money sometimes. George had scarcely bothered to consider the lord, but then he made his own money, which might account for it. Oliver was obviously in need of money, which might well be part of her attraction. She got out of bed, looked carefully in the mirror, then sighed in relief as she always did.

Thank God I am still good-looking, she thought, and got back into bed. Between them George and Mrs Cantripp would be rich, and that was good. George deserved to be rich, and perhaps Mrs Cantripp did, too. I must find out her first name, Natasha thought. If we are to be friends, I can't call her Mrs Cantripp for ever. And they were going to be friends: there was so much to do for her. Her clothes, and the concert, and Slagsby. Slagsby would be interesting: she was sure of it. It would be in such a place that the English would start their revolution, according to Marx, but this time she would know what to do when it happened. Perhaps the lord knew, too. Perhaps the priest was right to be afraid of him.

Mrs Greenhalgh came in to tell her that her bath was ready, and that lunch would soon be ready, too. Sunday lunch. The vicar thought it the most important meal of the week. Natasha looked at her warily.

'Who cooked it?' she asked, and Mrs Greenhalgh smiled.

'The cook thinks she did,' she said.

Natasha got out of bed and took off her nightgown (not that it hides all that much, the other woman thought) and shrugged on the woollen dressing gown. She looked like a child dressing up in her mother's clothes, Mrs Greenhalgh thought.

Aloud she said, 'Shall I look out a day dress for you?'

Natasha seemed surprised. 'Yes, of course,' she said.

And when she came back it was the same process in reverse. Letting the dressing gown fall while somebody else finished drying her and she looked at the clothes chosen for her. No shame. Not even aware that there could be shame, any more than a baby. But she was a treat to look at, especially just out of her bath. She'd make some chap think it was his birthday, Mrs Greenhalgh thought, and then: She probably already has. And then: That's quite enough of that, Greenhalgh. This is the Sabbath.

Natasha picked up one of those newfangled brassières she'd seen advertised. Bought in Paris, no doubt. They have all those sorts of things in Paris. Like those knickers. So small you'd wonder why she bothered. If the vicar ever saw them he'd have a fit. His wife's had been— Again she had to admonish herself. Greenhalgh, that'll *do*. All the same I'd better wash her underwear myself, she thought. It would never do to hang them on the line.

'I don't like the dress you've chosen,' Natasha said.

'I daresay, miss,' said Mrs Greenhalgh, 'but the vicar likes modesty on the Sabbath.'

Natasha held up the dress. Dark blue with white piping, made by a modiste Léonide had patronised because she was a Communist, it had 'anxiety' written all over it: perhaps even 'despair'.

'The dark red silk?' she suggested.

'Too short, miss.' Mrs Greenhalgh was implacable. 'Far and away too short.'

Natasha sighed a martyr's sigh, and allowed herself to be covered in dark blue linen with white piping. No one could say that this dress was too short. She reached for her lipstick, and Mrs Greenhalgh coughed.

'The Sabbath, miss,' she said.

Natasha looked close to tears, then suddenly she brightened.

'It's all right,' she said. 'I am Russian Orthodox,' and went to the mirror.

Sunday lunch was a disappointment. A vast piece of beef cooked rare, as she liked it, vegetables that were crisp but not raw; all very right and proper. But there was no wine. The priest had something called a Sunday School to conduct, and he could not do that, he insisted, with alcohol on his breath. His sons accepted it automatically, and at last Natasha accepted it too, but oh! How that beef cried out for a good claret . . .

After lunch the priest and his younger son set off for the church, where George taught a class in the Sunday School. Oliver it seemed was excused, no doubt because of his uncertain temper.

Natasha went to the drawing room and yawned over the Sunday papers, and longed for *Le Figaro*, but at least the English papers told her there would be racing at York quite soon. It would not be Longchamps, she thought, but better than nothing.

Then Oliver followed her in, which did not surprise her, and quite soon began to make love to her, and that did not surprise her either. Not that he leaped at her or anything: there were far too many servants about for that. It was the way he looked: the way so many men looked come to that, when they had to talk to a girl and be thoughtful and kind and loving, when all they wanted to do was tear her clothes off. But without the thoughtfulness and kindness and love the clothes stayed very firmly on, and gracious how they resented the fact – and how difficult it was for them to hide the resentment.

'How charming you look,' said Oliver.

This was nonsense and they both knew it. She wondered if he knew how long it would take to get to York by train.

Oliver said quickly, 'Of course you've always looked charming every time I've seen you, but today you look charming in the right way.'

'The right way?'

'My dear cousin,' said Oliver, 'it isn't an easy matter to look both charming and appropriate in an English vicarage on a Sunday.'

That was better, she thought, but it was still a rotten dress.

'I called you cousin,' said Oliver. 'Would that be correct?'

Was there a threat hidden in the question?

'The French would say that we are cousins *á la mode de Bretagne*,' she said. 'That means any sort of relative.'

'I can hardly call you "my dear relative",' said Oliver.

He's waiting for me to say, 'You shouldn't call me dear at all,' she thought, but I'm not such a fool.

'Then cousin will have to do,' she said.

He shifted his leg slightly, the one that had been wounded – to remind me, she thought, that he was shot in the service of his countrymen, and that includes me, since I too am now a Tyrrwhitt.

'Your leg is painful?' she asked.

'It doesn't like cold weather, and it's jolly cold for August, wouldn't you say?'

She shrugged. 'In Russia it will be much colder soon.'

Her shrug had pleased him: her answer had not.

'The South of France,' he said. 'That's where we should be.' She gave no answer. 'Have you ever been there?'

'Certainly.'

'With the Jacquards?' She nodded. 'Not with your parents – before the war?'

'Before the war I was considered far too young to visit the South of France.'

'All that gambling in Monte Carlo and Grand Dukes with their mistresses?' She was silent once more. This one uses silence like a weapon, he thought, and she gets through my guard every time. 'Tell me about your parents,' he said.

She shook her head. 'No.'

'But why ever not?'

'To talk about them is painful to me. Please do not make me.'

'How could I possibly make you?' said Oliver, but her only reply was more silence.

Damn, he thought. She's done it again. But he couldn't give up, not with one as pretty as this, and exotic too.

'I was thinking this morning that Ireland must be rather like Russia.'

She looked startled. 'But how could it possibly—'

'Not the climate or the landscape,' he said. 'Ireland's green, and gentle enough for the most part, and it rains a lot but there isn't much snow. No. Not the landscape but the people – poor and overworked peasants. Hating their masters. Priest-ridden. Isn't that what the Russians are like?'

'Not priest-ridden,' she said. 'Not any more.'

'Commissar-ridden instead?'

Again the silence. Ah well, he thought. If I'm not to receive, I'd better give.

'You knew I was a Regular,' he said.

'Regular?'

'Regular Army Officer. It was to have been my life – and not a bad life either when I went to Sandhurst in 1913. I'd become a subaltern in a decent regiment – well, at least I achieved that – then there'd be India and polo and tiger-shooting, and the odd brush with the Afghans in the hills. Only I didn't get it. The war saw to that. Funny thing was, the war didn't bother me. I mean I was a soldier, so obviously fighting went with the job.'

'You got a medal for it,' she said. 'A Military Cross.'

'Who told you that?'

'Your father.'

'He was proud of me in those days,' said Oliver. 'I was wounded a couple of times, too. Probably saved my life. Sounds Irish, doesn't it?'

'A little,' she said. 'How could being wounded save your life?'

'I missed the Somme,' he said.

Not Irish at all, she thought. The most brutal kind of logic.

'Then when it was over the War Office started cutting down on chaps like me. Too many of us, you see. Too many survivors . . . I

34

could hardly believe it. The ones they looked at hardest were the chaps who'd been wounded. Would they be fit enough for peace-time? In war it didn't matter, we'd soon be dead anyway, but in peace – one wound was bad enough. Two was a real worry, even if I did have an earl for an uncle, so I volunteered for the Black and Tans.'

'The Black and Tans?'

'What you might call the Army of Occupation in Ireland. Only I got shot in the leg by a peasant – and three wounds was a bit too much for the War Office, even if my uncle had been a duke.'

She began then to feel sorry for him. A little, anyway. Only he went and spoiled it.

'That's why I'm here,' he said. 'Alone and palely loitering, instead of playing polo in Amritsar. Though I can still ride. Did my father tell you that?'

'No.'

'I even hunt in the season – when I can get a horse. It's the foot-slogging I can't manage.'

'Is there nothing else you can do?'

'Nothing,' he said, then: 'You're thinking of poor old George.'

'Why should I?' she said.

'He was in the Army – and he's got a job. A nice, fat job with a nice, fat firm.'

'But he's fit and well,' she said. 'He wasn't wounded.'

'Indeed he was,' said Oliver. 'Twice. But I bet my father didn't tell you that.'

'No,' she said. 'But why didn't he?'

'Can't you guess?'

'Perhaps I do not wish to,' she said, 'but surely a wound is an honourable thing. There can be nothing shameful in it.'

'Almost always what you say is true,' he said. 'But there are exceptions.' She waited. 'Look here,' he said. 'It's a family secret, but you're in the family now. There's no reason why you shouldn't be told.'

'Not if it's something disgraceful,' she said. But she longed to know.

Oliver said, 'Not disgraceful, precisely. More unfortunate. Funny, certainly. Perhaps sad, as well. It all depends on how you look at it.' He paused – for dramatic effect, she thought. 'He was shot in the backside.'

Her hand went at once to her mouth: no doubt to hide a smile.

'Twice,' said Oliver.

The hand stayed where it was. Behind it she said, 'The poor man.'

'It made his Army career a short one,' he said.

She took her hand from her mouth: there was no smile. 'It probably saved his life,' she said. 'Just like you.'

Go on, he admonished himself. For God's sake go on. You've got to win one round at least.

'He was close enough to the front line to qualify for wound stripes. Both times,' he said. Again that silence, more eloquent than a tirade. 'You see, the first time it was his colonel who shot him,' said Oliver.

'His own colonel? Did he think that George was running away?'

'It was early 1917,' said Oliver. 'By that stage of the war I don't think George's colonel was thinking at all. He'd been in it since the beginning, you see.

'What happened was that George was with his company commander back at Battalion HQ, being shown around, so to speak. There was a little hill just by the château where headquarters was, and from there you could see the German lines. George and his company commander were up on the hill behind some sandbags, taking a look when the colonel came out of the château. He was carrying a rifle – the CO, I mean. He used to do that sometimes. Take pot shots at rabbits. Hit 'em too, with a 303. He was a damn good shot. Anyway, he saw George's breeches up on the hill.'

'His breeches?'

'That's what he said later. They were brand new, you see. Perfectly correct, of course, but a rather pale colour. God knows what the colonel thought they were.'

'He was drunk?'

'He hadn't been sober since the summer of 1916, but he could still shoot straight. Aimed and fired and that was it. In one cheek and out the other.'

'Poor George,' she said.

'Yes, indeed,' said Oliver. 'Bad for his breeches, too. It was hushed up, of course,' Oliver continued. 'George was very decent about it and the colonel was sent back to command a depot in Middlesbrough.'

'Did he shoot anybody there?'

'He never handled a rifle again,' said Oliver.

'And George recovered?'

'Oh yes. All the Tyrrwhitts heal quickly. You must have noticed that yourself.'

She shrugged because he liked to watch while she did it, and then was silent because he hated her silence. Pleasure must be paid for, after all.

'The second time,' Oliver said at last, 'was during George's first and only visit to the trenches. The Germans fired a mortar shell that was bang on target for once and it landed very close to George, who was of course blown up into the air. He was above the parapet for no more than a second, but even so a sniper got him. German snipers were very good shots.'

'Better than George's colonel?'

Oliver thought: I loathe and detest this woman, but oh how I long to have her.

'As good, anyway,' he said, 'but George's colonel was exceptional. Anyway, there it was again. In one cheek and out of the other. Neat and tidy as you please.'

'Was George wearing the same breeches?'

'As a matter of fact he was. He'd had them dyed, of course.'

'Of course. Darned too, no doubt,' said Natasha.

Oliver's fists clenched. 'For some reason he still has them,' he said. 'He's rather proud of them. But he doesn't ride, naturally. Not any more. It would be too painful. Unkind persons call him Dimples, you see.'

'And was that the end of his military career?'

'It was,' said Oliver. 'The second lot took rather a long time to heal, and even when it did there was the risk of gangrene. He was honourably discharged and went to Oxford and read law. Two wound stripes – and he never talked about his wounds. He was very much liked at Oxford.'

'He's a likeable man,' said Natasha, and at that moment George returned with his father. By an enormous effort of will Natasha managed not to look at his bottom, chastely covered in pin-stripe, but for the life of her she could not forbear wondering what that bottom looked like. Dimples indeed. Would they be neat, symmetrical holes like the stops of a piccolo? She lit a cigarette. At least that would irritate the priest and so divert her mind.

'We saw Mrs Cantripp in church,' said the priest. 'She was surprised that you weren't there.'

'I've no doubt you explained my absence to her,' said Natasha.

The vicar was silent. It was much too early, and too painful, to tell anyone that a Tyrrwhitt belonged to the Russian Orthodox Church.

George thought, I bet he's told her about my war wounds. He always does, first chance he gets. Besides, he could tell at once by the way she looked at him. A bit much to go and tell such a thing to a well-brought-up young lady – and a Tyrrwhitt, too.

He turned to his brother. 'Madeleine Cantripp was saying she's seen a horse that might suit you. A gelding. Bit long in the tooth but still goes well. Good for at least two more seasons apparently.'

'How much?' said Oliver.

'A hundred and twenty.'
'I can't possibly afford that,' said Oliver.
'Too bad,' said George.

MICHAEL

4

The first thing to do was get out of bed. He couldn't achieve anything until he'd done that. On the other hand, what was there for a thirty-two-year-old orphan like him to achieve? Not much. Not enough to make getting out of bed a matter of urgency, and anyway, he'd drunk far too much Bundy rum the night before to make getting out of bed more than a remote possibility.

Funny, that. Dad being a Pom had always called it Bunderberg rum, giving it its full title, but then Dad knew a fair bit about titles one way and another. His mum had called it 'that-filthy-stuff-you-should-be-ashamed-and-if-your-head-aches-don't-come-crying-to-me!' His head ached all right – banging more like the Somme than Gallipoli, and he didn't have a mum to go crying to, not any more. Lost her years ago.

Lost her. Now there was another funny thing. When somebody died, people always said you'd lost them, like you'd been careless or something. Seek hard enough and you'd find her again. But he'd never find his mum no matter how hard he looked. He knew that. He'd held her in his arms and watched her die . . . He'd watched a lot die in his time – not that he'd kept a list. But the rest had all been blokes. Mum had been the only woman: the only one he'd cried for.

He hadn't seen Dad die. He'd have been in his house in Brisbane, or else in that posh hospital with a private room. It would tell him in the letter more than likely, but he'd been drunk by the time he'd finished it. Stupid thing to do. Bachelor of Arts of Melbourne University, and all he can do is get drunk. But then, what else could he do? There wasn't a girl in miles, not one he fancied, and anyway looking for a sheila would have shown a lack of respect, which for some reason getting drunk didn't, not even on Bundy rum. It was all stupid anyway. Aloud he said, 'I must get up,' and tried it. Not a good idea.

From outside came the sound of hooves and a poddy calf bawled; must be Chalky and the blokes moving stock over to the big paddock like he'd asked them yesterday before he got the letter. He hadn't told them about Dad, and they had a right to know. He said again, 'I

41

must get up,' and this time he meant it. Somehow, he achieved the vertical as Dad used to say, but would say no more.

He found that he was naked, which saved a lot of trouble. Sandals and a towel in case Tabby, the cook, was about, he shambled into the light, which made the headache even worse. Still he got as far as the water hole and fell in by a combination of accident and design, drifted out of his depth and faced his second choice of the day: swim or drown? It was a lot easier than get up or stay in bed.

Despite what had happened, he found that he had no wish to die, absolutely none, and struck out in a cautious crawl. What I'm after is survival, not exercise, he thought, then back to the house and about a gallon of tea. And a shave. He owed Dad that much. Dad had shaved every day of his adult life.

Still slow, but a bit more easy, he swam to the bank, climbed slowly out, used the towel in a vague sort of way, and set off back to the house. He was dry before he'd walked five steps, and then the sweat began. One thing you could say about Queensland, it was a great place for sweating. Maybe it would help shift some of that rum. Back in his room, a huge mug of tea was waiting, and a jug of hot water. It looked like Tabby thought he should shave, too. He picked up his razor and inspected his hand. Not shaking all that much. He was in with a chance . . .

Shaved and dressed he looked for the letter. It was underneath the Douai Bible his mother had bought him to take to the Uni. Symbolism there, he thought, and tried to analyse it, but his head ached too much. He took an aspirin instead.

Dear Michael, (he read)
Forgive the informality, but in view of what I have to tell you I can hardly address you as Mr Walsh . . .

He turned over the letter's remaining pages and looked at the signature. *Yours sincerely, Edgar Tyrrwhitt.* Well, at least his sincere half-brother had written it all himself. From what he'd been told he might have left it to a lawyer, or even a secretary. But of course that was stupid.

Use your brains, he admonished himself. You're hung over, not stupid. Of course he wouldn't let somebody else write it. From what Mum had told him, Edgar would be far too ashamed to let anybody else know he had a bastard brother. And did that mean he was ashamed of Dad, too?

He went back to the beginning, back to *Dear Michael*, and read it through. Dad had died in his bed, at home: his Brisbane home. He'd much preferred the one here in the outback, but any place will do to die in: a beach, a shell-hole, a trench. It's when you're alive and happy that you're fussy about your surroundings. *Massive stroke*, he read, and *no suffering. The doctor has given his word on that.* But how could the doctor be so sure? He, Michael Walsh, was suffering that minute, but he bet it didn't show.

I'm enclosing twenty pounds, his brother had written. *That should cover your train fare to Brisbane and out-of-pocket expenses.*

Too right it would. The fare from Toowombah to Brisbane was only two quid return. But where was the money? He found the banknote at last, still inside the envelope. He really had been hitting the rum, and it wasn't fair to the blokes. None of them had ever even seen twenty quid all in one piece of paper. Supposing one of them had had to talk to him, come into his room? Then Tabby really did come in, and she had already been in his room at least once. Tea and hot water. And she could read. *And* she had eyes in her head. Like Zeiss binoculars, Tabby's eyes. She could see even better than Chalky.

Her proper name was Tabitha, and like the blokes she came from an orphanage for half-caste abos run by Franciscan brothers and Poor Clares. Running to fat, but still enough muscle to worry Jack Dempsey, and a brain to match the muscle.

'You were drunk last night,' she said.

'Too right,' said Michael Walsh. 'Did I make a lot of noise?'

'No.'

The monosyllable meant that being part abo she just knew, and clever as she was, she couldn't tell you *how* she knew. Or wouldn't.

'I made you some tucker,' she said. 'Are you man enough to eat it?'

'What is it?'

'Eggs and bacon.'

'I'm man enough.' A steak would have killed him, but breakfast he could cope with, just about.

She brought in a tray, and he found that he was hungry. No offence, Dad, he thought. It's just that I didn't have any supper last night, apart from the rum.

'You had bad news,' Tabby said.

More abo stuff; it had to be. Edgar Tyrrwhitt certainly hadn't written to her, and he knew beyond doubting that she hadn't read his letter, not after he'd put it under a Bible.

'Bad enough,' he said, and pointed to a chair and she sat, back straight, hands folded in her lap the way the Sisters had taught her.

'I got a letter,' he said. 'From Brisbane. My father died.'

'I'm sorry,' she said. 'He was a good man, your father. I liked him. The blokes, too.'

He went on eating. Starvation wouldn't bring Dad back.

Tabby said, 'If you don't mind my asking – when he died, was it like your mum?'

His mother had died of a burst appendix. Peritonitis. Agony.

'Stroke,' said Walsh. 'Very sudden. According to the letter, he never knew it had happened.'

'How could anybody know a thing like that?' she said, and then: 'I'm sorry, Mike. I just hope it's true.'

'Me too,' said Walsh, and thought, She's doing it again. Picking up my thoughts as if she's a wireless set. Thoughts I had ten minutes ago.

'I have to go to Brisbane,' he said.

'There'll be things to settle,' said Tabby.

'A lot of things.'

'No worries,' she said. 'Take your time. The blokes and me can look after the property.'

'Better than me,' he said, and rose to his feet. 'Time I told them.'

She nodded. Her face told him that the blokes already knew, but this was a death after all, an important death, and there were forms to be observed.

'Thanks for the tucker,' he said. 'Nobody can cook eggs and bacon like you can, Tabby.'

'I'll say a prayer,' Tabby said.

And a chant as well after I've gone, he thought, reaching out for other gods he couldn't begin to imagine. Tabby wasn't one to leave anything to chance.

The blokes were still over in the big paddock, having an early tea. A hundred tons of beef all round them, and they were eating snake. The blokes had every shade of colouring you could imagine, from Thomas, who was almost white, to Chalky, who had the blackest skin he'd ever seen. Yet according to the Brothers he too was a half-caste, and the Brothers would know. Chalky's real name was Barnabas, but he'd been Chalky from the day he'd arrived at the property. He was the best horseman in a hundred-mile ride.

When Walsh dismounted, Chalky offered him a piece of roasted snake. No irony intended, thought Walsh. He's far too decent for that.

'No thanks,' said Walsh. 'I just had breakfast. I got a bit drunk last night.'

'We heard,' said Thomas, and Chalky scowled at him. Who could have told them?

'I had bad news,' said Walsh. 'My father's dead.'

The men sighed together like one man: a sound like a breeze on which a bird flies upwards – but maybe that was just the last of the rum. At least he knew that they were sorry.

'He was a good man, your dad,' Chalky said. 'We'll miss him.'
'Me too,' said Walsh.
'Words are useless,' Chalky said, 'but prayers aren't. We'll pray for him. You too.'
'Thanks, Chalky.'
And like Tabby you'll chant for him, he thought, because you really liked him, and he liked you. All the way from Charterhouse and Oxford to the outback, and men from the Stone Age who could ride even better than he could, and they liked each other.
'I have to go to Brisbane,' he said. 'Things to arrange. You know.'
'Lawyers,' said Chalky. 'You be careful, Mike.' For some reason Chalky had a horror of lawyers.
'You and Tabby'll run the place,' Walsh told him. 'I shouldn't be long.'
'No worries,' said Chalky.
Nor would there be, Walsh thought, except that there was an abo tribe twenty miles away, and the blokes would probably take it in turns to ride over and inspect the talent, but Chalky could handle that, too.
First he had to get himself to Brisbane. That meant a ride in the buggy with Chalky to Toowombah Station. Suit and a collar and tie, too, but at least he could leave off the jacket and collar and tie till he reached the train. What he'd have liked to do was wear a flannel shirt and a bush hat and carry a swag, just to show half-brother Edgar where he stood, but that might be rushing things a bit, though he doubted it. He could still remember great chunks of half-brother Edgar's letter.
The track made a detour into forest, past trees like cathedral pillars, and orchids, and butterflies the size of plates. Koalas and snakes and waterfalls, too – the wild Australia a lot of people went for, until they found out about the flies . . . A kookaburra suddenly erupted into manic laughter, then another picked it up, and another and another. A game of Chinese whispers, he thought, but even a Chinaman couldn't whisper that loud. Dad had been mad about kookaburras – 'like kingfishers in deep mourning', he said. They reminded Walsh of that place near Cairns where O. B. Watson lived. Atherton, wasn't it?
Dad had been mad about Atherton, too. It was where he'd made his first hundred thousand Aussie pounds, in the goldfields. Make a strike and sell it, that had been his system, until he made the big one and sold it to a syndicate from Broken Hill. After that he left Atherton to the latecomers and tried his hand at sugar cane and cattle instead, and multiplied his hundred thousand by ten. Not a bad

businessman for a bloke that went to Charterhouse. The trouble was he'd needed capital for the Atherton strike, and so he'd married it and got Edgar as a dividend. It was three years later that he'd met Mum. There was no chance of a divorce – Mum was far too good a Catholic for that – but they'd had him nevertheless. Been good to him, too. Both of them . . .

Walsh put on the collar and tie, and the trilby hat he detested. He'd carry the coat till the last possible minute, he decided. Then he shook Chalky's hand and watched him turn the buggy and wished he was riding home with him.

Over to the ticket office then, an airless hole like a punishment cell, and to judge by the way the ticket clerk acted, it was. Just to give him hope, Walsh bought a first-class ticket. The journey was still awful: hard seats and air thick as soup. After the forest the scenery was boring, too. No more trees, or waterfalls, or orchids. Not like Atherton at all. Even the track, he remembered. Fourteen bridges, was it? Nine tunnels? Twenty-three miles of enchantment. But it wasn't just twenty-three miles. It was the rainbow where the pot of gold was. Till it ran out.

He took a cab from the station. A tram would have been cheaper, but he wasn't all that sure where the house was, and it was Edgar's money. Or maybe it was his. Dad had left him quite a bit: he'd told him so. Not that he needed it. He had the property, and was fit and strong enough to work it. All the same it had been Dad's money and now it would be his, and that was the way it should be.

The cab drove down wide, tree-shaded streets – Australia was never short of space and trees – and up towards St Lucia, and as they went the houses got bigger, richer, grander. Eventually, they stopped outside one that wasn't grand at all, just solid and secure in its own wealth. Grey stone, with a kind of English feel about it – sash windows, mahogany doors . . . but the garden was pure Australian. Plane trees and hibiscus and jacaranda, wattle, and bougainvillea – and parrots all over the place.

Walsh paid off the driver, and added a tip, Lord of Creation.

'Maecenas redivivus,' he said.

'And the same to you, mate,' said the driver.

5

The maid who opened the door was Chinese. Father came to work the goldfields, he thought. Mr Tyrrwhitt, so it seemed, was expecting him. Might as well get it over with.

He followed her obediently to what he supposed would be called a study, and found to his relief that he wasn't looking at a slightly older copy of himself. Half-brother Edgar was even fairer than Dad, with none of the dark Irishness his mother had bequeathed him. Edgar looked very – *English*, Walsh thought. Well-brushed hair, school or college tie, would it be? – and an anonymity of expensive clothing which well-born Poms seemed to achieve effortlessly, though Edgar, he suspected, had to work hard to achieve it at all. Even so, he looked a lot like Dad except for the eyes. Dad's had been blue, but Edgar's were grey – his mum, no doubt.

The room was very much Dad's. Big mahogany desk and padded leather chair, books wherever you looked, a college oar on one wall, Ackermann prints on the others, and about a hundred photographs... Most of them were of Dad and some local worthy or other, or Dad with some not-unattractive lady who must be Edgar's mum. Some were of Edgar, too, but there was no sense in getting excited about that. Dad had lived here, with Edgar and the lady, and now and again they'd had their pictures taken. He had an albumful at home of Dad and Mum, and himself, too, from the age of three weeks.

Edgar said, 'It was good of you to come so quickly.'

Pommy voice, Michael thought. Well-off Pommy. At once clipped and relaxed, like there was nothing in the world its owner had to worry about, because he'd been to a good school. Very like Dad's voice in fact, except that Dad's voice had never annoyed him.

'Least I could do,' he said aloud.

'Yes – well, it's all a bit difficult,' Edgar said. 'It was only three weeks ago I found out I even *had* a brother.'

'Dad told you when he was dying?' Walsh asked and thought, He doesn't like me saying 'Dad'. What's he expect me to call my own

47

father? 'Mr Tyrrwhitt'? All the same, take it easy. The bloke's still in a state of shock.

'That's right,' Edgar said at last. 'Sort of a deathbed confession.' He flushed. 'I'm sorry. I didn't mean—'

'That's all right,' Walsh said.

'Can I offer you something?' Edgar said. 'A glass of sherry?'

'I could do with a beer,' said Walsh.

'Yes, of course.' All the same he'd surprised him. Tyrrwhitts didn't drink beer. He rang the bell and told the gold-miner's daughter to bring some.

'That property's your permanent base, I take it?'

'That's right.' 'Permanent base' seemed a strange name for it. It was his home.

'Stony Creek? Isn't that the name?' Walsh agreed. 'And it's all cattle?' Walsh agreed once more. 'How many?'

'Couple of thousand maybe.'

'That must be a fair acreage.'

'She's big,' said Michael. 'Just how big that's hard to say. Wherever there's grass. Where the bush begins the property ends, so to speak.'

'You've no neighbours?'

'Six miles away. The MacIntyres run cattle too. There's room for both of us.'

'Suppose there's a drought?'

Walsh shrugged. 'You can't move cattle far in a drought,' he said. 'They can hardly move themselves. The MacIntyres have got a water hole and so have I. If they ever empty we're out of business. It hasn't happened yet.'

'You like living in Stony Creek?' Edgar asked.

So many questions, thought Walsh. Is my half-brother a lawyer? He shrugged. 'It's what I know,' he said. 'Yes . . . I like it. Provided I can go walkabout now and then.'

'Why do that?'

Walsh looked surprised. 'Wild oats, mostly.'

'You go for long?'

'Longest was three years,' said Walsh, 'but that wasn't wild oats. It was the Army.'

'Of course,' said Edgar. 'Who looks after the property when you're away?'

'Mum did. Only she died two years back.'

'So who's looking after it now? While you're here?'

Why don't you just sentence me and get it over with?

'I've got a good foreman,' said Walsh, and it was true, but now

48

wasn't the right time to say what colour he was. Then he added: 'I was fond of my mum.'

'Yes, of course,' said Edgar, which was as near as he was likely to get to an apology.

Edgar brooded for a moment. 'Would you like another beer?'

Walsh shook his head.

'I think perhaps I'll have a glass of sherry,' said Edgar, and poured one. 'It's a bit difficult,' he said again. Walsh waited. 'Stony Creek's mine, you see.'

The funny thing was, he was expecting it. Premonition, you could call it. Maybe it had started with the twenty-pound note.

'I never knew that,' he said.

Edgar looked at him suspiciously, but I can look guileless when I have to, Walsh thought, and I bet I'm looking guileless now.

'Father left a will,' said Edgar. 'Everything comes to me. Perhaps you know my mother died when I was quite young?'

Still guileless, Walsh said: 'I expect you were fond of her, too.'

'Yes,' said Edgar. 'I was.'

Is it possible he means it? Walsh wondered. He sounds as if he means it.

'Dad left it all to me,' Edgar repeated. 'Years ago. The sugarfields, the mill, the money in the bank, all three properties.'

'Congratulations.'

He's lying, Walsh thought, and he knows I know it. He also knows I can't do a bloody thing about it. The will he's talking about, Dad made years ago. Just before he met Mum, and he forgot to destroy it when he made the other one, the one that took care of me, the one my loving half-brother tore to shreds while he waited for the undertaker.

'Dear me,' said Edgar. 'I'm making our parent sound like a monster.'

Here it comes, thought Walsh.

'But he wasn't,' Edgar continued. 'By no means. He'd meant to provide for you, only he kept putting things off – not that that need worry you. Honestly. He told me precisely what he had in mind for you, and it's an obligation I intend to honour. A sacred obligation – if you'll excuse a rather high-flown phrase. He intended Stony Creek to be yours, and five thousand in cash.' And if I'm a good boy it will be, thought Walsh. Because there's more to come. There has to be. 'I'll be honest with you,' said Edgar. Now there was a novelty. 'While Father was alive I worked in the business, but I've decided to get out. Sell it. A bit at a time, of course.' Walsh nodded. 'Try to sell it all at once and people think you're going broke, and we can't have that.'

'Certainly not.'

Once more Edgar looked at him, but the guileless look was still in place.

'Investments, securities, that's what I'm after,' Edgar said, and looked at the wall to his right. A copy of the Gainsborough portrait of the Duchess of Devonshire hung there.

'Pictures?' said Walsh, and Edgar laughed.

'Far too risky,' he said. 'Even originals. No, no. Bonds, loan stock, stuff like that. Dull, solid and successful. I'm going into politics, you see.'

With that accent?

'Perhaps I'll hire you to give me elocution lessons,' Edgar said. Not so stupid then, his dear half-brother; dangerously perceptive.

'It wouldn't hurt,' said Walsh. 'The voters don't like Poms.'

'You know where I was educated then?' Walsh nodded. 'Charterhouse and Oxford. Only in Australia could that be a handicap, but we'll surmount it.'

'We?'

'How can I put this without being offensive?' said Edgar. 'The short answer is, I can't. You're a handicap too, old chap.'

'The Bastard from the Bush?'

Edgar winced. 'Well . . . yes. Not that it's your fault.'

'It's Dad's fault if it's anybody's,' said Walsh. 'And Mum's, of course.'

'They're both dead.' That put them out of the equation, it seemed. 'But you—'

'You don't want me running about saying you're my half-brother?'

'Precisely,' said Edgar.

'Then I won't.'

Edgar smiled, then – a smile at once amused and indulgent.

'I believe you,' he said. 'Of course. But I always think it's as well to have something on paper.'

'No worries,' said Walsh. 'All I want is Stony Creek, and five thousand quid. My name's Walsh, remember, not Tyrrwhitt. I don't even look like you.'

'That's a help, of course,' said Edgar. 'All the same—'

'When do you want me to sign?'

'Next week,' said Edgar. 'Wednesday say. My lawyers will have something ready for you by Wednesday. What will you do till then?'

'Go back to the property.'

'And after you've signed?'

'Go walkabout.'

'Splendid,' said Edgar.

On the train back to Toowombah he thought about it, stage by stage. Edgar really did want to go into politics. In fact, in the fullness of time Edgar wanted to be Prime Minister. There was no accounting for tastes. And he could understand that he, Michael Walsh, would be the hell of a handicap. Australia might be foul-mouthed, but it was strait-laced too, and the Irish were the most strait-laced of the lot. The fact that Mum had been Irish too would make it even worse if Australia ever found out who Dad was.

There'd been another Edgar with a bastard brother, he remembered. Gloucester's son, in Shakespeare's *King Lear* – and a right bastard that particular bastard had turned out to be.

He could hardly blame his own half-brother for taking precautions. Still, the fact that he was going walkabout had brought the roses back to Edgar's cheeks. With him out of the way Edgar could really get to work... It would be just as well to call on Bill Ormsby in Toowombah before he went back to Stony Creek, though. Bill was a mate. No worries there. Besides, he'd be paying him five quid a week. Seemed a bit mean when he thought of what he had coming, but any more and Bill would start to worry – and wonder.

Chalky was waiting with the buggy and drove him round to the pub where Bill was lowering beer against the clock. It didn't take much arranging: he'd done it before. All the same they sealed the bargain with another beer and Chalky drove the buggy home, then came in with Tabby for a chat.

When he'd finished Tabby said, 'Just like the other times?'

'That's right.'

But Tabby liked to get things clear. 'So I put Bill's clothes in your room and if any snoopers come calling I say he's been called away on business and send them to his house in Toowombah.'

'That's right,' Walsh said again, and then: 'I'm sorry, honestly. But the way things are—'

'No worries,' said Chalky. 'The way you arrange it we all get a bit of peace. You're going walkabout again?'

'That's the idea.'

'Do you good after your bad news,' Tabby said.

'Mind you enjoy yourself,' said Chalky.

'Do my best,' said Walsh.

Come at eleven, Edgar had said. The train arrived earlier than that, but the gold-miner's daughter let him in anyway and made him a cup of tea, then said that Mr Edgar would be visiting his lawyer, a fact he already knew. After she'd gone Walsh went up close to the Duchess of Devonshire. Lovely, but a bit of a handful by the look of her. He'd like to meet a woman like that, same as his Dad had done . . . Get on

51

with it, Walsh, he told himself. You came here to steal so don't dawdle.

He took out the keys Dad had kept at his place, selected the one with a blob of red sealing wax on it, then moved the picture to one side. It swung back on a hinge and there was the safe. Opening it was no problem at all.

There was a tray at the bottom of the safe, Mum had told him. He needed another key for that, the smallest on the bunch, and again it worked just as it should. The tray was stuffed full of paper. Bearer bonds, Mum had said they were: worth ten thousand apiece but as easy as money. Dad had acquired them in the early days, according to Mum; the days when he was never sure whether he'd end up poor or rich; to be on the safe side he'd hung on to them.

Just go to a bank, put one down, then on your way. There must have been a dozen of them, he thought, and helped himself to five. That lowered the level a bit, so he went to a bookshelf, pulled out a Kennedy's *Latin Primer* (*C. E. R. Tyrrwhitt, Upper IVth* on the flyleaf) and stuck it under the bonds, locked the tray then the safe, and put the delectable Duchess back where she belonged, before sticking fifty thousand quid under the spare shirts in his case. Every instinct said run, but he couldn't. It was the one thing that would make Edgar even more suspicious than he was already. Besides, he needed the Stony Creek deeds.

He went back to his tea, which had scarcely cooled. The whole thing had been so quick: fifty thousand quid in three minutes! What would Dad have made of it? he wondered. Laughed, probably. After all, emigrating to Australia hadn't been Dad's idea. More of an either/or proposition. Either you go to Australia, or you go to prison. Matter of a racehorse and a bouncing cheque . . .

Dad had chosen Australia and never looked back. Walsh wondered if Edgar knew why Dad had emigrated; wondered too if it worried him, made him ashamed. Idiot if it did, he thought. Most of the early Poms in Australia had gone there because of some naughtiness or other, and most of them in chains. At least Dad had travelled first class.

There was a magazine on Edgar's desk – a six-months'-old copy of the *Illustrated London News*. It would be. He went to the bookshelf and took down a copy of *Emma* instead. He had reached the bit where Harriet Smith was being nosy about Mr Knightley when Edgar came in.

'My dear Michael,' he said. 'Sorry to keep you waiting – but you were early, after all.' Behind the friendliness there was worry, until Walsh put the book down.

'Jane Austen,' Edgar said. 'Well, well.'

That's why I went to the uni, thought Walsh. So they could teach me to read and tie my shoelaces. All the same, Edgar began to relax a bit and rummaged in his briefcase, took out a document and a pile of notes.

'I went to the bank as well,' he said. 'For your five thousand pounds.' The thought depressed him. 'You know I was at my lawyer's?'

'Your maid told me,' said Walsh. 'He was Dad's lawyer too, wasn't he?'

'No,' Edgar said. 'Old Spofforth was a bit too pleased with himself. It was time for a change.'

Old Spofforth knew about the will with me in it, thought Walsh. Of course it was time for a change.

Edgar took a document from his briefcase. 'Just sign that and I'll get the deeds,' he said.

Walsh read it first, which irritated Edgar. He wanted Walsh out of the house so that he could begin his life as an only child. At last Walsh signed, and Edgar reached out his hand.

'Let's see the deeds first,' said Walsh. 'Do it properly.'

'Yes of course,' said Edgar. 'No offence old chap, but I'll have to ask you to turn your back just for a moment.'

They're in the bloody safe, thought Walsh, but even so, all he could do was turn his back and pray that the deeds weren't mixed up with the bearer bonds. There was the sound of the Duchess being moved, then one key turned, just one, parchment crackled, the key turned again and the Duchess was swung back into place.

'Here we are,' said Edgar.

He read the deeds too. There was an extra sheet of paper signed by Edgar, giving them to Walsh. Carefully he opened his attaché case and put the deeds and the five thousand on top of the shirts on top of the bearer bonds. Probably the bravest thing he'd ever done in his life, he thought.

He was on the train to Cairns before the thought struck him that it wasn't brave at all. For Edgar to accuse him would mean admitting that Walsh, his half-brother, was a bastard, and a thieving bastard at that. He'd never get to Canberra that way . . . He began to think about Mum, and how she knew about the safe and the bearer bonds. She always said Dad had no secrets from her. Maybe he'd told her what a mongrel Edgar was, too.

What he needed was somebody to talk to, which was why he was on his way to Cairns anyway. It was a long and boring journey, and the only thing Australians wanted to do on trains was eat steak and drink beer, and all he had to read was the papers. There hadn't even been time to buy another copy of *Emma*. Still, half-brother Edgar would never think of looking for him in Cairns. No politician, drunk or sober, would look for anybody in Cairns – unless it was his constituency. Canberra, that's where he would look – or Sydney. Melbourne at a pinch. But never Cairns. Just as well O. B. Watson lived there.

Walsh ordered a steak and a beer, and tried not to worry about what was in his case.

6

He hadn't phoned. To begin with he didn't have the number – always supposing O.B. *had* a phone – and anyway he didn't have time to go chasing telephone numbers. He wanted to leave Brisbane. Two steaks and one eggs and bacon later, the train pulled into Cairns, and Walsh, man of substance, hired the only cab, its driver mildly irritated at being woken up. At least he knew where O.B. lived, which was a bit of luck. A house built on the outskirts of whatever town Cairns was: and it was a nice house, too, built of Australian timber – jarra and redwood mostly, a long, relaxed sort of house with verandahs wherever there was shade.

He knocked at the door, and at once dogs barked, big dogs by the sound of them, then the door opened and O.B. stood there, with a couple of Queensland blue heelers for company. Walsh was glad O.B. was a mate of his. Blue heelers were burly dogs with a kind of arrogant courage all their own. They needed it, too. They were cattle dogs, trained to chivvy and snarl at calves, or cows, or even bulls. The nervous ones never lasted long. At the last count Walsh had owned five, but he wouldn't risk them in the house.

O.B. Watson said, 'My God.'

Big and tough-looking as ever, thought Walsh, but more relaxed than he'd expected, considering what he'd been through, and yet sad, too. Well, at least *that* made sense.

Walsh said, 'How are you, mate?' and offered his hand.

'Mike Walsh,' O.B. said. 'It is Mike, isn't it? Come on in. There's still some beer left,' and he grabbed his hand, almost pulled him into the house.

Walsh followed him through a cool, dim hall to a cool, dim room where a fan lazily whirled.

'All mod cons,' he said.

'Generator,' said O.B. 'That's what keeps the beer cold, too. While the petrol lasts.'

A bit cryptic, thought Walsh. Still, there's no rush.

O.B. turned to the dogs. 'This gentleman's a mate of mine so behave yourselves. Tell him a few jokes while I get the beer.'

55

He left and the dogs slumped to the floor, watching him with an unblinking stare till O.B. came back with beer.

'They seem to have lost their sense of humour,' said Walsh.

'Just as well,' O.B. said. 'They're guard dogs.'

'They got names?'

'Certainly they've got names,' O.B. said, and pointed. 'That one's O'Mara and that one's Haig.'

O'Mara and Haig. The two men in France they'd hated most: their platoon sergeant and the British commander in chief.

'If they're as nasty as their names you've got nothing to worry about.'

O.B. chuckled. 'If only that was true,' he said, then stopped.

'Go on,' said Walsh.

'You didn't come all this way to hear my troubles,' O.B. said.

'I didn't know you had any,' said Walsh. 'I came here to tell you mine, but let's have yours first.'

'Money,' said O.B.

'Well, of course.'

'Yes, well . . .' O.B. said, and then, 'You remember I was training to be a teacher before the war?'

'I remember,' said Walsh.

'After I left the Army I went back and qualified. Only I found it was a mistake.'

'Any particular reason?'

'Three years of fighting grown men. Kids was boring after that.'

'Fighting them?'

'Everything about them. So I thought I'd better do something else. It turned out I tried just about everything else.'

'Such as?'

'Barman, boundary rider, deck hand, car mechanic, cinema projectionist, encyclopaedia salesman. That was the worst. Of all of them, selling encyclopaedias was the worst. You remember I used to be a bit quick-tempered?'

That was like saying you remember that Everest is a biggish hill, thought Walsh, but all he said was, 'Yes.'

'I still was,' said O.B., 'even after I was wounded.' He waited then, but Walsh said nothing. 'It doesn't help when you're trying to sell encyclopaedias.'

'How many did you sell?'

'One,' O.B. said. 'To a randy little sod who asked if there were pictures of sheilas with no clothes on. I showed him a few and he paid up on the spot and I resigned.' He sighed. 'Not even pimping,' he said. 'Just going through the motions.'

56

'So what did you do then?' said Walsh.

'I bought an aeroplane.'

Walsh looked startled. 'What on earth for?'

'To fly, what do you think?' said O.B., and then, 'You mean where did I get the money?'

'Well, where did you?'

They had once been good mates, after all. The question could be asked.

'Not by stealing. Well, not much anyway.'

Walsh tried not to wince. He'd made far more money in three minutes' stealing than in a lifetime of honesty.

'After I – got wounded, the government gave me a pension. They still do.'

'You earned it.'

'Yeah, well – we'll talk about that later,' O.B. said. 'The thing is, it's enough to live on – so the jobs, the wages – I put it in the bank.'

'You're allowed to work?' said Walsh.

'I never asked,' O.B. said. 'Anyway, my dad left me a bit of money. Left me this house an' all.'

'Stockman, was he?'

'Builder,' O.B. said. 'Good one too, if he laid off the grog. Only he didn't. Go and look out of the kitchen window.'

Walsh went. Beyond the kitchen was a paddock, and in the paddock was an aeroplane. He went back to O.B.

'What did you see?' O.B. asked.

'It's a plane right enough,' said Walsh.

'It's a three-seater Avro 504K, you ignorant Mick,' said O.B. 'G for Gertie. The only girl I ever loved.' He sighed again.

'Then what you laughing so hard for?' Walsh asked.

'I've got to give her up,' said O.B.

'Money?' Walsh asked.

'Money's a bastard,' said O.B. 'Always was. Always will be.'

'Savings gone?'

'Savings, what my dad left, the loan on this house. Aeroplanes eat money when you're starting off. Maintenance, insurance, petrol, pilot's licence.'

'You mean you've got one?'

'Of course I've got one,' O.B. said. 'How do you think I fly the thing?'

'I thought maybe you hired some joker to fly it for you.'

'What do you suppose I bought her for?' O.B. asked. 'Nobody makes love to my girl but me. Till next Thursday anyway. After that she's somebody else's girl.'

57

'Are you any good?' Walsh asked.

'The flying school seemed to think so,' O.B. said. 'Anyway, what kind of bloody nosy question's that? Unless you're after a joyride. That's what got me started: I went for a joyride in Brisbane. Two pounds ten. If you wanted to loop the loop as well they charged a fiver. I had five quids' worth. I'd never known anything like it.'

'Weren't you scared?'

'Terrified,' O.B. said. 'For a start. Then gradually I knew I'd be all right. But it didn't stop there. It wasn't just being safe. It was the most wonderful excitement I'd ever known, like going over the top and knowing the Jerry machine guns couldn't hurt me. Nothing in the world to match it – except flying one myself. So I bought one and flew her.' He finished his beer. 'Want to try it yourself? There's still a bit of petrol left.'

O.B. hadn't lied to him. He was a good pilot: hadn't lied about the feel of it, either. Looping the loop was scary all right, but the rest of it – it was amazing. Sixty miles an hour in a straight line and nothing in the way. And the view – even through O.B.'s second-best pair of goggles the view was incredible. Limitless outback or limitless ocean, all you had to do was choose. O.B. chose the ocean, and Walsh was certain he was happy. Even the back of his neck looked happy, he thought, then he peered down at the ocean once more, and began to worry, just a little, about drowning. It seemed that he didn't quite share O.B.'s shining vision after all. But then they reached the Barrier Reef, and O.B. flew lower, lower, and Walsh forgot about drowning. There was just too damn much to see, before O.B. began to climb once more and they headed for home, and a neat three-point landing made as easily as he, Walsh, might rein in a horse.

Walsh sweated his way back to the house in helmet and flying jacket, took them off and mopped his face with a handkerchief as O.B. poured another beer. Walsh lifted his glass in a toast.

'You're bloody good,' he said.

'It ought to be a consolation,' said O.B., 'but it's not. What good's a stockman without a horse?'

Walsh said, 'My dad died a couple of weeks back.'

'I'm sorry, mate,' said O.B.

'I didn't see all that much of him,' said Walsh. 'I mean, what with the war – and other things. All the same we were close. Only—' He hesitated.

'Only what?' said O.B.

'Only he and my mum weren't married. Couldn't be. He was already married and Mum was a Catholic.'

'So there you were,' O.B. said.

'There I was. Happy as a possum up a gumtree till the war came. But I got home all right, so I went back to being happy. Till Mum died, and then Dad.'

O.B. said carefully, 'And that was the end of being happy?'

'Very likely,' said Walsh. 'But it was also the start of being rich.'

'Your dad?' said O.B.

'My dad,' said Walsh. 'Bless him.' He sipped at his beer. 'How much d'you need to keep your plane?'

O.B. looked at him. 'You wouldn't kid me – not about a thing like that?'

'Of course I wouldn't,' said Walsh. 'Us rich blokes never kid about money.'

'But—' O.B. was floundering.

I'm offering him salvation, thought Walsh, and he's finding Hell hard to leave. And yet he was so happy in that plane of his.

Then out it came. 'It's a fair bit,' O.B. said at last.

'How much?'

'Five hundred.'

'Give you it now,' said Walsh, and went to his suitcase.

'Might even be more,' O.B. told his back.

'If it is I'll give it to you,' said Walsh, and began to count out ten-pound notes as O.B. watched.

'Forgive me,' he said at last, 'but you did say your dad was already married.' Walsh nodded; still counting. 'Don't you have brothers and sisters?'

'One brother,' said Walsh. 'Half-brother anyway.' It was a bit late for O.B. to start developing a conscience, and what he didn't know wouldn't hurt him, even if he was a good mate.

'Don't worry,' he said. 'There was more than enough for both of us.' And that was the truth, after all. It was half-brother Edgar who'd got it in for bastards. Just like in Shakespeare.

He offered the wad of notes and O.B. took them, not quite snatching, but keeping them out in the open instead of in his pocket. More doubts to come.

'I can't tell you when I can pay you back,' O.B. said at last.

'When you can,' said Walsh. 'I know that. But don't start to starve yourself just because you owe me a few quid. Make that plane of yours pay, and then we'll talk. And if I lose all my money I can always come back here and live off you.'

O.B.'s hand, which had been on its way to his pocket, stopped again.

'That was a joke,' said Walsh. 'I've no intention of losing my money.'

At last, O.B. pocketed the notes. 'You staying here long?' he asked.

'That's up to you,' said Walsh. 'I've got a bloke back in Stony Creek looking after the property for as long as I like.'

O.B. looked puzzled. 'You're welcome to stay here, of course,' he said, 'but—'

'Not here,' said Walsh.

'Where then?'

Walsh shrugged. 'I thought I'd go walkabout for a bit,' he said. 'See the world.'

'Any particular reason?'

'Sheilas mostly.'

The look on O.B.'s face alone was worth the price of admission.

'Don't worry,' Walsh said. 'I don't want you selling me any live encyclopaedias. I want you to take me somewhere.'

'In the plane?'

'My very own magic carpet,' said Walsh.

'Where we going to go?' O.B. asked.

'That's something I want to talk about,' said Walsh.

Over tea O.B. said, 'This walkabout – you weren't thinking of Australia?' Tea had consisted of steak, chips and tinned vegetables, cooked by O.B.

'Too right,' said Walsh.

'What about the Dutch East Indies?' O.B. said. 'I could get you there, no worries.' He paused, then added delicately, 'If you're not in a hurry, that is.'

Walsh said, 'You reckon I'd like it there?'

'I did,' said O.B., swigged at his tea as if it was rum before a bayonet charge, then looked at it as if surprised to find a cup in his hand. 'There's something I have to tell you if you don't mind listening,' he went on. 'Only I couldn't tell it on tea.'

He got up, went into the living room, and Walsh followed and watched as O.B. took a bottle of whisky from a cupboard

'Part of Dad's legacy,' he said. 'I've had it since he died. Time we got rid of it.' He found a couple of glasses and poured.

'You know my name?' he said.

'Well, of course. O.B. Watson,' said Walsh.

'But what's the O.B. for?' Walsh waited. 'I've got names, you know. Not just initials.' Again Walsh waited. 'I didn't just get to be called that in 1917.'

'Well, of course not,' said Walsh. 'You were O.B. when I joined.'

'Too right I was,' said O.B. 'Osbaldestone Bernard Watson, that's me. No wonder I answered to O.B.'

'*Osbaldestone?*'

'I don't blame you for being surprised,' said O.B. 'I was surprised myself when I found out that's who I was. I mean, Bernard's bad enough, but Osbaldestone . . .' He shook his head, still bewildered. 'The thing was, my mum had this uncle back in Adelaide. A bachelor. Undertaker. Man of substance, as the saying goes.'

'He'd never run short of clients,' said Walsh.

'He should have gone to the Somme,' O.B. said. 'Half a day's work and he could have retired. Still, my mum got to thinking – only she wasn't all that good at thinking – but she wrote him the glad tidings of my arrival, and said she was going to name me after him. Osbaldestone . . .' He swallowed whisky and brooded.

'And she never heard from him again?' Walsh asked.

'Certainly she did,' O.B. said. 'He wrote back by return. We're a very close family.'

'Well, then?'

'Delighted, he said he was. *And* honoured. He sent Mum something else as well. A photograph of his new bride.'

'Rotten luck,' said Walsh.

'It gets worse,' O.B. said. 'She was a widow. Five children.' In the paddock a kookaburra gave way to its dreadful laughing scream. 'You and me both, mate,' O.B. said, then topped up their glasses.

'Now the point is this,' he said. 'That was thirty years ago – and I got away with it that time because in the Army I was O.B. and at school I'd learned enough sense to tell everybody my name was Os. If they thought about it they probably thought it was some kind of patriotism. Os short for Australia. But kids don't think much. Like my mum.' He drank more whisky. 'October the third, 1917,' he said.

'What about it?'

'Pozières,' said O.B. 'Weren't you there?'

'I was in hospital,' said Walsh. 'Malaria.'

'Courtesy of Gallipoli,' said O.B. 'You were lucky, mate. October the third was the day Haig had one of his brain waves. Shorten the line, he thought. Advance fifty yards nearer to Berlin. And O'Mara was there to see we did it.'

As they heard their names the two dogs stood, then lay down again for all the world, thought Walsh, as if they were taking a bow.

'So off we went,' O.B. said, 'and I got my second wound stripe and my discharge and my pension all at the same time. Only by then O.B. had acquired a new significance.' He broke off and looked at his glass suspiciously.

'Sorry about that,' he said, 'but we educated chaps do get polysyllabic now and again. No offence meant.'

'None taken,' said Walsh.

'O.B. Watson from there on meant One Ball Watson,' O.B. said. 'Jerry couldn't have done a neater job if he'd used a bacon slicer. I suppose you heard?'

'Soon as I got back,' said Walsh. 'The whole battalion knew.'

'Who told them?'

'The stretcher-bearers,' said Walsh. 'It's not the sort of thing you can keep a secret, is it? Not in the Army.'

'Had a good laugh, did they?'

'A few,' said Walsh. 'Most of them were worried sick. There but for the grace of God—'

O.B. said, 'But you wrote to me. You still do. And yet you never mentioned it.'

'How could I?' said Walsh. 'It was up to you to tell me.'

'And now I'm doing it,' said O.B. 'You don't want to see it, I take it?'

'Christ no.'

'A lot of blokes did. In the hospital. Convalescent home, too. I walloped most of them. One thing I hadn't lost. I still enjoyed a good stoush in those days.'

'Not any more?'

'I learned a bit of sense,' O.B. said. 'In Bali. Good place for learning sense. It was after I packed in the teaching. I signed on as a deckhand on an island steamer. Timor, the Celebes, Java, Sumatra. All over the place. It was a good life – and none of the crew knew I'd suffered a loss as you might say . . . I'm not boring you, am I?'

'Not in the least,' said Walsh.

'Only I want to talk about it. After all these years. You see, there were two people who helped me come to terms, so to speak. The first was the surgeon who rescued the survivor. Pom, he was. Bloody good bloke. He told me we were given two balls like we were given two kidneys. One was a spare – just in case. Like my case.

'"I've done my best for you," he said, "and the other one seems undamaged. No reason why it shouldn't be. Only remember – it's the only friend you've got left. Don't go working it too hard," and I told him I wouldn't. In fact I didn't work it at all.'

'Why ever not?' Walsh said.

'Supposing he was wrong? Supposing I was a bloody eunuch?'

'There was only one way to find out,' said Walsh.

'Too right,' said O.B. 'But I was too scared to try it. Till one day we put into a port in Java – Maderva. Lot of Dutch there. Randy sods. Fussy about their girls, though. And I was off watch and I saw the blokes going ashore and I thought to myself, Show a bit of sense, Osbaldestone Bernard Watson. You're about as far away from Cairns as you're ever likely to be, so why not give it a go?'

'And did you?'

O.B. nodded. 'I chose the best place in town,' he said. 'I was going to do it in style even if it was a dud shell so to speak, and being the best place in town you wouldn't get any low, common sailors there.' He smiled. 'It was a wonderful night – real Joseph Conrad. They always are over there at the right time of year. Just enough breeze, and the scent of hibiscus and spices, and the sound of the ocean no more than a sigh. And a gamelan orchestra playing somewhere, sweet as syrup. Just right if you were after a bit of romance, but I wasn't. I was after a fact. Just one.

'The girl I got was pretty – but then they all were. Like I said, it was the best place in town. Spoke a bit of English, too. The kind of English they speak over there.' Again O.B. hesitated, poured more whisky. 'You still sure you want to hear this?' he said.

'I'm sure.'

'Well, when she saw me – *it* – she looked at it as if she couldn't believe it. I'm not exactly Michelangelo's David. Not any more – but it wasn't that.'

'What then?' Walsh asked.

'She was sorry. For me. Not patronising. Sorry. Compassion. She asked me how I got it and I told her, and she still didn't laugh. She still was sorry.'

'She sounds nice,' said Walsh.

'She really was,' O.B. said, and paused again, then continued. 'Anyway she looked at me – *it* – like a plumber might look at a tricky piece of pipe. Like it might fit, and then again it might not. And then she got to work, and after a bit of tinkering the pipe fitted, as you might say. Best moment of my life till I took up flying. Then she said something in her own language and I asked her what it meant.'

'"God is great," she said. I wanted to marry her.'

'But you didn't,' said Walsh.

'How could I?' O.B. said. 'I had no hope of bringing her into Australia, the colour she was.'

'What was her name?'

'She told me at the beginning, but it didn't mean anything. And before I could ask her again—'

'Go on,' said Walsh.

'She had another customer waiting. So I gave her all the money I had on me and went back to the ship. It was just before I went aboard I remembered something.'

Walsh waited.

'God is great,' said O.B. 'She's a Muslim. They all are out there except the Balinese, and the Dutch. "God is great" is what they say when something good happens.'

Walsh reckoned the girl's next customer must have been a Dutchman, but he was too tactful to say so.

'So now you're the same randy bastard you used to be?' he said.

'That's just it,' O.B. said. 'Oh, I might fancy a girl now and then, but if there isn't one, it doesn't bother me.'

'G for Gertie?'

'The love of my life,' said O.B. 'Marriage made in heaven – thanks to you. But God is great. It set me thinking. What I mean is, there we were in that decrepit tub sailing all over the Indian Ocean and everywhere we went people believed. God was part of them, like rice for their dinner. I'm not saying they were any better or worse than we are, but they were different, because their God is always there.

'Then we got to Bali. They're Hindus in Bali – except for the Dutch – and the gods really do live in Bali. They're everywhere. Temples and shrines all over the place, and every house with its own little god – or maybe just a bit of cloth to keep the devils away. And it works. I never saw a devil all the time I was there.' Once again he smiled. 'Pretty sheilas, too. Walking around in just a sarong and nothing on top. I don't mean the prostitutes. All of them. It's got nothing to do with sex.'

'What then?'

'It's because it's hot. And it is. All the same they were a sight to see – and I spent all my spare time in the temples. I reckon that's why I got the aeroplane.'

'You've lost me,' said Walsh.

'Nearer to heaven,' said O.B. 'Finding out about yourself: "A lonely impulse of delight, Drove to this tumult in the clouds".'

'That's Yeats, isn't it?' said Walsh, and O.B. nodded. 'I never thought I'd come here for a tutorial.'

O.B. grinned. 'Reading gets to be a habit,' he said.

It took a few days, of course. There were creditors to be paid; suspicious blokes who needed to be absolutely certain that O.B. hadn't robbed a bank before they handed over the receipt.

The first day, Walsh stayed at O.B.'s place with Haig and O'Mara for company, but once he was left on his own he found that all he could think about was Edgar. Taking the money didn't worry him, and the fear of Edgar's wrath didn't worry him, either – so long as he didn't go to prison. It was just – the whole thing stank, and when you got right down to it he was no better than Edgar. No wonder he hadn't told O.B. *his* secret. He was too ashamed.

So after that he travelled on the pillion of the elderly motorbike O.B. drove far worse than he did the plane, and skulked in pubs while O.B. tried to force money on his creditors. A couple of times he bought a newspaper, but there was no headline screaming 'Politician Denounces His Bastard Brother', and the stuff that had got into print was boring. Except for one item.

Edgar had made a speech at a Liberal meeting in Brisbane, and a very good speech it must have been, since at the end of it he'd been adopted as candidate for a very posh part of Brisbane indeed – the sort of place where the Liberal always got in. Edgar Tyrrwhitt, M.H.R. in waiting. His own dear brother. Member of the House of Representatives. That should have made him feel more secure than ever, he thought, since Edgar now had even more reason to fear a scandal. But it didn't. For some reason all it did was make him even more disgusted with himself, until O.B. came back and they had another beer before they tackled the motorbike.

And then at last it was time to go, and he packed his shirts and his money while O.B. handed over Haig and O'Mara to a neighbour who doted on them. When he came back he looked worried.

'What's wrong?' said Walsh.

'You'll need a passport,' O.B. said.

'I've got a passport,' said Walsh. Too right, he thought. Just as soon as I took possession of my birthright.

'We'd better be off then,' said O.B.

They went out into the paddock, and Walsh swung the propeller the way O.B. had taught him, then scrambled into the double seat behind the pilot and the Avro bumped forward, building up the speed for takeoff, until at last the ground ceased nudging and the plane began to climb.

Maybe one day I'll buy a plane, thought Walsh. I've got the money. And maybe you won't, mate. He looked down below to where cattle were grazing. Down there's where you belong. You love it down there on the property . . .

He settled back in his seat with the luggage for company. The sun was shining and that should be a good omen, except that the sun usually was shining in Northern Queensland.

NATASHA

7

On the train home she thought about her day. The racing had been a good idea. York was not Longchamps of course, and most of the women were sadly lacking in chic, but that merely meant that most of the men looked at her, which was all very well at the races, but one had had to be careful at the – *mont de piété?* The pawnshop – that was it. But Dimitri had warned her about that, too. Really Dimitri had known about practically everything, and it was very difficult to manage without— but a train was no place for tears, she told herself. Not on one's own. You should have saved your tears for the pawnshop.

In Newcastle she had bought a raincoat of the dowdiest kind, and a cloche hat that was most unbecoming, and on the train she had tried to imagine that she was Madeleine Cantripp. This was difficult, but as Dimitri had told her, if you wanted to achieve a particular accent then you had to mimic a particular person, and Madeleine was the only one available. Dimitri said it was all because of a man called Stanislavsky, who had been in charge of the Moscow Arts Theatre and had invented this system, but her parents had disliked Moscow, and gone there only when it was necessary. Stanislavsky had brought his players to St Petersburg too, Dimitri said, but she couldn't remember. There were many things she couldn't remember . . . But that didn't matter. According to Dimitri, what mattered was that she was a good actress. All successful liars were.

Madeleine. 'Please call me Maddy,' she had said to Natasha, when at last they began to be friends. A quite extraordinary request, but she had complied. Her house at first had seemed to be full of dogs, but in fact there were only three, all loud, assertive and greedy. Rather like Oliver, Natasha thought. One of them, the bulldog, even had a limp. But Oliver would never do for Maddy, even though she seemed to think he would, which was tiresome. Maddy would be much happier with George.

In her head she listened to Maddy speak: about her house, her garden – and her major. Phrases came to her unbidden. 'So conscientious', 'never a shirker', 'the Army was so different before the war'. They gave her no idea what the major was like, not even whether he was good to sleep with, but then they weren't intended to. It was Maddy's voice that she was after. She couldn't speak aloud, not in a carriage with three other people, but she'd already practised on her own, and listening had its advantages. It brought Maddy to her so clearly. Soon she would begin to look more English, she thought. No rouge, and only a very little lipstick. Almost nondescript. That of course was dreadful, but it had to be done.

There were many pawnbrokers' shops in York. Perhaps it was because of the racing, or it might be the priests. In St Petersburg the priests were always seeking money, but that was because they drank . . . The shop she chose was in a quiet street, but it looked busy even so. A good sign. Deliberately Natasha began to remember Dimitri, until the tears were almost there.

Earnshaw looked up from his ledger as the young woman came in. Another officer's widow, he thought. Must have been quite pretty in her day. Please God don't let it be her husband's medals. They always cry when it's the medals, and this one's near tears as it is. He looked at the clock on the counter. French. Nineteenth century, with a fiver owing on it – and a fat chance of getting it back. Five to twelve.

'Good morning, madam,' he said.

'Good morning.' That cool, upper-class drawl without a trace of good Yorkshire. All the same she'd been pretty once, even if her coat and hat were terrible. Somebody else's most likely, he thought. Cast-offs.

'Can I help you?' he said.

'Oh, I do hope so,' said the woman. 'I would like to pledge these.' From a brown paper bag she produced two objects wrapped in tissue paper. Earnshaw unwrapped them: a watch and a bracelet – good quality stuff. This one really had known the good times.

'How much are you asking, miss?'

'Can't you advise me?' the woman said.

So often they say that, Earnshaw thought. Don't they realise I'm here to do them down? All the same, with stuff like that he could afford to be generous.

'Twenty-five?' he said.

In her mind Natasha screamed out: '*Thief! Murderer! Bolshevik!*' But she knew that if she began to argue she would be Natasha at once. Maddy would never argue.

'Thank you,' she said.

She walked back to the station and the left-luggage office where she had stored her other coat and an appropriate hat, then went into the Station Hotel to a lunch which was by no means to be compared with the Closerie des Lilas, though much better than anything attempted by the cook who had to be watched. In the restaurant men looked at her, some of them rather rudely (she had renewed her make-up) and she wondered which of them would attempt to pick her up. She hoped it would be one of those dressed for racing. That would save a taxi fare.

In the end it turned out to be what in Paris she had learned to call an 'Oh I say', because no matter what one said that was their invariable reply. He came over to her with a diffidence she found charming. No doubt it had taken all his courage to bring him from his table to hers. Quite pretty, too. She waited.

'Excuse the impertinence,' he said, 'but haven't we met somewhere?'

'You know perfectly well that we have not,' said Natasha.

Then out it came. 'Oh I say.' It never failed.

'But you may sit down,' she added, and he did so, rather abruptly.

'But weren't you at Lady Marshall's party in Eaton Square?'

'No.'

'Sorry,' he said. He looked spent – wasn't that the word? As if he had just lost a very long race.

'You're supposed to tell me your name,' she said.

'Bobby Wentworth,' he said. 'I came up last night. I have a horse running.'

No more than twenty-three, she thought, and he owns a racehorse. Perhaps more than one. She smiled at him.

'Natasha Tyrrwhitt,' she said, and offered her hand.

He took it, rather gingerly. 'Any relation to Lord Kielder?'

'My uncle,' said Natasha. This was not the time for nuances.

First he looked relieved, then disappointed. Being an earl's niece made her a lady, and he knew how to conduct himself with ladies. On the other hand what one definitely did *not* do with ladies was try to pick them up for carnal purposes.

'Oh,' he said at last. 'Your friend didn't turn up, I take it?'

'She sent me a telegram,' said Natasha. 'She missed the boat train.'

'A foreigner?'

'French,' Natasha said. 'Léonide Jacquard. She's a poet.'

'Oh I say,' said Wentworth.

Two in three minutes. Really, that wasn't bad.

'We were going to the races together,' she said.

He brightened at once. 'Perhaps you'll allow me to take you?'

'If you think my uncle would approve,' Natasha said.

Wentworth was sure of it. Moreover, he paid for her lunch.

He had a car too, a Rolls-Royce complete with chauffeur, who opened the door and saluted as she got in. Natasha walked past him as if he were invisible, Wentworth noticed, which is *not* the English way, but then her accent wasn't very English either, nor was the jade cigarette holder she took from her handbag. Even so he lit her cigarette for her.

'You live in these parts?' he asked.

'Sometimes,' said Natasha. After all, Northumberland wasn't so very far away. 'Mostly I have lived in Paris.' There just wasn't time to bother about Russia.

'Oh I see,' he said.

'What do you see?'

He blushed. 'The way you speak,' he said. 'The accent.' Manfully he added: 'It's very pretty.' Then even more manfully: 'And so are you.'

She looked ahead. The glass partition between them and the chauffeur was closed, but even so. 'You must not say that,' she said. 'The accent perhaps, but not the person. I think perhaps you are a *séducteur*.'

'Oh I *say*!' said Wentworth.

Three in one meeting. Really that must be some sort of record, she thought, and crossed her legs, whether as punishment or reward she was not quite sure.

The race meeting was a great success. There was a members' enclosure, and champagne, lots of champagne, and lots and lots of 'Oh I says' and their ladyfriends, most of whom Bobby Wentworth knew; many of them admired her, which was nice, though their ladies did not, which was nicer. Some gave her tips, and she looked around for a bookmaker, but Wentworth wouldn't hear of it. He sent an attendant instead. As for taking her money, he wouldn't dream of it.

'You can give me a cheque later,' he said. 'If you have to.'

She was pleased for him as well as herself when the horse won. It was Wentworth's horse.

After that she just drank champagne for a while. The rest of them spent most of the time looking through field glasses and shouting, but she didn't bet any more until quite late, when they went to look at the horses in the paddock and she saw one she liked. Its name was 'Old Comrade'. No Lenin, no Trotsky, would carry her money, but an 'Oh I say' explained it meant an old soldier, and half the people she'd known had once been that, including Dimitri. She put a tenner on it and it won at twelve to one. She told Wentworth that she would have to leave. He sent the attendant for her money and was, she was sure, about to offer her a lift to wherever it was she wanted to go, when another attendant, a rather grand one, came up and spoke softly to him. Wentworth looked at her wistfully.

'Summoned by royalty,' he said. 'I can't argue with that.'

'Of course not.'

'The Pragger Wagger at that.' She looked at him, puzzled. 'The Prince of Wales,' he said. 'Heir to the throne. All that. Try to stay till I get back.'

'I'll try.'

But her money was in her purse and she had drunk enough champagne, so that Wentworth was of no more use to her. The attendant led him away as another race began and all the other 'Oh I says' put their glasses to their eyes. Wentworth had forgotten his, and she picked them up absentmindedly and went in search of a taxi.

She returned to find the vicarage in uproar: only Mrs Greenhalgh seemed unperturbed, which for some reason agitated the vicar even more, as he spoke of murder, kidnapping, perhaps even worse. Oliver feared none of those things, but made no effort to reassure his father. He was far too busy worrying about his own conviction that Natasha had simply grown bored with the pack of them and gone back to Paris. George, summoned urgently from his office, was no help either, the vicar thought. All he did was agree with everything his father said. The gossip. The scandal. The shame. The shadows of Earl and Archbishop alike grew longer and longer.

Then suddenly she appeared. Radiant of course in a stunning and quite indecent dress, carrying a large and elegant bag, which contained, among other things, a dowdy raincoat, an unfortunate hat, and a pair of field glasses.

'Where on earth have you been?' said the Reverend Mr Tyrrwhitt.

Natasha put down the bag and took from it her handbag, then a cigarette and her holder and the little gold lighter Léonide had given her.

'Newcastle,' she said. 'Surely I told you?' She lit a cigarette.

'*For nine hours?*'

'Oh, I understand,' she said. 'You were worried about me. In that case I forgive the question.'

Tyrrwhitt flushed. 'You are my guest here,' he said. 'Naturally I was worried.'

'That is kind.' she said, 'and I thank you for it. I also went to York.'

'*York?*' For Tyrrwhitt that could only mean an Archbishop.

'It is quite easy,' Natasha said. 'On a train, you know.'

'But why?'

'There were races there. It was quite exciting. I won.'

'Much?' said Oliver, and she looked at him as if in disbelief at what she saw. 'It's a fair question,' said Oliver.

'It is totally irrelevant,' said his father. 'Whatever the custom may be in France – or in pre-Revolutionary Russia for that matter – in England it isn't done for unaccompanied young ladies to attend race-meetings.'

'Then that explains it,' said Natasha.

'Explains what?' said George.

Every bit as tiresome as his father, thought Natasha, but with much more charm. Perhaps it is his bottom, which I doubt that I will ever see. Far too much trouble. Better to let Maddy see it, though it might be as well to warn her before the honeymoon.

Aloud she said, 'Some of the gentlemen did act rather strangely.'

'Which gentlemen?' said Oliver. For some reason he seemed angry.

'In the Members' Enclosure.'

'How in the world did you get into the Members' Enclosure?' said George, and she nodded approval. It was a much more intelligent question.

'I was invited,' she said. 'You must not think I intended to – gate-crash?'

'Now look here,' Oliver began, but behind him Mrs Greenhalgh coughed, and he was silent. She spoke to the vicar.

'If you please, sir,' she said. 'Miss Natasha's bath is ready, and she should change for dinner.'

'Yes, of course,' said Tyrrwhitt, then to Natasha: 'Mrs Cantripp is dining with us. I shall of course inform her of what has happened. No doubt you will have much to tell her.'

'About York Races?' Natasha said, and then: 'I see. You mean because I won and there will be money for the barefoot children. Of course.'

'If you please, miss,' said Mrs Greenhalgh and opened the door for her, wondering if the little minx had the faintest idea of the chaos she created. But how in the world could she ask her that? It might spoil all the fun.

In the bedroom she helped Natasha to undress, but half-naked the younger woman said, 'I almost forgot,' and opened her purse. She took out a roll of banknotes, smoothed them carefully.

Lovely things, Mrs Greenhalgh thought. Paper as white as icing sugar: all crisp and crackling. And the letters black and gleaming as tar.

'You must have one of these,' Natasha said, then screwed one into a ball and threw it to her. 'Here.'

Mrs Greenhalgh fielded it neatly. A fiver, she thought. Not bad money for running a bath. Carefully she smoothed it, then gasped aloud.

'Oh miss,' she said. 'It's for twenty pounds.'

'So are most of the others,' said Natasha. 'I won them at the races.' She looked more closely at Mrs Greenhalgh. 'What is wrong? It is not enough?'

'It's far too much, miss.'

'Nonsense,' said Natasha, then went to her and kissed her cheek. 'Already you are worth much much more. Now choose a dress for me.'

She took off the rest of her clothes, put on the vast, unflattering bathrobe, and went to her bath. Mrs Greenhalgh looked at the twenty-pound note. Lovely it was. Really beautiful. From a lady. A real lady, and generous with it. All the same she couldn't help wondering if Miss Natasha hadn't bought her, like one of those serfs she'd heard her go on about. The red, she thought. The red really suited her – but then they all did, but tonight she'd put out the red. Bit of her own back, that would be. Red was the communists' colour after all.

Maddy wore blue of a kind that became her, and the dress showed a *great* improvement, though she still covered up far too much. But in time she would teach her.

'Maddy darling,' she said, and kissed her. Maddy blinked. The red dress was rather revealing, even by Natasha's standards.

'How lovely you look,' she said.

'Of course,' said Natasha. 'I won at the races.'

The gentlemen already had drinks: sherry for George and the vicar, whisky and soda for Oliver, but at a nod from his father Oliver opened champagne and poured two glasses.

'Oh, I don't think—' Maddy began.

'It is *good*,' said Natasha. 'Really you *must* drink it.'

Maddy sipped obediently, and found that Natasha was right. But how does she do it? she wondered. Champagne at the vicarage. Like a miracle! she thought, then wondered if that might not be blasphemous.

Dinner was bad (Mrs Greenhalgh had thought only of her twenty-pound note) but the Burgundy was good. At the end of the meal the ladies left the gentlemen to their port.

'You must speak to her,' the vicar had said, and Maddy Cantripp, biddable as ever, had said that she would try but oh, how she wished she'd refused that second glass of Burgundy. On the other hand she very much doubted if she could 'speak' to Natasha without it.

'The vicar says you went to York.'

'Mm,' Natasha nodded. 'Such fun. Lunch at the hotel—'

'On your own?'

'Who could I invite?' said Natasha. 'One of your children with no shoes? And then I went to the races in a Rolls-Royce. I won twice. Next time you must come with me.'

Oh dear God she means it, Maddy Cantripp thought. 'In a Rolls-Royce?' she asked.

'It belonged to a man called Wentworth. He had a horse, too. It won.'

'A man?'

This time there was no disguising the horror in her voice. Or was it envy?

'Very young,' Natasha said. 'I think probably a virgin.' Suddenly she looked hard at Maddy, then got up from her chair, went to her and kissed her. 'Don't worry,' she said. 'So far as I'm concerned he is still a virgin.'

It was unfortunate that the vicar should come in at quite that point. Two young ladies embracing – it was positively Sapphic – and Natasha as usual employing inappropriate language. But his sons were behind him: there was no escape.

'Do I interrupt?' he asked.

'Not at all,' said Natasha. 'I was telling Maddy about a man called Bobby Wentworth. We met at the hotel before the races.'

The vicar thought it best to sit, and his sons followed, George wary of the hearth rug.

'The hotel?' said Tyrrwhitt.

'Where I had lunch,' said Natasha.

Oh dear God, the vicar implored. Why me? Have I been so wicked?

'Nice lunch?' Oliver asked.

'I have eaten worse,' she said. Black bread in Siberia. Nothing at all in Siberia. Here, in this house.

'So you knew him?' said Tyrrwhitt.

'I do now,' said Natasha. It needed but that.

'Was he a bookie?' Oliver asked.

Natasha thought. 'He did not look like a scholar,' she said at last.

'A bookmaker.' Oliver sounded waspish. 'A man who takes bets.'

'He makes them,' said Natasha. 'I was telling Maddy. He had a horse that won. Also a Rolls-Royce.' She turned to Maddy. 'Darling, that blue is so good for you,' she said.

76

'Thank you,' Maddy Cantripp said. 'Blue can be a tricky colour sometimes—' But the vicar was looking at her: reproachfully the only word. Her voice faded.

'Do I understand that this rascal attempted to pick you up?'

For once it was George who interrupted his father. 'Young chap?' he asked. 'First name Robert?'

'Bobby,' said Natasha, and then, because she couldn't help it, 'Oh I say.'

To her delight he smiled: he had understood her. Then he turned to his father.

'Viscount Wentworth,' he said. 'He owns the pits in Wedderburn – the village next to Slagsby.'

'Good lord,' said Tyrrwhitt, and in his mind he prayed: Oh thank you God, for Lord Kielder had told him that Wentworth was a youth of blameless morals, a fact that Kielder attributed solely to Wentworth's mother, but a fact nonetheless.

George smiled at Oliver. 'Not unduly bright, young Wentworth. But rich. Really quite enormously rich.'

Oliver scowled, and looked at the coffee pot. Natasha, busy lighting a cigarette, ignored him, and Maddy poured.

'You have met him?' she asked.

'Once. Business of Lord Kielder's,' said George.

'He's sweet,' said Natasha, 'but that may be because his horse won. I had a fiver on it.'

The vicar thought: The Lord giveth, and the Lord taketh away, then added, because he at least tried to be a Christian: Blessed be the name of the Lord.

'You gambled much?' he asked.

'But that is what the races are for,' said Natasha. 'You think it is immoral?'

Immoral was not a word Tyrrwhitt liked to hear used in mixed company.

'Unwise,' he said.

'But I won quite a lot of money,' said Natasha. 'What is unwise about that? And anyway, all my family gambled, all the time, and yet they gave money to the Church. Especially when they won.'

'Would you like coffee?' Maddy asked.

'No,' said Natasha, 'but I will play the piano if you wish.'

Mozart because he had been Dimitri's favourite, and Bach because the priest thought that everything Bach wrote was holy, and then at last Chopin, because Bach made Maddy bewildered. She played badly – far, far too much champagne – but they applauded even so. At last Maddy said that it was time to go, and again it was George who offered to walk with her to her house. Oliver's wounded leg has its advantages, Natasha thought, but George tripped over the hearth rug as he left, and for a little while Oliver was happy. He began to search his pockets.

'Left my pipe somewhere,' he said.

'Then go and find it,' said his father. 'I want a word with Natasha.' Oliver limped out. Really, Tyrrwhitt thought, Madeleine Cantripp had been hopeless. Quite hopeless. But then Natasha was not an easy person to rebuke.

'This Viscount Wentworth,' he said. 'You would say he behaved like a gentleman?'

'Like some gentlemen,' said Natasha, 'but by no means all.' She thought for a moment. 'This title – this Viscount – it is what the French call a *vicomte*?' Tyrrwhitt nodded. 'Then our kinsman is greater. He is an earl.'

'Greater in some ways perhaps, but by no means as rich.' Doggedly the vicar returned to his duty. 'He did not attempt to molest you?'

'Sexually?' said Natasha. The vicar was glad that his sons were out of the room.

'I do not think Bobby Wentworth has molested any woman. Not yet. But he is nice.' She shrugged, and again Tyrrwhitt was glad that his sons were not there. Especially Oliver. 'You weren't happy that I went to York Races?' she said.

'No, I was not.'

'But I didn't go for immoral purposes – unless you include the gambling. And that is a family custom. Lord Kielder gambles too, and he owns horses. The Jacquards told me.'

'Lord Kielder is a man. Young ladies do not gamble.'

'Now there you are wrong,' Natasha said. 'In the Members' Enclosure *all* the ladies gambled.' She smiled. 'Many of them lost.'

The Members' Enclosure made it rather better. 'So you didn't go to a bookmaker?'

'Of course not,' said Natasha. 'Bobby Wentworth took care of everything.'

Tyrrwhitt sighed in relief. 'All's well that ends well, but please remember to be discreet, Natasha.'

She looked at him, her eyes wide open, guileless. 'How could I forget?' she said.

8

When she went to bed she fell asleep almost at once – so much
champagne, and claret and Burgundy, too – and soon she began to
dream, and because she had thought so much that day of Dimitri, she
dreamed of Siberia.

Ivan's gang of thieves had been defeated at last. This was
because they had robbed a Party Member. They had not intended
to do so, of course – that would have been inexcusably foolish –
but they did not find out until too late. Moreover the man had
escaped, and sent for the police immediately. Not that they were
called the police any more. 'Militia' was the word the people must
use, because where was the need for police in a Workers' Paradise?
Yet the militia did exactly the same things as the old police.
Indeed, many of them *were* the old police. Once she had tried to
explain this to Léonide, who had told her she was politically naïve.
It had been hard not to laugh.

They had sent her to what was called a Re-education and
Rehabilitation Centre, which was mostly lectures on Marxism-
Leninism and being beaten for not paying attention. The food was
atrocious, too, and she had run away, of course, but a guard had shot
her. The bullet scored her ribs and she had bled a great deal. She still
had the mark: she would always have the mark, but she had lived,
even though the hospital was much, much worse than the Re-
education and Rehabilitation Centre: the setting for her very worst
nightmares. Afterwards they had sent her to Siberia, to Camp 19.

The train journey too was bad: it was March after all, and the
trucks were shut tight to keep out the cold, but when she arrived the
first person she saw was Dimitri. At first she thought he was a guard
because he ordered everybody about and wore better clothes than
anyone else, but he was not. He was a prisoner like themselves – but a
unique one. The camp's commandant valued him highly, for he was
the only one there who could organise things, and he also knew how
to forge the sort of letters and permits that made life so much easier
for the commandant.

Dimitri took one look at her standing there shivering with the other new arrivals, and came to her. 'Name?' he said, and she told him. He looked at the list of names. 'Ah yes,' he said. 'Fluent French, English, and German.'

'Not German,' she said, but her voice was weak. No one else heard.

'German,' he said firmly.

'Yes, comrade,' she said.

Dimitri went to the lieutenant in charge of the camp guards. He was drunk.

'I have found my new assistant,' Dimitri told him. 'The commandant will be pleased.' This of course meant that the lieutenant was pleased, too.

'Did anybody bring any vodka?' he asked.

'It will be waiting for you,' Dimitri said.

The lieutenant smiled, and walked to a sledge, lay down and fell asleep. Dimitri tucked a fur blanket round him. As he explained to Natasha later, a drunken, useless lieutenant suited his purposes far better than a sober, efficient one.

The guards lined up the prisoners, and Natasha moved to join them. Dimitri restrained her.

'Not you,' he said. 'Didn't you hear? You're my assistant. You stay with me.'

A soldier drove the lieutenant's sledge, and the column followed, the prisoners' feet crunching the hardpacked snow.

Dimitri walked into the station, a pinewood shed with no buffet, no ticket office, no waiting room, just a pile of crates stacked in one corner, and a soldier from the train to guard them. He handed over a wad of money, and the soldier stowed it carefully away.

'Same stuff next time?' the soldier asked.

'More vodka,' said Dimitri, 'and a typewriter.'

The soldier nodded. 'Should be all right,' he said, then: 'What about her?'

'She's my assistant,' said Dimitri.

'She's the prettiest all right,' the soldier said, 'but I doubt if she'll last very long.'

'Give me a hand with the crates,' said Dimitri.

There was another sledge outside the station, and two men stacked the crates on it as she waited, shivering, till the soldier had left. At once Dimitri opened the crates, took out felt boots, a heavy coat and a fur hat, and shut up the crates again as she put them on.

'How did you know I spoke French?' she asked. 'Was it written on that paper?'

'Of course not,' he said and then: 'Do you speak French?'

'And English,' she said. 'But not much German. And anyway, what does it matter in this place?'

He climbed into the sledge, and she crouched beside him.

'We forge things here,' he said. 'Or rather you and I do. Sometimes it's in foreign languages. Passports, identity papers – stuff like that.'

'But why?'

'For the OGPU,' he said. 'You know what the OGPU is?'

'Secret police,' she said. 'They used to call it the Cheka.'

'Know it all, don't you?' Dimitri said.

'Not all,' she said. 'I don't know why you chose me. Unless it's because I am the prettiest – but then perhaps the soldier is right. Maybe I won't last very long.'

'It isn't as simple as that,' he said. 'Anyway, I haven't had time to think about it yet. But you'll last as long as me – I'll see to that.'

He shook the reins and the horse moved off, through a pine forest that seemed to have no beginning and no end, the only sound their voices and the crunch of snow beneath the sledge. As they drove he told her that he was a prisoner too, and that even if he did have great power, it would end the moment he failed to deliver what the commandant needed.

'And me too?'

'You too.'

'And what is the alternative?' she asked him.

He looked at the forest. 'Do you see yourself as a successful woodcutter?' he asked.

'Is that what the other women will be?'

'Most of them. A nurse, a good cook might get something better, but the rest of the women and all the men – the forest will get them all.'

'It will kill them,' she said.

'When it does it will be sent some more,' Dimitri said.

'I think I shall be an assistant forger,' she said, 'though I don't know if I'll be good at it.'

'You don't have to be,' Dimitri said. 'I am superb.'

They came to a clearing, barbed wire, watchtowers, guards with rifles.

'You haven't asked me why I don't run away,' Dimitri said.

'Because there's nowhere to run?'

'Not for hundreds of miles. Even alone I would have no chance.'

He was silent then as a sentry opened a gate, and they drove through. The new prisoners waited in a line to be registered, counted, examined, as they drove past the long prison huts. Natasha tried not to look at them, but she could not escape their hatred of her.

'They know,' she said.

'The guards will have told them,' said Dimitri, 'and it is sad. I agree that it is sad. But there is nothing that you or I or even the commandant can do about it.'

'What happened to my predecessor?'

'Vladimir? He had a heart attack.'

'*Vladimir?*'

Dimitri chuckled. It was the first time she had heard it: the sound that she could still remember.

'Don't jump to conclusions,' he said. 'Vladimir really was a forger.'

He pulled up at the back of one of the huts. A small house had been built on to it, a sort of annexe that used the hut as a shelter from the wind.

'Your palace, princess,' said Dimitri. 'Go inside and look around. I have to give this lot to the commandant – except for this.' Beneath the crates was a smaller one that he pulled free. 'Think you can manage it?' he said.

'Of course.' She took it and found it to be heavy enough to match what strength she had left, but forced herself to walk easily, naturally, until the sledge moved away.

There were three little hallways, each with its own door, to insulate the house from the unrelenting cold, but inside the place was warm: a stove glowed, wood was stacked, and she was glad to take off her hat, coat and boots before she looked about her. The place was small: a bedroom that was mostly a bed and a washbasin, and a packing case for clothes, though the bed was covered with a wolfskin blanket. The other room was bigger, and packed with all kinds of things: a hand press, a typewriter suffering from extreme old age, a desk with drawers stuffed with different kinds of paper, bookshelves of raw wood, though the books they contained – encyclopaedias, diction- aries, works of reference for the most part – were expensive and well-kept. She pulled one out at random. Inside was the bookplate of a Tsarist general. She had been to his daughter's fourteenth birthday party . . .

There was hot water, too; at the back of the stove, a basin, even soap. She stripped and began to wash herself. If he came back and saw her, then he saw her: she supposed it was what she was there for anyway, but at least she would be clean.

She looked at her body and wished she had a mirror. Not slim any more, she thought. Skinny. That hospital really had been a rehearsal for Hell. Still the man whose assistant she was didn't appear, and she dressed and found a samovar, made tea. At last he came in, and the cold came with him, until he shut the door.

'Do you like our little palace?' he asked.

She poured him tea. 'It's different,' she said.

'From your other palaces, princess?'

'Why do you call me that?'

'Isn't it what you were?'

She shrugged. 'That's all over. It's true I lived in a palace, but I also lived in a prison hospital. And now I live here, it seems.'

'The hospital in Leningrad?' She nodded. 'The worst of them all,' Dimitri said. 'We must build you up, princess.'

'Caviar, perhaps, and salmon, and roast chicken, and wine?'

'Caviar certainly,' Dimitri said, 'and food out of tins. Fish when the river thaws, but wine only when we're lucky. We're lucky today. Comrade Berin is pleased.'

'Comrade Berin?'

'The commandant.'

'Those cases?' she asked.

'Partly that. He will make a lot of money selling boots and hats to the prisoners.'

'But they have nothing.'

'Most of them have something,' Dimitri said. 'A watch, a ring. Even a gold tooth. Here felt boots are more important. But I gave him something else. Something that would have made him think of Christmas, if Christmas weren't illegal. A piece of paper.' She waited. 'A piece of paper signed by a commissar to say that Comrade Berin had filled his timber quota, and that Comrade Trotsky himself was pleased.'

'You wrote it?' Dimitri nodded. 'But suppose you are found out?'

'Then we'll all die. You. Me. Comrade Berin. But we'll all die anyway.'

He produced cigarettes, the first she had seen since the Rehabilitation Centre, and she inhaled one so fiercely her head swam. It was bliss.

'Easy,' Dimitri cautioned. 'Gently. Carefully. Here it's the only way.'

He opened the little crate he had given her. Tins of soup and stew and chicken – even caviar. Then he opened a cupboard. In it was more food, and vodka. He poured a glass for each of them.

'I am going to fatten you up. You will be quite safe till then,' he said.

They ate caviar and stew and black bread, and drank red wine from Georgia that the commandant had given Dimitri. Suddenly a klaxon sounded.

'Bed-time,' Dimitri told her. 'We retire early here, princess. Get up early, too.'

He lit a candle then turned out the lamp, and led the way to the bedroom. Natasha followed because there was nowhere else to go.

'Your clothes will be lousy,' Dimitri said . 'Best take them off. You can wear this shirt of mine.'

He passed one to her, and she undressed and so did he; then she put on the shirt and he searched under a pillow for pyjamas. A good body, she thought. Too good for her, the way she was now. He looked at her.

'No, no,' he said. 'First I must fatten you up.' Then he got into bed, pulled back the sheets so she could do the same, then covered them both, the wolfskins on top. 'Goodnight, princess,' he said. 'I'll get you some new clothes tomorrow.'

But already she was asleep.

That was how it was for the first few weeks. Food and sleep, and in between meals Dimitri at work and she helping him: translating documents in French and English, learning to use the terrible typewriter, fetching and carrying while he worked the press. The camp was all around them, brooding and silent for most of the day, when only the cooks and the sick and the off-duty guards were left behind: noisy with barking dogs, guards bawling orders, the crunch of footsteps when the prisoners set out for the forest and when they returned. She and Dimitri never went to watch, not even from the windows. We are too ashamed, she thought. We eat, we are warm, our work will not kill us. Of course we are ashamed. I am afraid, too, because if ever we fall from grace, if Comrade Berin has no more need of us and we too are sent to the forest, the other prisoners will kill us.

She hated Camp 19 – the guards, the dogs, even the other prisoners, because they hated her and shamed her too. She hated them all, except for Dimitri. She had decided that very early. It wasn't because he hadn't taken her when she was ill: that sort of romantic nonsense had no business in the camp. She loved him because of what he was, strong yet devious, cunning in survival – and not at all bad-looking, but it went beyond even that. He was there, and she loved him, and together they hated the rest of the only world they had.

One day the commandant came to the hut. To see if I'm the prettiest? she wondered. To take me from Dimitri? All the guards had a woman: the commandant could have a whole harem. And so he had, Dimitri told her later. He'd even brought one with him. A boy. What was the word the English had once used? His catamite. She had found it in some book or other, and asked her governess what it meant, but Miss Harrison had said that no lady should ever concern herself about such things. Even so the boy was very pretty, and terrified that the commandant would tire of him, and send him to the forest.

Berin was the only contented man in the camp. Even the guards hated it, but for the commandant it was his magic kingdom, a genie's gift. He was neither handsome nor clever, but thanks to his uncle, an economics adviser to Comrade Zinoviev, he had this wonderful job, with the pick of the prettiest boys and a clever and talented prisoner to do all the work he couldn't do himself. He watched Natasha as she worked at a translation, looking at her as he might look at a picture or a view; without a hint of desire. I thank You for this, oh merciful God, she prayed.

Then he turned to Dimitri. 'What is she doing?' he asked.

So I must not even speak, she thought. How happy I am to obey.

'She is translating an application form for a Belgian passport,' Dimitri said.

'Good God – why?' Berin asked, as if God still existed.

'No doubt because the OGPU wishes it,' said Dimitri.

Berin nodded. It was reason enough. Then he squeezed the cheek of the boy beside him: squeezed it too hard, too long, but the boy continued to smile.

'Come,' Berin said at last. 'It is time for our nap.'

That night she said to Dimitri, 'You have fattened me up enough.'

'Take your clothes off and we'll see,' he said, and she did so.

'Do I please you?' she asked.

'Of course,' he said.

'How much?'

'Come here and I'll show you,' Dimitri said.

It was protracted and fulfilling, as she had prayed it would be, and it was obvious that he had known a lot of women, but that didn't bother her. That was in the past. Now he was hers.

At last he said, 'Siberian tigress.'

'Me?'

'Of course you. Who else is here?' He lay back and said, 'What a wonderful way to destroy a man,' then he chuckled. 'You certainly are fattened up enough.'

He produced cigarettes and lit them. 'Why did you decide it was to be tonight?' he asked.

'The commandant.'

'Such a Cupid. Will you tell me why?'

'Because he can destroy us. I had no wish to be destroyed without ever—' Her hand reached out to him.

85

'Tigress, princess,' he said. 'Don't you know that a man must rest?'
'There may not be much time for resting.'
He took away her cigarette; his arms embraced her again.

9

Work by day, love by night: an islet of content in a sea of suffering. From time to time Dimitri went to collect more supplies when the prison train arrived, for the forest was always hungry, but she would not go with him. She could not endure such hatred a second time. When she needed exercise, she and Dimitri would walk around the camp while the other prisoners were in the forest, but for most of the time the two rooms were their world: a world that never changed, except that at last there were two typewriters instead of one.

One day he told her why he was in the camp. He had studied law for a while at St Petersburg University, but the academic life bored him, and when his parents died he left, drifted, tried his hand at acting, painting, engineering – until one day he discovered a printing press. 'The other great love of my life', he called it. His parents were bourgeois, but they had left him far less money than he had expected, and so he turned to forgery, and made a success of it too, from the very beginning, until at last the police began to be suspicious, and it was time to take a holiday abroad. To Switzerland.

A demure and friendly place before the war, he told her, where one could live quite well with the help of a little forgery. Printing, too. The legitimate kind. There were many Russian exiles in Switzerland before the war, and they all wrote pamphlets. Inevitably he had picked up some of the jargon of Marxism-Leninism, but he was never a believer.

'How could I be?' he asked her. 'I was a criminal even then, when I needed money. To a criminal private enterprise is sacrosanct.'

But he learned the big, important words: he even met Lenin.

'What was he like?' she asked.

'Strong,' said Dimitri. 'In the will. Very strong. He would have made a good crook.' From him that was praise.

'That's what he is,' she said, but he ignored it. Politics bored him.

When the war came he went back to Russia, which was foolish. He was safe in Switzerland. Perhaps that's why he went back, she thought. Security bored him, too – and look where recklessness had got him.

'I joined the Army,' he said. 'Saw a little fighting. Not much. Then I was wounded. Nothing serious, but it was silly to go on. We were obviously going to lose. So I forged my discharge papers and went back to Leningrad while it was still St Petersburg.'

'How did you live?'

He looked surprised. 'By forging,' he said. 'People always need papers. Money, too. Lovely notes in the Tsar's time. Even in Kerensky's.'

'You wouldn't forge money now?'

'No point,' he said. 'What is there to buy? Only food and warm clothes, and we've got them anyway.' He paused, holding her, his hands delighting in what they touched. 'In Kerensky's time I also got married,' he said.

'I hope she was a nice girl.'

'I hope so too,' said Dimitri. 'But it wouldn't be very often.'

'Pretty?'

'Of course,' said Dimitri, and before she could ask the question, 'but not as pretty as you. Also, she was fair.'

'What happened to her?'

'First the Communists came, then the famine, and she went to live with a commissar because she was hungry – only before she left she told him what I did for a living.'

'But why?'

'She wasn't sure what I might do if I stayed in St Petersburg, and neither was I, but the problem didn't arise. The commissar got me a single ticket to Siberia instead.'

'You've lived like this ever since?'

'*Like this?*' Very gently, he shook her. 'I had to work my way up to these great heights of ours. I began in the forest like everybody else.'

'Except me.'

His hand covered her mouth. 'I didn't hear that,' he said. 'You didn't say it. Cross yourself.' She did so, and so did he.

'It wasn't so bad for me,' he said. 'I was a crook, you see.'

'Well, I know that,' she said.

'What I mean is, I wasn't a political. The politicals were the ones who got the worst of it because their crimes were far worse than mine.'

'What crimes?'

'Being a bourgeois, failing to understand Marx, not listening to Lenin. These were terrible crimes. We crooks were just thieves or murderers. What we did was hardly a crime at all. More of a misdemeanour. So I got the easy jobs – and easy jobs meant easy pickings. A chance to steal food, even vodka sometimes, for people who could pay.' She shivered.

'Then my great opportunity came,' he said. 'Berin had just arrived –

and he'd been told about me. Somebody in Moscow needed a forger, and I was the best. What was needed was a Nansen passport for a refugee trying to get into the United States, and I made it for them.'

'Them? The OGPU?'

'They were still the Cheka in those days, but it would be them. Bound to be, though I wasn't fool enough to ask.'

'Of course not,' she said.

'Berin also had trouble with his quota returns,' said Dimitri, 'and I was able to help him there, too. Help him quite a lot. So first I got my little palace, then I got an assistant, and now I've got you.' He moved closer, easing her to him.

'I loved you from the moment I saw you,' he said, 'Which is a reaction so ridiculous I refused to believe it. The wrong word, I told myself. Stick to "like" or "need" or "desire", but it was love all right. From the very beginning.'

'Let us see how much,' she said, and he chuckled yet again.

Of course she became pregnant; it was inevitable. At first she had worried about the future of a child born in Siberia, but at last she realised that that was not the point. The point was who the child's father was, and since its father was Dimitri, the child's future would be better than that of most babies born in Siberia. And perhaps it would have been . . . if she and Dimitri hadn't taken a walk that particular day at that particular time. Exercise, Dr Brodski had told her, was most important. Dr Brodski had been trained in France and the United States, and with such a background he, of course, was a prisoner too, but the commandant would not allow him near the forest: not since he'd cured the commandant's gonorrhoea.

So they had taken a walk while the other prisoners were in the forest. How far gone had she been then? Three months? Four? Enough to show, anyway. Not that Berin and the guards gave a damn – in the camp women were always getting pregnant. And a cook suddenly ran out of the kitchens and kicked her in the stomach. She was mad, of course, but that did not stop Berin from having her flogged, then shot. It did not stop her from losing the baby, either. Brodski did his best, but it was not enough. The cook had still had a great deal of strength left in her . . .

When she was well enough, Brodski told her things about her insides, quite fascinating things, including the fact that she had had a hysterectomy, but she begged him not to tell Dimitri the other little details. A girl should have some secrets, after all.

When she was well enough she went back to work, and they were lovers again. The first time, she almost had to rape him, such was his fear of hurting her. But after that they were happy enough, until the day he said, 'It's time for us to go.'

89

'Go where?' A stupid question, but then his statement was senseless too.

'Away from here.'

'But how can we?' she asked him. 'You said yourseif—'

'If we stay here we'll die,' he said.

'We're to be sent to the forest?'

He shook his head. 'Cholera.'

'Here?'

'Almost certainly. Camp 23 had it, and Camp 23 is now wiped out. Just two weeks ago we had seventeen prisoners from Camp 23. Five of them are now in hospital.'

'Who told you this?'

'The guard commander. He wanted me to forge a railway warrant for him.'

'And did you?'

'Of course,' Dimitri said. 'But it isn't very good. He won't get far.'

'What about Berin?'

'He's in love again,' said Dimitri. 'Far too busy to read reports about Camp 23.'

'But where will we go?'

'There's a train,' said Dimitri. 'Not the prison train. Mostly it's for coal, but there are also carriages for important people – nice carriages. I wouldn't want you to be uncomfortable, princess.'

'Can we do it?'

'There's a spur line three days' ride from here. It's where they load the coal. We'll join it there.'

'But how can we?'

'Horse and cart,' he said. 'We have all the papers. It's worth a try.'

'You think we can do it?'

'I think we must,' he said.

Next night they stole the horse and cart, and set off by moonlight, taking only the very best of their stores, and a new dress for her, a suit for Dimitri. As they drove away – the guard on the gate was drunk on Dimitri's vodka – there came the sound of shots.

'They've heard about the cholera, poor devils,' said Dimitri. Later there were more shots, and then the glow of flame.

'Confusion,' he said. 'The answer to our prayers.'

'Will they all die?' she asked him.

'Most of them. But that's why they were sent here, after all.'

He shook the reins and urged the horse to a trot, but was cautious not to tire it. There was a long way to go, and in summer the weather was hot – too hot for galloping.

'It will be good to see St Petersburg again,' said Natasha.

He put one arm around her. 'Among the many things I love about you,' he said, 'are your courage – and your optimism.'

Dimitri made it look easy, but of course it wasn't. It was frightening. In order to get seats on the train they had to be important and that, in theory at any rate, was not so difficult. He was a high-ranking official in the Department of Justice, and she his secretary. They had a briefcase apiece to prove it, and he a new suit, she a new dress, all stolen from Berin. God alone knew what use Berin found for the dress, but it fitted her well enough. Worn by one of his boys, no doubt . . . They also had papers – the best Dimitri could make, and letters from the Minister marked *Urgent* and *Secret*.

But important officials, no matter how convincing their documents, do not travel by horse and cart, unless there has been a serious misadventure, and so they invented one. They had had a car, a good car, made in Germany and impounded after the war, with a chauffeur and bodyguard, and were on their way to Camp 19 to investigate certain irregularities there. Unfortunately the chauffeur and body-guard had heard of the cholera outbreak in the camp, and had fled. In the car. Comrade Director Rykov had been forced to commandeer the horse and cart so that they could make their way to the train. They had neither the intention nor the desire to visit Camp 19 until the situation there became calmer.

As they travelled they tested the story, probing it for loopholes. Dimitri would do all the explanations. As Comrade Director it would be expected of him, but even she, his secretary, was a person of some power. It must show in her demeanour. Haughty manner, Dimitri told her. Sneer a lot. The haughtiness came naturally to her, but after a little practice she sneered well, too. It must be the fear, she thought. If we are found out it will be terrible. How wrong Dimitri was to call me an optimist.

When they reached the spur line the train was in, and railway gangers were coupling up the coal wagons. Of the passenger coach there was no sign. A militia man came up to them, and saw only the horse and cart driven by a man in need of a shave.

'What the hell are you doing here?' he asked.

Dimitri snapped his fingers, and Natasha opened her briefcase, took out his papers and gave them to him.

'Take us to whoever's in charge,' he ordered, and showed the papers to the militia man.

It was obvious that the militia man couldn't read, and equally obvious that he was terrified of those who could when they spoke like that; terrified even of the expensive paper Dimitri held, and its elaborate printing. He ran off at once.

'Insolence,' said Dimitri, for the benefit of anyone who might be listening.

'Yes indeed, Comrade Director,' said Natasha.

The militia sergeant scurried up, took one look at the papers and wondered what he was supposed to have done and who had denounced him. 'Ministry of Justice' could only mean the OGPU.

'Have you an office?' Dimitri asked.

'Yes indeed, Comrade—'

'Comrade Director Rykov,' said Dimitri. Natasha sneered.

'This way, if you please,' said the sergeant. 'May I carry your briefcase?'

'You may not,' Dimitri said, and the sergeant worried that that too might be a crime.

The office was passably clean and had two chairs. Dimitri took the one behind the desk, Natasha the other, and the sergeant stood.

'Now listen to me,' Dimitri began. From outside there came a hiss of steam. 'What is that?'

'The train is about to leave, Comrade Director.'

'No, it is not,' said Dimitri. 'Go at once and tell the driver to wait.'

'Yes, Comrade Director.' He went off at the double.

'Really I'm quite pleased at the way this is working out,' said Dimitri. 'There is so much to do in Moscow, wouldn't you say?'

'Always, Comrade Director,' said Natasha.

'Let me see the Berin file,' Dimitri said, and she handed a file from the briefcase. Dimitri turned the pages.

'What a rascal the man is,' he said. 'A positively bourgeois greed for money.' He turned more pages. 'And a homosexual, too.'

'Good gracious,' said Natasha, and then: 'What will happen to him?'

'He will be dealt with. I'll telegraph Headquarters when we reach the next station. They'll send someone – probably someone quite junior. Now that I've reviewed the case—'

The sergeant returned, and Dimitri stared at him unblinking. Natasha looked haughty and sneered.

'You gave the driver my instructions?' Dimitri asked.

'Yes, Comrade Director.'

'Then let me tell you what has happened to us,' Dimitri said.

Out the story came and the sergeant took it without a blink, pitying the chauffeur and bodyguard, but despising them too for thinking they could escape such a man.

'My visit here is most secret,' said Dimitri. 'You will tell no one. Nor will the guard on duty. I shall hold you responsible for this.'

'Yes, Comrade Director,' said the sergeant. 'Do you want the carriage?'

'Of course.'

'I'll have it coupled up at once.'

'Send tea,' said Dimitri. 'Hot water. And a razor. I need to shave.'

'Immediately, Comrade Director.'

He dashed off again, and Natasha started to speak, but Dimitri said softly, 'I think there's a man listening beneath the window. Probably that guard. Talk about Berin.'

'We're making trouble for him?' she said, her voice as soft as his.

'My God, I hope so. If he's still alive.'

The sergeant carried their suitcases to the carriage, but not the briefcases, and handed them to a railway attendant. The coach was luxurious, a survivor of the old days, with decent furniture and comfortable beds. The servant looked like a survivor of the old days too, thought Natasha, though his fear of the OGPU was entirely contemporary. She had not been looked after so well since before the Revolution.

They changed trains several times, and their stories varied, but whatever story they told involved the threat of the OGPU. There was no trouble. They reached Leningrad at last. Dimitri took her at once to a house in a street that had once been charming, but now seemed in danger of collapse, but inside it was well-preserved and warm. The people who lived in it were like themselves – criminals, deviationists, fugitives, but they were the first ones to come back from a camp, which made them heroes: yet to live in Leskov Street worried her.

'But how can we live here?' she asked.

'Nobody lives here,' said Dimitri. 'It was condemned years ago.'

'But your friends. Us too. We have to register where we live.'

'We live nowhere,' Dimitri said. 'We don't exist.' He smiled. 'Officially it is true. Camp 19 was almost wiped out, and our hut was burned to the ground. We have been reported dead.'

'Who told you this?'

'A clerk who needed money. I gave him some of my best. The Comrades think we're dead, princess. To look for us would be foolishness.'

'But the militia—'

'We bribe them. One of them brings his girlfriend here, and we don't tell his wife. We're nice – when people are nice to us.' He kissed her.

'Princess,' he said. 'I was in Camp 19 for three years and when I came back my house was still here. Trust me.'

'I have no choice,' she said, 'but I do anyway.'

He began forging again almost at once. Business was brisk; permits, internal passports, even money. At night they went and gossiped with the others: the former Preobrajenski Guard major, the former

Professor of Rhetoric, the burglar, the pickpocket, the painter, and their girls who were so sweet to her because she had survived the camp. It was like being back in Ivan's gang all those years ago, except that they were all grown-ups, but it was nice to have people to talk to – until Dimitri died and she went to work in the cigarette factory.

The people in Leskov Street found her a doctor who was as vulnerable as the rest of them, but he knew his business. Heart, he told her. Perhaps he had been subjected to undue physical pressure? Worry? Anxiety? All three, she thought, and love. Love, too, can kill . . .

The people in Leskov Street were very kind, but even so they abandoned Dimitri's body in wasteland a long way from where they lived. To Natasha it was not important. Wherever Dimitri was, it was not in that lump of dead meat that wore his clothes, but the others expected her to weep for him, and so she did, and afterwards she left them, to become respectable, one of the masses, and wait for Léonide Jacquard. It was easy to be respectable. The papers Dimitri had forged for her achieved even that.

The next morning, Natasha went down to breakfast in the vicarage wearing what she thought of as her Sunday dress, and Mrs Greenhalgh looked surprised. Natasha smiled.

'Today I go to Slagsby,' she explained.

Mrs Greenhalgh smiled, too. 'Yes of course, miss,' she said. 'Lunch with Mrs Cantripp, I'm told. Perhaps you'd better have an English breakfast.'

'Who will make it?'

'Me, miss,' said Mrs Greenhalgh. It was delicious.

Afterwards Maddy came for her in a car she had hired for the day, and a chauffeur. It wasn't as good as the English *vicomte*'s car, but good enough, and the chauffeur gaped when he saw her in a most satisfactory manner, despite her dowdy dress. On the way Maddy talked of Oliver, which was tiresome.

'He drinks too much,' Natasha said.

'All military men do,' said Maddy. 'Even the major, but he was always a gentleman, even in his cups.'

'Oliver too is always a gentleman,' said Natasha, 'because he *is* a gentleman, but when he is drunk he swears. He's rude, too.'

Maddy sighed. She had no doubt that what she heard was the truth.

'George doesn't get drunk,' Natasha said, and Maddy sighed again.

'Did I tell you that the vicar has fixed the date for the concert?' she said. 'September the fifteenth. A Friday.'

'You have all your performers?'

'Natasha, please call them artistes,' said Maddy. 'They much prefer it, and really it's very difficult to persuade them to – to appear. A little flattery does wonders.'

'Of course, darling,' Natasha said. 'Who will – appear?'

'Mr Sowerby will play his flute,' Maddy said, 'and Mrs Gorton her cello – if her rheumatism will let her.' Natasha snorted.

'Yes, I know.' Maddy giggled. 'But that's exactly what she said. I knew you'd enjoy it. Then there's Miss Golightly, who sings, and so does Mr Binns.'

'It seems I shall have a busy night.'

'You will indeed,' Maddy said. 'There's your solo, too, but we also have Miss Digby, who recites, and Commander Harper, who tells funny stories. Respectable ones of course.'

'Of course,' said Natasha.

'And the school choir, but they sing unaccompanied.'

'An exciting evening,' said Natasha. Maddy looked at her suspiciously, but Natasha could always look guileless when she chose to.

'Will there be tickets?' she asked.

'Admission will be by programme only,' Maddy said. 'Price one shilling.'

Dimitri would have adored to print the programmes, Natasha thought, and forge an extra one for himself.

They were in the country now, a sort of moorland that Maddy called fells, that was mostly heather and sheep and trout streams, then the car climbed to the crest of a hill, and everything changed.

'Here we are,' said Maddy.

A hill that was not a hill, but a heap of waste dug from below the ground: a hollow tower called a shaft, with wheels on top, which Maddy said was a winding engine, lowered the miners below the ground in an enormous sort of lift, then brought up the coal they dug. A few sheds nearby, some ageing bicycles and the manager's car – and that was all there was to see of Slagsby Pit. All the rest was beneath their feet.

Further off there were the miners' cottages, terraced in long, precise rows; small and cramped, smoke-blackened and mean. Not Camp 19, thought Natasha, but I would hate to live in one. A few women in shawls or cardigans and aprons hurried in and out of the shops, a few men squatted by the kerbside, gossiping.

'Miners,' said Maddy.

They wore terrible clothes, of course – cheap blue suits, clumsy boots, caps that seemed glued to their heads, and they were pale because they spent so much of their lives below ground, but at least they looked as if they ate quite often. Better than Camp 19.

95

'But where are all the children without shoes?' she asked. 'At school?'

'Indoors,' said Maddy. 'They're not allowed to go to school.'

She pointed to a building of grimy brick with pointed railings around it that Natasha had thought was a prison. Perhaps it was. Near it was a church, also built of brick, and also grimy. And no wonder, thought Natasha. Even on that mild August day every kitchen chimney smoked, but then they had to, it seemed. The kitchen fire not only warmed its occupants, it cooked their food and heated their water, too. As they drove down the street men and women alike turned and stared. Cars in Slagsby were a treat not to be wasted.

They pulled up at a house near the church; a house as mean and grimy as all the others, but on its own, not part of a terrace, and with some attempt at a garden. Maddy knocked, the door opened at once, and one more shabby woman in a cardigan – a large one this time – stood and stared. Servant, thought Natasha, but it was the curate's wife.

'Mrs Carrick,' said Maddy, 'how nice to see you. May I introduce my friend Miss Tyrrwhitt?'

Cautiously Natasha offered her hand. The woman looked strong, but somewhere she had learned to be gentle, and took it carefully.

'How do you do?' she said, 'may I get you some coffee?' and continued to stare. She is memorising what I'm wearing, Natasha thought. Probably pricing it, too. And I don't even like what I'm wearing. Boring coat, unsuccessful dress, a hat that Greenhalgh despises. That Mrs Carrick would know all about her she had no doubt.

'Tea,' she said firmly. 'I should like tea.'

'Me too,' said Maddy.

'Yes, of course,' said Mrs Carrick. 'I'll just take you in to Arthur first.'

'Arthur?' Natasha said.

'My husband,' said Mrs Carrick. 'He's in the study.'

Rather a grand name for it, Natasha thought, but there were books and a writing desk, a gramophone and an aspidistra plant by the window. The junior priest – what was it? – *curate*, that was it, seemed more pleasant than his wife, and at least as strong. For a priest he didn't look like much of a drinker, either, but then in England priests quite often weren't. Tea was all that she would get.

Again Maddy introduced her, and again she received an appraising stare, more furtive than his wife's.

'I was told that Mr Tyrrwhitt had a relative staying with him,' said Carrick. 'Have you travelled far?'

'From Paris,' said Natasha.

At once Carrick looked arch. It was extraordinary how many Englishmen looked arch when one mentioned Paris.

'You must find Haydon Priors very dull, after Paris,' he said.

His clerical suit was old, worn, and not very well cut, but it was neat and clean, and his – dog collar did they call it? – gleamed. His accent was not like Mrs Greenhalgh's, but it was the accent of a region even so: *not* of a public school. Rather a common sort of man, Maddy had called him, but it might be possible to pity him.

Even so she spoke severely. 'There is much to do in Haydon Priors,' she said. 'The concert for the bootless children.'

'Shoeless,' said Carrick.

'But most of the ones I have seen wear boots,' said Natasha.

'Yes, but – forgive me – the word "bootless" has another connotation which might lead to confusion when applied to children.'

'What other connotation?'

'Useless,' said Carrick sadly. '"Bootless children" might be understood to mean "useless children", and that I hope and pray they are not. Merely deprived ... You are involved in the concert?'

He knows perfectly well that I am, thought Natasha, but he does not wish us to know that he gossips, which is nice.

'Miss Tyrrwhitt is our pianist,' Maddy said. 'She will play a solo, too.'

'Splendid,' said Carrick.

'And I wondered,' said Maddy, 'if there is any talent in Slagsby we might call upon.'

Carrick considered. 'There is talent,' he said at last, 'but most of it is of a rather dubious nature.'

Natasha longed to see it, but knew it was impossible.

'There's Slagsby Band,' said Maddy.

'It's a Temperance Band,' said Carrick. 'Most of them are Nonconformists. They wouldn't go near a church.'

'But it will not be in the church,' said Natasha, as Mrs Carrick brought in the tea-tray. 'It will be in the church hall. And anyway, I don't go near the church either.'

The tea-tray wobbled; the best china tinkled.

'You don't?' Carrick was astounded.

'I can't,' said Natasha. 'I'm Russian Orthodox.'

The Carricks looked at each other. The information pleased them. Perhaps it is because Tyrrwhitt is ashamed of my faith, she thought. Perhaps it appears shameful to them, too, and they dislike Tyrrwhitt very much.

'Will you join us, my dear?' Carrick asked.

'Yes please,' the large woman said. 'I brought another cup just in case.'

As she poured the tea, Natasha produced her cigarettes and holder, but the Carricks scarcely even blinked. They were still enjoying the thought that she didn't go to Tyrrwhitt's church.

'Are there many on the list this time?' Maddy asked.

'Far too many,' said Carrick. 'Of course the weather is mild at present, but autumn begins early in this part of the world, and even in summer-time they shouldn't go about barefoot. And of course they miss school as well.'

'Why is that?' said Natasha.

'If they're barefoot they are far more vulnerable,' Carrick explained, 'and if they had an accident the school would be held responsible. There simply aren't enough funds to cope with that.'

Mrs Carrick took a notebook from her husband's desk and leafed through it. 'Twenty-nine pairs,' she said. 'Average price ten shillings a pair. That's fourteen pounds ten – and the fund is down to its reserves.'

'Two hundred and ninety programmes,' said Maddy, sounding dismayed.

'We must hold a collection also,' Natasha said, 'and a – a raffle.'

'Gambling?' said Mrs Carrick. 'Mr Tyrrwhitt might not like that.'

Maddy said firmly, 'Mr Tyrrwhitt's feelings are one thing; barefoot children another.'

Again the Carricks looked pleased. Natasha in turn was both pleased and surprised at her friend's spirit.

'I take it they are all genuine cases?' Maddy said at last.

'I'm not entirely sure about Mrs Elstob,' said Mrs Carrick.

'Now Dolly,' Carrick began. 'Her life's extremely hard.'

'Harder than the others?' said Natasha.

'She's a widow,' Mrs Carrick said. 'I rather suspect she takes her children's shoes to the pawnshop.'

'She drinks, you see,' said Carrick.

What useful places pawnshops were, thought Natasha, but there were limits. One's children's shoes were beyond them. And yet to be a poor widow in Slagsby would be very unpleasant, especially if one could not drink.

'Are we to meet her?' she asked.

'In the church hall,' said Mrs Carrick. 'After we've finished our tea. We'll meet all of them.'

10

Twenty-nine sad mothers, all with pinafores over their dresses, all with cardigans or shawls, all of them memorising the clothes she wore. Some of them had brought their children, as if to prove they had no shoes, and they stared too – and always at me, Natasha thought, though today Maddy is dressed quite prettily, but then she didn't come here from Paris or go to York Races with a milord. Natasha had no doubt that the vicar's servants had handed on every juicy morsel. Servants always did.

How old the women looked, to have children still at school, but then the children also looked old. Poverty did that, and deprivation. Camp 19 had proved it again and again, and there had been so many poor and deprived in Camp 19. She followed Maddy and the Carricks down the hall, past the mothers and children who sat on benches, to where chairs and a table had been arranged for them. Before she could take out her cigarettes, Carrick began to pray. The mothers and children clasped their hands and closed their eyes, and Natasha looked at them. Some were obviously lousy, two of the children had ringworm, and one had a sort of iron contraption on his legs, though his feet were bare. She wondered how he had got to the hall. Perhaps his mother had carried him. It was good that she hadn't smoked, she thought. For a little while God had been near.

Carrick finished his prayer and spoke to them.

'Now you all know why we're here,' he said. 'It's a sad and distressing business, and since the government won't do anything about it, then it will have to be charity.'

Is this priest a Bolshevik? Natasha wondered.

'The ladies with me have arranged a concert in Haydon Priors,' Carrick said. 'The money for the shoes will be raised, I promise you.'

His audience sat, impassive, until a small, fierce woman put up her hand like a child in school.

'Yes?' said Carrick.

The woman spoke in an accent far stronger than Greenhalgh's.

'When, sir?' she asked. 'I mean we're all very grateful, believe me, but it'll be cold soon, and the bairns are missing their schooling.'

'Two weeks,' said Carrick. 'The fund's rather low at the moment, but it will be in two weeks, I promise you.'

'It must be now,' said Natasha.

'But my dear Miss Tyrrwhitt—' Carrick began.

'I will advance the money,' Natasha said.

'We both will,' said Maddy. 'I can't think why it never occurred to us before.'

Because Tyrrwhitt would dislike it, thought Natasha. He detests everything that concerns Slagsby, because it makes him ashamed. Once again Carrick and his wife looked at each other. They too knew that Tyrrwhitt would be annoyed.

'Very well,' Carrick said. 'What can I do but accept your very generous offer?'

'Hear, hear,' said his wife, and the small, fierce woman applauded, and the rest of them joined in. Natasha sought and found in her handbag a ten-shilling note, and folded it unseen into a small, neat square.

'If there is no other business—' Carrick said.

'If you please,' said Natasha. 'I have a question.' She looked at the women in front of her. 'I come from Russia,' she said, and they all sighed in unison. All the stories from Haydon Priors vicarage were true. They waited, eager for more.

'In my country,' Natasha continued, 'when we visit a new place, it is considered good luck to shake hands with a widow, particularly a widow with a child.'

This was the most utter nonsense, but Slagsby – the whole world, for that matter – would believe anything at all about the country that had produced Rasputin, Lenin and Trotsky in rapid succession.

'Is there a widow here?' she asked.

The small, fierce woman said, 'I'm a widow. Name of Elstob.'

'Would you please shake hands with me?' said Natasha.

'Be a pleasure, miss.'

Mrs Elstob came up to her, carefully wiped her hand on her apron, and grasped Natasha's: the ten-shilling note found its new owner.

Only for a second did Mrs Elstob look bewildered, then softly she said, 'Thank you, miss.'

'My pleasure,' said Natasha. 'You will bring me luck.'

Mrs Elstob went back to her seat, her hand in the pocket of her pinafore, and then, for no reason that Natasha could understand, the women applauded once more. When they left she saw that Mrs Elstob's child was the one with irons on its legs. How could the poor woman survive without a drink?

They went back to Maddy's house for lunch: a neat house with a neat garden, neat maid, neat furniture – everything neat except the dogs. Neat food, too, thought Natasha, which fitted exactly on the Royal Doulton plates. Even the wine was neat, inasmuch as there wasn't enough of it to spill over in the glass. But even so, Maddy was improving. The first time she'd eaten in her house there had been no wine at all.

'How will we do it?' Maddy asked at last. 'The money, I mean. For the shoes.'

'Just give me your half,' said Natasha. 'George will see to it.'

'Not Oliver?'

Natasha said severely, 'George is a solicitor,' and Maddy said, 'Oh yes. Of course.'

They began to talk of the concert, and its music.

When the chauffeur drove her home, Natasha went at once to the piano. She had drunk very little wine, and needed the practice. Chopin, she thought. That damn Pole yet again, but it was expected. The *Polonaise Militaire* because it made so much noise, and for the encore – she would take an encore whether they applauded or not – a waltz. The one they all loved so much, the one they all called the *Minute Waltz*, though it took at least twice that time no matter how well one played. And so she practised, in the only way that made sense: the same section, even the same phrase, played over and over until it was as good as she could make it. When at last she rested, Mrs Greenhalgh tapped at the door.

'Tea, miss?'

'Oh yes,' said Natasha. 'Tea at once.' And in it came.

'Greenhalgh,' Natasha said, 'I could not live in this house another minute without you.'

Mrs Greenhalgh poured. 'Slagsby was bad, miss?'

'Terrible,' said Natasha.

'Like Russia, miss?'

Natasha sipped her tea. 'Nowhere else in the world is quite like Russia,' she said, 'but it is very bad.'

'I was born there, miss,' said Mrs Greenhalgh.

'Then it was very sensible of you to go away,' Natasha said.

Mrs Greenhalgh took it in her stride. It was just the way miss was, after all. Say what you like and to hell with the consequences. Her Herbert had been the same. She liked it.

'The red dress tonight, miss?' she asked.

'No, the yellow,' said Natasha, and then: 'I must get some new ones.'

The door slammed, and heavy footsteps made their uncertain way up the stairs. Oliver had been to his club in Newcastle again. Halfway up, he began to sing, loudly, as he always did when he was drunk.

> *'There is a happy land,'* he bawled,
> *'Far, far away,*
> *Where I achieved a stand,*
> *Five times a day.'*

Mrs Greenhalgh giggled for a moment, and Natasha thought hard. It was indecent. It had to be. He was always indecent when he was drunk.

'Explain it to me,' she ordered, and Greenhalgh did so. Really without her she simply *couldn't* have survived here.

'So it's a hymn?' she said.

'Sort of Salvation Army kind of hymn,' Mrs Greenhalgh said. 'Different words, of course.'

'Of course.' Natasha took out her cigarettes. 'I simply *must* get some new dresses,' she said.

The solution came through the letterbox next morning, in a letter to her from Léonide. The priest seemed frantic to know what was in it, perhaps because of the French stamp, or perhaps simply because it was for her. After breakfast she told him.

'My cousin Léonide is in London,' she said. 'She wants me to go to stay with her there.'

The Savoy and Covent Garden for bait, she thought, and a rally of Marxists that she would not attend. She would go to Harrod's instead.

'But how could you possibly?' said Tyrrwhitt.

'By train.'

'On your own?'

On one's own is far better than with forty others, she thought, and with only one big bucket for a lavatory.

'I came here on my own,' she said.

'I should be happy to escort you,' said Oliver.

'Out of the question,' his father snapped.

'Besides,' said Natasha, 'you might find it necessary to sing.'

Oliver flushed, and George watched closely. A foul blow, and a hard one, too. He'd obviously been to his club yesterday, he thought. He shouldn't sing such songs where Natasha could hear. All the same she could take care of herself, even though he wished she couldn't.

The priest could not have been more anxious if she had been his own daughter, and seventeen years old. Young ladies in his day did not travel on their own, and all this gadding about made her seem so restless. And where would she stay?

'The Savoy,' said Natasha. 'Léonide has invited me.'

'Golly, she must be rich,' said George.

'Well, of course she is,' said Natasha, and the priest looked relieved. Better not tell him that she is amorous too, but only with young ladies. She went upstairs to watch Greenhalgh pack her suitcase and gossip. When she came down again, Oliver was waiting for her.

'I'm sorry about the singing,' he said. 'I was drunk.'

'I know.'

'You saw me?' he asked.

'I heard you,' said Natasha, 'and so did Greenhalgh. Really Oliver, it is not gentlemanly to embarrass a servant like that.'

In the taxi on the way to the station she thought of what she had said. Greenhalgh hadn't been in the least embarrassed, but Oliver couldn't possibly know it, which was all that mattered.

The trip to London was a great success. To begin with Léonide was in love again, and not with her for a change, so that she had been spared all those tears and tantrums at bed-time.

'But why did you invite me?' she asked.

'Simply to look at you, _chérie_. It's a great pleasure to look. Touching is better, of course, but looking is nice.'

'It must be because you are a poet.'

Léonide had seemed baffled at that, but pleased also.

'Do you know,' she said, 'I think that perhaps it is.'

Natasha had been spared the political meeting, too. It was to be a large one in a dreary hall miles from the good shops, but there was at least the possibility that there would be police spies there, which made it sound exciting. On the other hand, Léonide had said, there will be some real Russians there, and therefore it was impossible for Natasha to attend. In the dining car of the train to Newcastle she had wondered if Léonide considered her to be an _un_real Russian, and if she might perhaps be right.

She sipped her claret and looked about her. No young aristos anxious to seduce a woman on her own, which meant that she would have to pay her own bill, but it also meant that she had time to think, and there was much to think about. Especially Harrod's. She wished it were possible to ask the priest whether it would be possible to go to a sort of Harrod's when one died (if one were young and quite pretty) but the priest would dismiss this as frivolity, though she wasn't sure it was. Certainly Dimitri's idea of heaven had been a vast and superbly equipped printing shop, where he could forge Tsarist thousand-rouble notes throughout Eternity. He'd told her so himself. But

103

Harrod's had simply everything. It was true that there were wonderful shops in the rue de la Paix, but in Harrod's one need never go outside.

She had bought dresses – five was it? Six? – and lots of silk underwear and stockings and shoes, then stolen a travelling clock, a crystal vase and a jar of caviar. It had been so simple. First she had bought flowers, but no wrapping paper. In Harrod's they wrapped the gifts themselves, but the roses were of exactly the shade of red to bring out the smooth pallor of her skin: a red that Léonide would adore. After that she went up to a man in a morning coat and demanded to be taken to whoever looked after the cheques. The man looked at the French couture dress, Cartier ring and hand-lasted shoes, and took her to the lift, and then, after a brief wait, to an office where another man sat behind a very large desk.

'My name is Natasha Tyrrwhitt,' she told the man behind the desk. He wore simply a lounge suit, but it was of excellent cut, and he looked wary.

'Formerly I was the Countess Natalya Krilova,' she said, 'but after what has happened in Russia it was thought best I use my mother's name. Tyrrwhitt. She was English.'

'Yes, Miss Tyrrwhitt?'

'Oh yes. Life was – difficult in Russia after the Revolution, and so I went to Paris. I have relatives there. Their name is Jacquard. Perhaps you have heard of them? He makes motorcars.'

'I've heard of them,' said the man. 'In fact I drive one sometimes.'

Natasha nodded. So many people do, the nod said. Rich people, anyway.

'But then I thought it best to come to England,' she said aloud. 'I have an English passport after all. I was to stay with my uncle, but he is in Kenya. Big game, you know.'

'Quite so,' said the man.

'So I stay with my cousin instead – but not in London ... Northumberland. He is a – priest. Surely that's not right?'

'Parson?' suggested the man.

'It is very boring so I came to London to stay with my cousin Léonide Jacquard at the Savoy and for the shopping. Only it will be easier if I pay with cheques. I wish to buy dresses, you see.'

Really, she thought, I did that very well. Russian aristocracy, French millionairess, and the Savoy – not to mention the shopping, all in one speech.

'May I ask your uncle's name?' said the man.

'Kielder,' she said.

'Lord Kielder?'

'The Earl of Kielder. Isn't that the same?'

'Pretty well,' said the man. Now was not the time to explain the English aristocracy's mystique. The Russians no doubt would have their own. All the same, Natasha noticed, he was beginning to crumble. The Earl was her Ace of Trumps.

'If you will excuse me,' the man said. 'Just for a moment. There is something I must attend to.'

'Of course,' said Natasha, and he scurried off, to telephone the Savoy, no doubt. She looked at the papers on his desk. His name was Simkins, and he seemed important. If Dimitri had been alive she would have taken some of the writing paper, so that he might forge it. She sat down and lit a cigarette, and Simkins came back and smiled.

'We shall be very happy to accept your cheque,' he said. Definitely the Savoy. 'May I offer you a cup of coffee?'

'No thank you,' she said. 'I have *lots* of shopping to do.' His smile broadened.

She had bought dresses only from Paris, couture dresses, and it had been a very enjoyable experience: the changing rooms and the fittings, and the sewing woman to do the alterations. Fuss, fuss and more fuss. She loved all that. Then she took a look round that vast and gleaming store to decide what to steal, before she went to choose her shoes and lingerie. A simply marvellous afternoon. Dimitri would not have approved of her stealing: he would have argued that the Jacquard legacy was more than enough, which was true, but it was also boring. Besides, the English charged far too much for caviar.

But really at Harrod's they were very good. No doubt they had cleared her cheque at record speed, but they had also agreed to arrange for the delivery of her dresses to Haydon Priors, except for one that had needed no alteration. She would wear it at dinner quite soon. Her one excitement, she thought. A new dress to show off to George and Oliver and the priest. Greenhalgh would appreciate it, but even so . . .

This Lord had better come back soon, Natasha thought, or I shall go somewhere else. This is all so boring. Since Dimitri left me, everything is so boring. It would be pleasant to drink cognac instead of coffee, but I must not. When I get back the priest and his sons will be asking questions. That much at least the three men had in common. They all had the desire – or perhaps the need – to find out what she had been doing.

So it was. Greenhalgh did nothing but admire the dress, a Poiret, in blue, and said thank you for the enormous box of chocolates that

Natasha had bought her. Not so the Tyrrwhitts. She went down to the drawing room and champagne was produced at once. To loosen my tongue, she thought.

'Nice trip?' George began.

'Very.'

'See any shows?' Oliver, this time.

'The opera. The ballet. The opera was *Turandot*, the ballet *Giselle*.'

Oliver grunted. Opera was meaningless to him and the ballet meant pansies.

'How was the Savoy?' Tyrrwhitt asked.

'Very comfortable.'

'Luxurious, surely?' Tyrrwhitt said.

'That, too.' She finished her champagne and held out her glass. Reluctantly Tyrrwhitt filled it.

'And your Cousin Léonide? How was she?' More questions. Champagne never comes free.

'Well,' she said. 'And as active as ever.'

'Active?' said George.

'For the Party,' Natasha said. 'I told you she was a Communist. One reason she came to London was to attend a meeting with some Russians.'

'Good Lord,' said Tyrrwhitt. 'Did you go?'

'Certainly not,' said Natasha, and the priest looked relieved. 'I went to Harrod's instead.' For some reason that made him angry.

'Why on earth did you do that?' he wanted to know.

'To buy dresses. Couturiers are better – though perhaps not in London – but there was not enough time. Harrod's was excellent.' Next they would want to know the price of the dresses, she thought, and said, 'I told Léonide about the Shoeless Children's Concert.'

'She approved?'

'Not in the least,' said Natasha.

'But if she's a Communist—' Oliver began.

'It's *because* she's a Communist.'

'Do you think you could explain that?' said George. At least he was polite about it.

'Shoes for poor children is charity,' said Natasha, 'and if charity is effective, it impedes the Revolution.'

'Prevents it, you mean?' said Oliver.

'Nothing can prevent it,' Natasha said. 'Postpones it.'

'Good God,' Oliver said. 'How can you possibly believe that?'

'Of course I don't believe it,' Natasha said. 'You asked me what Léonide thinks.'

106

'But—' the priest looked bewildered and, for a little while, endearing. 'But if they are not to accept charity, what are the parents of those unfortunate children to do?'

'Take shoes from the feet of the children of the bourgeois,' said Natasha. 'Or better still, take over a shoe shop. Nationalise it.'

'But that would be stealing.'

'Stealing is a bourgeois concept,' said Natasha. 'We are talking of expropriation.' She remembered what they had taught her in the Re-education and Rehabilitation Centre. 'From each according to his ability: to each according to his need.'

'You really have got the hang of that stuff,' said George.

'Léonide does talk rather a lot.'

'She's not married, is she?' said Oliver, as she emptied her glass once more. 'Why not?'

'She is a Revolutionary,' said Natasha.

'You mean she has lovers?'

'I mean that she finds the Revolution more important than you men,' she said, and of that there could be no doubt. She held out her glass once more to the priest, and he poured into it the rest of the bottle. Were there priests at Caana? she wondered. But of course not. They would be rabbis. Just as well there was no Pommery left, but even so I shall not play tonight – not if there is claret.

'I thought all those Bolshies went in for free love,' said Oliver. He sounded disappointed.

His father said repressively, 'Speculation on such a topic would be pointless, since Natasha is hardly in a position to enlighten us.' Oliver looked as if he didn't believe a word but the parlourmaid came in to announce dinner.

It was just like the OGPU, Natasha thought. Like the bloody OGPU. All that was missing was the knout.

Next day she lunched with Maddy (fish that was really rather good, but still not nearly enough wine) and told her about Harrod's. She *must* marry George, she thought. He is very fond of wine.

'It sounds divine,' said Maddy.

'It is,' said Natasha, and then: 'You have never been there?' She was appalled.

'Dreadful, isn't it?' said Maddy.

'Then we must go,' said Natasha. 'Once the concert is over.'

'I'd love that,' Maddy said, 'but not the Savoy.'

'You would prefer the Ritz?'

Maddy sighed. Natasha was not the easiest person to explain things to.

'I had a letter from Mr Carrick,' she said. 'The Temperance Band will send us a quartet. But there will also be a trumpet solo. More work for you.'

'So long as he has music,' Natasha said.

'It's all they have got, the poor things,' said Maddy, and Natasha smiled at her. She was far too good for Oliver.

Before she dressed that night she said to Greenhalgh, 'Did you ever eat caviar?'

'Just the once, miss,' Greenhalgh said. 'Herbert sent me some from Murmansk.'

'Did you like it?'

'Loved it, miss.'

Natasha took out the jar Harrod's had supplied. 'What we need is very thin toast,' she said.

'Melba toast. Yes, miss. And lemon. I'll see to it at once.'

She came back not only with the toast and lemon but a bottle of champagne in an ice-bucket as well.

'It's one the Earl gave me, miss,' Greenhalgh said. 'My contribution, as you might say.'

Champagne from earls was something that had to be thought about, but not when consuming champagne and caviar.

After suitable murmurings Greenhalgh said, 'You remember Mr Oliver and his song, miss?'

'Vividly,' said Natasha. 'I – what do you say? – ticked him off about it. It wasn't true of course that he upset us, but it made him feel rotten.'

'That's what he told me, miss.'

'Did he? When?'

'While you were away, miss. The vicar was out and Mr George was at the office.'

Unasked, she spread more caviar on her toast, but Natasha remained unperturbed. She was pouring out more of Greenhalgh's champagne, after all.

'Rang the bell and asked for me, and when I went up, "I behaved badly," he said. "Singing rude songs like that where females could hear them. I apologise."

'"That's all right, sir," I said. "My Herbert could sing worse than that when he'd had a few." "Your Herbert wasn't a gentleman," he said, and God knows that's true. He was a company sergeant major, and if he'd tried to act like a gentleman he wouldn't have lasted five minutes. I remember—'

There was a peremptory tap at the door, and Tyrrwhitt's voice, in tones of awful sarcasm, said, 'Natasha, if you could spare Mrs Greenhalgh to the rest of us for a little while—'

Natasha said, 'You cannot come in. I am naked.' She remembered the priest's prudishness. 'Well, almost. Please wait.'

Greenhalgh winked and hid the champagne and caviar in the wardrobe. Natasha counted to twenty slowly, then stood up, folded her hands in front of her, and nodded to Greenhalgh, who opened the door, contriving to look censorious as she did so.

Tyrrwhitt almost began by apologising to her, but his eyes went at once to Natasha – to reassure himself that I am adequately clothed, she thought. Well, so I am, and by Poiret. Somehow she looked demure and mildly shocked, as if he, a parson, had only just been prevented from doing something improper.

'My dear Natasha,' he said, 'do forgive me. I had no idea—'

'Please come in,' Natasha said.

'No, no,' said Tyrrwhitt. 'I wouldn't dream of it.'

As if Greenhalgh would lock the door while I tore all my clothes off, she thought. It might be amusing at that, but not when there was caviar.

'But you wished to tell me something,' she said. 'About all of you wanting Greenhalgh. I don't understand that, I'm afraid.'

'A figure of speech,' said Tyrrwhitt. 'If it was unfamiliar to you I apologise. All I meant was that Mrs Greenhalgh normally keeps an eye on Cook at this time of day.'

'I'll go down at once, sir,' said Greenhalgh, but made no move to do so.

'You can't,' said Natasha. Both of them knew there was one more glass each left in the bottle. 'You haven't finished dressing me.'

Greenhalgh looked at the vicar. 'That is true, I'm afraid, sir. And I can't be in two places at once, now can I?'

'Then by all means finish Miss Natasha first,' said Tyrrwhitt, 'but be as quick as you can. Mr Oliver contrived to obtain some lobsters, and Cook is not very good at lobsters. So sorry, Natasha.'

Natasha, who adored lobsters, said at once, 'No, no. Greenhalgh will not be long.'

Tyrrwhitt apologised once more, and left, and Greenhalgh waited for a moment, then closed the door. The two women looked at each other, and Natasha giggled. Greenhalgh snorted, then she began to giggle too as she brought out the champagne and caviar.

'You're a wicked one, miss,' she said. 'I can't remember when I've enjoyed myself so much.'

'Yes, but you must finish telling me about Mr Oliver,' said Natasha, and filled their glasses.

'Well, that was about all there was,' said Greenhalgh. 'He said he was sorry and slipped me a ten-bob note.'

'Shouldn't he slip me one too?' said Natasha. 'I heard him as well.'

'If I may say so, miss—' Greenhalgh began, then hesitated.

'Of course you may,' said Natasha, 'only please get on. You have to watch Cook with the lobsters.'

'It's not a ten-bob note he wants to slip you,' Greenhalgh said, then admonished herself. You've gone a bit too far this time. You never did have a head for champagne.

'Well, of course it isn't,' said Natasha. 'He wants me in that Happy Land of his. Did he ask about me?'

'Not half,' said Greenhalgh. 'Questions you wouldn't believe. More like being in the dock than a drawing room. That's what the money was for, miss. I knew straightaway ten bob was too much for an apology.'

'What sort of questions?' Natasha asked.

'Impertinent ones,' said Greenhalgh. 'Like had you told me who your parents were, and had you anything to prove you were a cousin of the Jacquards, and had the Earl ever heard of you.'

Impertinent certainly, thought Natasha. But clever, too. Really extremely clever. And then she remembered. Oliver had been a member of that strange-sounding Black and Tans, whose business was to find out secrets. Sort of a British OGPU. Of course he would be good at interrogation.

'What did you tell him?' she asked.

'I said your parents were the Count and Countess Krilov,' said Greenhalgh, 'and surely he must know that better than I did.'

'And he said?'

'Well, seeing you were always called Miss Tyrrwhitt he just wondered if I knew we had foreign nobility in the house.'

Clever Oliver. 'And the Jacquards?'

'I said I didn't know what relatives of yours they were, but you seemed fond of them. Not surprised, he said.'

'He probably meant that if Léonide hadn't helped me I'd still be in Russia,' Natasha said.

'That's what he said, miss, but he still kept on about how close you and this Léonide were.'

'Close?'

'Good friends, miss. He said she must be fond of you if she treated you to a stay at the Savoy. Very palatial, the Savoy, he said. I told him it wouldn't be the first palace you'd stayed in.'

Natasha clapped her hands. 'And the question about the Earl?'

'Did His Lordship know about you? I said I'd no idea. How could I? And he said didn't I used to work for the Earl once upon a time? It

110

was his wife I worked for. Lady's maid. Only that wasn't what Mr Oliver was getting at.'

'No indeed,' said Natasha.

Greenhalgh said, 'What you're thinking – about the Earl and me – it was quite true, miss.'

'Of course it was,' Natasha said.

'Until I met Herbert,' the older woman said. 'It was time I settled down, anyway. And he was never one for sharing. Not Herbert.'

Natasha kissed her on the cheek. 'Dear Greenhalgh,' she said, 'I'm sure you made the Earl very happy, and Herbert too.'

'Thank you, miss,' said Greenhalgh. 'And I must say I never had any complaints from either party.' She swallowed what was left of her champagne. 'Better go downstairs and see what she's doing to those lobsters,' she said. 'Thank you, miss. I haven't enjoyed myself so much for a long time.'

'I also,' said Natasha, and let her go. Apart from the lobsters there was Oliver to think about.

MICHAEL

11

He hadn't really told O.B. the whole story, but then how could he?
He wasn't just after a naughty, but what he *was* after was impossible
to explain, even to as good a mate as O.B. Then O.B. had been
straight with him, that was the point: told him the truth, the whole
truth and nothing but the truth, so to speak. For O.B. the naughty
had been a matter of establishing a fact which, once established, gave
way to O.B.'s own peculiar brand of monasticism in which the
Avro took the place of the Blessed Virgin Mary.

For him it hadn't been like that. True enough his needs were carnal
– how could they be anything else? – but it wasn't just that. Funny
thing was, O.B. hadn't reacted at all when he said he wanted to go to
Indonesia. Two reasons for that, he supposed. The first was he could
afford it. Getting there was not a problem, and having got there he
could afford the best. The second reason was the girls themselves. So
many of them were pretty; so many of the best of them (in terms of
the places he'd been to) were beautiful. Exotic, you might say. Well,
of course they were. The Mystic East and all that, though there wasn't
all that much mysticism about the way they paid the rent, but beauty –
it was there wherever you looked.

Colour was part of it. 'Brown girls', they would have called them
in Australia, but brown didn't come near. Gold, that was their
colour. Gold of every shade the goldsmith had ever made, from red to
yellow, and like the metal itself, so their skin gleamed and glowed:
but unlike the metal, their skin was firm yet yielding, and it smelled of
hibiscus or jasmine or sandalwood. Brown eyes, black hair, gold skin
– but never two the same: the bodies saw to that. Gold must be
shaped; the bodies shaped themselves. Small and elegant, female and
shapely: all of them were that, and yet they were all different, all
memorable.

All good at what they were there for, too, he thought. That was a
part of their success, their price. Not like the ones he had sought out
in Melbourne, never mind Brisbane. Not that there'd been all that
many. There had to be more to it than that. In France, too. Daughters
of Joy. Joy hadn't been much in evidence . . . Hurry up, Digger, don't

you know there's a queue? That was more the attitude. Money. Cash in advance. That was why they were there. And the golden girls too, of course, but with them – if you were nice about it, they were nice too, like dessert after a good dinner. Of course they expected an extra tip but why not? In another world he'd have brought them flowers.

Now we're getting close, he thought. Flowers and good restaurants and not forgetting her birthday. Not just a matter of what the blokes in B Company called sinking his sausage; he wanted a girl who liked him. Of course the golden ones all pretended to like him, classy ones like them had to be actresses as well as everything else, but it wasn't the same, although it was better than nothing. Far better. Then suddenly it wasn't. He woke up one morning and found he couldn't be bothered. In Sumatra, that was. He'd had his brekky and read a week-old copy of the *Straits Times* instead, then went off to the bar to drink gin and lime and soda with a mob of Dutchmen who were telling some Poms about how good it was back in dear old Holland. From the way they talked, Holland sounded like Belgium, which was quite a bit like Northern France, and they could stuff it.

He'd be better off in Stony Creek now he'd got over this need for sheilas, except for one who liked him, and where would he find her? Should he set off on the next ship bound for Oz? One of the nice things about money was that you didn't have to worry about it as long as it was there. Just walk into the shipping office and ask for a first-class ticket. Being on a ship by yourself wouldn't be all that wonderful, but at the end of it he'd see Tabby and Chalky and the blokes again, and find out what sort of a job Bill Ormsby had made of running the place. Never gone near, not if he knew Bill . . .

Beside him the Dutch blokes were talking about dogs. Not cattle dogs like O'Mara and Haig, but it seemed these particular Dutch dogs worked for a living, too. They pulled little carts. One of the Dutchmen was getting quite tearful about it, making himself homesick. Dogs and gin. What a way to do it. He'd never cried for Stony Creek, not even after was wounded, but all the same he missed it. On the other hand he still hadn't been to Bali, and the way O.B. had gone on about it, Bali was *the* place to see. Not the golden, bare-breasted girls – that was out of his system for a while – but the place: the mysticism, the – what was the word? – the religiosity. An orphan with two wound stripes could do with a bit of that.

The Dutchmen had moved on to winter-time now, and how good it was to feel cold and go ice-skating. And you can stuff that too, Walsh thought. I've tried it. Slithering on duckboards and frozen mud. You can keep it. I'm off to Bali where it's warm.

A Dutch ship. Well, it was bound to be. But at least it meant comfort and decent beer. Decent grub too, even if they did go in for too much *rijst-tavel*. He didn't have to eat it of course, but when he didn't his waiter sulked, and the waiter was the only one he had to talk to. The privations of the wealthy. Still, he had plenty of Jane Austen left, and people to watch. Not just Dutch, either. Yanks, Poms, all kinds. Richer than him, a lot of them, and off to Bali to see the sights, and dance and drink cocktails on the way. He had nobody to dance with, but the cocktails weren't bad at all.

It was a pity that he didn't have a dancing partner, though. His dad had insisted that he learned how to dance before he even went to the uni. Sitting at the bar, listening to some joker at the piano making a mess of *Get Out and Get Under*, he could still remember the conversation.

'I'd feel a fool,' he'd said.

'No, you wouldn't. Not if you can do it properly,' Dad had said, and how right he'd been.

'But what use is dancing to a stockman?'

Knockout punch that should have been, but Dad just shrugged it off.

'You're a gentleman,' Dad had said. 'A gentleman should know how to dance.'

'Me? A gentleman?' If he'd sounded indignant he had good reason. To call an Australian a gentleman was even worse than calling him a poofter.

His father had grinned at him then: a grin at once mocking and sympathetic.

'You've got no choice,' Dad had said. 'You're a Tyrrwhitt as well as a Walsh.'

And so Dad had seen he learned how to dance, just as he'd seen that he learned how to shoot and tie a bow tie and read Horace and drink red wine. Cricket and horse-riding took care of themselves: school and Stony Creek saw to that. But all the same, Dad had been right. Dancing was the only way he could hold a girl in his arms: a girl of the kind they called respectable, anyway. He wondered if Dad had made sure that Edgar learned to dance, too.

The two women came in, or more precisely, the two lady Poms. One a bit older than him; the other a bit younger. Both fair and pretty, both married, according to their rings, but neither of them with a husband. Toffs, he thought. Débutantes not all that long ago, curtseying to the King and Queen with feathers in their hair, and they still sat the way they had been taught, prim and upright and knees together. Pretty as pictures -- and he'd no more find the nerve to ask either of them to dance than he'd go out on deck and bay at the moon.

Still, they were nice to look at. Not like that encyclopaedia-buying customer of O.B.'s – nothing like that. They were just something nice to see, like the moonlight on the water – and light years away from Stony Creek. Mayfair, more likely, and hunt balls, and shooting deer in Scotland at the appropriate times. Dad could go on for hours about that sort of stuff. Better than the *Tatler* – but it wouldn't do for him, Michael Walsh, even if he did have money. Better to stick with Jane Austen. He reached for his copy of *Persuasion*.

The pianist was doing what he could with *Varsity Rag*. What he could do wasn't much, but at least he got the beat right. All the same, Anne Elliot didn't like it, and no more did he. He'd been in love with Anne Elliot since Jane Austen first introduced them.

'I say.'

Walsh looked up. It was the younger of the two.

'Forgive me,' she said, 'but do you speak English?'

'A bit,' said Walsh cautiously.

'Oh,' said the woman. 'Are you Dutch?'

'Australian,' said Walsh.

She laughed. Real upper-class laughter, according to what Dad had told him: at once tinkling and very loud, like handbells shaken by a weightlifter.

'I wonder,' the woman said, then hesitated. 'May I sit down?'

'Please,' he said. 'May I get you a drink?'

'Dry martini,' she said, and looked about, and a waiter came at the double. Whoever she was it seemed she had influence. Enough for two, maybe.

'My name's Margaret Bonner,' she said. 'Mrs Margaret Bonner as a matter of fact.'

'Michael Walsh,' he said. 'Mister.'

Once again there came that tinkling bellow. It was a pleasant thing to do, to make her laugh – if only people wouldn't stare.

'My friend's name is Felicity,' she said. 'Felicity Winthrop. She's a widow.'

'The war?' said Walsh.

She nodded. 'You were in it, too?'

'Everybody was,' said Walsh. This time there was no laughter, nor had he intended that there should be.

'Bob Winthrop had just got his battalion,' the woman said, 'when a sniper got *him*. At least, that's what they told her.'

'Why would they lie?'

'A sniper meant a clean death, wouldn't you say?' And indeed it usually did. 'My husband survived it,' the woman went on. 'Blest if I know how.'

'Luck,' said Walsh. 'It was the only reason.' *Please God don't let her go on about the war. I want to go back to Anne Elliot.*

'Is that why you're here on this antiseptic Dutch home from home?' she said. 'Luck? Anyway, I didn't come here to talk about the war.'
Oh good.

'My friend Felicity is dancing,' she said, and pointed to the dance floor, which was about the size of a large carpet, where Felicity indeed was making all the right movements in the arms of a man younger than herself; a handsome and rather awed young man who nevertheless hung on grimly because the British always won the last battle, provided they survived.

'Scrumptious, isn't he?' said Margaret Bonner.

'Looks like a jackaroo,' said Walsh.

'That's a perfectly beastly thing to say,' the woman said, and then: 'What exactly *is* a jackaroo?'

That isn't her second martini, Walsh thought. Maybe not even her third. All the same, she was nice to talk to.

Gravely he said, 'A jackaroo's a young man of good family, usually British, who works on a property to learn about cattle farming, mustering the mob – all that. The word's origins are obscure, but I should think they're Aborigine.'

She looked at him warily. 'You know, most of the time what you say makes total sense,' she said, 'and then suddenly you lose me. I mean, where does politics come into it?'

'Politics?' His bewilderment was absolute, and she smiled. She was still in the fight.

'Mustering the mob,' she said.

'That isn't politics,' said Walsh. 'It's driving the cattle to the stockyard.'

'A round-up,' she said. 'Just like the cinema. Tom Mix – Golly! Is that what you do?'

'That's it.'

'Then why are you reading Jane Austen?'

'Because I like Jane Austen,' he said. He picked up his book. 'It was nice talking to you, Mrs Bonner.'

He was halfway to his feet when she touched his arm.

'No wait, please,' she said. 'That was clumsy of me and I'm sorry, but everybody's clumsy sometimes. Please don't go.'

He remembered the time he'd asked O.B. where he got the money to buy his Avro, and sat.

'It was just – so unlikely. What you do and what you read. Surely you can see that it's unlikely?'

He smiled then. 'I suppose it is,' he said, 'but nobody can write

119

prose like she can. Is that what you came over for, to discuss my taste in novelists?'

'Certainly not,' said Margaret Bonner. 'I came to ask you to dance with me.' He gaped at her. 'You *can* dance?' she asked.

'Of course I can,' said Walsh, 'but back in Australia it's usually the bloke that asks.'

'There you go again,' she said. 'Bloke. You mean chap, I suppose. But you would never ask me to dance, Mr Walsh. You're much too shy.'

'How do you know?' Walsh asked.

'I saw you watching me. Now please don't start sulking. Being shy's endearing usually, but now there just isn't time. It's Felicity, you see. For the moment she's rather smitten with that – jackaroo, but if I don't have a chap to dance with she'll feel it's her duty to sit out with me. Please come and dance, Mr Walsh.'

'Be a pleasure, Mrs Bonner.'

It was, too. She danced very well, and it was nice to watch her surprise when she discovered that he danced even better than she did. At last Felicity and her jackaroo went out to look at the moon and it was time to sit down, order another drink.

'Goodness you do dance well,' she said. He smiled at her.

'How very un-British,' she said. 'If you were English or Scottish or Welsh – or even Irish – you'd say "Oh no, not at all, but thanks awfully".'

'I'm Australian,' he said.

'Indeed you are. This ranch of yours—'

'Property,' said Walsh.

'Property then. Where is it?'

'Queensland,' he said. 'Not far from Toowoomba. A place called Stony Creek.'

'Stony Creek,' she said. 'Oh, what bliss.' Then almost at once she added, 'Please, please don't start being touchy again. I meant that. It *is* bliss.'

'I'm not touchy,' he said. 'But what's so blissful about it?'

'A place called Stony Creek. What you do. It's a million miles from what I know. And the way you talk—'

'I talk Australian,' he said.

'Sometimes. But sometimes you talk like – like a scholar. A University man.'

'I was a University man.'

'Then why do you talk in that other way too?'

'You mean like a stockman? Because I am a stockman. I was a soldier, too.'

120

'You mean a comm— you weren't an officer?'

'A common soldier,' he said. 'Right. I bet you never danced with a common soldier before.'

She blushed. 'You think I'm a snob,' she said.

'Well yes,' he said. 'Sometimes – but then so am I. Sometimes. But I know what you mean. University man. Vast acres of land.'

'Are your acres so vast?'

'Enormous,' he said. 'By Pom standards. Don't interrupt. So why didn't this Australian imitation of a gentleman get a commission?'

'Why didn't you?'

'It never occurred to me.'

'But surely your friends—'

'Some did, some didn't,' he said. 'We still spoke to each other. This was our Army, not yours. Haig hated us for it.'

'I should imagine he would,' she said. 'He's unbelievably pompous.'

'You've met him then?'

'Oh yes,' she said. 'One does. Because of Tom's profession. He's a soldier, too. Have you met him?'

'One did,' he said. 'Just once,' and she laughed her loud, enchanting laughter.

'I shall have to go,' she said. 'Felicity has seen enough moonlight for one night. Will you dance with me tomorrow?'

'Be a pleasure,' he said.

'Rather a lot of it will be mine.'

She stood up, and he did, too. No public schoolboy could have done it better, but it would have been disastrous to say so. She smiled instead: one of her best ones.

Walsh sat on over his drink. When it was done he would go in to dinner, and Anne Elliot. He loved her as much as ever, but if he didn't watch it she'd have a rival.

'I say.'

Oh my God, another one, he thought, but this time it was the jackaroo.

'Do you mind if I ask you something?' the jackaroo said. 'My name's Carlton, by the way. Edward Carlton.'

'Michael Walsh,' said Walsh. 'Sit down. Can I get you a drink?'

'Oh no,' Carlton said. 'Thanks all the same. What I wanted to say was – I saw you dancing with Mrs Bonner.'

He can't be going to challenge me to a duel, Walsh thought. Not when I saw who he was dancing with.

'No law against it,' he said.

'No, no,' said Carlton. 'No indeed. The thing is, she's a jolly good dancer. Pretty, too.'

'I suppose she is,' said Walsh, as if it had just occurred to him.

'What I mean is, you're a jolly good dancer too. You looked jolly well together.' Walsh stayed silent, and Carlton began to flounder. 'What I mean is – dancing. It's important in one's social life, so to speak.'

'Oh, absolutely,' said Walsh. Carlton looked at him warily, but Walsh seemed bland enough.

'I just wondered where you learned to dance,' Carlton said.

'A place in Punt Road,' said Walsh.

'Is that in London?' It was Walsh's turn to look wary, Carlton's to look bland.

'It's in Melbourne,' Walsh said at last. 'In Australia.'

'Oh,' Carlton said. 'I see. But you still looked well together.' And then he was gone – and make what you will of that, thought Walsh . . .

'Felicity's in love,' said Margaret.

'With the jackaroo?'

'Of course,' she said. 'Who else?'

'Seems a bit young for her,' said Walsh.

'Well, of course he is,' said Margaret. 'It won't last. It can't.'

'I thought you said she was a widow,' said Walsh.

'For the moment,' said Margaret, and then was silent as Walsh negotiated a hesitation spin. Modern waltzes needed all one's concentration.

'She's going to Singapore to look at one of her other chaps,' she said at last. 'Rather a grand chap. I think perhaps she'll marry him. He's a general *and* he's got a K.'

'What's a K?' said Walsh.

'Oh sorry,' she said. 'A knighthood. My Tom's his ADC just at the moment.'

'Now I do know that one,' said Walsh. '*Aide de camp.*'

His French accent, she noted, bore no trace of Australian. She started to speak, then decided against it. The dance floor was no place for what she had to say. Perhaps no such place existed.

'Can we go on deck?' she said. 'I could do with a breath of air.'

Just the hint of a breeze, but here the air was never really cold. They stood demurely apart, watching the ship's gleaming wake.

'Felicity wants to be alone with him,' she said.

'Lucky jackaroo.'

'But the only place to be alone is our cabin – and they can't exactly be alone with me there.'

If I were a gentleman and a Pom, he thought, I'd offer her mine and sleep on deck, but I'm not. Love will find a way, so they say. Let love start looking.

'She really is fond of him,' said Margaret, 'and she's a jolly good friend, so I just wondered' – he waited and she drew a deep breath – 'if I might share yours?'

'Share it?' he said. 'Fair dinkum?'

Margaret said cautiously, 'I'm not sure about the "fair dinkum" bit.'

'It's Australian for "honestly".'

'Well, of course share,' she said. 'I could hardly ask you to sleep on deck, could I?'

Con man, thought Walsh. Or rather woman. She could hardly be another golden girl, not on a liner . . . could she?

'The thing is I've become rather fond of you,' she said.

In twenty-four hours? No, not even that. Four charlestons, a waltz, a tango and two foxtrots – oh yes, and three dry martinis.

'I'm fond of you too,' he said. 'That's why I was too shy to look at you.'

'You'll do it then?'

'Be a pleasure.'

'That's what you said when I asked you to dance with me.'

'This'll be a bigger pleasure,' he said.

'Goodness I hope so,' she said, and then: 'You're supposed to kiss me, you know.'

'Yes, Mrs Bonner,' he said, and put his arms about her.

She kissed with a delicate and pleasing skill that intensified as she realised that he had no intention of mauling her or sticking his tongue in her mouth; realised too that he held her in a most delightful way. Really this could turn out to be rather a good idea. She drew away from him at last.

'How strong you are,' she said. Men always liked to be told that, but this time it was true.

'Let's hope so,' he said, and she laughed once more. She really was rather fond of him.

'Just one thing,' she said. 'No matter what happens later on I want your solemn promise that you will never *ever* call me Peggy.'

He raised his hand. 'I swear,' he said.

12

She's got to be a con person, he thought. It's the only thing that makes sense – but then that meant that Felicity and the jackaroo were con persons too, and who could believe that the jackaroo could con anybody? Unless it was part of his technique, of course, and anyway it helped to explain why the bloke had told him how well he and Margaret Bonner looked together. He was definitely being conned, Walsh decided, so he might as well enjoy it.

There were rules, it seemed. A couple more dances, and one drink before dinner, but not dinner itself. That he took on his own: just him and Anne Elliot, who obviously disapproved of the whole thing. The jackaroo also ate on his own, and ate voraciously. Love took people in all sorts of ways, thought Walsh, and anyway the bloke couldn't be more than twenty. Probably be graduation night for him. Just as well to keep his strength up.

When he'd finished Walsh went out on deck again, and smoked a cigar. More people out then, enjoying the moonlight and the phosphorescent wake chopped out by the ship's propellers. No sign of don't-call-me-Peggy though, or Felicity, or the jackaroo either. Putting the final touches to the master plan on how to fleece the wild colonial? Well maybe, but he'd give them a game.

The cigar was a good one; the Dutch knew what they were doing when it came to cigars. He thought about a brandy to go with it, then decided against it. You needed a clear head to be conned, and anyway if there was to be any naughtiness, which he was beginning to doubt, alcohol was not the answer. He'd have one after he'd been conned. For the moment he'd make do with Anne Elliot, even if she was more disapproving than ever. When he decided to go below she threw up her hands in despair, but he shut her up even so, and went to his cabin.

What to wear? That was the problem. The Poms were always formal, whatever the occasion. For the golden girls the problem scarcely existed, but this was an English lady and a con artist. He could hardly just stand there in the nuddy. In the end he settled for pyjamas and dressing gown, stuff he'd bought at a Chinaman's shop in Djakarta. White silk pyjamas: dark blue dressing gown. They didn't exactly transform him into Rudolph Valentino, but at least they were well-cut.

There should have been flowers, and champagne. For between rounds so to speak, always supposing they ever got as far as 'Seconds Out', as he very much hoped they would. It was all very well to tell himself that he'd only do it when there was affection, but with Margaret Bonner there *was* affection. From him anyway. He reached for *Persuasion* again, but Anne Elliot would scream the place down. He began a letter to O.B. instead.

When she finally arrived she had changed from her evening dress to something much simpler, and she carried a vast handbag. He wondered if there was a revolver in it. There could well be. There could even be a sawn-off Lee Enfield in it, the kind they used to carry on trench raids.

'Let me take that,' he said, and she surrendered it at once. No Lee Enfield.

'It's got all my things in it,' she said. 'At least I hope it has.'

'Heavy enough,' said Walsh.

'I brought some champagne for later,' she told him. 'There's ice in a box, too. I can't stand warm champagne.'

He opened the bag and took out the champagne and ice. The rest of its contents was mostly silk of one kind or another: all intriguing.

Suddenly she came to him, embraced him and said, 'I know this is hardly the time to say it, but I'm nervous.'

She was, too, he thought. Her body was as hard as a board, and on deck it had had a yielding firmness he'd found enchanting.

'Me too,' he said, and she relaxed a little.

'The unknown,' she said. 'One always fears the unknown. Suppose I'm not—'

He put his hand to her mouth. 'Don't spoil it,' he said. 'We're not here for supposing. We're here to find out.'

'Yes, all right.'

She picked up her bag. Nice that he too had a suite, she thought. She could undress in the bedroom, take her time, will herself to relax. Because really he was an awfully nice man, and what she was going to do to him wasn't nice at all.

'I'll change in the bedroom,' she said. 'Then I'll call you.'

He watched her go, head up, shoulders squared, back as rigid as a guardsman's. Was that what her Tom was? he wondered. Come on, mate. This isn't the time to start thinking about her husband.

Better, far better, to think about his beautiful con artist, who for once in her career seemed to have stage fright, and for that he had to remember the golden girls, and that wasn't being nasty, either. It was because of the things they had taught him. His idea of love – well, amorous lust – wasn't just plank 'em and get back to the pub. The way he saw it, there not only had to be pleasure, it had to be reciprocal, but it was the golden girls who'd shown him how. All those wasted years, he thought, but at least he'd started to catch up. He wondered if Margaret had, too.

She called him at last, and he took off his dressing gown and pyjama jacket and went in. She was wearing a silk nightdress. There was far too much of it even if the electric fan was going full blast. He lay down beside her and she moved to turn off the bedside light, but his hand prevented her.

'No,' he said. 'I'm hopeless in the dark. I keep losing my way.'

Her laughter gurgled for a moment, then died as the stiffness returned and she tugged up her nightdress, opened her legs. Again his hand stopped her.

'What's your rush?' he said. 'We've got all night.'

She looked bewildered, and he drew her into his arms to kiss her, gentle still: always coaxing, never demanding, till at last her mouth opened and flowered, and he pulled down the straps of her nightgown to admire her breasts, to touch and tease.

And very pretty breasts they were, he thought. Bigger than any of the golden girls', but every bit as firm and rounded. He coaxed and kissed, and watched the nipples harden, darkly glow, and Margaret-not-Peggy sighed in content because someone at last was doing it right. Still taking his time he found the hem of the nightgown and pulled it over her head, and for a moment she tensed, but all he did was stroke her, most adorable of pussy cats, tummy and buttocks and thighs, until at last she began to purr and tugged at his pyjamas, pulled them down.

'Golly,' she said.

'Fresh air,' he said. 'Exercise. Mustering the mob.'

'I don't think—' she began.

'You're not here to think.'

His hand touched the inside of her thigh, that was firm and smooth and moist and creamy-white. Up and up it went and again she tried to speak, and once more he kissed her, another sweet and undemanding kiss, while his hand made all the demands imaginable. Up and over, to where, to where – she pulled her mouth from his.

'What on earth are you doing?' she said.

'Don't you know?'

She would have laughed then, but what he was doing was so delicious that she lay back instead and said 'Ooh,' then sighed, and her breasts swelled and he kissed them and it was all too wonderful. His fingers had a cunning life of their own that seemed to know what she wanted even

127

before she knew it herself, and she wriggled to his touch and cried out aloud. 'Oh, *please*,' she said, and he answered her summons and came into her, and there was no pain at all, only the most unbelievable pleasure. But even then he had to tell her what to do, and it should have been too shaming, were it not for her delight, as her arms and legs came round him, his thumb flirted and teased, and he came into her deeper, deeper, until at last she could take no more and yelled out loud, and he too stiffened and was still.

He eased himself from her and touched her cheek. Her face was rosy with fulfilment, blue eyes shining, exulting in what they had achieved.

'My God,' she said. 'Where on earth – but I mustn't ask that, must I?'

'What would be the point?' said Walsh. From ladies who were not your colour, and maybe the thought would disgust you, but oh, Margaret-not-Peggy, how very fond of you I am.

'All the same I'm glad you went to another dancing school,' she said. 'I've never known anything like it.' She sprawled back, wanton, in a way he was sure that she had never shown herself to any other man. As a compliment it would be hard to match.

'What do we do now?' she said. 'Drink our champers?'

'We have a bath,' he said.

'A bath?'

'We're hot. I'm sweating and you're glowing the way ladies do. Certainly a bath.'

She sighed again, and her breasts reacted appropriately. Walsh began to worry about how long he would last.

'All right,' she said resignedly. 'Who goes first?'

'We go together.'

'What a perfectly marvellous idea,' she said.

It was a sitz bath just big enough for both of them, with a scoop that they could use as a sort of shower. They took turns pouring water over each other, until at last she reached out and grasped him.

'Not much good to you now,' said Walsh.

'Nonsense,' she said, and gently tugged. 'He's full of potential.' Then, still holding him, 'Do you mind my saying that? I've never done this before, you see.'

'I love your saying that,' said Walsh. 'I love your doing it too.'

What kind of con artist is this?

'Will we do this again?' she asked him.

'That's up to you,' he said.

'Then we'll do it. You're not the only one with ideas. Now let's go and drink champagne.'

But first they dried each other, then she found her perfume and splashed it on herself, and him, so that they might smell the same, and then the champagne at last as they lay on the bed and the fan softly whirred: but not too much, she said. They still had a great deal to do. But not quite yet.

For the moment they sipped and talked and he made her giggle and she discovered that not only was it possible to flirt stark naked, it was the only way to flirt. She asked him about Melbourne, and he told her he'd gone to the uni there.

'What's a uni?' she asked.

'I might have known,' he said. 'Don't you Poms know anything? It's a university. We abbreviate everything in Australia. It's because we're lazy.'

'Not you. Not always,' she said, and he chuckled.

'Can I ask you something serious?' he asked her.

'Maybe.' But her hand that had held his moved away.

'Do you have any children?'

'Not even one,' she said, and her voice for the only time was bitter. 'What I have is disappointments.' He tried to speak then, and she added: 'That's all I want to say about that,' and he put down his glass and hers so that he might hold her, and at once the stiffness yielded.

'You're the most beautiful sheila I ever knew,' he said. 'Clever, too. Witty. Well-connected. And now I know why you're sad sometimes.'

He kissed her, very gently, on the mouth, and when he had done her fingers found the scar of the exit wound on his back: a puckered roughness where the rest of him was smooth. An inch to the right and I'd be lying in three feet of French mud, he thought, instead of alongside this fantasy made flesh.

'Sheila?' she said. 'That's girlfriend in Australian?' He nodded. 'So I'm your sheila – for the time being, anyway.'

'Too right,' he said.

Her hand moved round him, downward seeking. 'It's time you went back to work,' she said.

'Do my best,' said Walsh. 'Just give me a bit of encouragement first.'

Later she said, 'And a very good best it was.'

'That was because of the encouragement,' said Walsh.

'Thank you, kind sir,' she said and smiled, and yet she wept.

'What's wrong?' he asked.

'Shortly I'm going to do something ghastly,' she said. 'I'm going to leave you. Darling, do you realise how ghastly that is?'

'Yes,' he said. 'I reckon I do,' and her tears flowed faster.

'Oh you,' she said. 'You can hurt a girl without even trying.'

'Without even wanting to,' he said.

But already her thoughts had shifted. A mind like a swallow in a breeze – and what was wrong with that?

129

'I called you darling,' she said. 'What will you call me?'

'Anything you like,' he said. 'Anything except Peggy.'

The tears ceased to flow at last, and she dried her eyes on the corner of the sheet. 'I bet I look dreadful,' she said.

'Not from here.'

'Pour me another glass of champers and then I really must go.'

He poured the wine and she washed her face and dressed, used lipstick and powder.

'It was good,' she said. 'Wasn't it good?'

'It was the best.'

'Even if you're lying you said that very nicely,' she said. 'What time is it?'

He looked at his watch. 'Ten past four.'

'Even Felicity will have had enough by now,' she said.

'If she hasn't the jackaroo will,' said Walsh.

'Too right, sport,' she said, and he snorted with laughter, but then she added: 'We have a saying: "Practice makes perfect". Do you say it too?'

'Certainly,' he said. 'We can all speak English when we want to.'

'Well, what I was thinking was this. We haven't had nearly enough practice – at least, I certainly haven't – so if you've nothing better to do I thought we might practise again tomorrow night.'

'Practise what?'

'Fair dinkum,' she said, and kissed him and was gone.

Not a con lady, he thought. Definitely not. But if not, what was she up to, apart from being delightful? He lay back on the bed. He was far too tired to think about it – or anything else.

She came back as she had promised, and it was just like before, but my God how she worked at it, and so inevitably he worked at it too, not only because he was a gentleman according to his lights but because there was no other option. This was definitely a game for two players, except that it wasn't a game, not for her. She made it seem far too important for it to be the game of love: more like labour – the labour of love, and hard labour too. She insisted on that.

Two more nights like the second one and I'll be in hospital, he thought. If I had O.B.'s affliction I'd already be dead. But there was only one more night; after it they arrived in Bali. Margaret and Felicity would change ships and move on to Singapore, and he would go ashore. Where the jackaroo would go he had no idea. Into intensive care, most likely.

But before that they had their last night: a kind of Olympic love gymnastics that shattered record after record, until at last he begged for mercy because what else could he do? He was a big tough Aussie with war wounds to prove it, and she couldn't weigh more than eight stone, but all the same he was whacked.

'Greedy, aren't I?' she said.

'Too right,' said Walsh, 'and I love it.'

'I like to think I can make you happy.'

'Ecstatic,' he said, 'and that's only when we start.'

She sat up to look at him then, and once more he looked at her body, rejoicing in its prettiness. Rejoicing for her, because she deserved a pretty body. For him at that moment the pleasure was aesthetic, no more.

'Let's bathe,' she said. 'To use your tactful phrase, I'm glowing like anything.'

In the bath she said as she poured water over him, 'I'm glad I made you so happy. It would have been jolly unfair if you hadn't been, after what you did for me. What we did – I didn't know it was even possible. Did you realise that?'

He took the ladle and poured water in his turn.

'I don't suppose we'll see each other again,' she said, but it wasn't what she meant. What she meant was: Please don't even try to see me again. Not ever.

'I suppose not,' he said. 'It's a fair cow, isn't it?'

'Is it?' she said, naked and bewildered.

'I mean it's awful,' he said. 'The most awful thing that ever happened to me.'

'Worse than being wounded?'

'Being wounded began in pain and ended in healing,' said Walsh. 'For me loving you began in pleasure and will end in grief.'

'Please don't make me cry,' she said, and then: 'This is the end of it for me, you know.'

His turn to be naked and bewildered. 'End of what?'

'Sex, cavortings, amorous couplings.'

'Oh, come on!' he said.

'Tom has rights – or at least he claims he has,' she said, 'and it's easiest just to let him get on with it. But it isn't like you – my God, no. Nothing could be.' She touched his cheek. 'Just remember. Whatever you may hear about me, you were the only one I could do this for.' Her hand moved down his body and grasped him. 'The one and only.'

'I'll remember,' he said. 'How could I forget?'

'Let's go and lie down,' she said. 'I'm not glowing any more – and I'd rather like to glow just once more.'

'I don't think—' he said, but she tugged at him carefully.

'You don't have to think,' she said. 'We'll try the perfume again – or better still, I've brought my talcum powder. That could be rather fun . . . Please, darling. Can't I be your sheila just once more?'

'You can try,' he said.

As they dried each other she said, 'I haven't got a present for you.'

'Nor I for you.'

'I didn't realise,' she said. 'How could I? All the same I want to give you something.' She thought for a moment. 'Do you bet on horses?' she said at last.

'Of course I do,' said Walsh. 'I'm Australian.'

'Could you get a bet on an English race in Australia?'

'You can get a bet on anything in Australia,' he said.

'This is sort of a family secret,' she said, 'but I think I can call you a friend of the family. Of one of them anyway. The Wentworth Handicap. Can you remember that?'

'Well, of course,' said Walsh. 'My dad lost his shirt on it once.'

'Well, now's the time to win it back. There's a relative of mine called Bobby Wentworth – Viscount Wentworth as a matter of fact, but don't hold it against him. It could happen to anyone.'

Walsh thought of Lord Kielder. 'Too right,' he said.

'He has a horse entered for it. If the going's firm bet all you can spare. If it's soft don't touch it. The horse is called Brillig. Can you remember that?'

'Ridden by Slithy Tove. Trained by Gyre and Gimble.'

'You'll remember,' she said, and grinned. 'Do back it, darling, if the weather's firm – and so will I. Will you?'

He nodded.

'Oh super,' she said. 'We'll be sort of together again if the going's firm. Talking of which . . .' She shed her towel, pulled away his, and reached for the talcum powder and an enormous powder puff. 'Now this won't hurt a bit,' she said. Nor did it.

At last he said, 'The Poms won the Ashes that time,' and she kissed him.

'I have to go,' she said, as if she couldn't believe it. 'I have to leave you.'

She began to dress, bent to kiss his lips and said, 'Shut your eyes please, darling, I can't bear it if you watch me go.'

He shut his eyes and the door clicked and she was gone.

13

Next morning he gave his steward a fair wad of money – there were talcum powder and perfume and wet towels to be explained, and money was the best explanation of all – then went ashore. On his way the purser saluted him, but then he'd given the purser a fair wad of money too, to make sure that Margaret's new cabin would be filled with orchids. Then it was time to drive to his hotel. Sailors loaded his trunk on to a taxi – more money – and they were off.

The heat was nothing to marvel at for a Queenslander, but it was there, hard and assertive, and in the taxi it was hot indeed. The windows were almost shut to keep out the dust. Margaret would glow in here all right, he thought, but now was not the time to think of Margaret.

Think of the island, think of Selat Lambok, of this city, he told himself – the dust on this road that seems only half-completed: the traffic on it that must be the most haphazard traffic in the world. Not many cars, but lots of rickshaws to make up for it, and carts and bicycles and a buffalo, and once two pigs on a lead, happily trotting in front of their owner as if they knew precisely where they were going. And every conveyance seemed to be following its own inclination. There was simply no point in trying to find out whether you drove on the left or the right because you didn't. You drove wherever you fancied driving so that the traffic didn't flow, it jumbled itself together and hoped for the best. And a very good best it was, thought Walsh. Throughout the drive no one was hurt, or even injured: not even the pigs. Perhaps the gods looked after them. According to O.B. they were a very religious people.

They were certainly a very pretty people, men and women alike small and graceful, the bare breasts of the women much in evidence; the breasts for the most part framed by a sort of embroidered jacket that should have been erotic but wasn't. Margaret had taken care of that, he thought. He'd lost the last Test by an innings at least. And they were a cheerful people, too, smiling for the most part or even laughing out loud, even if they were going into a temple, and there were plenty to choose from. Every tenth building seemed to be a temple.

They arrived at his hotel, which was, of course, the best: the only kind of hotel the rich were allowed. The room was good, shaded and cool, with a ceiling fan that whirled efficiently enough, and a large, luxurious bathroom. A shower, too. He had never taken a shower with Margaret . . . He opened his small case, the one with the bonds in it, and took out his book. Maybe Anne Elliot had forgiven him by now.

At first he slept a lot, which wasn't surprising, and ate a lot too, and that wasn't surprising either, but after a couple of days he began to explore the place. The temples first. Some were old and majestic, some as cheap and tawdry as the churches in Ireland his mother remembered from her childhood, but all of them proclaimed the fact that a god lived there, again just like the Irish churches. But unlike them, the temples were cheerful places: the smiling and laughter continued inside them. There was chanting, too, prayers and the ringing of bells, even holy water, poured by the priests into the cupped hands of the worshippers. Walsh visited half a dozen on the first day alone, and no one questioned his presence – no one so much as stared, so long as he remembered to take his shoes off.

After a couple of days he hired a guide, an amiable half-caste called Cornelius, who came equipped with a Model T Ford. Together they looked at the island of Bali as if it were a picture gallery, ancient temples like monasteries complete with monks, gigantic statues, terraced rice paddies of a green more intense than emeralds, the volcano that gave life to the island because of its soil, and had once brought death: might do so again. Cornelius marvelled that Walsh should bear the island's heat so easily, and Walsh explained that Queensland was just as hot, but Cornelius didn't believe it. White men came from a place called Holland, and sweated and turned red when the sun shone, and called out for beer . . . But even so he smiled because his mother was Balinese, and when a white man spoke of impossibilities what else could he do but smile? The white man seemed to approve of it, even if he didn't do much smiling himself.

At the end of the week Walsh paid off Cornelius and took a trip to the ocean shore. Close to the land men fished from boats that didn't look much bigger than his steamer trunk, casting their nets in a way that St Peter would have found familiar. He walked to the sand that was of a white almost blinding, but the brim of his straw hat gave him shade, till he reached a palm tree, and took off his jacket and sat looking out at the lazy ocean, as blue as the paddy fields were green, sapphires to match their emeralds, and the lifting waves were no more menacing than the froth on champagne. No wonder they smiled so much here.

Gradually he began to recall things: Gallipoli, and then France. Pozières, the hospital, O.B. missing when he got back. Missing for nearly a decade, he thought, though finding him had been no problem. Missing because I'd been happy and didn't need him, though I went to him fast enough when the happiness was over. Off like a bride's nightie. And he'd taken it without a blink. 'Sit down. Have a beer.' Even before I knew he needed money ... And maybe that was why he had the blue heelers. It would take a bloody brave bailiff to move in on those two and start removing the furniture.

O.B. knew he was a bastard. The whole company knew because it was there in the records and the clerk who kept them was a gossip. But O.B. never mentioned it, any more than the others did, though he wasn't the only one, not by a mile, but it wasn't that. O.B. was his mate, and there were some weapons he just wouldn't use, not even when they quarrelled, and they usually ended up with a stoush after too much beer. Good bloke, O.B. Good mate, and Walsh felt glad he'd been able to help him. God was good to both of us that time, he thought.

God of course meant Mum. God was never far away from the property when Mum was alive. Every Sunday a buggy ride to the little church in Toowombah, as ugly as any in Ireland, according to Mum, but God was there all right. Never left the place. Tabby and most of the blokes thought so too, but he'd let it all slide a bit after Mum had gone. With Dad it had all been different. Dad had been Church of England, and his churches had been old and beautiful, set among trees, looking down on the sort of green where cricket was played, or else cathedrals bigger than a nobleman's mansion: stained glass and choirs and vestments, and incredible English – prose? poetry? it was impossible to tell – that only Shakespeare could match. But Mum and Dad were dead now, and they'd sort it out between them. He'd go to her Heaven one week, and she to his the next.

Margaret. All this thought had been leading up to her, because now he was ready to think about her, to put her, when you came down to it, among the human beings he had held most dear, the living and the dead. Four days he'd known her, slept with her three times, but that wasn't it. That didn't even begin to be it. Think deeper. A lady. A sad, unhappy, witty lady; the wit for the most part triggered by the unhappiness. A rotten love-life with a rotten lover. Her husband. But God knew, he thought, that there were plenty of them about. I could have been like that with her myself if it wasn't for the golden girls. Come to think of it, the first time she expected me to be like that.

Legs apart, pulling up that terrible nightie as soon as I lay beside her, and the terror in her eyes as if it were five seconds to zero hour, and she'd faced the Jerry machine guns too many times already . . . Then why face them again?

At the start, even the champagne she'd brought had been no more than an award for her own valour. She didn't know then that I could help her to enjoy it all. For all she knew I could have been another bull at a gate called Tom. And yet she'd just lain there and waited. *Why?* A reward for him letting her share his bedroom? It didn't make sense. And then when she'd got the hang of it she acted like she couldn't get enough, and yet she wasn't a nympho. Couldn't be. Somewhere there was an answer but he didn't want to know it. It was her problem after all, her private property, and he had no right to trespass. In a weird sort of way he felt afraid to trespass. Leave it. Leave it all. The Pom lady's voice, the pretty, greedy body, the loud and pleasing laughter. It was what she wanted after all. But he'd had enough of being alone, of not knowing a single soul. It was time to go home and see what sort of a mess Bill Ormsby had made of the property.

O.B. said, 'That's quite a story.'

In his mind he'd called it 'a fantasy made flesh', but 'quite a story' would do.

'Pom sheila?' O.B. said. He'd told O.B. everything except the name: never the name.

'Upper-class Pom,' said Walsh.

'The Princess and the Peasant?'

'More like Beauty and the Beast,' Walsh said.

'And you just let her go?'

'It's what she asked me to do,' Walsh said.

O.B. considered this. 'She might not have meant it,' he said at last.

'She meant it.'

'But you loved her and let her go?' Walsh nodded.

'Like I say, quite a story,' O.B. said. 'All the same, I don't like it. It's too bloody sad. Let's have another beer.' He went to the kitchen and Haig went with him; O'Mara stayed where he was. No chance of putting anything across those two, thought Walsh. Not that he intended to try.

Telling O.B. had been a good idea. He'd had to tell someone, and O.B. wouldn't talk. He was his mate. Owed him money, too. Now that's enough, he admonished himself. That's nasty. O.B. was his mate, and his mate was the only one he could tell, now he'd stopped sharing his secrets with the priest.

O.B. came back with the beers, Haig two steps behind him, giving Walsh that Don't you try it look that was a carbon copy of O'Mara's.

'You want to talk about it some more?' O.B. asked.

Walsh filled his glass. 'Let's leave it,' he said. 'I've bored you long enough.'

'I told you,' O.B. said. 'It isn't boring, it's sad. Anyway, you listened to my troubles. Not that I've got any. Not any more.' He looked towards the paddock where the Avro waited. 'Thanks to you.'

'Money can't solve everything,' said Walsh.

'Like my plumbing problem? A girl in Java took care of that and told me that God is great.' He swallowed beer. 'Which He is. When do you want to go back to Stony Creek?'

'Tomorrow if it's possible,' said Walsh.

'Got a job tomorrow. Taking a grazier down to Brisbane for an operation. Thursday do you?'

'Thursday's fine.'

Flying over the bush wasn't as good as over the ocean, except when the plane's engine startled a bunch of kangaroos. He'd never seen them move like it; not till they startled a flock of emus that moved even faster. If Brillig goes like that, he thought, and then – *Leave it. Let it be.*

They circled the house because Tabby had never seen a plane close to before, and she was due for a treat. She shot out from the house like a rabbit from its burrow, and waving as she ran. O.B. selected a level stretch of paddock, and put the Avro down smooth and gentle, cut the motor as Walsh climbed from the plane and ran to Tabby who was racing towards him and yelling all the way. When they met she embraced him, and O.B. blinked, but it wasn't that. More like she was his aunty, if you could imagine Mike with an aunty that black. Then another half-caste appeared, a man this time, on a horse, then another and another. Suits me, O.B. thought. They can give me a hand with the cabin trunk.

Tabby said, 'Your mate's staying the night?'

'Too right,' said Walsh. 'Those things can fly, but they can't see in the dark.'

'I'm glad you came in it,' she said. 'It's the first I ever saw.'

'Would you like a trip in it?'

'Show some sense, Mike,' she said. 'Why should he take me?'

'Because he's my mate.'

She smiled. 'When I was younger I might have taken you up on that. Not any more.'

'Why not?'

'Too scared,' she said.

'You?' said Walsh. 'You're not scared of anything on God's earth.'

This time she laughed aloud. 'That's not when I'm scared,' she said. 'It's when it's up in the air. Lamb chops for your tea?'

'Fine,' he said, and looked round his bedroom: immaculate as always. Dusted every day. 'Bill Ormsby bother you much?'

'Not much,' she said. 'No need. Chalky took care of things. Only—'

There was the sound of footsteps in the hall. O.B. had left the Avro at last.

'Tell you later,' said Tabby. 'Get your mate a beer.'

But it was Bill Ormsby who told him. Nine people in Toowombah had seen the plane fly by, and four of them were sure it was heading for the Walsh place. That was good enough odds for Bill. He rode over first chance he got, and Tabby showed him in. To Walsh it was obvious that she knew why he was there, and equally obvious that she wanted to tell him herself, but all he could do was smile.

'G'day, Bill,' he said. 'Beer?'

'Yeah,' Ormsby said. 'Great. Thanks.'

'Everything OK?' Walsh asked.

'No worries,' Ormsby said, 'except—' He looked at O.B., who at once got to his feet.

'Better take a look at the Avro,' he said.

'Kiss her goodnight?' said Walsh.

'She frets if I don't.' O.B. got up and left them to it.

'Let's have it,' said Walsh. 'That's a mate of mine. I don't like driving him away without a reason.'

'There's a reason all right.' Ormsby searched through his pockets and came up at last with an old, battered envelope. 'Bloke with a funny name.'

'How funny?'

'So funny I couldn't spell it,' Ormsby said. 'I had to write it down.' He peered at the envelope. 'Tyrrwhitt,' he said. 'T-Y-R-R-W-H-I-T-T. First name Edgar. Lives in Brisbane. Mean anything to you?'

'No.'

'He's looking for you,' Ormsby said. 'Wants a word. Urgent, he said. I told him you were away and hadn't left no forwarding address. "I need to speak to him," he says. "It's important. As a matter of fact there could be a few bob in it for anyone who could tell me where he is".'

'A few bob?'

'Ten quid,' Ormsby said.

No wonder he looked so miserable, Walsh thought. Ten quid just for an address.

'He must be rich,' he said.

'Like his old man owned a gold mine,' said Ormsby. Well, he wasn't far out there.

'Posh bloke?'

'Too right. Talked like a Pom half the time. Not that he was one. "I'm in the book," he said. Now what's that supposed to mean?'

'The telephone book,' said Walsh.

'I didn't think it was the Bible.' Ormsby swallowed beer. 'Not trouble, is he?'

Walsh shrugged. 'How can he be? I don't even know him. Maybe he wants to buy this place.'

'Not him,' said Ormsby. 'He might get his hands dirty.' He swallowed what was left of his beer. 'I'll leave you to it,' he said. 'Just thought I'd mention it. It could have been important.'

'Another of Life's great mysteries,' said Walsh. 'Like the *Mary Celeste*.'

'Saw her in Brisbane before the war,' said Ormsby. 'Farewell tour. Come to think of it, there was a resemblance.'

He got up and left Walsh shaking his head like a punch-drunk boxer. Queensland could get you like that sometimes.

It was after O.B. left that Tabby came in to see him. One look and he knew why.

'My visitor?' he said. 'The one who thinks it's worth ten quid to know where I am?'

'He didn't get any takers,' said Tabby. 'Even if we'd known we wouldn't have told him.'

'He asked you all?'

'That's right,' she said. 'Whatever it is, it's important.' Then without a pause she added, 'He's your brother, isn't he?'

'Half-brother, anyway,' said Walsh, 'but don't you tell me he looks like me.'

'There's a look of your dad sometimes,' Tabby said, and if she said it, it must be true. 'Is he trouble?'

'Not trouble, no,' said Walsh, 'but he tried to take what's mine and I didn't let him.'

'You wouldn't.' She smiled, delighted. 'But if he's your dad's son – he'll be rich.' Walsh nodded. 'Richer than you?'

'A lot richer,' said Walsh. 'He's legitimate. He's the heir.'

'He must be a millionaire,' said Tabby.

'Probably.'

'Dear God,' said Tabby, and crossed herself. 'I've been thinking, Mike.'

'We'd better sit down then,' said Walsh. 'I know what I'm in for when you start thinking.'

She sat and faced him. 'He's a hard one to read,' she said. 'It's all there if I could find it, but—'

Tabby, Walsh knew, was famous as a seer among the blokes, and even the abos in the bush, but Edgar had been too much for her. It didn't surprise him.

'But I did get something,' she said.

From where? he wondered. What had she been doing? But that was pointless. She would never tell him. This wasn't Tabitha, the good Catholic. This was the aborigine who walked into the Dream Time as if it were a familiar road; then turned and looked into the future, and waited for the clouds to part.

'Let's have it,' said Walsh.

'You should go away again,' Tabby said. 'I don't mean you should be scared of your brother – your mum and dad and Chalky and me, we didn't bring you up to be scared – but I get this feeling. You should go away.' She looked at her hands as if the answer was written on them, but it was too small to read.

'Where?' Walsh asked, but she didn't answer: not at once.

'You lost a woman,' she said, and he nodded. 'I knew it as soon as I held you. Sadness. All over you. Perfume, too.'

No good trying to get her to explain that. 'Where?' he said again.

'Where your dad came from,' she said. 'You never went there during the war, did you?'

'My name's Walsh,' he said. 'Why should I?'

'You should go now,' she said. 'He was your *dad*.'

Back to the tribe, he thought. The Tyrrwhitt tribe. What would they use for boomerangs? All the same, what Tabby saw would be there. It might be distorted, but it would be there.

'Give me a little time with you and the blokes and I'll go,' he said.

Again the smile. 'You're a good boy, Mike. I wish you luck.' She rose to her feet. 'Your brother,' she said. 'He left a magazine behind when he was here. Pom magazine. Shall I get it?'

'Yes, please,' said Walsh.

It was the *Tatler*, opened halfway through. The nobs were on the grog in Singapore, it seemed. Fancy uniforms and evening dress and all the champagne they could shift. The Governor General looked as if he'd shifted his share already, and who should blame him with Felicity Winthrop heading towards him, full steam ahead.

He looked at the caption below the photograph again. The man next to the Governor General was his ADC, Captain Bonner, married to Margaret, a cousin of Viscount Wentworth. Walsh looked more closely. Tall and lean and dark was Captain Bonner, just like him, Michael Walsh. Suddenly he knew the reason why the captain's wife had made him so happy, and wondered if Tabby knew it too.

NATASHA

14

The housemaid said, 'There's only Miss Tyrrwhitt at home, my lord.'

'She's the one I want to see,' said the Earl, and handed her his hat and gloves. 'You needn't announce me. I know the way.'

No sense in sharing the first encounter with a servant, he thought.

The housemaid said, 'Very good, my lord,' and curtseyed. She's disappointed, thought the Earl, which shows I was right.

He went into the drawing room, and the sound of the music. Really quite pleasant music – Chopin, and by no means easy. She was using a fair amount of whip and spur, but that wasn't necessarily a bad thing. It didn't do to give the Pole too much time to brood.

A pretty girl, he thought. Remarkably so. Old Russian nobility written all over her. Yellow dress. Very nice. Expensive, too. Harrod's, wasn't it? but made in Paris. She reached the end of the piece, and he coughed. Natasha spun round on the stool.

'There is no one at home,' she said. 'The parson and George are at the Parochial Church Council.' Her voice was as enchanting as the rest of her, and totally unsuited to words like 'Parochial Church Council'.

'And Oliver?'

'In bed.'

'Is he unwell?' the Earl asked.

'Drunk,' said Natasha. 'I think it is time for you to tell me who you are.'

'Of course,' said the Earl. 'Forgive me. To use a favourite word of the parson, I am a kinsman of yours, Lord Kielder, if indeed you are Natasha.'

She stood up then to sweep him a curtsey even a ballerina would have approved. No doubt a ballerina had taught her.

'No need for ceremony, child,' he said.

'But indeed there is,' said Natasha. 'You are the head of my family.'

'Delighted,' said the Earl. 'I mean that. But surely you belong to the Krilov family, Countess?'

145

'There is no Krilov family,' she said. 'Only me. So now I am Miss Tyrrwhitt. It was Léonide's idea.'

'Clemency's niece?'

'Yes. A Communist and a poet also.'

'Sounds a bit of a handful.'

'If you let her,' said Natasha. 'I did not.'

The Earl took it without a blink. 'Of course not,' he said. 'Why is Oliver drunk?'

'Let us sit down,' she said, 'and I will tell you.' But not all, she thought. By no means all. I think I am going to like you, but these are early days. 'He is unhappy,' she said.

'That is an adequate excuse for drunkenness?'

'To a Russian it is the most adequate of all. May I offer you a drink, by the way?'

'Will you join me?'

'Champagne,' said Natasha and rang the bell. The housemaid positively scurried in, and not all of it was curiosity, the Earl thought. There was a goodish dash of fear as well.

'Champagne,' said Natasha. 'Quickly.' The housemaid scurried out again.

Really the absolute essence of the Russian nobility, he thought. The house isn't hers and the champagne is almost certainly mine, and yet she offers it as if she were at home in St Petersburg. He watched in delight as she produced cigarettes and a jade holder. The picture was now complete.

'Please smoke if you wish,' she said, and the Earl took out a cigar.

'Why is Oliver unhappy?' he asked.

'Because he can no longer be a soldier,' she said.

'Then he will be unhappy for the rest of his life.'

'It is very possible,' she said, 'especially as he is poor and has no woman.'

The Earl said gravely, 'Those are cogent contributory factors, certainly.'

'If you are going to use difficult words I shall have to consult a dictionary,' she said. 'But I think I know what you mean.'

The housemaid scurried back in, this time with glasses and champagne in an ice-bucket, and Natasha continued as if she simply wasn't there.

'He sang a very rude song,' she said, and the maid turned red and almost dropped the ice-bucket. The Earl fielded it deftly. 'I'll open the bottle,' he said. 'You can go.'

The housemaid left even faster than she'd entered.

'Did you understand it?' he asked.

'Certainly,' said Natasha. 'It was quite – explicit.' She looked at the Earl in triumph: she too had achieved a difficult word. 'Perhaps you know it? It goes like this:

> *Oh, my little sister Milly was a whore in Piccadilly,*
> *And my mother was another in the Strand,*
> *And my father—*

The Earl said hastily, 'Yes, I have heard it, as a matter of fact. Usually sung to the tune of *The Road to the Isles*, I believe.'

'The Scottish folk song? But the original is not obscene, surely?'

'Far from it,' said the Earl. 'I found it dull, when it wasn't incomprehensible.'

'Oliver's song was not dull,' said Natasha. 'I think perhaps its obscenity gave him relief of some sort.'

'No doubt,' said the Earl, 'but it also embarrassed your housemaid. He must have sung very loudly for her to have heard him.'

'He always does,' said Natasha. 'Did you grow tired of killing beasts?' The Earl looked puzzled. 'Shooting big game,' she explained.

'I thought it time to come home,' he said. 'I was right.'

She smiled, acknowledging the elegance of the compliment. 'It is good that you came. Now you can attend the concert tomorrow. It is for the children with no shoes. I think many more people will come if you are there.'

'One day isn't much notice.'

'I shall tell Maddy Cantripp,' said Natasha, 'and Greenhalgh, and they will tell everybody else.'

'Daisy looks after you?' said the Earl.

'Daisy?' She sounded puzzled.

Dear God, thought the Earl, she doesn't even know her first name, and yet Daisy adores her. But is it so surprising? If I'm not careful I'll adore her, too.

'Daisy Greenhalgh,' he said aloud.

'She is very good,' said Natasha. 'But surely you must know that.'

'Must I?'

'She worked for you,' Natasha said.

'For my wife,' said the Earl, 'but she is very good. You're right.'

'I am very fond of her,' said Natasha.

'I also.' Far, far too late the Earl realised that the words should not have been said, but all Natasha did was smile once more.

'Today is her day off,' said Natasha. 'Did she come to see you?'

'She came to see my cook,' the Earl said. 'She didn't know that I was back at home.'

147

Natasha looked at him. An aging man, sixty at least, but lean and strong: brown face, blue eyes, white moustache neatly clipped.

'It must have been a delight for her,' she said, and held out her glass. The Earl filled it. She had been perfectly serious.

Then the parson and his son came in, dammit: the parson babbling apologies for not being in when his kinsman called. The Parochial Church Council meeting had gone on for far too long, and in any case he'd had no idea—

'Quite all right, Matthew,' said the Earl, watching George make for Natasha like a hungry man to a beefsteak. Nothing wrong with the boy's eyesight, he thought, but why does he walk like that? He can't be drunk too. Not at a Parochial Church Council. And then he remembered. George was clumsy.

'Perhaps we should have more fizz,' said the parson, pleased with the raciness of the word, and Natasha rang the bell.

'That is a very good idea,' she said.

'You have met Natasha, I take it?' the parson said, and Kielder nodded. 'It is a pleasure to have her staying with us.'

'A great pleasure,' said George.

'Yes,' said the vicar, stretching out the word, his agreement provisional at best. 'She has shown a lot of interest in our parochial affairs.' Tentatively, relying on the persuasive powers of champagne, he approached his problem. 'There is to be a concert in aid of the Shoeless Children's Fund. Natasha has arranged it.'

'And Maddy Cantripp,' said Natasha, her eyes on George.

'And, as you say, Mrs Cantripp.' The vicar turned back to his kinsman. The Earl approved of good works, he knew, but he did not like to be rushed. 'It is tomorrow evening, which is very short notice I admit, but I was wondering if it would be possible, provided you have no previous engagements, that is . . .'

'Don't worry,' said the Earl. 'I've had my orders. I'll be there.'

'*Orders?*' The vicar was appalled, but the Earl was smiling. Cautiously he began to relax, as the maid brought in more champagne. 'It seems a pity that Oliver wasn't here to welcome you,' he said. 'Unwell, poor chap.'

'Ah yes, Oliver,' said Natasha. 'There was something I forgot to tell you. Usually when he sings obscene songs they are pastiches of his own.'

Deft as ever, the Earl fielded the ice-bucket once again.

'They are often quite clever,' Natasha continued.

'You understand them all?' the Earl asked.

'If I do not, Greenhalgh explains them to me.'

The Earl noticed that the parson had achieved a colour he had never before seen: something between an aubergine and a pinot noir grape. He twisted the wire from the champagne cork.

'But not this time,' he said. 'I wonder why not?'

'I think he was too drunk,' Natasha said.

What a good idea it was to come back home, thought the Earl, but all the same I'd better stop bowling her lobs. My kinsman can't take much more.

'I hope he'll be fit to attend the concert tomorrow night,' he said at last. 'He's very fond of music, I believe.'

'He'll be there,' the vicar said.

So that was it, thought the Earl. Oliver is broke again, with only his father to turn to. He looked again at his niece, if that's what she was. Oliver had always been nosy, and doubtless the spell in the Black and Tans had sharpened that talent. He'd know she had money: couldn't fail to know how attractive she was, just as his brother had done, but the Earl didn't give much for his chances. Natasha was much too clever for him; fastidious too, if what Daisy said was right, and it usually was.

When she went up that night, Greenhalgh was waiting for her.

'But it is your day off,' Natasha protested.

'I know, miss,' said Greenhalgh, 'but I wanted to know what you think of him. Lord Kielder, I mean.'

'I like him,' said Natasha. 'I like him very much. Also he is clever.'

'Oh yes, miss,' said Greenhalgh. 'He was in the Diplomatic Service.'

'So the priest told me. He was in St Petersburg years ago – when I was a child.'

You're not much more than a child now, thought Greenhalgh, not if you measure by years, but that's not the way to know about you. It's what you've been through, and if my guess is right you've already had enough to last a lifetime. She began to unbutton the yellow dress.

'Oliver was drunk tonight,' said Natasha. 'He sang.'

'So I heard, miss. A very rude one, too.' The two women smiled. They could have been discussing a naughty child.

'Perhaps his rudest,' said Natasha, who now considered herself something of an expert on Oliver's repertoire of bawdy. 'You know, for a soldier he has a very weak head for alcohol.'

'You're wrong there, miss,' said Greenhalgh. 'It's the quantity. When he gets the miseries he can do a whole bottle.'

Natasha said, 'That is what I told Lord Kielder. About the miseries.'

'What did he say, miss?'

'He was angry because Oliver sang loudly and the housemaid heard. He thought she would be upset.'

Greenhalgh snorted. 'I don't think,' she said. 'Give Molly Parker a couple of pale ales and she'd join in the chorus.'

Natasha unhooked her brassière. 'Molly Parker?' she said.

'The housemaid, miss.'

'Is that her name?' said Natasha, and kicked free of the yellow dress. Greenhalgh dived to pick it up.

Might as well give us bleeding numbers and be done with it, she thought, and then: That's not true, Greenhalgh. She's fond of you. You could be the only person alive she is fond of.

Natasha yawned and stretched, and her bosom firmed prettily. Had His Lordship noticed that pair, she wondered, but of course he had. He noticed yours, and a few others. Not that he'd lay a finger on Natasha. He had his rules, and he stuck to them. All the same he'd notice all right. He liked pretty girls, sight as well as touch, especially when they had the style this one has. Maybe Miss Natasha would grow fond of His Lordship too. She hoped so. There was more than enough of her to share.

Next day she lunched with Maddy at the vicarage, and took a medicinal swig of the vodka she had brought from Harrod's first. This would be a long and trying day. Maddy began talking as soon as the housemaid had served them.

'How exciting for you to meet the Earl,' she said. 'It was so sweet of you to telephone me about it.'

I needed you to spread the news, Natasha thought. 'I like him,' she said.

'Mmm,' said Maddy. 'I do too.'

You are too young for him. Also I need you for George.

'And will he come to the concert?' Maddy asked.

'Of course.'

'Darling, how *did* you manage it? He hates all that public-life sort of thing.'

'I smiled at him,' said Natasha.

'You smiled?' Maddy looked incredulous, then her brow creased. She was thinking. I must tell her about that, thought Natasha. At her age it is bad for the skin.

At last Maddy said, 'You smiled and he said yes. Of course he did.' The frown vanished. 'It must be marvellous to be able to do that.'

'To smile?'

'To make people obey you because you smile.'

'I think you mean men.'

'Well, of course men,' Maddy said. 'It would be wasted on a woman'

Natasha thought of Léonide, but was silent.

'Please don't be angry,' Maddy said, 'but I want to ask you something.'

'Ask,' said Natasha. 'I can't say I won't be angry because I have a very bad temper, but I promise I will do my best.'

Maddy took a deep breath. 'Did you have to practise, or was it always there?' she asked at last.

'I think I had it when I was born,' Natasha said. 'It is like a light switch. On and off as and when I please. But I do not use it so very often. Only when I need it.'

'I wish I had it,' said Maddy, but Natasha headed her off ruthlessly.

'Oliver was drunk again yesterday,' she said, and told her about the song, but not the words. Maddy was nothing like as shockproof as Greenhalgh.

The rehearsal was as bad as she had anticipated, but then they always were, she thought, remembering the despair that clung to the Conservatoire like a fog, and the ballet rehearsal at the theatre in St Petersburg she had once seen with her *maman* before a charity gala: uproar and swearing, and a man and two girls in hysterics, and afterwards a controlled and disciplined beauty that was like no other she had ever seen. There was no controlled and disciplined beauty at Haydon Priors church hall, but there was plenty of despair, quite a lot of it hers.

It was not that they were downright bad. They almost always hit the right notes in the right order: Mr Sowerby with his flute, Mrs Gorton with her cello, Miss Golightly and Mr Binns with their voices. But there was no passion, and certainly there were no hysterics, so that the chances of disciplined beauty were nonexistent. Mrs Gorton perhaps had possibilities, but she simply didn't have the time to reduce her to hysterics, let alone build her up again. Besides, she had lost an earring, one of the pair from the rue de la Paix that went so happily with the red dress. It was all very irritating.

The children made her feel better. They were not very good singers, but somehow their teacher had persuaded them that singing was a pleasure, and their happiness reached out to her. *Nymphs and Shepherds. In Scarlet Town. Drink To Me Only.* It was all very English and very *nice*.

Then the players from the Slagsby Brass Band arrived,

Nonconformists to a man, so Maddy said, and as wary as virgins in a brothel, even if it was the church hall. But Carrick and his wife were with them, and it was obvious that they trusted Carrick and his wife.

A brass quartet. Two cornets, trombone and tuba. Where in the world had they found the money for them? Natasha wondered. The instruments were old and battered but they cost something, and these men were much too God-fearing to steal. But the instruments had been polished till they gleamed, and they played them superbly: *The Lord's My Shepherd*, Handel's *Largo*, a Beethoven Minuet.

Then the first cornet had to rehearse his solo, and she went to the piano, newly tuned but feeling its years, and motioned to the cornet player to take centre stage. A young man in a terrible suit, a white muffler around his neck instead of a collar and tie, fingernails grimy because there was no means of getting them clean, but there was something about him, she thought. The hysterics are over; let us try for the disciplined beauty. But his piece was by Rimsky-Korsakov, *The Flight of the Bumble Bee*. Every show-off in the world tried for it once, but few succeeded. For this item one didn't need beauty: one needed technique.

She nodded her head, and the young man plunged in: the notes pure and separate and true. And overwhelming too, she thought, like Dimitri at his most ardent. There was no other way to describe it. He made music as Dimitri had made love – as if it were the one thing in the world that mattered and it had to be perfect. That they finished together was God's wish and hers, and that too made her think of Dimitri. She rose from the stool and turned to face him.

'You were superb,' she said.

'Thank you, miss.' Pale, undernourished, gaunt, with the eyes of a fanatic, but an artist of rare quality.

'It is not easy to keep up with you,' said Natasha, but he didn't say 'Sorry, miss,' he merely smiled. Very rare quality, she thought, but what would Mr Sowerby and the rest of the artistes make of him, and would they show it? And would he care?

Maddy came up to her. 'I've arranged for a cup of tea and a bikkie,' she said.

'For everyone?'

'Of course,' said Maddy. 'Mr and Mrs Carrick will take care of the chaps from Slagsby. They were awfully good, weren't they?'

'Awfully,' said Natasha. 'The cornet player was sublime.'

Maddy blinked. It was not the word she would have chosen to describe a miner from Slagsby.

'Let us take our tea in that little room at the back,' Natasha said. In her bag there was a small flask of vodka, much too small to share.

'I believe it is called the Green Room,' said Maddy, and tittered nervously. Green Room sounded so theatrical and racy.

'No doubt,' said Natasha, although the room was painted a sort of brown like the colour of the soup Cook made when Greenhalgh wasn't watching her.

Before she could look for her flask the gardener's boy from the vicarage was shown in to them.

'Mrs Greenhalgh sent this for you, miss,' he said, then handed over a small package and left at once. How odd they are, thought Natasha. A Russian servant would have stayed to see what was in the package.

It was her earrings. Greenhalgh had found the missing one, and sent her a note to wish her luck and tell her she would be there. Darling Greenhalgh. Natasha found her flask, and offered it to Maddy.

'Vodka?' she said.

'Oh no,' said Maddy. 'Thank you. I might get drunk.'

'Sometimes it is good to get drunk,' said Natasha, 'but not like Oliver.' Then she thought she understood her friend's reluctance. 'But not before the concert – of course not. Afterwards we shall see.'

It was a success. True, Commander Harper panicked at being in the presence of an earl and a parson sitting side by side, and forgot half his stories, and Maddy as prompter to Miss Digby was all too clearly audible when Miss Digsby was not. On the other hand the children's choir was warmly applauded (much of the audience were their parents) and the Slagsby brass quartet and their soloist took encore after encore. She herself was also well-received, despite the fact that she banged and crashed her way through everything in sight – or perhaps because of it. This was an audience who believed in *fortissimi*.

After the concert there was a party. In fact there were three. One for the gentry and wealthier bourgeoisie among the audience, one for the artistes, and one in Slagsby for the Slagsby quartet, who were supplied with tea and buns to celebrate their safe return from the wiles of the Anglican Church. Carrick, the Slagsby curate, and his wife had been invited to what Greenhalgh called the nobs' party, which was held at the vicarage. Greenhalgh was there too, and so was Viscount Wentworth, Natasha noticed at once, but there was no need to worry. The suitcase that contained his binoculars was locked. Lord Kielder led him over to her.

'I made him come,' he said. 'Heard he was staying in the country so I fetched him. He was about due for a bit of culture.'

'Oh I say,' said Wentworth.

Like a slot machine, she thought. Insert the coin and out comes the chocolate, and always the same chocolate.

'You know each other, he tells me,' said the Earl.

'He bought me a very good lunch and gave me racing tips,' said Natasha.

'So I hear,' said the Earl. He didn't look too pleased about it, and Wentworth blushed and was silent.

'Allow me to introduce my friend Madeleine. Mrs Cantripp,' she said.

'We do meet from time to time,' said Kielder, 'especially when she feels the urge to buy shoes. How much this time?'

'Ten pounds,' said Madeleine.

'Each,' said Natasha, and Wentworth's hand went at once to his wallet. She left them and went to Greenhalgh.

'What'll it be, miss?' Greenhalgh asked.

'Burgundy,' said Natasha. 'Lots of it. And food. I'm starving.'

Greenhalgh poured wine from a bottle produced, rather furtively, from beneath a white cloth, and Natasha sipped. 'The Earl's,' she said at once.

'Yes, miss,' said Greenhalgh. 'And it's not for everybody. Not by any manner of means.'

'Who then?'

'Just you and His Lordship, miss,' said Greenhalgh, and then: 'I see you got the earrings, miss.'

'Oh Greenhalgh, I am so sorry. I forgot to say thank you,' said Natasha, and kissed the other woman's cheek.

For a second, perhaps a little more, all conversation in the vicar's drawing room ceased, then resumed with added volume as if determined to show that nothing untoward had happened. Damn fools, thought the Earl, and then, No, that's not fair. One had to have lived there to see it for what it was. Wentworth was still speechless: Madeleine Cantripp the only other person in the room unsurprised that Natasha had kissed a servant, but then Natasha had called her her friend, which suggested that she was used to her. Natasha came back, holding a second glass of Burgundy, and a plate of sandwiches.

'You should drink now,' she said. 'You have been working very hard. Greenhalgh will serve you.'

'No please. Allow me,' Wentworth said, and set off at something close to a trot.

Is the young fool afraid she might kiss *him*? the Earl wondered. Or is it because Madeleine Cantripp's still a very pretty woman? Far prettier than I recalled. Or is that Natasha's doing? He must remember to ask Daisy.

Natasha looked about her. Most of the people in the room were strangers who looked rather boring, but Oliver was there, drinking lemonade in a self-pitying sort of way, and George had wedged himself in a corner, out of the way of rugs and footstools and other people's feet. Natasha waved to him, and beckoned him to come over, and of course he had no choice. All the same he crossed the room as if it were mined, and somehow contrived to join them without accident.

'Well George,' said the Earl, giving George and his glass plenty of room.

'Good to see you back, sir,' said George. Wentworth returned to them, bringing Madeleine her wine, and George watched him enviously. He did it as if it were no problem at all.

The Earl began to talk of grouse shooting and Natasha said firmly, 'Maddy has something she must discuss with you, but not here.'

'Oh really?' said George, and Maddy looked startled.

'Her accounts,' said Natasha. 'For the shoeless little ones.'

'They won't be shoeless for quite a while,' Maddy said. 'We've made simply masses of money. Topping idea of yours, getting the Earl here. He guaranteed a good turnout.'

'Natasha too,' said George. 'The whole village wanted to see her. Hear her, too.'

Either you are a liar or you know nothing about music, Natasha thought, and said aloud, 'You must invite George to lunch, Maddy.'

'Must I?' said Maddy, more bewildered than reluctant.

'*To discuss the accounts.*'

'Oh yes, do come,' said Maddy. 'Both of you.'

That was not a problem: it would be so easy to forget to go.

Just before he left, the Earl came up to her as she was talking to Carrick and his wife. She introduced them both, and if Carrick didn't wipe his hands on his clothes like Mrs Elstob before they shook hands, it was touch and go. The Earl drew her aside.

'Friend of yours?' he asked.

'He runs the church in Slagsby for–' Natasha smiled '–our kinsman. They are the ones who do all the work for the children with no shoes.'

'They and Mrs Cantripp and you.'

She gestured impatiently. 'Madeleine a little. I simply enjoy myself. Those two work hard.'

'Enjoy yourself?' He sounded incredulous. 'How?'

'Being bossy,' she said. 'I very much enjoy being bossy. Perhaps it is because I am good at it.'

'Perhaps,' he said. 'But perhaps it is because sometimes people have to be bossed if something good is to be done.'

'Which people?' she asked.

'Rich people,' he said. 'Rich people who do not know the responsibility of their riches.'

She followed his gaze: he was looking at Wentworth.

'I would like you to come to lunch with me,' he said.

'A party?'

'Not the first time,' said Kielder. 'You've chosen to join the house of Tyrrwhitt. It's only fair that you should see the house.'

'I should like that,' she said, and offered her cheek, and again the conversation died then resumed, like an engine on the blink. Bloody fools, thought the Earl, and went to collect Wentworth. Nice to drive home in another man's Rolls.

After the Earl and Wentworth had gone, the other guests too began to drift away. No reason for them to stay, Natasha thought. I am the only aristo left, and these days I am no more than Miss Tyrrwhitt, and anyway they can see me any time they want to.

Maddy yawned behind her hand. 'Forgive me,' she said. 'I'm *quite* exhausted.'

'No wonder,' said Natasha. 'So much work.'

'And so much money,' said Maddy. 'I'd better take it home.'

'I'll walk with you,' said George.

And then it happened. Later Natasha told Greenhalgh that it was bound to happen, like something in a Greek play. It was inevitable, but also like something in a Greek play it unleashed powerful emotions.

The trouble was that George had begun to feel confident, thanks to the soothing influence of Madeleine Cantripp. She had that effect on him, and others, Natasha thought. The sense that everything was as it should be, and could not be other than it was, so what was the point of worrying about disaster, even if one had been shot twice in the backside? Pride before a fall, thought Natasha, then, No, not even pride. Just misplaced confidence, but the fall was real enough.

Later she realised that it was one of George's better ones: the best she had seen, in fact. The corner of the rug had turned over again, as it always did when it was trodden on too much, and George, looking at Maddy, telling her how important it was that they purchased a cashbook, stepped into it and tried too late to free himself. It was spectacular: Natasha could not deny it. Something out of modern ballet. *Petrouchka*, say. At one moment George was talking earnestly, sensibly, to a pretty woman who needed his advice, the next he was spinning like a top – two and a half *tours en l'air* – before crashing into the door jamb and sliding to the floor.

This time the silence lasted for five seconds at least, then the vicar said quite audibly, not knowing that he said it, 'Oh dear God, is George drunk too?' and Oliver began to laugh, a jeering bellow that was one of the ugliest sounds Natasha had ever heard. Then the whole room joined in.

'How absolutely disgusting of him,' said Maddy.

But which one? Natasha asked herself. Her best, her only hope was that Maddy had meant both of them, that they would start again from scratch. She went across to help George to his feet. That he had hurt himself was obvious, but the laughter continued.

'Are you all right?' she asked, and he nodded, not sure how his voice would sound. 'You are sure?'

He cleared his throat. 'I'm sure,' he said and then, more softly, 'who laughed first? Oliver?'

She made no attempt to lower her voice. 'Of course Oliver,' she said. 'He is a pig.'

All over the room the laughter stopped, and Oliver's head whipped back as if she had struck him. George looked where Maddy had stood. She was gone.

'Do you think she'll still expect me to lunch with her?' he asked.

All in all it had been a memorable day.

15

Oliver sought her out two days later. She was sitting under an apple tree's shade in the sunlight (nothing so bad for the skin as direct sunlight). He said, 'May I fetch you a glass of wine?' This was insolence. It was barely ten o'clock.

'No,' she said.

'I would rather like a word with you,' he said.

'Very well.'

'I should begin by telling you I—'

'You may have a word,' said Natasha, 'but not while you're standing over me. Fetch a chair.'

He found a deck chair in the garden hut, and sat down to face her. 'I heard what you said that night,' he said at last.

'I said many things.'

'About me,' he said.

'What did I say about you?'

Go carefully, Oliver told himself. Don't get rattled, and remember that she's clever as well as pretty.

'You called me a pig.' She made no answer; that trick of hers that could infuriate even when he knew it might be coming. Still no answer. Keep going, keep going. 'Please don't deny it.'

She shrugged: that other infallible method of distracting him.

'What is there to deny?' she said. 'I said it and you heard me.'

'Not a very nice thing to say in the middle of a party.'

'It was my opinion and I offered it,' she said.

'Because I laughed at George?'

'That was my reason at that time.'

'You have other reasons?'

'Certainly I do,' she said, 'but please do not ask me to enumerate them all.'

'There must be quite a list,' he said, but all he got for that was another silence.

Oliver took out pipe, tobacco, matches. 'Do you mind?' he asked.

'No.' That would have to do for permission, he thought, and he needed it. Tobacco would help him to relax.

159

'Pig's not a word that I like,' he said, 'when applied to me, that is, but I'm prepared to admit I can be nasty if I have to be.'

Still she didn't speak, but her face told him how readily she accepted his admission.

'I found that out in Ireland,' he said.

'When you were in the secret police?'

'*I was not in the secret police.*' Oliver found that he was shouting, and forced himself to finish lighting his pipe instead, and puffed out tobacco smoke. It drifted towards her, and she waved it away with her hand. He wanted to strangle her.

'Sorry,' he said, and cursed himself for the apology.

'Quite all right,' Natasha said. 'Your smoke did not reach me.'

Beat her first, then strangle her, thought Oliver. There would be pleasure in both.

'I was in the Black and Tans,' he said at last, 'as well you know.'

'Explain to me the difference,' she said, and lit a cigarette in her turn, assuming the air of one about to be given a lesson that might well be boring, but had to be endured even so.

'The Black and Tans' business was to combat revolutionaries,' he began.

'Just like the secret police,' she said. 'The ones we call the OGPU. They will tell you their business is to combat counter-revolutionaries, but it is much the same. And how did you combat them?'

'By force,' he said. 'We arrested them and put them on trial. If they resisted we killed them.'

'Exactly,' she said. 'It is strange to think of the English using such techniques. How did you know where to look for them? I assume that they did not wear uniform.'

'Of course not,' said Oliver. 'They looked like everybody else. We had to search for them – make people tell us where they were. That's where the nastiness comes in.' She waited once more. Pretty as a picture, he thought, and about as forthcoming.

'Bribery,' he said at last. 'That was the nice way. Bribery and informers. The nasty way was interrogation. Sometimes that could be very nasty indeed. You would know that if you'd ever been interrogated.'

Natasha remembered the militia and their way of asking questions: the Re-education and Rehabilitation Centre. 'Oh, but I have,' she said.

'I find that hard to believe,' he said, and again there was the silence that hurt like a blow. 'What I mean is that it's usually so obvious.' Again the silence – the trump that took the trick every time; a silence that was not really impolite, and certainly not dismissive, but nevertheless it told him: 'You are not merely rude, you are stupid, too.'

'Let me explain,' he said. 'A successful interrogation leaves its mark on a person. Takes away some of their self-assurance. Once you've been interrogated like that you are never quite the same again, and it shows.'

Unless you are lucky enough to find a Dimitri to reassemble the pieces, she thought. Aloud she said, 'That is most interesting.'

Calmly, willing himself not to shout, Oliver said: 'Yes, it is. But it doesn't explain why you are as you are.'

She nodded approvingly as if, for once, he had said the right thing.

'No, it doesn't, does it?' she said. Suddenly Oliver lost control, and jumped to his feet.

'No it bloody doesn't,' he yelled, 'so don't give me any more of your lies. I want to know what you think you're up to.'

Behind him a voice said, 'I was wondering if you'd like to change before you went to His Lordship's, miss.'

Oliver spun round, snarling, and his lame leg punished him for it. Greenhalgh stood facing him. She was looking at his hands, which were clenched into fists. He opened them and realised that he had dropped his pipe. It lay at his feet.

'I think perhaps I should,' said Natasha. 'I will feel better.'

'Very good, miss.'

The lame leg throbbed, and Oliver knew that he couldn't hope to bend to pick up his pipe. 'I wonder if I might ask you to pass me my pipe,' he said. 'My leg's bad today.'

Greenhalgh bent and passed it to him, holding it as if it were the most disgusting object she had ever handled.

'Thank you,' said Oliver.

'Sir,' said Greenhalgh, and Oliver limped away. Neither woman doubted that the limp was genuine.

'You shouldn't provoke him, miss,' said Greenhalgh.

'Why not?' said Natasha. 'He does his best to provoke me.'

'He wants to hurt you, miss,' said Greenhalgh, then added, 'as well.'

'Of course,' said Natasha, 'but I shall not allow him to do either.'

'One day he'll try, miss,' said Greenhalgh. 'See if he doesn't . . . I reckon it's the war.'

'The war?'

'Mr Oliver saw a lot of dead men,' said Greenhalgh. 'And that leg of his, sometimes it hurts something shocking.'

161

'I have seen a lot of dead men too,' said Natasha. 'And women, and children. And I know as much about pain as Oliver.' Every word of it, Greenhalgh was sure, was true.

'But I don't roar and bully like him,' said Natasha. 'At least I try not to. Though it must be said that I drink rather a lot. What is Lord Kielder's favourite colour?'

'On a lady, miss? Blue every time.'

'Then it shall be the blue dress.' She stood up then, uncoiling like a spring. Earlier in the day she had seemed tired, Greenhalgh thought, but now she was fairly bouncing with life, as if the quarrel with Oliver were the very thing she had needed to set her to rights. This one's unique, Greenhalgh told herself. I'm glad I was here when she came to call.

Lord Kielder had sent a car for her: another Rolls-Royce. Perhaps there was a law that said all English noblemen must have one, a kind of protocol, but this one was older and somehow easier than Wentworth's, like one's favourite slippers.

The chauffeur drove along the Slagsby road, then turned off just before the pit village into moorland where the miners coursed whippets after hares, played a gambling game called pitch and toss, and sometimes even now, said Greenhalgh, held cock fights in the ruins of sheep farms.

Wild country, Natasha thought, hard and poor, and in the winter, if there were snow, pitiless. Gorse and heather and crumbling walls, mile after mile, until at last there was a stream and a little bridge, a stream like a frontier, because beyond it there was grass, and grazing cattle, and a meadow with horses, a gently sloping hillside studded with deer. The car climbed the hill, and she saw parkland and formal gardens, and beyond them Kielder House.

It was the sort of place her English governess had shown her pictures of, long years ago. A hundred and fifty years old perhaps, with a formal elegance that was somehow warm too, and welcoming, like a jolly gentleman in evening clothes made in Savile Row. How lucky the Earl was: but more and more she was beginning to think that he deserved his luck.

He was waiting for her in the hall. It would have been quite wrong of him to be at the door on her first visit, she thought, and so of course he wasn't, because on her first visit Cribb, his butler, would feel it was his business, perhaps even his entitlement, to open the door so that he might run his expert eye over the latest addition to the Tyrrwhitt family. That he knew all about her she was certain: Greenhalgh was a wonderful servant, but she had not taken a vow of silence.

162

The earl came over to her and held out his hand, and she took it, and offered her cheek to be kissed.

'Natasha, my dear,' he said, and kissed her.

Really a *very* nice man, she thought, for there was appreciation in his kiss, but not what that same governess had once called unseemly ardour.

'Chanel,' he said, 'my favourite. And a blue dress, too. My lucky day. Come along.'

He tucked her arm in his and led her to the drawing room, past paintings and statues and bibelots, to more pictures and furniture and a painted ceiling, then pointed to an ice-bucket.

'Champagne,' he said. 'I don't think I could keep up with you on vodka these days.' The butler quivered a little, and the Earl said, 'Pour us a glass apiece, Cribb, then tell Cook we'll lunch at one-fifteen.'

The champagne was the best yet: she was glad she had ordered the blue dress.

'Matthew has told me your story,' Lord Kielder began, 'to the best of his ability. I don't want you to think I was prying—'

'Of course not,' she said.

'It was just that I felt I ought to know a few facts about you – as your kinsman.'

'As the head of the family,' she said.

'So that's my rôle, is it?' he said.

'You will be whatever you want to be, sir,' said Natasha, 'and so shall I.'

He smiled. 'Jolly decent of Jacquard to send you to me,' he said, 'but what a fool he was to let you go.'

'He told me he was obliged to,' said Natasha.

'That daughter of his acting up?' the Earl asked.

'Yes, but Léonide was not the only problem,' said Natasha. 'I am not always an easy person to have in one's house.'

'Tyrrwhitts rarely are,' said the Earl, and began to talk of St Petersburg and her life there, in the great mansion with its endless servants, on the streets with Ivan's gang, at the Re-education and Rehabilitation Centre. It was tactfully done, and skilfully too, but it was a cross-examination. Not that she minded: it was his right, after all. She even told him about Dimitri – a little, anyway.

When she had done he said, 'I take it you loved him very much.'

'Oh yes,' she said.

'And he loved you.'

'If he had not I would not be here,' she said, 'but it wasn't for very long, was it?'

'Think of it as champagne,' he said. 'Only a glassful, but it was vintage Krug.' He offered her a cigarette box. 'Please smoke. I want to see you use that holder again.'

He lit their cigarettes, and poured more champagne.

'How are you enjoying life at the vicarage?' he asked.

She shrugged, and he thought of starving George and beefsteaks. 'I was afraid it would be dull,' she said, 'but really it's not so bad. That is mostly because of Greenhalgh. You do not mind that I have Greenhalgh?'

'My pleasure,' said the Earl. 'A lady needs a lady's maid.'

'You do not want her back here?'

'What would I do with a lady's maid?' said the Earl. 'And anyway, she wouldn't come. Not any more.'

He is saying they were lovers, she thought, and doing it so sweetly.

'Then there was the concert to arrange, and a trip to London.'

'Ah yes, Harrod's,' said the Earl.

Natasha said severely, 'And the opera and the ballet, too. I am not wholly frivolous.'

'And Madeleine Cantripp for a friend. Really, your life is packed with incident.'

'It is restful,' she said. 'After Russia that is no bad thing. Not that it will last.'

'I should hope not,' said the Earl. 'You need entertainment, excitement. Lots and lots of young men to dazzle.'

'I have two at the vicarage.'

'Oliver and George?' said the Earl. 'I was forgetting about them.'

'Are they so unmemorable?'

He snorted. 'Perhaps not. George has made a success of his professional life at least, but Oliver – Oliver made one ghastly mistake.'

'Joining those Black and Tans?'

'Yes,' said the Earl, 'and I rather think he'll spend the rest of his life paying for it.'

'Perhaps so,' said Natasha, 'but he must not expect the rest of us to pay for it also.'

'You're thinking of the way he laughed when poor old George tripped and fell and you called him a pig?'

'But you had already left by then,' said Natasha.

'This is the Northumbrian wilderness,' the earl reminded her. 'Like the African jungle without the sunshine – but the bush telegraph is every bit as efficient. Of course I heard. This is the place where everyone hears everything. You must remember that, Natasha.'

She was being warned, but of what she was not yet sure.

'He did not like it that I called him a pig,' she said.

'No man would,' said the Earl, 'especially one who loves you.'

Is that what you think? she wondered, or is it what Greenhalgh thinks?

'Love?' she said at last. 'Sometimes he would like to beat me, and sometimes he would like to sleep with me, 'but I do not consider either of those things to be love.'

'Does he, by God!' said the Earl. 'Do you want me to do something about it?'

She looked surprised and said, 'Of course not. Keeping Oliver out of my bed is my business.'

It was unfortunate that Cribb came in to announce lunch at precisely that moment, but at least it bore out the Earl's theory of the Northumbrian bush telegraph.

Lunch was excellent, as she had been sure it would be: *langoustines* and roast chicken and a *crème brûlée*, and with it a claret of which Jacquard too had approved – a Château Montrose. Since Cribb was present throughout the meal in what was called the Little Dining Room (twenty metres by twelve, perhaps) the talk was general: Paris, the Côte d'Azur, and above all, music. Kielder was knowledgeable, and teased her slyly about her performance at the concert, but she made no excuses.

'I didn't play for my pleasure,' she said. 'I played for shoes.'

'And very successfully from what I hear.'

'That was mostly Maddy. It was her idea to bring in the men from Slagsby.'

'They were superb, weren't they?' said Kielder. 'That cornet-player...' He struggled for words. 'There are so many things he should play. Handel for instance – *The Trumpet Shall Sound*. Does he even know that such a piece of music exists?'

'Perhaps you should tell him,' Natasha said.

'Perhaps I should.'

They went back to the drawing room and coffee, and brandy for the Earl, who made not the slightest protest when Natasha asked for some too, though Cribb was outraged, which was ridiculous. The brandy too was excellent.

At last Cribb left and the Earl said, 'Wentworth is still here. He has invited us to dine with him. Would you care to go?'

'Is his house like this?'

'Not quite so big, but it has a Tintoretto.'

'Then by all means let us go. I have never seen a Tintoretto, unless there is one in the Hermitage. I can't remember.'

'No more can I,' said the Earl, 'but aren't you curious about why Wentworth asked us?'

'He finds me attractive,' said Natasha. The statement wasn't offensive. Not in the least. It was as if she had said, 'Today is Tuesday.'

'The boy's got eyes,' said Kielder, 'and that's partly it – but only partly. He wants you to meet his mother – or rather, he wants his mother to meet you.'

'Shall I like her?'

'It's possible but unlikely,' the Earl said, and thought: really, this habit she's taught me of answering direct questions with the truth is most enjoyable.

'Then why should I meet her?'

'I rather think,' said the Earl, 'that he wants to marry you.'

'*What?*' For once he had startled her. Almost she spilled her brandy, but drank it instead, and held out her glass for more. 'Does he need his mother's permission to marry?'

'Approval, shall we say. He is rather an old-fashioned young man.'

'And he spoke to you about all this?'

'I am head of the family as you say, and he couldn't think of anyone else to apply to. Better me than my cousin Matthew, surely?'

She said, 'Yes, yes of course,' then brooded for a moment. Even scowling she looked enchanting.

It's a bore to be sixty, he thought, but at least one is safe.

'She didn't come to the concert,' Natasha said at last.

'She dislikes gatherings of what she calls the lower orders.'

'Neither you nor I are in that category. Nor is her son, nor Maddy. Nor is the priest.'

'The priest? Oh, you mean Matthew. Do call him the vicar, child. Calling him the priest confuses him.'

He doubted if Natasha even heard him.

'I have met him only twice,' she said. 'The first time it was lunch and then the races: perhaps four hours. The second time it was at the priest's house and that was minutes only.'

'The vicarage,' said the Earl.

'It was minutes wherever it was,' said Natasha. 'How could he possibly wish to marry me in so short a time?'

'Oh easily,' said Lord Kielder.

She bounced from her chair, embraced him, then sat down again and sought in her handbag for cigarettes.

'Let us be serious,' she said, and the Earl sat up straight. 'This Wentworth is very rich, so they tell me?'

'Enormously.'

'Richer than you?'

'Considerably. His mother's father made a great deal of money in South Africa. Diamonds mostly.'

'It was – discreditable, what his grandfather did?'

'Sometimes. Great wealth isn't achieved by obeying the Ten Commandments.'

'It sounds exciting.'

'I've no doubt it was. Alfred Grout was an exciting sort of man.'

'What sort of lord was he?'

'No sort,' said the Earl. 'An out-and-out commoner. He'd been a boxer for a while and a sailor – not an officer – then he jumped ship to try his luck looking for gold and found diamonds instead. Then he came home shedding fivers like sweets and every match-making mama in Mayfair was after him.'

'And one of them got him.'

'Just so,' said the Earl, 'And he sired Lavinia. He was the most enormous fun. Knew more jokes than anybody I ever met. "Call me Alf," he used to say. He was killed on the hunting field, which was odd in a way. Clipping rider. He'd been a National Hunt jockey for a while as well.'

'At least we know why his daughter dislikes commoners,' said Natasha.

'Because she's partly one herself?' He blew her a kiss. 'As clever as she's pretty,' he said.

Natasha said severely, 'We are still being serious.'

'Yes, miss. Very good, miss,' said the Earl.

Natasha ploughed on. 'You are not poor?' she said.

'Good lord no,' said Kielder. 'Do I look poor?'

'No, no,' said Natasha, 'but when I was young I met many men like you – men with palaces and dachas and land and horses and serfs. And when they died, often they had nothing.'

'When I die I'll have quite a bit,' said the Earl, 'but what use will it be when I'm dead? Get to the point, child.'

'If you really needed money – if you were liable to lose this house, for example, I would marry him,' Natasha said. 'The head of the family must live in the family house after all.'

'Such a tremendous sacrifice will not be necessary,' said Kielder.

'Tremendous sacrifice?' For once Natasha was startled. 'How dreadful Wentworth's mother must be . . .'

167

16

'Oh she *is*,' said Maddy. 'That is to say I've never met her, but everyone says she is.'

Natasha had called at Maddy's house for tea, and perhaps to show off a little. Maddy had never been invited to an earl's house for lunch, or a viscount's for dinner. Perhaps when they went to Harrod's and chose some prettier frocks ... but then what would she do with George?

'Will you go?' Maddy asked.

'Lord Kielder thinks it might amuse me,' said Natasha. 'So I shall risk the Viscount's *maman*.'

'Is he in love with you?' Maddy asked.

'Lord Kielder? He is far too old, though very attractive. And besides, we are relatives.'

'Lord Wentworth, silly.'

Maddy was her friend, but it didn't do to rush things.

'I have thought about that,' said Natasha, 'but I have met him only twice after all, though both times I was wearing a very pretty frock. Perhaps it is his mother who wants to meet me.'

'But why should she want to do that?'

'To ask questions about Russia,' said Natasha. 'So many English aristos want to ask about Russia. Damned if I know why.'

Maddy blinked. A child of the lesser gentry, she knew beyond doubt that young ladies must never, never swear. Perhaps what dear Natasha called the aristos weren't aware of the rule.

'Oliver talked to me this morning,' Natasha said.

'Did he?' Oliver's star, for the moment, was waning it seemed.

'He is an uncouth person,' said Natasha. 'Isn't that the word? Uncouth?'

'It may well be,' said Maddy, then curiosity overcame her, as it so often did. 'What was it he talked to you about?'

'His time in Ireland,' said Natasha.

'Those dreadful Black and Tans.'

Natasha said innocently, 'Were they so dreadful?'

'Almost as bad as the wretched Fenians.'

'Now you mention it,' said Natasha, 'he did talk a lot about how ruthless the Black and Tans had to be.'

'Good gracious,' said Maddy, 'that hardly seems to me the way to impress a girl.'

Oliver's star might be waning, but Maddy could still be jealous, and after all, to mention two chaps in five minutes was rather overdoing it.

'*Oliver?*' Natasha said. 'Trying to impress *me*? I can think of nothing more unlikely.'

'I'm not so sure,' said Maddy.

'But consider,' Natasha said. 'If he wished to attract me he would not tell me about all the terrible things he did in Ireland.'

'Did he do terrible things?' said Maddy, interested once more. 'What were they?'

'Using spies, and giving bribes. Bullying people. Frightening them. Shooting them sometimes.'

'Yes,' Maddy said. 'He could do that. My poor husband never could – except the shooting, of course. And even that was Germans.'

'Of course,' said Natasha, 'but the point is Oliver didn't tell me what a wicked monster he was in order to seduce me—'

I love her dearly, thought Maddy, but I wish she wouldn't use such words.

'Why, then?' she asked.

'Because I called him a pig,' Natasha said.

'So you did,' said Maddy. 'At the party after the concert. I'm afraid I'd forgotten.'

'That is because so often he is a pig,' said Natasha. 'It was his way of paying me back.'

'Trying to frighten you?' Natasha nodded. 'And did he?'

'Of course not,' said Natasha.

'Haven't you ever been frightened?'

Natasha thought of the Centre, the hospital and Camp 19. 'Many times,' she said, 'but not of Oliver.'

'Those Tyrrwhitts are pests,' Maddy said.

Poor George, thought Natasha, but she wouldn't give up. Not yet.

'George doesn't try to frighten me,' she said.

'Of course not,' said Maddy. 'He wouldn't know how to. But he's so clumsy. Everybody was looking at him and laughing. And at me.'

'Don't you think that there may be a reason for it?' Natasha asked.

Maddy said vaguely, 'The Army? It could have been that. He was in it for a while. I don't remember him being clumsy before he joined.'

170

So she doesn't know he was wounded, thought Natasha. Or if she does, she doesn't know where.

'I'd never been so humiliated in my life,' said Maddy.

'Let us talk about our trip to London,' Natasha said.

The dinner had not been a success. That was an understatement: 'total failure' would have been more to the point. Lavinia Wentworth had disliked her from the moment she had set eyes on her, though really she was looking extremely pretty – both Greenhalgh and the Earl had said so. But perhaps that was the reason. Perhaps to look pretty in Lady Wentworth's eyes was bad, and to look extremely pretty was unforgivable.

Natasha considered. It could be jealousy. Lady Wentworth was not ugly, but prettiness had escaped her, even when she was young. Of that she was sure. Or perhaps it was that her own prettiness seemed to increase her son's fondness for her, a fondness he was unwilling, or unable, to hide. He couldn't keep his eyes off her: not like Oliver, who stared as if he were tearing her clothes off, but in a timorous and somehow reverent way she found equally irritating. All the same she encouraged him, if only to punish his maman a little.

The Earl had enjoyed it. But of course he had. It was the sort of vignette of social comedy he found vastly entertaining, and he had contributed to it by being paternal with her, man to man with Bobby Wentworth, and flirtatious with his mother, who obviously had no taste for flirtation. Natasha was pleased that Lord Kielder had enjoyed himself, but then he hadn't been obliged to drink coffee with Lady Wentworth while he drank port with her son. There was no offer of brandy either, only a tiresome lecture on the evils of smoking followed by another, almost equally tiresome, on the importance of rank, of aristocracy, of breeding. All this from a mere viscountess whose father was a gold miner.

'I do understand,' Natasha had told her. 'I was a countess for many years.'

'So Kielder told me,' the boring one had answered, 'but not British, after all.'

'My mother was,' she had said, '*and* she was a Tyrrwhitt.'

It was not enough, it seemed. To be established in polite society one must be of noble lineage, *English* noble lineage. Even Scottish was suspect, and Irish out of the question. But why tell me all this? Natasha wondered, though the answer was obvious enough. She was being informed that for her to aspire to marry her son, her darling Bobby, was not to be thought of.

Well, of course it was, silly woman. She would be bored in no time: darling Bobby bored her already if the truth were known.

Natasha began to describe what fun she had had at a birthday party given for the Grand Duchess Olga. She had worn a pink dress, and the food had been wonderful. She had described it, and the guests, and the game of blind man's buff they had played, until Lady Wentworth became bored in her turn, so that when the gentlemen walked in she looked almost elated – until the Earl suggested that Wentworth take Natasha to look at the Tintoretto. Naturally Lady Wentworth stood up too, but the Earl intercepted her, saying that he and she were far too old to look at pictures.

'No no, Lavinia,' he said. 'You and I will stay here and gossip while the youngsters enjoy themselves.' The implications of this were so horrendous that Wentworth had hustled Natasha out if the room before his mother could exercise the power of veto.

The Tintoretto was the best part of the evening: that, and the Earl in his rôle of doddering old fogey. It was the portrait of some holy chap or other, according to Wentworth. A saint, most probably. St Peter, was it? St Paul? He was almost certain it began with a P. Perhaps it was St Philip, she suggested, or perhaps St Francis, and he said more than likely, and she wished that he would try to kiss her and get it over with, so she could go back to the drawing room and be rude to his mother.

Instead he'd wandered further down the gallery of which the Tintoretto was the focal point, to show her two more pictures. They were of racehorses: one by Toulouse Lautrec, whose work she knew, and one by an Englishman, Stubbs, of whom she had never heard. They were both superb – but of course they would be. Everything of Wentworth's – or perhaps his mother's – proclaimed itself the best of its kind. She thought of his binoculars, and managed not to smile. There was little else to smile at, apart from what he said next, and that she would have to think about . . .

Greenhalgh drew the curtains, and for once the sun was shining.

'Good morning, miss,' Greenhalgh said. 'I hope you slept well.'

'Very well,' said Natasha. 'There is nothing like being thoroughly bored to make one sleep.'

'You did say it was a bit hard, miss,' said Greenhalgh.

'It was insupportable, except—' she hesitated.

'Yes, miss?'

'There is something I must speak to Lord Kielder about, then I will tell you.'

'His Lordship's just been on the telephone, miss. He has to go into

Newcastle to see his lawyer and wondered if you'd like to go with him.'

'To see a lawyer?' Natasha's voice was sharp.

'To do some shopping and have a bite of lunch, miss.' So we don't like lawyers, thought Greenhalgh. I can't say I blame you. I don't much care for them myself. Apart from poor Mr George.

'Did you say I'd go?' Natasha asked.

'He said he'd call in on the way and ask you himself, miss.'

'Then I'd better get up,' said Natasha.

Not blue, she thought, not this time: she mustn't spoil him. Well, not too much. Instead she chose a dress of her favourite yellow, a neat cloche hat, vast tapestry handbag, and a coat so capacious it was more like a cloak, but elegant and cool too, because the sun was shining.

The Earl, when he saw the ensemble, nodded approval. 'I'd better take you to somewhere decent,' he said.

'Those are the only places you know,' said Natasha, unperturbed.

He left her at the department store, and she went at once to the florist's section and bought roses, and a boutonnière for the Earl, then the wrapping paper, and after that to the perfumery to buy perfume and a lipstick, all of which she paid for in cash. After that she went to what was called 'Ladies' Accessories', where she stole a diamanté necklace for Greenhalgh to match the earrings she had already given her. When she went outside, the Earl's Rolls was waiting. Almost she had hurried, even run, but it was a mistake to run after one had stolen something. Instead she apologised by tucking the boutonnière into his button-hole.

'How very kind,' he said.

'Am I not?'

'But why all the flowers? Matthew has a gardenful.'

'But not like these,' said Natasha, and indeed it was true, the Earl admitted. The flowers in Matthew's garden had a sort of grim determination about them that was far removed from the opulent red roses Natasha had bought.

When they got to the American Bar of the hotel where they would lunch, he called for Martinis for them both and water for the roses. If I were older, not even very much older, Natasha thought, I could be in love with this man.

Over lunch Kielder said, 'This is by way of making up for that terrible dinner.'

'You enjoyed it,' she said.

'I rather suspect that you did too,' said the Earl. 'Some of it, anyway. All the same I never thought that Lavinia Wentworth could be quite such a gorgon.'

'She does not wish me to marry her son,' said Natasha.

'Nothing could have been more obvious.'

'It should have been equally obvious that I do not wish to marry him.'

'Not to her,' said Kielder. 'She assumes that any unattached female would wish to marry him.'

'But why?'

'Because he's Viscount Wentworth.'

'Good God!' said Natasha.

'If I may ask,' said Kielder, 'did he propose to you when you looked at the pictures?'

'No,' she said, and ate more smoked salmon.

'I find that odd,' said the Earl.

'I also,' said Natasha. 'I was looking very pretty.'

'You always do,' the earl said.

'Exceptionally so,' said Natasha. 'I don't know why. Sometimes it just happens like that.'

And yet there's not an ounce of vanity in her, thought Kielder once more. She said it as she might say, it's warm today but yesterday was a real scorcher.

'I think his *maman* must have told him not to,' she said, and smiled. 'Poor chap.' She sipped her Chablis. 'Please may I ask you something about him?' she said.

'Of course.'

'Is he really so very stupid?'

'I think not,' Kielder said. 'It's just that he's never been allowed to think. Why do you ask?'

'If he gave you a tip for a horse, would you back it?'

The Earl thought for a moment. 'One of his own?' he asked, and she nodded. 'On balance I think I would,' he said, 'but not too much. He's got a very good trainer. Chose him himself for once, which is why I don't think him as stupid as all that. Care to tell me what the horse's name is?'

'I would love to,' said Natasha, 'but I promised I wouldn't.'

The Earl looked at her sharply. 'He must think it's a good 'un,' he said, then changed the subject. 'I have to go to York next week,' he said.

'There is racing?'

'No, no,' he said. 'We can't have you upsetting Matthew again. He still hasn't got over the last time. Board meeting. Dreary stuff. And maybe—' he hesitated. 'You can keep a secret?'

'I am Russian,' Natasha said, 'and I am a woman. How can I possibly keep a secret?'

'Blessed if I know,' said the Earl, 'but I'd bet my life you can.'

'Yes,' she said. She was entirely serious.

'Don't look so solemn,' he said. 'It's not such a deadly secret. It's this. While I'm in York I shall also have a round of golf with the Archbishop. He was my – we were at school together.'

'Your fag,' she said.

'Who told you about fagging?'

'George,' she said. 'He was a fag, too. It didn't sound very nice.'

'It isn't,' said Kielder, 'but in those days the Archbishop wasn't very nice either. Even now he—' The Earl paused for a moment. 'I always beat him, you see. Always. I can't help it. I'm a better player than he is. Mind you he tries a few tricks.'

'He cheats? The Archbishop?' Natasha was enchanted.

'Not to say cheats,' said the Earl, 'but when he's got a tricky putt he always says a prayer. I know he does – I can tell by his face. So just to be on the safe side I always cough or light my pipe when he's about to hit the ball. I mean to say, fair's fair. All the same it's a dead bore.'

'Then why do you do it?'

'Matthew,' sighed the Earl. 'He thinks if I stay on terms with the Archbishop he may get preferment.'

'I expect he wants you to let the Archbishop win,' said Natasha.

'That's the funny thing,' said the Earl. 'He doesn't – which just goes to show he's a better Christian than his CO, besides being a damn sight more innocent.'

The waiter came to remove their plates and Natasha said, 'That reminds me. Am I to continue living with the priest?'

At least the waiter did better than Matthew's housemaid, thought the Earl. A lot better: hardly a tremor, and waited for him to leave. When he had gone he said, 'I want you to promise me something.'

'Of course.'

'When there are servants about – housemaids, waiters, people of that sort – I want you to promise me that you will choose your words carefully before you speak.'

'But all I said was—' Natasha began, and then, 'Oh.'

'Precisely,' said Kielder.

Natasha giggled then: a delicious, gurgling sound.

'Yes, I daresay,' said the Earl, 'but if you don't put a curb on that tongue of yours I'll end up kneedeep in broken crockery.' Even so he was smiling, but when the waiter brought the next course she was silent until he had gone.

'Getting bored with Matthew?' the Earl asked at last.

175

'Not always. Sometimes it is far from dull.'

'Oliver?'

'George too,' she said. 'It is time that he was married.'

The Earl discovered that he had far more sympathy for George than he had suspected.

'Then there is Greenhalgh,' said Natasha. 'I cannot exist without her.'

'You mustn't even consider it,' said the Earl.

'But she works for the priest.'

'She works for me,' said the Earl, 'but since mine is a bachelor establishment I can loan her to you.'

'The priest cannot exist without Greenhalgh either,' said Natasha. 'She watches the cook.'

'He'll just have to find someone else to watch her,' said the Earl. 'Oliver never seems to lift a finger so far as I can see. Let him do it. Do you want to stay with me?'

'Not immediately,' said Natasha. 'I have certain arrangements to make at the priest's house.'

The Earl discovered that it was possible to feel sympathy even for Oliver.

'Then as you say, you have no wife now,' said Natasha. 'And as you also said, the priest is innocent. It was his idea that I should stay with you – but I do not know how such things are arranged here. What would Lady Wentworth say, for example?'

'Hooray, probably,' said the Earl. 'She'd suspect the worst, you see, which would mean that Wentworth would be safe from your clutches. She would also say that there's no fool like an old fool. People often say that in England.'

'But you are not a fool,' said Natasha.

'And quite often I don't feel all that old,' said Kielder. 'But quite old enough to be your grandfather.'

'Just about,' said Natasha. 'Oh, I do wish you were!'

'I too,' said Kielder, 'but I'll settle for great-uncle instead. As for staying with me, we'll work something out. I may have to shunt you off on one or two others, just for the look of the thing—'

'Not Lady Wentworth,' Natasha said firmly.

'No, no. Really rather nice people.'

'But will they want me to stay with them?'

The Earl smiled. 'My dear, they'll fight for the privilege. And then there's the Season, of course. You're missing all that.'

'I have read so much about the London Season,' she said wistfully. 'Maybe next year—'

'No doubt about it,' said the Earl, but she did not seem so sure.

'There is something else I must ask you,' she said. 'I want your permission to go to London.'

'I am wearing my head of the family hat, I take it?' said Kielder.

'Yes, sir.'

There was no mockery in her answer: she was serious. His rôle in her life was important to her, and he must live up to it.

'You will not go alone?' he asked.

'Good gracious no.' For once he had shocked her.

'Madeleine Cantripp?' She nodded. 'And where will you stay?'

'The Savoy,' said Natasha. 'It is pleasant at the Savoy. Maddy worries that she can't afford it – such a fuss – but once I have dressed her properly she will be better.'

'Harrod's?' said the Earl.

'Such a *useful* shop. With the right clothes it will be so easy to make arrangements for Maddy.'

Madeleine Cantripp took her place in what promised to be a fairly lengthy queue for the Earl's sympathy. All the same he let it be. Much better not to know.

'I see no reason why you shouldn't go,' he said. 'When will it be?'

'While you are away,' she said.

That was a compliment indeed. It must be rewarded.

17

It was a good trip to London: the Pullman comfortable, the Savoy everything a hotel should be, and Harrod's still everything a store should be. Moreover, Maddy was much better to share a room with than Léonide. There were no tears, no tantrums, no chasing around the bed. Altogether it was most satisfactory. And there was more. The Earl had bestirred himself, and when they arrived at the hotel invitations awaited them to far more parties than they could hope to attend. Dinners, cocktail parties, dances. Really, the head of the family had behaved splendidly, and Natasha prayed that he would beat the Archbishop at golf even more soundly than usual.

'But this is absolutely wonderful!' Maddy was ecstatic.

'Yes,' said Natasha. 'We must go to Harrod's tomorrow first thing.'

'Oh yes,' Maddy said, then suddenly looked downcast.

'What is the matter?' Natasha said.

'Francis.'

'Who is Francis?'

'My late husband,' said Maddy.

But if he is late why should he be a problem? Natasha wondered. Aloud she said, 'What about him?'

'His cousin and his wife live at Sunningdale. They'll expect me to visit them.'

'Don't tell them,' Natasha said.

'They'll find out,' said Maddy. 'They always do.'

'Are they awful?'

'The most ghastly snobs. They'll expect me to stay.'

'You can't do that,' said Natasha, 'but if they are snobs just go to tea to this—'

'Sunningdale.'

'—and tell them that you are acting as chaperon to a Russian countess to oblige Lord Kielder whose great-niece she is, and you cannot stay for more than tea because I am very wild.'

'They'll love that,' said Maddy. Natasha rang for room service, and ordered champagne.

179

* * *

Harrod's supplied everything of course, and really Maddy behaved very well, accepting all Natasha's suggestions. There was a little awkwardness about the underwear perhaps.

'What's wrong with it?' Natasha was baffled. Too revealing, it seemed. 'But if nobody else will see it, how can that matter?'

Maddy bought it, but there was a distinctly frosty look in her eye, and Natasha wondered if someone was going to be privileged to see it after all. Not Oliver, she thought, but whether George could cope with knickers like that she was by no means sure.

She stole nothing, because with Maddy by her side all the time she had no choice, but she bought more dresses, and shoes, and a hat, and Mr Simkins left his office to ask how she did, and it was all most satisfactory.

'Shall we send your purchases to the Savoy as usual, ladies?' Mr Simkins asked, and Natasha looked at her friend. For Maddy this was far, far more than satisfactory: it was bliss.

As they walked down Knightsbridge to a restaurant Lord Kielder had recommended, Maddy said: 'You know, it really is rather fun to have one's own money to spend.'

'I do so agree with you,' said Natasha, who had never had her own money in her life, but spent other people's like water.

In the restaurant two men lunching together tried to pick them up, but Natasha decided they weren't quite what she wanted, not after the invitations she had received. Even so, although she blushed a little, Maddy sat up very straight and smiled, and even pushed her chest out.

No doubt about it, thought Natasha, my friend has potential.

That night they went to a party in Eaton Square: cocktails, and dancing to gramophone music, and a host whose aging, still pretty mother remembered Lord Kielder well.

'He was one to watch,' she said, and Natasha would have liked to hear more, but not at a cocktail party. Maddy, she noticed, danced well. 'I took lessons in Newcastle,' she said later, which meant of course that she had intended from the start to come to London, and who could blame her for that? All those years of boring widowhood. After that, two far more eligible men took them dancing at the Ritz, but they were no trouble. They were both 'Oh I says'.

Next morning Maddy woke to find that she had danced with the nephew of a duke and the heir to a shipping line. It said so in three different newspapers, and was all very gratifying: in fact the whole week was – not just the parties, but the ballet, the opera and the theatre. Dear Natasha crammed them all in like a greedy schoolgirl with a box of chocolates, Maddy thought. But that was unkind, she reproached herself. She was doing the same herself. Even the obligatory visit to Sunningdale turned out to be fun. Francis's cousin and his wife had read the three newspapers too, and were overawed and acquiescent and most unlike the people she remembered, so that she was able to show off like mad and leave far too early. She was dining with a former ambassador to Paris and his wife, after all.

Natasha used Maddy's absence to go back to Harrod's, buy and pay for vodka and steal caviar, which was still ludicrously expensive. For a while she considered lunching at the Savoy Grill and finding a man to pay for it, but decided against it. Lord Kielder, she was sure, would not approve, and there was a good chance that he would know the man. He knew Bobby Wentworth, after all. Instead she went to her room and ordered an omelette and tested the vodka, which was not at all bad, and thought about Maddy, who was doing her credit.

Looking prettier by the hour, dear Maddy, and loving it, and no more nonsense about skimpy underwear. On the contrary. If they stayed in London for very much longer she might succumb to the temptation to show it to somebody – and what chance would George have then? Not that he seemed to have much of a chance now, she thought, but all the same one should try . . .

She yawned, and wished she had a piano to play or Greenhalgh to gossip with. Really she missed Greenhalgh desperately, though Maddy was getting better at doing her hair. Useful too that she was dark and Maddy was fair. The orchid and the English rose, one young man had said, and of course Maddy had blushed – but that helped, too.

Maddy returned in triumph and Natasha listened, delighted. Bullies and tyrants should always be attacked on sight, and at last Maddy seemed to be getting the hang of it. She kissed her.

'We must celebrate,' she said. 'I shall order champagne.'

'We're always drinking champagne,' Maddy said.

'We're always celebrating.'

And all Maddy did was grin. Such an improvement.

That night Maddy wore a blue dress, and Natasha was sorry that the Earl wasn't there to see it. Hers was of a dark and glowing red that paid no homage at all to Comrade Stalin. The ex-ambassador and his wife lived in a house just off Park Lane, and from across the road there came the sound of a dance band; taxis and cars queued to disembark their passengers.

'Debs,' said Maddy, watching a gaggle of girls climb the steps.

Young men, nervous or unconvincingly confident, followed. 'And their Delights,' she added. 'How glad I am to be shot of all that.'

'But you like dancing,' said Natasha.

'They aren't there to dance,' said Maddy. 'That's just the excuse. They're there to get married.' She paid off the driver and they went to the ex-ambassador's door, and the waiting butler.

'Mrs Cantripp,' the butler called. 'Miss Natasha Tyrrwhitt.'

Deliberately, though they had never rehearsed it, the two women stood side by side for the benefit of the dozen or so people already assembled, then moved to where Sir John and Lady Brett awaited them.

'Miss Tyrrwhitt,' said Lady Brett, and her husband said helpfully, 'Tom Kielder's girl.'

Lady Brett didn't look as if she was awfully good at remembering things, thought Natasha. Certainly she had forgotten to have those diamonds cleaned.

'Great-niece,' Natasha said.

'Yes, of course,' said Lady Brett. 'He wrote to us about you. Such a sweet letter.'

On the other hand she looks kind, thought Natasha, and not at all stupid.

'May I present my friend, Mrs Cantripp,' she said.

'He wrote to us about you too,' said Sir John, 'though he forgot to mention what absolute stunners you both are.' Again Maddy blushed: again it did no harm at all.

'You know the Jacquards, I believe,' said Lady Brett.

'I lived with them in Paris for a while,' said Natasha, 'after I left Russia.'

Sir John looked at her sharply and she saw at once that behind the old buffer compliments a very clever man was watching.

'Russia,' he said. 'That must have been interesting.'

'Fascinating,' she said, then more people arrived and it was time to move on.

Champagne appeared, and men: older than the Debs' Delights, their confidence much less of a bluff. One obvious *pédéraste*, she thought, but at least he makes no effort to hide it, two who are wondering how much money we have, and deciding, perhaps regretfully, that it won't be enough, and two who came up simply because it was nice to be next to pretty women and show off their party tricks in the hope that something exciting might follow.

One of them said, 'I'm Martin Brett, your host's son. In the Diplomatic like my father. I say – this is a bit of luck for me.'

'It is kind of you to say so,' said Natasha.

182

'The thing is, I was expecting a posting but it's been delayed so Mummy suggested I have this party. And the other thing is I've been learning Russian. Would you mind awfully if we spoke it for a while?'

Natasha said in Russian, 'For a little while. We must not be impolite.'

'Thank you,' he said, and told her about the posting that had not come through. Latvia. He spoke not a word of Latvian, but it seemed that everyone there spoke Russian, though they disliked doing so intensely.

'We used to own it, you see,' Natasha said.

She speaks of Latvia as if it were a Fabergé egg the Tsar had mislaid, he thought, and chattered on. At last he said, 'Do I sound like a Russian?'

'No,' she said. 'You speak it like an Englishman who has learned my language well.'

Back in school, he thought. Seven out of ten.

'I wish you luck in your new appointment,' she said. This time she spoke in French.

'Thank you,' he said also in French, and then, 'What next? German? Italian?'

'My German is not good,' she said, 'and my Italian consists only of words concerned with music – *mezzo forte*, *da capo*, *pianissimo*.'

She smiled at him. Did your father tell you to find out how fluent I am? she wondered – and was it the Earl who asked him to do so?

The man who had been chatting with Maddy turned to her, as Martin Brett approached her friend. Corbyn, was that his name? Andrew Corbyn? A banker, so Martin had said, but not the kind who stands behind a counter. And a soldier too, apparently, in the war they all talked about so much, here and in France, and in Germany too, no doubt. That would make him rather older than Martin, and no doubt very rich. She would have to watch Maddy most carefully.

Corbyn said, 'Your English is better than your Italian, I trust?'

'Much,' she said. 'My mother was English and so was my governess.'

'Jolly good,' Corbyn said. '*La plume de la tante du jardinier* is the best I can manage.'

'Even in France,' she said, 'that will not get you very far.'

He grinned at her. 'After dinner there is to be dancing. I hope you'll save me one.'

'Of course.'

After dinner there was indeed dancing, in a drawing room with the carpet rolled back, to the music of piano, drums and a saxophone. Sir John and Lady Brett and a couple of their friends sat and watched, while the young people waltzed and one-stepped and Charlestoned. The men, she thought, were no more than adequate for the most part, but the *pédéraste* seemed to know what he was doing. So relaxing to dance with a – what did the English call them? – a fairy, that was it. One could move in their arms in any way one pleased without raising false hopes. From across the street the dance band played on, serenading the virgins who hoped to be brides.

Martin Brett, too, heard the music. 'Did you have a come-out?' he asked.

'A début, do you mean? How rude you are,' said Natasha. 'By the time I was old enough for such things, the band no longer played.'

He apologised in English, Russian and French, and she wondered if that too would be reported to Papa, then Andrew Corbyn suggested they stroll on the terrace and look at the stars. It really was rather warm in the ballroom...

In the taxi to the Savoy, Maddy said, 'Andrew Corbyn tried to kiss me.'

'He's rather good at it, isn't he?' said Natasha.

'You mean you let him?' Maddy sounded horrified. The underwear was not yet to be revealed, one gathered, at least not to Andrew Corbyn.

'For a little while only,' said Natasha. 'It was much too late to do my make-up again.' She lit a cigarette: inserted it into her holder. 'He wanted to take me to Paris. It is odd how Englishmen want to take one to Paris. After all, I've just come from there.'

'It's disgraceful,' said Maddy, then added: 'He wanted to take me to Paris, too.'

'Would he take us one at a time, or both together?' Natasha asked, and Maddy giggled.

Corbyn had been good for her, thought Natasha, though it was as well she didn't want to go to Paris with him. Come to that he'd been good for her, too. Apart from the kisses he'd told her something very interesting.

'He's very persistent,' Maddy said.

'He is indeed,' said Natasha. 'Persuasive, too.'

'I told him to stop,' said Maddy, 'and he wouldn't.'

'Did you want him to?'

'Well, of course I did,' said Maddy. 'That is—' Natasha waited. 'Yes, I did.'

'You should have run away.'

'How could I?' said Maddy. 'The way he was holding me, I could hardly move. And anyway he's much, much stronger than I am.'

Natasha blew out smoke. 'Tomorrow I will show you a way to get free,' she said, 'but if you use it you must be quite sure you want to get free. It can be really very painful – for the gentleman.'

Maddy looked at her worshipfully. 'Oh Natasha,' she said, 'you know so much.'

This trick I learned before I'd even met Dimitri, thought Natasha. It was taught me by one of the girls in Ivan's gang, and it hasn't failed me yet.

All in all it was an excellent week and when the day to return to Haydon Priors arrived, Maddy seemed ready to weep, but packing the new dresses consoled her. They would cause envy and annoyance among so many of her friends. The trick to rid herself of too-persistent gentlemen had horrified her at first, but then curiosity and a sense of power overcame the horror.

'I see what you mean about being sure,' she said, and then: 'Francis—'

'Your husband? What about him?'

'He'd have been appalled,' Maddy said.

Because you might have used it on him? Natasha wondered, but there was simply no point in speculating about other people's love lives. It was like the wounds in George's bottom. There was no way of telling – unless she could persuade Maddy to marry him. She tried to talk about him on the train, but all Maddy would say was, 'Do let's try to look on the bright side.' Definitely not a good sign.

They took a taxi from Newcastle. Maddy dropped her at the vicarage and the gardener carried in her suitcases. To her astonishment he seemed to be the only one about. So far as she could gather, for his accent was very broad, the Sunday School Sports were being held on a playing field nearby, the vicar had given permission for everyone to attend, and everyone had.

'But why are you here?' she asked, as he carried her cases to her bedroom.

'Had to finish mowing the lawn first,' he said. 'And I have, so I'm going – if there's nothing else, miss?'

She gave him a shilling and he left at once. As if I might ask for change, she thought. Pity Greenhalgh wasn't there to unpack. A gossip was just what she needed. Not like her to be away when I return home, but then going probably wasn't her idea. The priest had ordered all the servants to go. He liked an audience. She remembered the concert and thought, I shall go downstairs and practise for a while, but first I shall have some vodka.

She had poured the second glass when Oliver came in. She looked at him: he seemed sober enough.

'You shouldn't drink that stuff,' he said.

She swallowed it at a gulp the way Dimitri had taught her. 'If it comes to that you shouldn't be here,' she said.

He continued as if she had not spoken. 'I've been thinking about you,' he said. 'All the time you've been away. Thinking and thinking.' She waited. 'You can't be who you say you are.' Again she did not speak, but this time it failed to upset him. He didn't want her to speak, he wanted her to listen.

'You're too much,' he said.

'That is a silly thing to say,' said Natasha.

'Don't interrupt. When I say too much I mean just that. Too clever, too beautiful, too accomplished – too good at carrying your booze, come to that. No Tyrrwhitt was ever like that. You can't be who you say you are. I wrote to a friend of mine in Paris who works on a newspaper and I asked him about your pal Léonide. His answer came yesterday. She's a lesbian.'

'Of course,' said Natasha. 'Also a poet, and a Communist.'

'I told you not to speak,' said Oliver. 'I won't tell you again.'

He's not nearly so sober as I'd imagined, she thought. Either that or he's having some sort of *crise*, and whichever it is I must be careful. She waited.

'That's how you wormed your way into this family,' said Oliver. 'She wanted you. Well, I can understand that.'

Natasha took out her cigarettes and holder, and the little gold lighter she had bought at Dunhill's.

'I don't like your smoking, either,' Oliver said. She lit her cigarette.

'I'll teach you about that in a minute,' said Oliver. 'I'll settle this first. You wormed your way in here when you'd made a nuisance of yourself in Paris – my chum said you had quite a reputation there before you left – and settled down to wait for the Earl so that you could make sheep's eyes at him and set him to waiting on you hand and foot as if he were bloody Greenhalgh.'

She winced at that, he noticed. Mustn't be rude about Greenhalgh, it seemed. Well, she was about to learn differently.

'What do you think you're going to do? Marry him – or just spend his money? Well, I won't have it whoever you are. Bloody countess my foot. You came out of the gutter and you can bloody well go back there.'

The odd thing was that in a way he was right. For a while the gutter had been her only home.

'They're all out at the Sports Day,' said Oliver. 'Won't be back for

an hour at least so there's no point in yelling – but you can speak now.
I'll allow you to do that. Tell me who you are.'

'You insist that I do this?'

'You'll tell me,' he said, 'or I'll beat it out of you.'

She thought that he intended to beat her anyway. 'There's no
need,' she said. 'I am Anastasia.'

'Anastasia who?'

'The Grand Duchess Anastasia. Daughter of the Tsar and Tsarina.
We didn't all die at Ekaterinburg. I survived.'

For a moment she thought that he believed her.

'Not that I was not hurt,' she continued. 'The soldiers shot at me
and I have wounds. No doubt you will try to see them. But I did not
die. Peasants – good people – they rescued me, nursed me, started me
on the long, long journey. Perhaps it is over now. I do not know.'

He looked bewildered, then slowly the bewilderment was replaced
by rage. 'You little liar,' he said, and leaped at her.

It was just as Dimitri had taught her. He was stronger, but she was
quicker. As his hands reached for her she squirmed to one side, and
lunged with the cigarette holder at his wrist. Her aim was a little high,
but even so the hot coal of the cigarette tip burned through his shirt-
sleeve and touched his skin. At once he yelled, and as he did so she
showed him the trick Svetlana had taught her in St Petersburg all
those years ago, and the yelling grew louder.

I am hurting him a great deal, she thought. It is because I play the
piano so much, and my wrists are strong. At last she let him go, and he
fell forward, whimpering.

'You—' he gasped. 'You—!'

'I,' she said, 'whoever I am. Attack me once more and you will
have no success with ladies, ever again. Do you hear me, Oliver? *Do
you?*'

Doubling over, sweating with pain, he whispered, 'I hear you.'

'Then listen to what I have to say. In 1917 you were found in a shell-
hole in Cambrai. Five more men were with you, but they were all
dead. You were unmarked, Oliver. Kind-hearted persons suggested
you might have concussion; others were not so sure. But the battle
was fierce and everyone was too busy, and so they gave you an aspirin
and you went back to fight and were brave, and the fact that you
might also be a coward was overlooked.'

'Who—?' he said. 'Who told?'

She shrugged, but there was no pleasure in it for him, not then.

'Does it matter?' she said. 'It's true, isn't it?' He made no answer.
'If you talk about me, I will talk about you.' She was implacable. 'Do
you believe that?'

'Christ yes,' he said.

'Then the choice is yours.' Let him write to his friend the journalist and ask about Anastasia. Paris was full of the story. The ones who knew everything said she was in Berlin. Such nonsense.

She looked at Oliver again. What an odd colour he was. White, with a tinge of green. The pain must be severe. She wondered if his having been a coward might explain why he had joined those Black and Tans he boasted about so much. A kind of revenge perhaps, when others too were afraid. It was foolish of him if it were true. There was no disgrace in fear, if the cause of it was strong. Suddenly she wanted to giggle, but was careful not to give way. All the same it was funny. 'No point in yelling,' he had said, and it was true. He had yelled like anything, and there was no one to hear.

'You must go now,' she said.

He was kneeling, his body bent in a posture that brought him relief: a very little. 'I can't,' he said.

'You must,' she said. 'I do not want you here. Go now or I shall hurt you again.'

He looked at her, appalled. Bewildered, too. He would not have lasted long at the Re-education and Rehabilitation Centre.

'I can't walk,' he said.

'Then crawl.'

But that was too much. Somehow he straightened up till he knelt upright, then grasped at her bed and pulled himself to his feet. Every movement was agony, but what did he expect?

'Will you tell anyone I came here?' he asked.

'Why should I?' she said. 'It was disgusting. Get out of my room.'

Slowly, every step another torture, he left her, and she poured more vodka.

It was over, she thought. Almost certainly it was over. He had gambled, and he had lost. Gambled for so many reasons. Jealousy because Kielder preferred her to him, and what was she to make of that? It couldn't all be money. Lust, of course, and the need to dominate, to hurt, because with Oliver that was a part of lust, and the kind of craziness that visited him from time to time because his war had lasted too long. Just as well that Andrew Corbyn had wanted to take her to Paris, she thought. Otherwise he would never have told her.

When Greenhalgh came back, babbling apologies, she was practising the piano, but they went to her room at once. It was as she had guessed: the priest had needed an audience, but that was because he had persuaded a bishop to present the prizes.

'Does he play golf?' asked Natasha.

Greenhalgh blinked, but she was becoming accustomed to miss's brand of logic. 'His Lordship only plays with the Archbishop,' she said. 'He likes to beat him.'

'He's been doing it ever since he was at school,' said Natasha. 'The Archbishop was his fag.'

Greenhalgh began to unpack. 'You brought some lovely things back this time, miss,' she said.

'The one on the top is for you,' said Natasha. Another enormous box of chocolates, and tied to its ribbon a little box that held earrings, gold hoops of the kind Natasha knew that Greenhalgh yearned for.

'Oh miss,' she said. and☎ kissed her. 'Oh thank you.' The only one I ever knew who doesn't give a damn about money, Greenhalgh thought. If she liked somebody, she gave, and when it was all gone she would get some more or do without – though being Miss Natasha the odds were she would get some more.

'Put them on,' said Natasha.

'I shouldn't, miss,' said Greenhalgh.

There was no risk, thought Natasha. Nowadays I pay for the things I give Greenhalgh. The Earl would not like it otherwise. Except for the caviar we share. Then she understood.

'The priest would not like it?' she asked.

'Nobody would except you, miss.'

'The Earl wouldn't mind.'

'He's still in York, miss.'

'The Archbishop had better not forget his prayers,' said Natasha.

The unpacking continued. She never gets it wrong, thought Greenhalgh. Never. Every one might have been made with her in mind, and every one was of silk, or of a cotton so fine it must be almost as expensive. Hundreds of pounds' worth – and she doesn't give a damn.

Natasha looked at her watch. 'It is time I bathed,' she said, and began to undress. Suddenly Greenhalgh gasped.

'I don't have a rash, do I?' Natasha asked.

'Mr Oliver,' Greenhalgh said. 'He never came to the Sports. The vicar was furious. You haven't seen him, have you, miss?'

'I believe I heard him singing when I first came up, but it wasn't rude. At least I don't think it was. I haven't seen him. Perhaps he's asleep.'

Greenhalgh sighed her relief, but even so insisted on enveloping Natasha in the bathrobe when the time came. Not that it matters, Natasha thought. Today I could walk into Oliver's room stark naked and all Oliver could manage would be a groan. Still, she had given her word not to tell, and so she belted the robe about her.

189

'Which dress, miss?' Greenhalgh asked.

'Is the Bishop dining?'

'Had to get back, miss. Choral communion in the cathedral tomorrow. There'll just be the family, miss.'

Natasha rather doubted that Oliver could walk so far, but all she said was, 'Mrs Cantripp is coming in after dinner for coffee. She bought some pretty things too. See if there's Benedictine. She has begun to enjoy Benedictine.'

And we all know who taught her, thought Greenhalgh, but where's the harm? I'm partial to a drop myself.

'The new red dress,' Natasha decided. 'And the ruby earrings,' and went off to her bath.

The red, thought Greenhalgh. It would be. The skimpiest of the lot. Show more skin than silk when she put that one on. Still, she had the skin for it. Seemed wasted on Mr George and Mr Oliver though. Then it dawned on her that it wasn't for their benefit at all; it was for the vicar, punishment for him because tomorrow was Sunday and she'd have to dress what he called respectably and she called like a dowd. One thing about Miss Natasha. She always paid in full, good or bad. Just as well Mr Oliver had kept out of her way . . .

NATASHA AND MICHAEL

18

Walsh looked at the house: neat, grey stone, sash windows, polished mahogany door. Desirable gentleman's residence circa 1780, according to what Dad had told him. He turned to the cab driver. 'This is the vicarage?' he asked.

The cab driver made almost unintelligible sounds that Walsh took to be affirmative, but then each man thought the other's accent outlandish. 'Aye, it is,' it had sounded like, but how could he ever know? The point was that the only priests' houses he'd seen before were of grubby brick with a corrugated iron roof. This place would be fit for the squire, he thought, always supposing they had one. Maybe they had Lord Kielder instead. He sought in his pockets for change. Paying off the driver almost called for an interpreter, so in the end he just held out the coins on his palm, and the cab driver took what he considered fair.

The door was opened by the housemaid, as neat and smart as a maid in a play.

'Mr Walsh?' she said.

'That's right.'

'The butler telephoned from Kielder Hall. Mrs Greenhalgh has just gone up to tell the vicar. He got back late on account of the prize-giving. The Bishop went on a bit.'

This time he could understand the words: it wasn't that. It was just that they didn't make all that much sense. The name seemed the best bet.

'Mrs Greenhalgh?'

'The housekeeper, sir. If you leave your case here I'll take you to the drawing room. Miss Natasha's there.' He wondered why the maid looked suddenly wary.

The woman was seated in a chair of cream brocade that might have been designed solely to show off the red of her dress. She was smoking a cigarette in a long green holder that looked like jade and he had absolutely no idea what on earth she could be doing in a parson's house.

The maid said, 'This is Mr Walsh, miss. He's come to stay with the vicar.'

'Then you had better bring champagne,' said Natasha, and the maid took off like a sprinter.

'Tell me about yourself, Mr Walsh,' said the woman in the red dress.

'I'd much sooner hear about you,' said Walsh.

She smiled then, as she might at a small boy who had said something intelligent for a change. 'No, no,' she said. 'I asked first.'

The accent was Slav and her name was Natasha. What the hell was a Russian doing here? And such a Russian.

He told her, and as he talked the maid brought champagne in an ice-bucket, put it down and sprinted out again. Natasha signed for him to open it, and he did so. The maid's terrified of her, he thought, then noticed the set of her small chin and the dark, smouldering eyes – and I'm not surprised. He poured the wine and told her about Dad and the Outback and Stony Creek, but not about Margaret Bonner.

'So you are related to the Earl?' Natasha said at last.

'My dad reckoned they were cousins.'

'And you came all this way just to see him?'

'Too right.'

She looked puzzled, and he realised he was talking Australian again.

'The thing is, I've never seen an earl before, but then I reckon the Earl's never seen a wallaby before, or even a man who's seen one.'

'What is a wallaby?'

'Let's save the Australian fauna for later,' he said. 'Tell me about you.'

She looked at him, and liked what she saw: a lean, tall man with a suntanned face, the tan burned in by day after day of working in the sun. A man who knew how to arouse her curiosity, too. Wallabies indeed. Nevertheless it would be possible to tell him things.

'Once I was the Countess Natalya Krilova,' she began, 'but now I am Natasha Tyrrwhitt. I also am related to the Earl – but not so closely as you.'

She told him about St Petersburg and her mother and the Grand Duchess Olga's birthday party, and as much about Léonide as was necessary. Suddenly she giggled.

'Mind if I share the joke?' Walsh asked.

'I just thought – you and I related to an English milord,' she said. 'I wonder if the poor man has any English relatives?' Then the smile vanished and a frown succeeded it, and even when she frowned she looked enchanting.

194

'I have thought of something else,' she said. 'If your father was a Tyrrwhitt why are you a Walsh?'

'My mum and dad weren't married,' said Walsh.

At once the frown vanished. 'Oh I see,' she said. 'You are a bastard.'

Stay calm, thought Walsh. English isn't her first language, perhaps not even her second – all those Russian aristocrats spoke French, too. She's just glad I cleared up a tricky point for her, and I don't mean to go crook about it because what would be the point? All the same it was a pity that a bloke in evening dress and a fancy dog collar should walk in just as she said it.

The vicar had been advancing, hand outstretched, all hospitable welcome, but at her words he halted as if he'd hit an invisible wall. The look he gave Natasha was not one of Christian charity, thought Walsh. This one was obviously a bit of a handful . . . an armful, too. *And that's quite enough of that.*

Somehow the parson got into gear again, came up to him, held out his hand. So there must be Christian charity available from him occasionally, thought Walsh, since he's heard what Natasha just said.

'You are Cousin Roger's son, I believe?' he said as they shook hands.

'That's right,' said Walsh. 'Name of Michael Walsh. I was explaining to Miss Natasha here—'

'Yes yes,' said the parson. 'I heard what Natasha said, but it's not something for which you should do penance after all.'

'The thing is,' said Walsh, 'I'd no idea I'd be bothering you like this. I mean, I telephoned Kielder Hall from Newcastle Station and the butler bloke told me I should come here first because the Earl was away in York.'

'Golf,' said Natasha. 'The Archbishop. He was Lord Kielder's fag.'

More mysteries. Walsh ploughed on. 'I reckoned I should go to a hotel,' he said, 'but the butler said to come to you.'

'I'm sincerely glad you did,' said the parson, and he seems to mean it, thought Walsh. 'My kinsman is away on business, but only for a little while. He will certainly want to receive you on his return. He had great affection for Roger.'

Me too, thought Walsh, but at least you took my bastard origins in your stride and I respect you for that, but before he could work out how to say so – if indeed it was possible to say so – another bloke came in. The parson's son by the look of him. Not a bad-looking bloke, but with an eye on the carpet as if it might bite him. Best leave it. Every household had its eccentrics after all, but they certainly piled them high in this one. Then he noticed how the younger bloke looked at the

195

Natasha sheila, and there was nothing eccentric about that. Normal as breathing, that was.

'George,' said the parson, 'this is your kinsman Michael Walsh. I told you he was here.'

'Yes, of course,' said George. 'I'm very pleased to meet you.' He offered his hand.

'G'day,' said Walsh. 'Pleased to meet you, too.'

Another bloke in a dinner jacket, and whatever little there was of Natasha's dress could only be described as evening wear.

'Maybe I ought to change,' he said. 'There's a dinner suit in my case.'

'Nonsense, my dear chap,' the parson said. 'Only a family party. No need to stand on ceremony. Have some more champagne. We'll join you.'

Natasha went to press the bell, for the bottle was empty, and as they waited the parson said to his son, 'Where on earth is Oliver? I thought I told you to inform him that we had a visitor?'

'I did,' said George. Oliver, whoever he was, seemed to cause him not so much concern as bewilderment.

'Well then?'

'He says he's not feeling well.'

'What on earth's wrong with him?' said the parson. 'He was perfectly well earlier.' He turned to Walsh. 'Oliver is my other son,' he said. 'George's elder brother.'

'He says he's pulled a muscle,' said George, and Natasha assumed a look of innocence a Botticelli angel might have envied.

'What muscle?' said his father.

'In the thigh. He reckons he was moving too quickly and suddenly twisted it.'

Natasha smiled, then frowned, and hunted in her handbag for a cigarette.

'Silly fellow,' said his father. 'Does he need a doctor, do you think?'

'He says not,' said George. 'Rest should do it, he thinks.'

Natasha lit her cigarette. Lots and lots of rest, she thought.

'But he said if you don't mind he'd rather not come down to dinner,' said George.

'Yes, of course,' said the parson, and turned to Walsh. 'Oliver was in the war. He was wounded. So was George, come to that. But Oliver sustained another wound in Ireland. He was in the Black and Tans.'

'I see,' said Walsh, and what else could he say? Even from as far away as Queensland his mother had hated the Black and Tans.

196

'Were you in the war, Michael?' George asked, and Walsh nodded. 'Where did you serve?'

'Gallipoli,' said Walsh, 'and then France.'

'The Somme?'

'Too right,' said Walsh.

'That is the second time you have said that,' said Natasha, 'and I do not understand it. Either something is right or it is not. How can it be too right?'

'It's Australian,' said George. 'A sort of affirmative.'

'A strong affirmative,' said Walsh, and then to George: 'How did you know?'

'The chap in the next bed to me was an Australian,' said George, and blushed a deep, unpleasing crimson, but why he did so Walsh had no idea. Walsh noticed that Natasha was regarding George with sympathy, perhaps even compassion, and admonished himself for resenting it. It did no good.

'You have not told me what a wallaby is,' said Natasha.

'Sort of a kangaroo,' said Walsh, 'only not so big.'

'You have seen kangaroos? They are real?' she said.

'Too—' he caught himself in time. 'Indeed they are.'

'They seemed like a fantasy when I read about them. The way they move, their babies in the pouches – it's like a fairy tale. But you do not like them, I think.'

'No, I don't,' said Walsh.

'But why ever not?' the parson asked.

'Roos eat grass, and some of it's my grass, and I'd sooner my cattle ate it,' said Walsh.

'You're a farmer then?' said George.

'Sort of. Back home we'd say I had a property.'

'You have lots of cattle?' Natasha said.

'A couple of thousand or so.'

She squealed in delight. 'You are a cowboy,' she said. 'I knew it. So brown!'

'Sort of,' said Walsh. 'Only back in Australia they'd call me a stockman.'

'Who cares what they call you?' said Natasha. 'You ride a horse and chase after cows and wear enormous hats. On Monday you must take me to the cinema and explain it all to me.' She turned to the parson. 'Imagine,' she said. 'A cowboy. Here in this house.'

And how am I supposed to compete with that? thought George, and what is the point in even trying? He was quite sure that Oliver had long since told her where he was wounded.

Even so it turned out to be rather a jolly evening. Maddy arrived

197

just as they all went to the drawing room for coffee, and Greenhalgh had managed to find some Benedictine. Moreover she was wearing one of her new dresses, the blue one, and it fitted her charmingly. Everyone was agreed on that except the vicar. There was more of it than there was of Natasha's, but not all that much more. He began to sulk as soon as he saw it, but then he'd had a trying day. A bishop, an Australian bastard and two half-naked women . . . it was all too much of a strain. Best to get out of his way.

'We ought to dance,' Natasha said.

'Oh yes,' said Maddy, and Natasha smiled her approval. Before London she would have waited for the vicar's permission without the slightest hope of receiving it.

'I see no harm,' the vicar said, 'provided you cease at midnight, of course.'

George rose. 'I'll get the gramophone,' he said. 'It's in Oliver's room. He won't feel much like dancing. Never does, come to think of it.'

'What's wrong with him?' Maddy asked.

'His thigh hurts,' said Natasha. 'He pulled a muscle.'

'Oh,' said Maddy. As an expression of grief it was barely adequate, but she was looking at Michael Walsh, and that would never do.

The vicar finished his coffee. 'I'll leave you young people to it,' he said. 'I want to go over my sermon for tomorrow.' He turned to Walsh. 'Our morning services consist of Morning Prayer at nine and Sung Eucharist at eleven,' he said. 'Which would you prefer? I need hardly say that you'd be welcome at both.'

'I'm awfully sorry,' said Walsh. 'I'm afraid I can't do that.'

'You're not an atheist, surely?' said the vicar.

'I'm a Roman Catholic,' said Walsh.

If I'd hit him with a hammer the parson couldn't look more outraged, he thought, especially when Natasha made a gurgling noise that she tried, unconvincingly, to convert into a cough. Even Maddy what's-her-name seemed taken aback. He'd thought he was doing all right with her, but owners of properties, it seemed, should be Anglican. Not that he was a particularly good Catholic. Since Mum died he hadn't bothered – even gone into Balinese temples. But Balinese Hinduism was one thing and the C. of E. quite another. To begin with Mum wouldn't have given a tuppenny toss if he'd been in a hundred temples, but the C. of E. was the Opposition. He couldn't do that to her. And he owed her memory something.

'Have you got a Catholic church here?' he asked.

'We have not,' said the parson, like I'd said Have you got a brothel here? thought Walsh. Scarlet Woman. All that. Then he looked at the scarlet woman in the cream-coloured chair, and wished George would hurry up with the gramophone.

The older man's expression softened. 'Your desire to attend a place of worship is commendable,' he said, 'but there is no Roman Catholic church nearer than Slagsby, and that of course would be wholly unsuitable.'

'What's wrong with it?' said Walsh.

'To begin with there is no bus there on Sundays,' said the vicar, 'and even if there were, it is an uncouth and violent village. Not at all the sort of place where a kinsman of ours would wish to worship.'

If I tell him I'll take a taxi it'll just start him off again, thought Walsh. All the same I did my best, Mum. Then George came back with the gramophone and the vicar fled. Lascivious dancing and popery...

Warily, George turned back the carpet with Walsh's help. Once it was done and all the small objects of furniture were pushed to one side he felt better. The problem was who to ask first? It should be Maddy because she was the visitor, but even so... He put the needle on the record, the band played *Look for the Silver Lining* and Walsh solved his problem for him by walking up to Natasha.

Maddy wasn't exactly overwhelmed by his invitation, but accepted since, given the dictates of polite society, she had no other choice. She was nice to hold, even as gingerly as he held her, but he couldn't think of a damn thing to say. At last it was she who broke the silence.

'Did he fall off a horse?' she asked, and his silence continued. 'Oliver,' she prompted.

'Oh,' said George. 'He can't have done. He wasn't wearing riding clothes and anyway he hasn't got a horse to ride just at the moment.'

'Perhaps he fell downstairs,' said Maddy.

'I'm the one who does that,' said George.

She looked up at him. He wasn't smiling, she noticed, but then he hadn't much to smile about. His business was to cause others to smile.

'I was very angry with you,' she said.

'You had good reason.'

'But it wasn't your fault. I should have realised that. You were just unlucky. Forgive me.'

'Nothing to forgive,' he said, and this time he did smile. It was a pity that she was looking at Michael Walsh as he did so.

'What do you think of my friend?' Natasha asked.

'She's nice,' said Walsh. 'Pretty too.'

'And attractive,' said Natasha. 'She has bought new dresses that make her so. We are – good for each other?'

'Contrast?' said Walsh.

'Exactly,' said Natasha. 'In London we were a *succès fou*. That means—'

'A wild success,' said Walsh. 'More literally, a *mad* success.'

'Where did you learn to speak French?' she asked, astonished. In England, nobody she had met spoke French except Martin Brett and his father, who had to – and perhaps the Earl. He also had been a diplomat.

'Melbourne University,' said Walsh.

'A cowboy should not attend university.' She sounded disappointed: even resentful.

'It was my dad's idea. He thought it was only fair. After all, he went to Oxford. And I didn't forget how to ride a horse while I was there.'

For the life of him he couldn't sound anything but apologetic, but how else could he sound, clasping that silk and skin, smelling that perfume?

'Would you like to talk French now?' she asked. He shook his head. 'Why not?'

'Because I'm quite sure your French will be almost perfect—'

'Not almost.'

'—and that means you would sound like any other beautiful Frenchwoman speaking French.' She took the compliment as no more than her due, and nodded her agreement.

'But when you speak English you speak it like no one else in the world I ever heard.'

'Then we're two of a kind,' she said.

The record stopped and it was time to change partners, which was a pity. It would be midnight all too soon. Tomorrow, she thought, Greenhalgh must see him. It was necessary to know Greenhalgh's opinion of all the things in her life that might be important . . . The gramophone record played *They Didn't Believe Me*, as she revolved dutifully in George's arms.

'He seems nice,' George was saying, rather reluctantly, she thought.

'Yes, he does,' said Natasha, 'except that sometimes his language is a little strange.'

'Language?' said George. 'You mean swearing?'

'No, no,' said Natasha. 'Not bad language. I can learn all I need of that from Oliver. I meant idioms, expressions.' Carefully, tactfully she helped George to reverse. 'Should Oliver see a doctor, do you think?'

'He says he won't,' George told her. 'Got quite ratty when I suggested it – but don't let's talk about my brother.' He took a deep breath. 'You're looking awfully pretty tonight.'

A bludgeon compared to the foil that Melbourne University cowboy used, she thought, but even so she smiled and said thank you.

Maddy thought that Walsh danced beautifully, and Natasha thought that George's dancing was almost competent, and that, when one thought about it, was really quite remarkable, when one knew that he spent every dance in terror of the consequences that might follow if he moved about a room while clasping another human being. Then suddenly it was five minutes to midnight and the vicar came in to tell them so.

Walsh's room wasn't bad at all, he thought. Same floor as George, which made it the one above Natasha (stay away from that) and the mysteriously injured Oliver, who didn't seem to be getting much sympathy. His father had twittered a bit but brother George was delighted and Maddy and Natasha had that serve-him-right look on their faces that women seemed able to assume at will, as if twisting his thigh muscle must inevitably be Oliver's own fault. Natasha had looked almost smug, which was ridiculous . . .

She'd given him a wallop or two about the uni, though. Didn't like to have her preconceptions contradicted, which was crazy – but then women *were* crazy from time to time. No doubt they thought men were. Lovely to hold though, lovely to coax a smile from, to touch . . . *Now that will do*, he told himself. Remember you're a dad now – or will be soon. Remember Margaret and her occasional craziness, remember holding *her*. Another gloss on preconception, he thought, and sure enough, conception had followed. As she had known it would – or at least hoped. 'All I ever get is disappointments,' she'd said. But maybe that was her husband's fault, if fault it was. Anyway she'd gone broody to the power of ten. Needed a baby the way a fish needs water, and if her husband couldn't do it she would try elsewhere. And he'd been the lucky feller.

And so he had been lucky. No question. She'd been wonderful with him. Of course there was a reason, but there was a reason for everything, and hers was a good one when you thought about it; to bring more life into the world. He'd taught her a few things too, and maybe that had helped, and when it was over he'd sent her orchids. A whole cabinful: the maddest, most loving gesture he could think of. Then he'd found out from those Pom magazines that he'd made her a mum: that he'd been chosen with that function in mind. Like Don Giovanni, the property's stud bull.

At first he'd hated her for it, which was stupid. Men and women did it all the time, and what could the result be but babies, no matter how careful they were? True, she'd lied to him about that – or half-lied, anyway – but nobody had forced him to her, nobody had pointed a gun. They'd have had to point a gun to keep him away from her, and even then they mightn't have succeeded.

And what was so awful about being a dad? Except he'd never see his son, or maybe his daughter. All he'd been there for, you might say, was to do Captain Bonner a favour. On the other hand, Captain Bonner had done him a favour too, and that wasn't something to snigger over – it was a fact, and more than a fact. A privilege ... Three nights of bliss and the end product with its name down for Eton or Roedean or wherever. And he'd never see the little ankle-biter. Never. Because whichever it was it might look like him, and that wouldn't do at all. Not if the gallant Captain was there too. Far better for it to look like its mum. In every way. His kid. With a posh Pommy accent like his own dad. Like the kid's paternal grandfather, come to that.

He wondered if he and Bonner were related: seventh cousins twice removed or something. After all, they both belonged to the English toffs, and English toffs did tend to marry each other more often than not. And they were both tall and thin and dark ... Make life a lot easier for Margaret, that would, provided he kept out of the way.

He'd thought he'd loved her, which explained all the rage and disgust he'd felt when he found out what happened – and now was over, thank God. But it hadn't been love – simply tremendous affection and joy and lust combined. And no doubt that was what she had felt too. And at the end of it, pain, and a yelling child, and nursemaids and governesses and prep school and a pony. And for the gallant captain, bills. Bills for the next twenty years or so. He'd have liked to help, even if he never saw the little beggar, but how could he?

He could try a prayer, though. If Mum had been alive she'd have been first furious, then understanding – it had happened to her, after all – but in the end she'd have prayed. When he got back maybe he'd ask Tabby to try a prayer, too. Mum had always reckoned Tabby was one of those God heard first. But in the meantime it was down to him. A woman's prayer, he thought, and searched in his memory, saying each word clearly in his mind. *Ave Maria, gracia plena, benedicta tu in mulieribus* ...

In no time at all he was asleep.

19

She had told Greenhalgh to serve him breakfast, and Greenhalgh, safely returned from Morning Prayer, had obliged. The cook had gone to Sung Eucharist, which rather imperilled lunch, but lunch would have been in peril anyway. The night before, Cook had discovered that she too liked Benedictine.

'He ate a good breakfast?' Natasha asked.

'Oh yes, miss,' Greenhalgh said. 'My Herbert reckoned all Australians eat well.'

'And where did your Herbert meet Australians?'

'Why France, miss.'

'The war,' said Natasha. 'Of course. Michael Walsh was in it too.'

'Yes, miss. Had it pretty rough I shouldn't wonder.'

Natasha thought of George. 'But he's all right, I hope?'

'Right as rain by the look of him,' said Greenhalgh. 'If you'd seen him eat you wouldn't have to ask.'

'What is he doing now?' Natasha asked.

'Sitting in the drawing room, yawning over the papers,' Greenhalgh said.

'I shall get up,' said Natasha. 'Did he speak of me?'

He's a man, isn't he? thought Greenhalgh. What else would he speak of?

'Your name was mentioned, miss.'

'I'm glad,' said Natasha, and went to the wardrobe.

'I got your dress ready here, miss,' said Greenhalgh.

'Not the dark blue one?'

'Yes, miss.' Greenhalgh was implacable.

'But we have a visitor,' Natasha pleaded.

'We've got the vicar an' all, miss,' said Greenhalgh. 'I'd get the push if I sent you down in anything else. The pretties will have to wait till tomorrow.'

He didn't look disgusted when he saw the dress, which surprised her, but maybe in Australia too there was a rule about looking ugly on Sundays.

'You've been let off too, have you?' he said.

'I am Russian Orthodox,' said Natasha. 'Your nearest church is in Slagsby, but mine is in Paris – or possibly London. I am never sure.'

'But I'm not allowed to go to Slagsby,' said Walsh. 'The people are vulgar there, apparently. What difference does that make? The way the parson looks at life, the whole of Australia's vulgar.'

'For a priest he knows very little about the soul,' Natasha agreed. 'If one's soul needs God, really needs Him, one would go to the place that's nearest. The rest is mostly pleasure, after all.'

'Pleasure?'

'Music, pictures, sculptures, incense. It is pleasing, but more for oneself than for God.'

'I have a friend who reckons he came to know God in Bali,' said Walsh. 'Not that he turned Hindu or anything. He doesn't even go to church. Just reckons he knows God.'

'But where does he go to pray?'

'In an aeroplane,' he said. She considered this.

'Are you quite sure,' she said at last, 'that he is not crazy?'

Only a Russian would have considered the implications of the aeroplane before asking that question. For Margaret it wouldn't have been even a question, merely the statement of an obvious fact. 'He's mad, of course,' she would have said, but maybe today was the day when he began to stop wondering what Margaret would have said.

'He's as sane as I am,' he told Natasha. 'Whether that answers your question or not is up to you.'

She smiled. 'He's an airman?'

Walsh nodded. 'Owns a fleet of one. I've been in it – but not to get closer to God. Just to travel.'

'Did he fly you to Bali?' she asked.

He shook his head. 'Too far. To get to Bali you need a ship.'

'I am told,' she said, 'that in Bali it is the custom for the girls to expose their breasts in public.'

'Too right,' he said, but she let it go.

'And are they nice, those breasts?'

'Some of them are very nice,' he said.

Apparently it was the right answer, for again she smiled that particular smile: that of the adult pleased by a small boy's rare flash of intelligence.

'Greenhalgh says I owe you an apology,' Natasha said. 'Greenhalgh is my maid. Also she watches the cook.'

'We met earlier,' said Walsh. 'She gave me breakfast.'

'Did you like her?'

'Very much,' said Walsh. Another correct answer, it seemed. 'But why does she reckon you owe me an apology?'

'I called you a bastard. That is rude, she says.'

'A bit strong maybe, but then I am one. It's the truth. It's when you call a bloke a bastard and he isn't one that it's an insult.'

'Explain that a little more, please,' she said.

'Say you were a bloke and my parents were married and you called me a bastard, there'd have been a stoush straight off.'

'Stoush?'

'Sorry. I'm talking Australian again. A fight.'

She looked at him. He would be strong, she was sure, far stronger than George, or even Oliver: his body hardened by heat and hard work, just as Dimitri's body had been hardened by hard work and the cold.

'I'm glad I'm not a bloke,' she said.

'Me too,' said Walsh. This time she gave him a quite different smile, then looked at her watch and rang the bell.

'This priest Tyrrwhitt is very strange,' she said. 'Because it is Sunday he insists we have no wine with our food. In Russia priests drank wine whenever they could get it – otherwise vodka.' Then another smile came, and this one told him as clearly as a statement on oath that Natasha had done something cunning and was pleased with herself.

'But I told him my doctor in France insisted I must drink champagne for the sake of my health,' she said.

'And he believed you?'

'Of course,' she said. 'Of a French doctor he would believe anything.' The smile switched off, and a scowl took its place. 'Where is that idiot maid?' she said.

No wonder the poor girl moves at the double, Walsh thought, but it was Greenhalgh who came in, bearing an ice-bucket, a bottle and glasses.

'I take it this is what you wanted, miss?' she said.

'Greenhalgh, you are as clever as you are beautiful,' said Natasha, as Greenhalgh uncorked the champagne.

'If it's all the same to you I'd sooner have a beer,' said Walsh.

'*Beer?*' Both women in unison. Both astounded rather than disgusted.

'You really like beer?' said Natasha.

'In Australia it's against the law not to like it,' said Walsh.

'Mr Walsh says that "bastard" is all right provided you are one,' said Natasha. Greenhalgh, who was about to pour, hesitated, but not a drop was spilt.

'I think he'd also tell you to avoid the subject whenever you can, miss,' she said. 'Specially when there's other people present.'

'Oh,' said Natasha, and her cheeks flushed. 'Yes, I see.' There followed a torrent of Russian, and then she looked at Walsh. 'I will remember,' she said. 'I promise.'

'No worries,' said Walsh.

'I'll get you that beer, sir,' Greenhalgh said, and left them.

'I am proud, you see,' said Natasha. 'Vainglorious – isn't that the word? I think I understand the English and their customs, and what can be said and what can not be said. But that is all madness and vanity. Nobody understands their customs except the English, and not all of them.'

'I'll drink to that,' said Walsh, 'as soon as I get my beer.'

Greenhalgh brought it. A bottle on a tray, and a silver tankard. The tankard had been presented to Oliver Tyrrwhitt for coming first in the half-mile race at some sports club or other in 1913. Everybody has their troubles, thought Walsh, but it keeps the chill in the beer.

'By the way, miss,' Greenhalgh said, 'I had word from the Hall. His Lordship will be back tomorrow. You and Mr Walsh are asked to lunch on Tuesday.'

'It will be good to have him back,' said Natasha.

'Yes, miss,' said Greenhalgh. 'It will.'

'Any news of Mr Oliver?' said Walsh.

'He won't be down to lunch,' said Greenhalgh, 'but he's walking a bit better.' She topped up Natasha's glass. 'Trays,' she said. 'As if Cook and Molly Parker and me hadn't got enough to do.' She left them.

'Doesn't anybody like him?' said Walsh.

'I do not think so,' said Natasha. 'At one time Maddy thought she did, then she realised that she was mistaken.'

The visit to the cinema was a success. The vicar had doubted that this would be so. A cinema play devoted to the behaviour of what he was led to understand were violent herdsmen had no place, surely, for a lady fluent in three languages and a graduate of a university which he had been led to believe was not without distinction. A low blow that last one, thought Walsh, but they went even so, and the Regal Cinema, Newcastle, did them proud. Plush seats, and chocolates on sale in the foyer, and a string quartet as well as a piano, and Buster Keaton and Felix the Cat as well as a screenful of cowboys. Natasha had brought along her flask of vodka too, but he only pretended to swallow when she offered it to him. The one time he'd tried it, it had just about blown his head off . . . When the film was over she took him to a pub – the nearest one, just up the street. It would be, he thought. All the same it was a good pub: what they called a cocktail bar.

'Well?' she said.

'What do you want to know?' he said. 'Whether it was accurate?'

'Of course,' she said. 'What was not was all *fantaisie* – isn't that it?'

'Near enough,' he said, and then: 'It was like most things. Some of it was right, some wasn't. The cowboys – not the hero but the others – they were right. Riding horses, working cattle. They were fine.'

'But not the hero?'

'No,' said Walsh. 'He was acting. He managed to look good on a horse because acting's his job, but the others – I reckon they really were cowboys not long ago, and it showed.'

'Could you do what they did?' she asked.

'All my life,' he said. 'Since I was twelve years old.'

A forger and a Cossack who went to university, she thought. Not the most obvious choices, but the first had been good. It would be interesting to find out if the second was, too.

'I would like some more vodka,' she said.

The view of the Hall was impressive, and he said so.

'Of course,' said Natasha. 'That is why it was built, to impress people. The man who caused it to be built is saying "Look at me, at how rich and powerful I am, and a creator of beauty too."'

'The Earl isn't like that, surely?'

'Not this one,' said Natasha, 'but the Earl of two hundred years ago was. He almost bankrupted himself to create the place.' She lifted the speaking tube and said, 'Drive on,' and the great car moved forward.

'Did you have a place like this in Russia?' Walsh asked.

'More than one,' she said. 'My family was very rich, you see. We had a palace in St Petersburg and others in the country.'

'You must miss it,' he said.

'Almost I have forgotten it,' she said. 'When I lived in palaces I was somebody else.' For a moment she looked bewildered, woebegone and about ten years old, and he wanted to hold her in his arms and comfort her as a child is comforted. Then she shook her head, admonishing herself.

'But I am still alive after all,' she said, 'and those others who lived in palaces are all dead, or else wishing they were.' She lit a cigarette. 'I have also lived in a hut,' she said, 'and even for a little while in the gutter, but those are stories for another time.'

207

The car came to a halt and the chauffeur got out to open the door so that they might climb the steps to where footmen and a butler waited.

'As good as the pictures,' said Walsh.

'Better,' said Natasha. 'It is free and it is real.'

Beyond the butler another man stood waiting, in a tweed suit he wore with an elegance Walsh knew he could never hope to imitate, but the man was smiling, almost beaming, which must be because Natasha was there.

'Michael Walsh,' the Earl said. 'How good of you to come!' and he offered his hand. He still had a grip, Walsh noticed.

'But it is wonderful,' said Natasha. 'You are so alike, you two.'

They looked at each other. Both tall, both lean, with the horseman's look, both strong featured, long-nosed – but there it ended, for one had white hair and moustache, while the other's hair was as dark as the beer he was so fond of, and there was thirty years between them. Even so, Natasha thought as they looked at each other, one saw the man he once had been, the other the man he would become.

'You're a Tyrrwhitt all right,' said the Earl. 'After lunch we'll take a look at a few portraits. If you went to a fancy-dress shop we could pass you off as any one of them.'

Natasha went to him and kissed his cheek. 'He doesn't need fancy dress,' she said. 'He is a cowboy.'

'Stockman,' corrected Walsh.

'He wears a big hat and a check shirt and corduroy trousers and riding boots, and he carries a whip.'

The Earl looked at Walsh. 'Do you, by God?' he said.

Walsh grinned. 'Only for the cattle,' he said. 'The last convict was set free years ago.'

'Come into the drawing room and tell me about it,' said the Earl, and smiled at Natasha. 'I suppose you want champagne?'

'We all do,' said Natasha, 'unless Michael wants beer.'

'Not today,' said Walsh. 'Natasha has told me about your champagne, sir. I'm looking forward to it.'

The 'sir' came out rather tentatively, but Natasha had told him it was what Lord Kielder preferred, and no Australian would say 'My Lord', let alone 'Your Lordship'; not unless he was being sarcastic.

The lunch was a success. The champagne was every bit as good as Natasha had promised, and so was the meal, and the Earl a witty and attentive host. That he doted on Natasha was obvious, but it was as a grandfather dotes on his favourite granddaughter: indulgence mingled with gentle teasing, but at that Natasha could give as good as she got.

Over the smoked salmon she said, 'You are his first Earl.' Cribb the

butler poured Chablis impassively, with the dogged look of a
Guardsman under fire. The Earl did not even look at him, but said to
Walsh, 'I hope I'm up to expectations?'

'Too right,' said Walsh, and this time Cribb's hand did tremble a
little, though, like Greenhalgh, he didn't spill a drop.

'But he thinks he has the advantage of you,' said Natasha. 'He has
seen an earl, but you have not seen a wallaby.'

'Not unless they have them in Regent's Park Zoo,' said the Earl.
'My nanny took me there when I was four, and I really can't
remember. You should go there on your next trip to London,
Natasha. Make a nice change from Harrod's.'

Thought she'd bowled him out but he got his bat in the way in time,
thought Walsh. This was an earl with his wits about him.

'What sort of stock do you breed?' Kielder asked. 'Apart from
wallabies, of course.'

'Wallabies don't need help to breed,' said Walsh. 'Any more than
rabbits. Mum and Dad settled on Herefords. They're survivors and
they give good meat.'

'Can they cope with the droughts?' the Earl enquired.

'They learn,' said Walsh. 'Anyway, the survivors do.'

'It sounds like a hard country,' said Natasha. 'Like Russia. Only
too hot instead of too cold.'

'That's about it,' said Walsh.

They were in the Little Dining Room – where the family ate, the
Earl explained, when they were on their own. Room for no more than
a dozen, but they went in for big families in those days. Afterwards
they went back to the drawing room, for coffee that even Natasha
said was drinkable.

When Cribb left them alone at last the Earl said, 'There was a time
when I knew your father quite well. I liked him.'

'He was a likeable bloke,' said Walsh.

'Yes, indeed. But you took your mother's name?'

'He was already married,' said Walsh.

'So I had supposed. Do you wish it to be known that we are
related?'

'It already is known,' said Natasha. 'Everyone in the priest's house
knows, so now everybody in Haydon Priors knows.'

'Yes, of course,' said the Earl. 'How stupid of me. I asked because
I'm not sure whether you wished your illegitimacy to be known.'

'Illegitimate!' said Natasha. '*That* was the word I needed.' She
turned to the Earl. 'Forgive me for interrupting, sir,' she said, 'but I
was rude to Michael without meaning to be.'

The Earl took his time thinking about it and said at last, 'Just as

209

well you're a girl.' Walsh grinned, but the Earl continued, 'That's all very well, but things could prove awkward for you.'

'Not when you are there,' objected Natasha. 'You are the Earl. Who will dare to ask you whether Michael is legitimate or not?'

'Best take it as it comes, sir,' Michael said. 'After all, I didn't have to come here and say I was a Tyrrwhitt.'

'No, indeed,' said the Earl. 'Why did you?'

'To see what you were like,' said Walsh. 'I mean – you're all the family I've got now Dad's gone.'

'I hope we're not a disappointment,' said the Earl, and Walsh thought: He means the parson, and even more he means Oliver. 'When did he die?' the Earl asked.

'A few months back,' said Walsh. 'Heart attack.'

'He was successful, I gather?' said the Earl. 'I mean, this property of yours—'

'He did better than that,' said Walsh. 'He had a gold mine once, and a sugar plantation, and I don't know what else. He was a millionaire.'

'Good Lord,' said the Earl. 'When I first knew him, the only thing Roger understood about money was how to lose it.'

'That's because he gambled,' said Walsh. 'When he got to Australia he stopped. He used to say that if you didn't gamble in Australia you couldn't help making money.'

'So you are rich,' said Natasha. 'That is good.'

'I've got enough,' said Walsh, 'more than enough. No worries. But I've also got an elder brother – half-brother anyway.'

No sense in beating about the bush, thought the Earl. 'A legitimate half-brother,' he said.

'Yes, sir.' Michael looked at the Earl, whose face told him nothing except that he was interested, and that very possibly he deserved that interest.

'You see,' Walsh continued, 'all I really wanted and needed was the property, and that's mine. But Dad left me a pile of money as well. More than I wanted, but Dad wasn't one for half-measures.'

Nor half-truths either, he thought. Dad had meant to leave him that money, certainly, but when you got right down to it he'd helped himself. Better get back to the truth, the whole truth and nothing but the truth.

'I'm not ambitious, you see,' he explained, 'but my half-brother is, so he copped all that was left. It didn't bother me.'

'Your brother's name is Edgar?' said the Earl, and Walsh looked at him warily, as if Edgar might be hidden in the vast oak chest beneath that portrait of a woman he didn't much like the look of.

'That's right,' he said. 'Who told you?'

'He did,' said the Earl. 'Or rather, he wrote me a letter. Like you, he proposes to sail to England and worship at the shrine of his forebears. He didn't tell you?'

'We don't talk much,' said Walsh.

'Ah,' said the Earl. 'Let's go and inspect a forebear or two. No need to bother about fancy dress since you're a cowboy.'

Walsh felt as if he'd been prodded in the stomach with a rifle barrel, but somehow managed to get to his feet and go out with the Earl and Natasha. There wasn't anything else he could do.

20

'So we stay on with the parson,' said Walsh.

'I have decided I like the priest's house,' said Natasha. 'It is exciting. I didn't think it would be, but it is.' She thought of Oliver, and smiled.

'The Earl's would be better,' said Walsh, 'but we can hardly stay there while he's in London. I see that.'

Natasha stretched out in the car and Walsh hoped he wasn't gawping too much.

'What's he going to London for anyway?' he asked.

He will not grab me when the chauffeur is in the car, she thought, and shrugged. It worked just as well on Michael as on Oliver, but with Michael it pleased her more. 'Directors' meetings,' she said.

'But you said that's what he went to York for.'

'That and to beat the Archbishop at golf. Certainly. But he is on many – *boards* – is that right? It sounds odd.'

'Odd but right,' said Walsh. 'He must be rich.'

'Yes he is,' said Natasha, 'but not so rich as Lord Wentworth.'

'Lord Wentworth?' Margaret, it seemed, had not quite finished with him yet.

'He is quite a young lord – but imm–ense–ly rich.' It took her all of three seconds to say 'immensely'. 'Even Lord Kielder says so.'

'Have you met him?'

'At York Races. And later I dined with him at his castle. He wishes to marry me.' Walsh's reaction to that was all she had hoped for, but even so she took pity on him and added: 'His mother was there also. She dislikes me. Lord Kielder thinks I would be wasted on Wentworth.'

'But if he's so rich—'

'He is also so boring,' said Natasha. 'You will meet him quite soon.'

'He's coming here?'

'In September there are races here,' she said. 'He owns horses. One of them will run in a race that was paid for by his father. The Wentworth Handicap. He is bringing a – group?'

'Party,' said Walsh, and thanked God the mother of his child was in Singapore. If he'd been on his own he'd have crossed himself.

'You're not listening,' said Natasha. She sounded as if she had a whip handy. Probably a knout.

'Sorry,' he said. 'I was just thinking how much I like races.'

'You are far too big to be a jockey.'

'The kind of horses I ride wouldn't win anyway. I like race-meetings. It would be a pleasure to take you to this one.'

'There is no need.' She waited for the scowl but it didn't come. He learns far more quickly than Oliver, she thought. 'Bobby Wentworth invited me. He said I could bring friends.'

'Am I a friend?'

'So far,' she said, then after a pause: 'Also I will invite Maddy Cantripp and George.'

'But not Oliver?'

'If I did he would get drunk,' she said. 'He will probably get drunk if he attends the meeting by himself, but at least that will not be my fault.'

'Does it a lot, does he? Getting drunk?'

'As often as he can afford it, Greenhalgh says. And when he is drunk he sings rude songs. Some of them are amusing, but of course they are disgusting too.'

Walsh looked at the window that divided the chauffeur's seat from theirs. It was shut, but even so he was sweating.

'Not the sort a lady would sing,' he said.

'The Earl said that too,' Natasha said. 'It is most unfair.'

There had been brandy with the coffee, and she had drunk her share; the Earl hadn't batted an eyelid, even though he'd almost certainly never before in his life offered brandy to a lady. But then Lord Kielder didn't think of her as a lady, Walsh decided. To him she was an original, and an enchanting one, and he treated her as such, as a reward for being enchanted.

'What will you do when we get home?' he asked her.

'Rest for a while, then change for dinner.'

'Rest was your French doctor's advice?'

'This one was English,' she said. 'I saw him in London.' The tower of Haydon Priors' church became visible. 'I hope Oliver has managed to get downstairs,' she said.

He had. He wore pyjamas and dressing gown and was drinking tea. Just as well, thought Walsh. I had more than I'm used to at lunch, and it's far too early to start again.

'Michael Walsh?' said Oliver.

'Oliver Tyrrwhitt?' said Walsh.

214

Oliver made no offer to shake hands, and Walsh stayed where he was. They'd just heard Natasha call out for Greenhalgh. Two dogs and only one bone...

'You've been to the Earl's for lunch, I hear,' said Oliver, and Walsh nodded. 'I trust His Lordship fed you well?'

'He did.' Walsh rang the bell to ask for another cup and saucer. Australians drank a lot of tea, too.

'You went with our female – cousin? Would you call her that?'

'It's what she is,' said Walsh.

'Is it?'

'Once or twice removed,' said Walsh.

'Removed.' It was hard to know what Oliver meant when he used the word. There was regret, certainly, but there was a kind of anger, too. Removed to a prison, perhaps, or back to that Camp 19 she'd told him about.

'A lively one, our – cousin,' said Oliver. 'Not exactly the conventional type.'

'Never met one like her,' said Walsh.

'Nor I,' said Oliver, and shifted in his chair as if the pain, wherever it was, still persisted. 'A young lady who likes her own way and usually gets it.'

'Is that a fact?' said Walsh, and the housemaid brought in fresh tea.

'I thought your lot drank beer,' Oliver said.

'Who are my lot?'

'Australians,' said Oliver. 'That's what you are, isn't it?'

'We drink beer when we feel like it,' said Walsh. 'At the moment I feel like drinking tea.'

'I gather Natasha doesn't,' said Oliver, and squirmed again in his chair. Suddenly Walsh knew beyond doubting that it wasn't Oliver's thigh that hurt, it was his bollocks, and that Natasha had done it. No need to get excited, he told himself. Oliver's the one in pain after all. But it didn't make it any easier to like him.

'Sooner drink champagne,' said Oliver.

'*Chacun à son goût*,' said Walsh equably, and Oliver blinked. Australians weren't supposed to speak French.

'You were in the war?' Oliver asked. Walsh nodded. 'Where?'

'Gallipoli, France,' said Walsh.

'You must have seen some action?'

'Too right,' said Walsh, and again Oliver blinked. 'Too right' didn't belong in the same mouth as '*Chacun à son goût*'.

'Wounded?' he said, and Walsh remembered that Natasha had said he'd been in the Black and Tans, and his mother had said that the Black and Tans were an especially nasty sort of coppers. He certainly

215

asked questions like the worst kind of copper: worse than a
Melbourne walloper. Even so, 'Always be polite as long as you can,'
his father had told him, and he nodded.

'Where?' Oliver asked. He made no answer, and Oliver continued
at last, 'My brother George was wounded. Twice. In the backside.'

And that's a fine thing to tell a man you've only known twenty
minutes about your own brother, thought Walsh.

'Don't you think it's funny?' said Oliver. Walsh shook his head.
'Everybody else does.' Walsh stayed silent. 'You're a sulky sort
of—' Oliver broke off. 'Forgot what I was going to say,' he said at
last.

'Up yours for the rent, mate,' Walsh said amiably, and got to his
feet.

'What's that supposed to mean?'

'Think about it,' said Walsh, and left him to it.

He was tying his bow tie when George tapped at his door, came in
and closed it, then manoeuvred his way carefully to a chair at Walsh's
invitation.

'Forgive me,' he said, 'but I came home when Oliver and you were
talking in the drawing room. I couldn't help overhearing—'

'I should think you couldn't,' said Walsh. 'Oliver doesn't exactly
whisper.'

'About my wounds,' said George.

Carefully Walsh adjusted his tie, turned from the mirror and
offered a cigarette. 'You got shot, I got shot, and so did Oliver,' he
said. 'What's so extraordinary about that?'

'I bet you weren't shot in the bottom,' said George.

'In the chest,' said Walsh. 'Lucky one. Went straight through.
Missed what the doc called the vital organs. Made a mess though.'

'People don't laugh at you,' said George, 'but they laugh at me.'

'Am I laughing?'

'No,' George said. 'You're not. Extraordinary. I can't believe it.'

'Not extraordinary at all,' said Walsh. 'I know a bloke who had it a
lot worse than you.'

'Forgive me,' said George, 'but I don't think that's possible.'

'He had a ball shot off.'

George winced, but even the thought of it seemed to take his mind
off his own troubles. All the same perhaps I should have said testicle,
thought Walsh.

'You don't mean to say people laughed at him?' said George.

'Not laughed at him,' said Walsh. 'It made them curious. They
wanted to see it. Some of them offered him money.'

'What happened to him?'

'He was discharged,' said Walsh. 'The board reckoned he'd given enough for Australia.'

'No,' said George, 'I mean—'

'About his love-life?' George nodded. 'For a long time he didn't have one. He was too scared to try. The way he looked at it – what if he was never going to do it ever again? Then one day he decided that not knowing was even worse. He was a sailor in those days – deck-hand. He went ashore some place in the Dutch East Indies to find out.'

'Well?' said George.

'He finds out he's home on the pig's back,' said Walsh.

'I beg your pardon?'

Walsh reminded himself he was supposed to be comforting George, not giving him a course in colloquial Australian. Talk like Dad, he told himself. You can if you concentrate. 'He found out it still worked,' said Walsh.

'I'm glad,' said George, 'because you're perfectly right. It is worse than mine.'

'Does yours hurt?' Walsh asked.

'Not any more. It did at first. The second one was infected. That's why they discharged me, too.'

'Scars bad?'

George smiled then. 'How would I know? Nothing spectacular, from what I've been told.'

'Then what's your problem?'

'Before I got shot I wasn't—' he hesitated.

'Wasn't what?'

'Wasn't clumsy,' said George. 'You'll have noticed how clumsy I am?'

'Yes,' said Walsh. 'I've noticed.'

'Of course you have,' said George. 'You must have been told about the time I tried to teach Maddy Cantripp how to do a rugger tackle. She was furious.'

'Can you blame her?'

'As a matter of fact she's been jolly decent about it since,' said George. 'A lot of people aren't. Like my father. Because I look foolish it makes them look foolish. It sounds ridiculous, doesn't it? I get shot in the backside and spend the rest of my life tripping over things because of it.'

'Any idea why?'

'None,' said George. 'Except that perhaps at the back of my mind there's the fear I might be due for a third one and that puts me off balance.'

Could be, Walsh thought. Being one short caused O.B. Watson to take wing.

'It isn't rational, I know,' said George, 'but—'

Walsh thought of the unreasoning fear he had that he'd meet Margaret Bonner again. 'It makes sense, whatever it is,' he said.

George looked at his watch. 'Is it true Maddy's dining with us tonight?'

'Yes,' said Walsh. 'Natasha asked her.'

'We'd better go down then. Father likes us all ready and waiting when the guest arrives.'

Walsh opened his door and let George go first. Halfway down the stairs he realised why.

The parson and Natasha were already there. Oliver too, white shirt, black tie, all that convention demanded — except he wore what Dad said was called a smoking jacket of dark blue instead of a black one. To prove he was still among the walking wounded no doubt, thought Walsh. The parson wore his usual ecclesiastical dinner outfit that made him look as if he were about to conduct an orchestra in Vienna in the 1880s. Natasha wore a dress of a colour he had never seen before, and which, by her standards, was demure, except that, as she was wearing it, demure was not the first word one thought of.

He likes it, thought Natasha, which proves he has taste. She had known it would be a difficult dress when she bought it, but she had faith in Greenhalgh, who had not failed her. Taffeta, the colour of apricots, and her skin was so pale, but Greenhalgh had known exactly how to apply her rouge. None of her jewelry had worked either, but Greenhalgh had loaned her the golden earrings and they were all that was needed. How could she live without Greenhalgh? Tomorrow they would eat the caviar.

The priest had begun to speak. 'Unfortunate accident,' he was saying, 'to trip on the carpet at his age, too. So unlike Oliver. So clumsy.' He looked at George, then away, but George for once did not seem upset, Natasha thought.

'His wound no doubt exacerbated his condition,' said Tyrrwhitt after a pause.

In more ways than one, Walsh thought.

'And so Oliver is going to leave us for a little while, take a holiday,' said his father, 'and return to us rested and refreshed.'

'Good idea,' said George. 'Where are you going?'

'Somewhere quiet,' said Oliver. 'I thought perhaps the Yorkshire coast.'

'Nice was mentioned at one point,' said his father, 'but I always think that Scarborough is hard to beat.'

Natasha smiled, and Oliver allowed himself to relax a little. The bitch was so quick, and he hadn't finished with her yet: by God he hadn't.

Then Maddy arrived, and asked Oliver how he was.

'Pretty well, thank you,' said Oliver.

'That's all right then,' said Maddy, which wasn't what Oliver wanted at all, not when she was wearing a blush-pink dress of which his father instantly disapproved. Natasha rang the bell for drinks . . .

After dinner Natasha played, but not Chopin. Not this time. Schumann, whom only Michael had ever heard – but then his father it seemed had also been musical. She followed this with Mozart, Haydn, and a Beethoven sonata, the *Waldstein*. The Tyrrwhitts, father and sons, seemed mildly surprised that he'd written another one besides the *Moonlight*. When she'd done she saw that Maddy was sitting beside Michael, and that would not do. Maddy's place was beside George.

'Maddy darling,' she said, 'the strap of this dress is twisted. Do come and help.'

They went into the corridor, and when they were outside Maddy said, 'The strap seems fine to me.'

'It is,' said Natasha, 'but I have a secret for you. I know why Oliver is going away.'

'His father said it was a holiday.'

'More like convalescence,' said Natasha, and Maddy looked bewildered, which suited her. 'Svetlana,' said Natasha.

'Svetlana?' Maddy, still bewildered, looked even prettier.

'Oliver attacked me,' said Natasha.

'Svetlana!' cried Maddy. 'She was the one who showed you how to— How to—' Natasha nodded. 'And you did it?' Another nod, and a smile. 'And *that's* why he's limping?'

'That is why,' said Natasha.

'Oh gosh,' said Maddy. 'I think you're absolutely wonderful!' and hugged her, then drew back and looked at her anxiously. 'He didn't—?' she said.

'How could he?' said Natasha.

Oliver, she knew, was finished. Whatever he did or said, from now on Maddy would ignore him. For a man who needed money so badly, Oliver could be very stupid, which was as well. The problem now was George, but when they went back inside the priest and Michael were talking to Oliver and George was on his own. She went to him at once, and of course Maddy followed, and it was not long before Michael joined them. The priest continued to talk to his elder son, who rather looked as if he would like to get away, but wasn't quite up to it yet . . .

Natasha smiled at Michael and lit a cigarette, and when he went to fetch her an ashtray she went with him.

'What instrument did your father play?' she asked.

'Violin,' said Michael, 'but he wasn't in your class.'

'I think the priest's wife must have been good,' said Natasha. 'I found some very interesting pieces in the piano stool. Come, I will show you.'

They went to the piano, and even further away from Maddy and George. As she sorted through the music she said, 'What were the three of you talking about?'

'The fleshpots of Scarborough,' said Michael, 'and the need for economy while enjoying them.'

'That was the priest? He's paying for Oliver's holiday?'

'He is,' said Walsh. 'It seems that all Oliver has is his pension and what his father gives him. And an occasional hand-out from the Earl.'

'He need not be so very poor,' said Natasha. 'He lives here free, and he spends money only on whisky when he goes to Newcastle to get drunk. Are there really fleshpots in Scarborough?'

'I've no idea,' said Walsh, 'and I don't intend to find out.'

'There may be racing quite near,' Natasha said, and then: 'Here it is – Debussy. I met his widow once at the Jacquards and she did not approve of my piano playing. "*Trop slavon*," she said.'

Walsh would have liked to argue that, but his father had thought highly of Debussy. His widow would surely know what she was talking about . . . Not that he gave a damn. He loved the way Natasha played.

'*La jeune fille aux cheveux de lin*,' said Natasha. 'Do you know what that means?'

'The girl with the flaxen hair,' said Walsh.

'Flaxen. That is pretty.'

'Rather like Maddy,' said Walsh.

'If rather German.'

Then she played it, and whether it was too Slavonic or not, it was a pleasing rendition of a remarkable piece of music – gentle, evocative, luminous as moonbeams, he thought, committing what his poetry professor had denounced as the greatest crime in the critical calendar: evaluating one art form in terms of another. But don't blame me, Professor, he thought. Blame the young lady who's playing it.

When she had done he said, 'Thank you,' and she smiled, acknowledging that there was nothing else he could say, then turned and looked into the room. Every other person in it was staring at them, thought Walsh, and not looking any too happy about it either. Their faces showed emotions ranging from bewilderment (Maddy, and once again very pretty) to, in the priest's case, incredulity, perhaps with a touch of outrage, too.

'Why do you stare so?' Natasha asked.

Good girl, thought Walsh. *L'audace, l'audace, toujours l'audace.* You and Georges-Jacques Danton.

'That music,' said Maddy. 'Darling, it was so strange.'

'Sounded a bit French to me,' said George.

'Of course it's French,' said Natasha. 'It's by Debussy.'

But Walsh knew that by 'French' George meant naughty. Just as well she hadn't found a piano arrangement of *Prélude à l'après-midi d'un faune'*, he thought. That *would* have roused the parson's wrath – not that it needed much rousing as it was.

'French?' the parson was saying. 'It was downright immoral!'

'Come to corrupt us clean-living English, Natasha?' said Oliver.

Automatically his father said, 'That will do,' then returned to the attack. 'I had always considered music to be the innocent of the art forms,' he said, 'devoid of innuendo and salaciousness. But these sly hintings, these *nudgings . . .*'

Farewell moonbeams, thought Walsh.

'*Where did you get it?*' the parson asked, and not very politely either.

'From the piano stool,' said Natasha.

'Are you suggesting that my wife indulged herself in such – such—'

'I suggest nothing,' said Natasha. 'It is not my way, suggesting. You ask me where I got it and I told you and that is all.'

L'audace! L'audace!

George said, 'Steady on, Father. It wasn't that bad. I mean, the chap was French after all.'

It seemed that, to George, the French were sexual maniacs to a man and (with a bit of luck) woman.

The vicar's anger turned to puzzlement. 'But why would she wish to play such – such—?'

Natasha said, 'It is – difficult. Not technically. Technically it is almost easy, but to catch the mood and express it just so – that is not easy at all. But I shall not play it again since it displeases you. When the Earl returns I must ask him if I should give up playing Debussy altogether.'

And there you have her, thought Walsh. An apparent retreat, then a blast from her heaviest gun.

'You are very good,' said the parson, lying through his teeth. 'I hope you don't think I'm making a great issue out of something trivial?'

'Of course not,' said Natasha, lying through hers.

Walsh decided he might as well have a turn, too. Rather like cricket, he thought, or maybe net practice. The parson flashing his bat in all directions, and the ball getting through anyway and hitting him where it hurt.

'Natasha and Lord Kielder were talking about some cornet-player. Saying how good he was.'

'Cornet-player?' said the parson.

'At the concert I missed,' said Walsh.

'Oh yes.' To Tyrrwhitt, when the poor were no longer visible they ceased to exist. 'What about him?'

'He was brilliant,' said Natasha.

'For an uneducated man he acquitted himself more than adequately,' agreed the parson.

'Lord Kielder said he was brilliant too,' said Walsh.

'But then I am a poor judge in such matters,' said Tyrrwhitt.

'He was wonderful,' said Maddy.

'Top-hole,' said George.

Oliver pulled a face. Sulking because we're talking about somebody else and ignoring his afflictions, thought Walsh.

'The Earl thinks he should do something for him,' he said.

'*Do something?*'

But this time it wasn't the priest yelping in outrage: it was Oliver.

'What can he possibly do for an out-of-work miner?' Oliver asked.

'A scholarship,' said Walsh. 'Send him to college to study.'

'But that would cost hundreds of pounds!'

'He's got it,' said Walsh, 'and even if he hadn't I wouldn't mind helping.'

'I also,' said Natasha.

'Me too,' Maddy said. 'I couldn't manage very much but I'd be delighted to help.'

Everybody seemed to be looking at George, who was silent for a moment. Calculating the odds against having to cough up? But George was shy, wary of pushing himself forward – and not without reason.

'Count me in too if I'm needed,' he said at last.

'You're very generous all of a sudden,' said Oliver.

'We may not have to be,' said Walsh. 'The Earl seemed very keen on the idea.' He looked to Natasha. 'Didn't he?'

'He did,' Natasha said. 'When he returns from London he will drive straight to Slagsby to see the priest Carrick to find out where the cornet-player lives.'

'*What?*'

This time it was the parson, and Walsh marvelled at how much outrage he could cram into one syllable.

'I do not understand you,' said Natasha.

'Are you telling me that Kielder – our kinsman – intends to visit Slagsby to call on a workman?'

'Out-of-work more likely,' said Oliver. 'They're a lazy lot up there – *and* he's a musician. They're the worst. Bone idle, the lot of them.'

'How dare you insult my friend?' said Maddy. 'How dare you!'

By God, she means it, thought Walsh. Any more unkind remarks and she'll slap his face.

'I didn't mean Natasha, obviously,' said Oliver. 'I was thinking of my company bugler.'

'Your company bugler is beside the point,' said his father. 'What concerns me is that Kielder should visit Slagsby.'

'But why on earth shouldn't he?' said Walsh. 'He owns the place.'

'Because it is full of lawless and combative men who might very possibly insult him.'

'Mr and Mrs Carrick seem to survive there perfectly well,' said Maddy.

'In many ways they are not unlike the inhabitants themselves,' said the parson repressively.

Why doesn't he just say natives and have done with it? Walsh wondered. Or abos?

'He must be warned,' the parson fretted. 'Warned for his own good. But where to reach him, that's the problem.'

'Doesn't he have a house in London?' Walsh asked.

'The town house was sold years ago,' the parson said. 'He has a flat – rather a large one, but I cannot remember where I put the address. I must look in the study.'

He left them at a kind of scurrying run, and Walsh thought that this was a better than average game to play once you got the hang of it, but Oliver didn't. He thought it was time he went to bed. He needed someone to help him do it, and there was only George. That put him at risk of course, but when Walsh offered to help, Oliver wouldn't hear of it.

Then Maddy outmanoeuvred Natasha so brilliantly that Natasha was proud of her, and so simply, too. It was time she went home, she said. Such a long day. And who was there to escort her but Walsh?

Natasha fluttered over to kiss her goodnight like a cygnet in *Swan Lake*. Really, Maddy was learning admirably, but Michael was not for her. She was certain of it. Her destiny was George.

21

When Walsh returned Natasha was in the drawing room alone, playing the piano. Bach: *Jesu Joy of Man's Desiring*. Nothing in that to bring the blush of shame to the parson's cheek. He sat down and waited until she had finished.

'Another treat,' he said. 'My lucky night.'

'Not yet,' she said, and then: 'Is Maddy home safely?'

'No cutpurses,' he said. 'No highwaymen. No sturdy beggars. She's fine.'

And yet, she thought, he is puzzled. 'What happened?' she said.

'Nothing happened exactly,' he said. 'It was just—' He broke off, still puzzled.

'Do tell me,' she said. 'If you may, of course.'

'No big secret,' he said. 'We got to talking about when I was in the Army. She was interested, she said, because her husband had been a soldier, too.'

'He was a major.'

'Right,' said Walsh. 'And I was a private. When I told her that, she sort of left me.'

'Ran away?' Natasha managed to sound at once horrified and delighted.

'No, no,' said Walsh. 'She became somebody else. I promise you I didn't try to molest her.'

Better and better, thought Natasha, and then: 'I am quite sure you would have no need to molest her.'

'I thought we were friends,' said Walsh, still puzzled. 'But when I told her I was an O.R. – other rank and not an officer, she sort of moved away as if I had some contagious disease. And I'll tell you another thing,' said Walsh, more baffled than ever. 'Her husband's been dead for years and years—'

'Indeed he has,' said Natasha.

'—but I got the impression that by walking with a common soldier she thought she was betraying his memory. It doesn't make sense.'

'My poor darling,' said Natasha, and kissed him because he was so

225

upset. It took rather longer than she had intended, because he knew how to kiss. She wriggled free at last.

'I think I can explain,' she said.

'I'd sooner kiss you again.'

'No doubt,' said Natasha, 'but the priest is still looking for Lord Kielder's address and George is helping him and I have stopped playing the piano. Now, let me tell you why Maddy behaved so foolishly. It is because she is English and, so Lord Kielder tells me, she was not only born into an Army family, she married into another. And by "Army" she means officers, Michael. For her to be close to you meant not only betraying her husband but her entire class.'

'She should have met my half-brother,' said Walsh.

'He was an officer?'

'Captain,' said Walsh. 'In the Imperial Light Horse. Very grand.' He went back to brooding. 'I still don't understand it. After all, I only wanted us to be friends.'

'Perhaps she didn't.'

'Mind what you're saying,' he said. 'My head's big enough as it is. That's why I wear a big hat.'

'Michael, Michael,' she said. 'I told you her husband has been dead for years – and she bought all those pretty frocks at Harrod's. How many eligible young men like you come to Haydon Priors, do you suppose? But all is not finished for her.'

'It isn't?' Still he sounded wary.

'She had almost decided on Oliver when I arrived – but that would never do. On the other hand George will be just what she needs, and I am arranging it.'

'You are?' Not wary now – incredulous.

'Somebody must,' said Natasha. 'They seem incapable of doing it for themselves.'

'You know about his wounds?'

'Of course I do,' said Natasha. 'Oliver told me. But that will give them something else to do on their honeymoon. Oh, how I wish I could see them too.'

'Out of the question,' said Walsh.

Natasha sighed. 'That is true,' she said, 'unless I seduce him, and how can I when I want him for Maddy?'

Walsh waited. He was being teased, even punished a little, and if he waited long enough he would find out why.

'But Maddy would tell me,' Natasha said at last. 'After all, she has told me everything else,' and then in the same breath: 'I think we should make love, you and I.' He waited once more. Another tease?

'Not here and now of course,' said Natasha, 'because the priest is still looking and soon he will come in to tell me so, and see why I have stopped playing. But soon.'

Apparently she meant it.

'How soon?'

'After Oliver has left we must make an excuse to go away for a little while.'

'Why after Oliver goes?'

'Because he was in the Black and Tan Secret Police. He will suspect. Oliver always suspects if it is me.'

And not without reason if what *I* suspect is true, thought Walsh. Aloud he said, 'Fair enough.'

'You do *want* to make love to me?' said Natasha.

'Very much.'

'Such passion,' said Natasha. 'How much is that?'

'From the moment I saw you I've wanted you,' said Walsh.

'You did not show it.'

'Parsons, solicitors, Black and Tans, earls, chauffeurs, even officers' widows. What chance did I have?' said Walsh. 'But it's true, and if you keep on looking at me like that I'll show you it's true, even if the parson does find the Earl's address.'

Natasha tried to look demure. 'We must wait,' she said. 'It will be so much better.'

'I hope to God Oliver leaves tomorrow,' said Walsh, but the vicar came in as he said it, and he was holding a piece of paper as if nothing else mattered.

'It was in my Bible,' he said. 'I was using it as a bookmark. A quotation for a sermon, as a matter of fact. Leviticus chapter sixteen, verse ten. "Let him go for a scapegoat into the wilderness." The theme of my sermon was repentance.'

George came in. 'I've put the books away for you,' he said.

'Most kind,' said his father. 'I hope you haven't muddled them up.' George looked away. 'Kielder has a flat in Berkeley Street,' his father said. 'I shall write to him tomorrow. Or perhaps I should telephone.'

And what will you say? Walsh wondered. Not that it's any of your business, mate. Save your strength for Natasha.

'I think I'll be off to bed,' said George. 'Goodnight.' He stumbled on the rug as he left, not too disastrously. A side-table rocked, but did not fall. Even so his father clicked his tongue audibly.

'I too,' said Natasha. 'Greenhalgh will be waiting. Goodnight to you both.'

227

The two men rose as she left them, and Walsh enjoyed her body's sway. The parson looked at his piece of paper as if it contained the secret of Eternal Youth.

When the door had shut the parson said, 'I was unkind to George.' This was manifestly true, and to deny it would be both cowardly and foolish.

'He helped me,' said the parson. 'He went to great lengths to help me. He always does. Oliver does not, even when he is capable of doing so, and yet I am rarely unkind to Oliver. I love them both and yet I am unkind to only one.'

It will be Jacob and Esau next, thought Walsh. He has no business to be telling me this, but all the same I have to listen because he knows he's done wrong and he's telling me so. Father Walsh. Late night confessions a speciality.

'Was your father unkind to you?' the parson asked.

'Unkind? No,' said Walsh. 'He'd give me a hiding now and again when I was a boy, but that was because I'd asked for it, but he was never unkind. Not that I can remember.'

'George will never be able to say that of me. Yet I know him to be a Christian gentleman: generous, thoughtful, hardworking. Why should I treat him so unpleasantly?'

He doesn't really expect an answer, thought Walsh, and lit a cigarette instead.

'It is, as you have no doubt deduced, his clumsiness,' said the parson. 'His one major failing, but one that I cannot endure. It makes him look so foolish, you see, and I cannot bear it when he looks foolish. Why does he do it? He never used to be like that.'

You were never in it, mate, thought Walsh, and if you weren't in it nobody can tell you what it was like, or explain how it made George the way he is.

'I should like to ask you a favour,' the parson continued.

'If I can,' said Walsh. 'What is it?'

'Pray for me.'

Walsh got into bed and lit a cigarette. There was a lot to think about. The parson, for one. 'Pray for me.' Well, he had: knelt by his bedside and said an Our Father and a Hail Mary for him, then a prayer of intercession he'd made up as he went along, asking the soul of his mother for help as he did so. All the same it was an odd one: an English parson all public school and Oxford asking a Roman Catholic bastard to pray for him – and yet that same parson had ransacked his house for an address so that he could implore his most illustrious relative not to hobnob with the poor. Why?

Maybe it's because I'm a Tyrrwhitt too, he thought, or maybe it's even simpler than that. Maybe it's because he's human, with the good and bad so intertwined it's sometimes hard to tell which is which. But why *me*? Why did George want to discuss his problem with me, come to that? Because I'm a bird of passage, maybe? Because soon I'll be gone, never to return? Well, at least I said a prayer when I was here, and told George something that might do him good. (The side-table hadn't gone crashing after all.)

Snobbery didn't rank high in the list of Australian sins, except perhaps in Melbourne. You could argue that Australians hadn't much to be snobbish about, although that wasn't the way he looked at it. Australians just hadn't got around to being snobbish yet, except when it came to the abos... He sat up in the bed and looked around for the ashtray. He couldn't go to sleep yet: he still had things to consider. Edgar...

But where was the sense in thinking about Edgar? Either he knows I'm here or he doesn't, and whichever way it is he'll want his money back. Well, he won't get it, not without a fight. If he wants a blue he can have it. That must mean I'm staying, he thought, and then – well, of course I'm staying. The only reason for me to go is Edgar, and if I can't handle him I don't deserve to stay. It's not as if he can prove anything. And anyway, Dad left that money to me, and the way things are shaping up I'm going to need it.

Which brings us to the main event, he thought. Natasha Tyrrwhitt: the Countess Natalya Krilova. Take your pick. The second woman in his life who'd ever meant anything to him, and both of them had made the first move. More than that. They hadn't just left the key in the lock, they'd left the bloody door wide open. Of course, with Margaret the reason was obvious. She was frantic to have a baby. The pleasure they had shared had been no more than a bonus: she'd have put up with pain if she'd had to. Thank God he'd spared her that.

But Natasha – what reason had she to throw the key away? He wasn't all *that* rich – and she hadn't even bothered to find out how rich he was. And he was no Rudolph Valentino either. And yet she had said it. '*I think we should make love, you and I.*' She couldn't possibly have said that unless she meant it. Nine hundred and ninety-nine girls out of a thousand wouldn't have said it even if they did mean it. Which meant she was different. Not promiscuous; at least he didn't think so. How could she be promiscuous in Haydon Priors? And though he had no doubt she'd been up to something in London, he didn't think it was sex. In Haydon Priors she'd had only George and

229

Oliver to choose from; George she pitied and Oliver she detested, but even apart from that he knew it wasn't sex. Nor greed either – not when she'd turned down a viscount loaded with racehorses and coal mines. And anyway, she seemed to have enough money of her own. Look at her dresses. It was great looking at her dresses with her inside them.

Oh dear God, he thought, she can't want to make me a dad again? But that was ridiculous. To begin with she wasn't married, and anyway marriage hadn't been mentioned. He wouldn't have minded if it had been, but it hadn't. To kiss her was not to be unfaithful to Margaret Bonner: it was to forget that she had ever existed. Just like the parson and Slagsby's poor, he thought.

He stubbed out his cigarette. Time for some beauty sleep, and he'd bloody need it to be worthy of that one. The parson had said Oliver would be off to sunny Scarborough in a couple of days, which wasn't nearly enough time to look like a feller who could share her bed. A hundred years might do it . . . like the Sleeping Beauty . . . His eyes closed.

Oliver went walkabout, and next day it was his turn: sudden impulse to visit the Lake District, always been fascinated by the Lakeland poets, etc, etc. And the truth of it was that he could just about remember two lines of Wordsworth's *Prelude*. Fortunately the parson couldn't remember any, and was so glad to be rid of what he obviously regarded as an embarrassment, especially on Sundays, that he almost helped his guest to pack . . . And yet he meant it when he asked for my prayers, thought Walsh. Somewhere inside him was the makings of a good priest, but there was a lot of sad stuff to be rid of before it happened.

First he went to Newcastle, to buy a couple of books of poetry, and some walking shoes, and to hire a car. After that he really did go to the Lake District, and looked at Dove Cottage and Scafell and Grasmere, and almost as many sheep as he'd seen in Victoria. He read the poetry too, and remembered how much he'd enjoyed it. 'Wait three days,' she had told him, 'then join me in Newcastle, and we'll go on to somewhere quiet.' He'd worried about that. Suppose someone saw them? But she didn't give a damn and he did as he was told and took the car back and joined her at Newcastle station. The somewhere quiet, it seemed, was London. Well, at least he didn't know anybody there – provided he didn't bump into Lord Kielder.

She looked as she always did: chic, beautiful, and about as anonymous as a budgerigar in a flock of sparrows. Behind her toiled a porter with a barrow heaped with luggage. They'd be gone for three days . . . She ran to him at once and kissed him.

'Darling,' she said. 'You're on time. How gorgeous.'

He blinked. It was Natasha, no doubt about that, but the voice was Maddy's. He passed his suitcase to the porter, who added it to the pile.

'Well of course,' he said, his accent modelled on his father's. Wouldn't have missed it for quids, as you might say, only I can't because I'm not supposed to talk Aussie.

'Wouldn't have missed it for anything,' he said. 'Absolutely top-hole, in fact.' The porter took it unflinchingly, so it seemed that he'd got it right.

She took his arm. 'You won't spend the whole time on dreary business, will you?' she said. 'I do hate to be neglected – and there's so much in London I want us to do.'

It was a relief when the train came in, and the porter found them an empty compartment where they could talk as themselves.

'Why the Maddy imitation?' he asked.

'People always remember foreign accents,' she said. 'I should have warned you. But you talked like an Englishman anyway.'

'Like my dad,' he said. 'But how did you manage it?'

She told him about Stanislavsky, and a very little about Dimitri. This was not the time to invoke so powerful a ghost.

'Was it good in the Lake District?' she asked.

'Wonderful country. I walked for miles.' She made a face. Walking held no charms for her. They had been very keen on it in the exercise yard of the Re-education and Rehabilitation Centre, regardless of the weather.

'Where did you go?' he asked.

'York,' she said. 'For the racing.' And it was true, but not the whole truth. Scarborough was quite near York, and it was as well to be sure.

'And where did you say you were going?'

'London,' she said.

'On your own?'

'I told the priest I had a gynaecological problem and must see a specialist,' she said. And that is true too, she thought, except that I've already seen him.

'He said I should take Maddy, but I said I was too shy. As a matter of fact I think he was shy too. He turned a very strange colour.'

'Like a red dessert grape?' said Walsh. 'I know. What did Mrs Greenhalgh say?'

'Sometimes you are very clever,' she said.

231

Nine out of ten, thought Walsh. Very Good Indeed. Go to the top of the class, Michael Walsh.

'She looked at me for a long time then she smiled and said, "Now you be careful what you're up to."'

'Looks like she's clever too,' said Walsh.

Over lunch she showed him her wedding ring, which he admired dutifully. 'Where did you get it?' he asked.

'Woolworth's,' she said. 'Imagine – it costs only sixpence to be married.'

'Natasha—' he began.

'More claret please,' she said, 'and no seriousness. We are here only for frivolity. Your name is Thomson, by the way. So is mine.'

'You've made a reservation for us?'

'Certainly,' she said. 'I do not intend that we should sleep in the park. But not in an hotel. In something called a service flat.'

And who told you about them? he wondered. He decided it must be Greenhalgh because of her Earl, but better not to ask.

'I telephoned when they were all out,' she said. 'I was your secretary. I used my Maddy voice.'

'And did you use it when you bought the ring?'

'There was no need,' she said. 'All you do is give them sixpence, but I did wear the dark blue dress, the one that Greenhalgh makes me wear on Sundays.'

'How about when we arrive at the flats?' he asked. 'Will you speak like Maddy then?'

'I shall not speak at all,' she said. 'You are the husband.'

'And how do I explain my sun-tan?'

'If anybody should be so impertinent as to ask,' she said, 'you will say you are a businessman who has just returned from the Far East. You are in molasses. It is a word I found in the dictionary. It sounded important.'

'And just what I need,' said Walsh. She giggled and gave him a smile, but even so she thought, Please God, help me to be right for him, and make the train go faster.

They made love as soon as they had unpacked, and the champagne had been delivered, and once again he acted as the golden girls had taught him, but this time there was no exhibition of bewilderment. This time there was a sigh of relief rather than surprise, but then Natasha, he discovered, was something of a golden girl herself, and a noisy one at that. When at last they could do no more, she said, 'Someone taught you well.'

'You too,' he said.

'You should be glad,' she said. 'We have only three days. If I had been a virgin it would have taken so much longer.'

'So I am glad,' he said. 'Glad I'm here. Glad I'm in molasses. Glad you used—'

She interrupted him. 'I did not use protection,' she said.

Oh dear God, he thought. Why didn't I? Except she said she didn't like – *capotes anglaises*, she had called them. English over-coats.

'That is not exactly true about protection,' said Natasha. 'I don't need it.'

Exactly like Margaret, he thought. Exactly. I'm going to be a dad again, only this time I'm going to have to marry her, and what's wrong with that?

She was as naked as he was, and from the start there had been no shyness, only delight, and sometimes surprise – he had been rather proud of that surprise – but now she looked shy; not attempting to cover herself because she knew he liked to see her, but shy even so.

'Let me explain,' she said.

'If you want to.'

'I must.' She told him about Camp 19, and Dimitri, and Dr Brodski who had saved her life, and how the fee she'd had to pay was never to have children. If Dr Brodski had not made that impossible, she would be dead.

'What happened to Dimitri?' Walsh asked.

'There was cholera at the camp, and we escaped. It was very exciting – amusing too, sometimes. I learned to sneer like this –' she sneered for him '– but when we got to St Petersburg he died because of his heart and after a while I met Léonide and she fell in love with me.'

'My poor darling,' he said, and kissed her very gently. A friend's kiss, she thought. Oh Dimitri I am sorry, but I love this man.

'What will we do now?' she said.

'Take a shower,' he said, 'then drink champagne. Not too much for me, though. I've still got work to do.'

They showered together and she dried him, and then it was his turn. As he patted her with the towel the first stirrings of his need began again, which was most satisfactory, but first she wanted champagne.

'You do not mind that I have marks?' she said.

'Marks?' said Walsh. 'Oh, you mean scars. Why should I mind? I've got marks, too.'

She kissed them, front and back. 'My brave soldier,' she said.

233

'Not always,' he said. 'Believe me.'

'And some pig of a German shot you. But God was good. He was saving you for me.' Her hand reached out for him. 'I was shot, too. By a pig of a Russian. Here.' She touched the scar, still livid against the whiteness of her skin, but Walsh took her hand away and kissed the mark left by the bullet before his lips moved down to the other. Natasha yelped like a delighted puppy.

'First champagne,' she said. 'Just a little for you, and then your molasses.' But as she looked into his eyes, he saw that they were serious, worried. 'We don't have to hurry, do we?'

'If we hurry we'll spoil it,' he said. 'Slow and easy's our motto, Mrs Thomson.' At once her eyes danced: she poured out the wine.

'*Santé*,' she said, 'and when you have finished I will do some things that you may find amusing.'

In the morning they made love again, then she lay in his arms and asked, 'You are happy with me?'

'You know I am,' he said.

'Yes,' she said. 'I do know, and it amazes me.'

'Why on earth should it?'

'My marks – scars – and the life I have led.'

Walsh said, 'Wait till I tell you about the life I've led.'

'I very much want to hear,' she said, 'but not about your ladies.'

'You told me about your gentleman.'

Her eyes were sad again. 'How could I not? I had to explain.'

He began to stroke her, and she shivered, and so he kissed her, picking his targets, till she called out in joy, then later she said, 'We must get up.'

'When I get my strength back,' he said, and she giggled.

'The priest says we're the weaker sex.'

'Much he knows,' said Walsh, then added: 'Poor feller.' And then, 'Why must we get up?'

'Because we must have breakfast,' she said. 'I must keep you strong. And then there is shopping, Mr Thomson.'

'I thought there might be,' said Walsh. 'But suppose we met Lord Kielder?'

'He went to Brighton three days ago,' Natasha said, and added: 'Greenhalgh has a week's holiday.'

'Lucky Lord Kielder,' said Walsh. 'But not so lucky as me. I wonder if the parson managed to telephone him?'

She shrugged. It was even better when she had no clothes on. 'Greenhalgh will tell him anyway,' she said.

He began to touch her in the way they both liked so much, but she wriggled free and found her dressing gown – not the one to protect her from Oliver's lustful gaze. This one offered very little protection from lustful gazes, nor was it meant to.

She would not go with him to Harrod's, because she had stolen caviar there, but Greenhalgh had told her of another place called Fortnum & Mason. They sold caviar there, too. And frocks. Also, she must buy things for Michael.

'We will go shopping,' she said, 'and have lunch, and come back here, then we will go to the ballet, and supper at the Savoy, and come back here, and we will see how strong you are.'

Caviar to be put in the refrigerator, and frocks and a nightgown and silk and lace underwear. She kept bringing things to him and asking if he liked them while the whole store watched, and waited to hear what he would say, but he had already decided what he would do about that. He answered her in French and the whole store lost interest. The French were capable of anything. It also solved the problem of their words of endearment: *chéri*, *ma chère*, *mignon*. She threw in a few Russian ones, too. Almost he was beginning to enjoy shopping.

The ballet was Stravinsky's *Firebird*, which she adored, and which he saw for the first time, and he adored it too, just as he adored dancing at the Savoy. She wore a new dress of the blue Lord Kielder liked so much, and a sapphire necklace he had bought her that morning in Bond Street. Let Edgar try to get his hands on that, he thought. He's not going to get back a single quid. Give him enough practice and spoiling Natasha would become an art form.

They took a taxi back to the service flat in Grosvenor Place, and somehow he achieved enough to pass muster (the afternoon had been an orgy for two) and fell asleep with his head on her breast, then awoke soon afterwards to the smell of tobacco, the ruby glow of her cigarette in the darkness. He touched her cheek: it was wet.

'Natasha,' he said, 'what's wrong?' then switched on the light to find his own cigarettes, the case and lighter she had bought him that morning.

'You should not do that,' she said. 'I look ugly when I cry.'

'You look beautiful when you cry,' he said, and passed her his handkerchief. 'What is it?'

'I was remembering Camp 19,' she said.

'Dimitri?'

'Him also. He was part of it, and I would do wrong to forget him. Without him I would not be here, after all. But I am here, and he is dead. But not just Dimitri. Camp 19 was like a special kind of Hell, *mon cher*, where it is always cold and you are always weary and soon it will be worse . . . And now I am here and I am crying because it is all too much and I honestly do not know how I must feel. Sad for Dimitri, or happy for myself. Did you ever escape from Hell, Michael?'

'Pozières,' he said.

'What is that?'

Incredible that she shouldn't know, but then she wasn't Australian, not yet – and she'd had other things to think about in 1917.

'A battle,' he said. 'Yours was a Hell of cold; mine was a Hell of mud. It was so deep men got stuck and couldn't move. I nearly drowned in it.'

'What saved you?'

'The Germans. A shell landed nearby and blew me out – and before I could go down again a mate of mine grabbed me. O. B. Watson. Lifted me clear.'

'A good – mate.'

'The best,' said Walsh. 'I told you about him. He's the one who says his prayers in an aeroplane. Next day I got this –' he touched his chest '– and he carried me to the Dressing Station. From there I went to hospital. Heaven after Hell – till they patched me up and sent me back to Hell.'

'And what happened to Mr Watson?' she asked, and Walsh told her.

'But that is terrible,' she said. 'Far, far worse than George.'

'George thought so too – until I told him O.B. could still manage to do it.'

'Oh *good*,' she said – and she means it, he thought, but then I did tell her O.B. had saved my life.

She thought for a moment, then asked him: 'Did you think that if he knew about Mr Watson it would make him feel better?'

Walsh thought of the side-table. It had wobbled, not fallen. 'Perhaps it will,' he said. He looked at her. She was serious still, but the happiness was returning. It was as if she had never cried in her life.

'Why is he called O.B.?' she asked.

'Because his full name's Osbaldestone Bernard Watson.' He yawned. 'He likes O.B. better.'

'Of course he does,' said Natasha.

Walsh stubbed out their cigarettes. 'After it happened some of the blokes said O.B. stood for One Ball,' he said.

Natasha curled herself against him. 'Some of the blokes were very cruel,' she said, but it was too late. Walsh was already asleep.

236

* * *

Their three days passed in a blur. Another ballet, *Giselle*, more shopping, and much, much more love. On their last night, as they lay together, he asked her to marry him.

'Because of this?' she said, and did one of her amusing things, but it was too soon. His body was not ready for her.

'Because I love you,' he said, and she let him go.

'And I love you,' said Natasha, 'but would I love Stony Creek?'

'I shouldn't think so,' said Walsh. 'Not for long, anyway. We'd live somewhere else when you wanted a change.'

'Where?' she asked.

'Anywhere you fancy,' he said. 'Melbourne, London, Paris. Haydon Priors even.'

'You would sell Stony Creek?'

'I couldn't do that,' he said. 'Not with the blokes and Tabby being there.'

'I think you must explain,' she said.

'Well, of course.' He turned to look at her, not wanting her again, not yet, simply delighting in what he saw.

'They're not abos,' he said. 'They're half-castes, all of them. Tabby's looked after me since my mum hired her – and the blokes are some of the best cattlemen I've ever seen. The foreman – Chalky – he taught me to ride. He's the best brumby breaker in Queensland. That's a bloke who breaks in wild horses.'

'Ride him cowboy,' she said automatically. 'But if he is a half-caste, why do you call him Chalky?'

'Because he's the blackest of the lot,' said Walsh. 'Sort of irony of opposites. Very Australian. Same reason we call a red-haired man Bluey. But what I'm getting at is this. We don't treat the abos all that well in Australia – or the half-castes.'

'You do,' she said.

'Because my mum did. She was that sort of Christian, which was why she hired them in the first place. She taught my dad to do the same. I sort of grew up with it, but if I sold Stony Creek they'd never get another job like it.'

'Couldn't they stay on?'

'I doubt it,' said Walsh. 'Who else would want them?'

'But if they're so good—?'

'They're still half-castes,' Walsh said. 'Not a hope in Hell. I had an idea I might give it to them, but if I did, some smart white man would find a way to cheat them out of it. Probably a lawyer.' He thought for a moment, then added, 'Or a politician.' He touched her cheek: a gesture that was almost pleading. 'You do understand, don't you?'

237

'Yes,' she said, and took his hand from her cheek to kiss its palm. 'I am also beginning to understand why I love you so much.'

She began to do an amusing thing again, his favourite, and this time he responded splendidly. 'Wait,' he said. 'You haven't said if you'll marry me.'

'That's because I do not yet know,' she said, 'but I will come to bed with you whenever you ask me.' She rolled on top of him. 'Or even when you don't.'

22

They travelled north together as far as York. From there, he told her, he would make his way to Howarth, and a parsonage far different from Haydon Priors. Different parson, too, and different parson's children. Far different. But if separation from her was to be his fate, he would give English literature another go: see where Emily and Charlotte and Anne had written that astonishing fiction – though without Natasha he would be far more likely to follow in brother Branwell's footsteps and go on the grog. She smiled at him mistily, the tears not far; and he in his turn realised how much she loved him, and wished she would get a move on and say yes . . .

Greenhalgh looked at her and thought, she's had the time of her life. The pussy cat who's had all the cream, and the goldfish for a second course. If she glowed any more she'd light up in the dark. But then maybe I'm looking a bit that way myself. At least I was careful to turn the lights down a bit in front of Molly Parker and Cook.

'Oh Greenhalgh,' said Natasha, 'how happy you look.'

No fooling this one, Greenhalgh thought, but then why should I want to?

'I brought the champagne and Melba toast, miss,' she said.

'Good on yer,' said Natasha, and Greenhalgh blinked. Well, at least we know where we stand, she thought. She began to spread caviar on the toast: Fortnum & Mason this time, but still Beluga.

'You look happy too, miss,' she said.

'Well, of course,' said Natasha.

'Had a good win at York, did you?' Natasha put out her tongue at her.

'The service flat was excellent,' she said. 'Thank you.'

'Not at all, miss.' Greenhalgh uncorked the bottle, poured out wine, and waited.

'We were very happy together.'

Greenhalgh stared at her then; her eyes shrewd, unwavering. 'You sure, miss?'

'Believe me, I know,' Natasha said. 'The kind of life I've led – I have to know.'

Greenhalgh smiled. 'That's all right then,' she said, and then, politely ironic: 'I don't suppose you found the time to do any shopping, miss?'

Natasha pointed to a brand new suitcase, and they ate caviar and drank champagne as Greenhalgh unpacked.

You never pick a wrong 'un, do you? she thought. Every dress just right for her, and the underwear hardly more substantial than the froth on their champagne. Lucky Mr Walsh. All the same, she approved of him, or she'd never have let miss go. Be sensible, Greenhalgh, she thought, How on earth could you have stopped her? But she knew she would.

At the bottom of the pile was a jewel case. 'Shall I put this with the others?' she asked.

'Look first,' said Natasha, and Greenhalgh opened the case. Sapphires, and not from Woolworth's, either – not like that wedding ring she'd found in the ashtray.

'Oh miss,' she said, 'they're beautiful.'

'There is an expression I learned,' said Natasha. 'The wages of sin.'

'Mine was diamond earrings,' said Greenhalgh, and Natasha bounced from her chair and embraced her.

'Darling Greenhalgh,' she said, and kissed her. 'How marvellous. Show me.'

'Not here, miss,' said Greenhalgh. 'But I will. I promise.'

'You were happy,' said Natasha. 'Truly?'

'Truly, miss.' There could be no doubt that she meant it.

'Such fun to be wicked,' said Natasha. 'Profitable, too.' Then the smile vanished. 'He wants to marry me.'

'So I should hope,' Greenhalgh said.

'Yes, but – I am not so sure,' said Natasha.

'Why ever not?' said Greenhalgh. 'Straight as a die, that one, or I miss my guess. And that fond of you, and I don't just mean sapphires neither.' She put her glass back on the table. 'You don't mean you've turned him down?'

'Not that, no,' said Natasha. 'But I said I must consider. He thinks it is because we will have to live in Australia – sometimes, that is – but really it is because of what I told you.'

'You can't have children?' Natasha nodded. 'Does he know?'

'Oh yes,' said Natasha. 'Of course. I told him. The things we did . . . If I could have children I'd be pregnant now.'

That's my lady, thought Greenhalgh. Straight out with it because it's the truth and she knows no other way. But if poor Mr Walsh knew what you'd just said he'd never look me in the eye again. But you'll marry him, my love, because you're mad for him just like he's mad for you, and you daren't risk losing him.

'You marry him, miss,' she said. 'After all, if you want children you can always adopt.'

Natasha thought of all the half-castes in Stony Creek and wondered whether perhaps she already had.

'Greenhalgh,' she said, her voice coaxing. 'If I may ask . . .'

'Am I going to get some more diamonds?' Natasha giggled. 'His Lordship has a plan, miss. Only it's had to be postponed on account of he had to go back to London.'

'Again?'

'To see an old chum, miss. Sir John Brett. You went to his house.'

'So I did,' said Natasha.

'His Lordship rang him up to see how you'd enjoyed yourself, and Sir John said his son Martin's got the idea he wants to marry you, miss, and so Lord Kielder had to go and tell him he can't, on account of he thinks you're already spoken for.' She sipped her champagne. 'So it looks like you are, miss.'

'It is beginning to seem so,' said Natasha. 'Tell me about Lord Kielder's plan.'

'Well, His Lordship thinks that when he gets back from London you and Mr Walsh should stay with him.'

'Both of us?'

'Only fair, miss. You're both relations. Can't have one without the other, so to speak.'

'I can understand that,' said Natasha, 'but is that all the plan?'

'Of course not, miss. But if you go, then I'll have to go too. You couldn't manage without me, now could you, miss?'

'I never want to even try,' said Natasha. 'How clever of him.'

'His Lordship always was a clever one, miss.'

'Tell me,' said Natasha. 'Do you always call him His Lordship?'

'Well of course, miss,' said Greenhalgh.

'Even when you make love?'

'Not then, miss. It would be silly.'

'What *do* you call him then?' Natasha asked.

'That's between me and him, miss,' said Greenhalgh, and by the look on her face it would remain so: one of the things not to be achieved, like the sight of George's wounds.

Best to change the subject. 'Oliver is not yet back?' she asked.

'No, miss. And not so much as a postcard from Scarborough. Really vexed, the vicar is.'

But Oliver is not in Scarborough, so how can he send a postcard from there?

'Seems a daft place to go, when you've pulled a thigh muscle,' said Greenhalgh.

'Daft?'

'Foolish, miss. It's all ups and downs.'

Like my life, thought Natasha, which is now going up and up and up and will continue to do so. I have no intention of allowing Oliver to pull me down. If necessary I shall hurt him again, but I do not think it will be necessary. He was not a Berin after all, not even a camp guard – but he must be stopped. He would be. Forget him for now.

'Did the priest telephone to Lord Kielder in London?' she asked.

'Not that I know of, miss, and I'm sure he would have told me. But why should the vicar phone? You never did tell me.'

'To advise him not to go to Slagsby.' She told Greenhalgh about Kielder's scheme for the cornet-player.

'As if His Lordship would take any notice of what the vicar says. Obstinate as a mule, is His Lordship. Not that it isn't a good idea. He played lovely,' she said, and smiled at Natasha. Not the smile of a servant for her mistress: more like a mother for her daughter. 'Almost as good as you,' she said.

'Me? I lost too many years, but that Slagsby man, if he listens to Lord Kielder, he could do very well.' She looked at her watch. 'Time for me to change,' she said, and swallowed the last of her caviar and champagne. 'Is anyone dining?'

'Only Mrs Cantripp, miss. Which dress will you wear?'

'You choose,' said Natasha. 'Anything except the new blue. I want to save that for Lord Kielder.' She began to unbutton her dress. 'At least I won't have to wear that horrible dressing gown since Oliver's away.'

'Indeed you will, miss,' said Greenhalgh. 'He might come back when you were halfway down the passage. Always one for doing what you don't expect is Mr Oliver.'

It would be as well to remember that, thought Natasha.

'I still think you should have taken me with you,' said Maddy.

'To see the gynaecologist? He might not have let you in, and even if he did I would be shy.'

'And that was the only reason you went to London?' Natasha nodded and sipped her coffee. Greenhalgh had made it.

'But you bought dresses,' said Maddy accusingly.

'One could not go to London and not buy dresses,' said Natasha.

Maddy, a fair-minded young woman, agreed that that was so. 'But the gynaecologist says you're all right?' she said. 'No – problems?'

'Absolutely none,' said Natasha, and Maddy knew it must be true because she smiled so happily.

She accepted a cigarette from Natasha and said, 'George told me that Mr Walsh drinks beer.'

Mr Walsh indeed. Romance *must* be dead.

'He told me it's because he's Australian,' said Natasha. 'It's compulsory there.'

Almost the bewildered look returned, but in the end Maddy said, 'He has a very odd sense of humour.'

There was more to come, but to judge by the next pause it was difficult; though not impossible, for out it came at last.

'This is not easy for me to say, but I think you should know,' she told Natasha. 'Mr Walsh is illegitimate.'

Natasha looked shocked. 'George told you that?'

'No, no, of course not,' said Maddy. 'It was my maid. You know how servants love to gossip.'

Then the gentlemen joined them. They never lingered over their port, it seemed, when Oliver was away. George made his way to sit beside Maddy, who watched anxiously as he approached, but when he sank triumphantly into his chair, she smiled. Like a young mother who watches her infant take its first tottering steps, Natasha thought. Then Maddy's look changed again. Hard to describe it this time. Perhaps like a woman contemplating a dress she'd thought at first she disliked, then decided that, on the contrary, it might do very well. George, it seemed was on trial.

'Are we to have music?' the priest asked her.

'Yes, but not Debussy,' Natasha said. 'I have not yet had a chance to speak to Lord Kielder.'

It was dull without Michael. Unbelievably dull. There had not been much dullness in her life. Joy, misery, fear, delight . . . an abundance of those, but never dullness. It was like the beginning of a headache that never got worse; just went on, bearably painful, hour after hour, except when she talked about him to Greenhalgh, and that could not be for long. Greenhalgh had to watch the cook, or else the priest grew angry. And Michael would be away for three more days . . .

Mon cher, you know too many clever things, too many pleasing things, she thought. Also you are rich and can make me laugh, and you are kind and do not know it, and it is altogether impossible for me to have a life without you, although whether I can marry you or not I do not know for a certainty, no matter what Greenhalgh says. She wished she could talk to a priest, a proper priest from her own Church, but there was only this Tyrrwhitt, and even if she did go to him her problem was mostly gynaecology, and the subject terrified him.

She lit a cigarette and looked at the ceiling through the smoke. At least she was resting as the gynaecologist had told her, and she should be able to sleep because the house was so quiet. George was in his office, and the priest visiting the sick – surely the sick had troubles enough without a visit from him? – and Greenhalgh had been sent to Newcastle to order asparagus, which was a nuisance, since they could not talk. She thought of vodka, but it was no longer a pleasure on one's own, and so she thought yet again of Michael, and that first time, and how little champagne he had drunk while she had finished the bottle, and how she had rewarded him for his sacrifice. Then the door slammed downstairs, and she knew that the dullness was over, for the time being at least.

The footsteps on the stairs were still a little cautious, and unsure of themselves too, which made her certain that it was Oliver. Softly Natasha rose from her bed, sat down by the dressing table and began to file her nails. It was a very long nailfile, the point sharp enough to cause pain. I'm all on my own, she thought, and just as well. If my Australian stallion were here he would trample him dreadfully. The footsteps limped and lurched towards her room, then passed her door. How very odd, she thought, and then – of course. He is going to the bathroom to soak his head and be not quite so drunk when he comes to frighten me. My very own – what is the word? Bogey man. That's it. How fortunate I drank no vodka. Now my head will be at least as clear as his. Suddenly he began to sing, bawling the words.

> *'In Dublin's fair city,*
> *Where I first saw a titty*
> *'Twas one of a pair on sweet Molly Malone.'*

Then the bathroom door closed, and Natasha giggled softly. It was really rather amusing this time, though she was not sure she understood all the nuances. She would discuss it with Greenhalgh before she told it to Michael, but when she did she would have to be careful not to say too much and make Michael angry . . .

The footsteps came back towards her room, Oliver's movements perhaps a little steadier, but there was no doubting the limp. Even so he hurled the door open with a vehemence that even a Russian might have envied.

'Why Oliver,' she said. 'You're back. Do come in.'

'I am in,' said Oliver. He did look pleased with himself.

'And looking so much better,' she said. 'Scarborough has done you good.'

For a moment he flinched, and then recovered, as if remembering that he had been dealt a hand with rather a lot of trumps in it.

'I didn't go to Scarborough,' he said.

'I didn't suppose you did,' said Natasha. 'Very hilly, Scarborough, for a person with your affliction. Where did you go, may I ask? Paris?'

'Yes I did, as a matter of fact,' said Oliver.

'And does your father know? After all, he paid.'

Oliver lurched towards her. 'Now look here,' he said, then stopped. She was holding the nailfile like a dagger: a dagger aimed at him. A dagger aimed very low.

'Sit down,' she said, 'and try not to shout – if you want us to have secrets.'

He went to a chair, and its ease helped him to recover.

'Dad won't be pleased I lied to him,' he said, 'but I'll risk that because I don't think you'll tell him. I found out about you, you see.'

'You went to Paris to see Léonide?'

'Of course not,' he said. 'You duped her, too.'

'Who then?'

'A friend of mine. He was a brother officer once. Now he's a journalist – Paris Correspondent for Empire Press.'

She had begun to file her nails again, and listened as if she were not bored precisely, but only just this side of boredom.

'He has people you might call informers,' said Oliver.

'All journalists do,' said Natasha. Léonide had told her that and it was true.

'One of them is Vitali Chomsky.'

Natasha inspected the finger she was working on, and filed just a little more. 'Oh him,' she said.

'Yes him,' said Oliver. 'My friend says he's the best informed White Russian there is.'

'*Chomsky?*' Natasha's voice held a note of incredulous amusement. 'He's the one who said that the Grand Duchess Anastasia was living in Berlin.'

'You tried to tell me you were Anastasia,' said Oliver.

'And didn't you want to believe it? And even if I were, I've never been to Berlin. Chomsky will say anything that keeps him in vodka.'

She's doing it again, thought Oliver. Tying you in knots. But this time she isn't going to get away with it. Stick to the facts. Deliver your ultimatum. This time *you're* going to win.

'Chomsky says that *all* the Krilov family are dead,' he said.

Natasha shrugged. 'Chomsky said that Anastasia is alive.'

'He says he knows someone who can prove it. The Princess Makarova.'

'A very old lady who lives in Finland.' Natasha continued to file her nails.

'My friend is thinking of visiting her. He thinks there may be a story in these lies of yours.'

245

She held her hand out and looked at her nails and was satisfied. Even so she held on to the nailfile.

Oliver said at last, 'He won't go after this story unless I let him. He owes me a very big favour and he'll keep his word, I promise you.'

She examined the nails of her other hand and Oliver said angrily, 'This is what I'm prepared to let you do. You can stay here till I'm better, then we'll go to bed together, then you can bugger off and find another lot of mugs – but it won't be the Tyrrwhitts. And no more bloody nonsense about Cambrai either. Do you hear me?'

'Certainly.'

'And what the hell does that mean?'

'It means I hear you,' she said. 'But don't you think you ought to lie down for a while? You look far worse than when you came in.'

He got to his feet. 'Two days,' he said. 'That's all I'm giving you. After that I'll send a telegram to Paris,' then he lurched to the door.

'The Scarborough air did you no good at all, did it?' said Natasha, and the door slammed.

All the same it was a nuisance, perhaps even a problem. Chomsky was not important but the Princess, even at ninety, had an excellent memory . . . She poured a glass of vodka. Really she needed it after such a trying interview, and Michael surely would not begrudge her just one. She had barely finished it when there was a tap at the door. She filled the glass with water from the carafe.

'Yes?' she said, and the priest opened the door to stand just inside the threshold. 'Forgive me,' he said. 'I hope I don't intrude.'

'How could you?' said Natasha.

'Very kind. The thing is that our kinsman has returned. I thought you would like to know.'

Be calm, she told herself. Mildly interested, but calm.

'Did he visit Slagsby?' she asked.

'I fear so,' the priest said, 'but he is in excellent health.' He hesitated for a moment then said, 'I understand that Oliver also is once more with us.'

'So I believe,' she said. 'I think I heard him go to his room when I was resting.'

'Was he – noisy?'

'He can't have been,' Natasha said. 'At least not terribly. I went back to sleep.'

The priest looked relieved. 'I had better go to him,' he said.

'Tell him I hope Scarborough has done him good.'

'I will indeed,' said the priest. 'Thank you, my dear.'

Then he left her to visit the sickest of all, but she had no time to think of that. She had to telephone Kielder Hall at once.

246

23

'Am I to spend the rest of my life watching you break the hearts of eligible young men?' said the Earl. 'First Wentworth, and now young Brett.'

'Was he so very disappointed?' Natasha asked.

'I expect so,' said the Earl.

Natasha tried to imagine herself in bed with either of them, doing even a fraction of the things that she and Michael did so effortlessly, and found she couldn't.

'I know I would have been at his age,' said the Earl.

What a darling he is, she thought. He *deserves* Greenhalgh.

'But he is a very strange young man,' she said.

'Strange?' The Earl looked wary.

'Suggesting we speak Russian in the middle of a party.'

'He's in the Diplomatic,' said the Earl.

'Yes, but even so,' said Natasha, 'this was a *party* – rather a nice one, too. Not that his Russian was so very bad, but even so . . .'

Lord Kielder discovered that this particular way Natasha had of looking at one, challenging, unwavering, could make a chap damned uncomfortable.

'I expect he wanted to show off,' he said at last. 'Any young man would, for a girl as beautiful as you.'

Just about the perfect answer, milord, she thought, but much too late. I don't know how you suggested it, but suggest it you did, so you, too, have your doubts. But how delicately you express them when I compare you with Oliver.

'You do not mind that I am glad you refused him?' she said.

'What business is it of mine?' said the Earl.

'I would have refused Wentworth too,' she said, 'but if you had wished it—'

'I remember,' he said. 'You thought I might be broke and if you'd married him you'd help me to some of his money. But why, child?'

'You are the head of my family.'

'Your kinsman, you mean?'

'Oh that.' Her hand made a gesture that broke the word 'kinsman'

247

into a thousand pieces. 'You are the one to whom I owe obedience: respect.'

Dear God, he thought, she means it. But how can she? Except that they were all like that . . .

'You're safe from both of them,' he said, 'but that wasn't why you came to see me.' The word 'kinsman' still lingered. 'Was it Matthew?'

'Oliver,' she said. 'He came back to the priest's house today. He—'

'*Oliver?*' His Lordship was suddenly furious. 'What the devil has he been up to? He didn't—' I wish Daisy were here, he thought. Don't quite know how to put it on my own.

Natasha had no such problems. 'As a matter of fact he did try from time to time,' she said, 'but that is not the point.'

'Of course it's the point.' The Earl was furious. 'Molesting you. I'll skin him alive.'

'But he didn't molest me,' said Natasha. 'I was taught years ago how to stop that, in St Petersburg. What I want to tell you is—'

'Just a minute,' said the Earl. 'Oliver's six feet tall and twelve stone if he's an ounce, *and you stopped him*?'

'Yes, but that isn't why—'

'Bear with me, please,' said the Earl. 'He's been away, according to his father. Convalescing – after he had pulled a muscle in his thigh, so he went to Scarborough to get over it. Damn queer place to cure a thigh strain.'

You and Greenhalgh, she thought. How you belong together. Then suddenly he was looking at her as she had looked at him.

'It wasn't his thigh, was it, Natasha?' he said.

'Not precisely,' she said, and cast down her eyes.

The Earl wheezed and choked with laughter until she had to pound him on the back, then at last he stopped and gasped, 'Ring the bell. I think we both deserve a drink. Especially you.'

As Cribb poured the wine he said, 'Has he recovered yet?'

'Not completely,' said Natasha.

'Dear God.' The Earl looked at her warily, but that was understandable. He was someone she loved, but he was also a man: he knew what Oliver had endured.

When Cribb had left he said, 'Is that what you want to tell me about?'

'Oh no,' she said. 'That is over. I warned him I could take care of myself, and I did.'

'What, then?'

'Oliver didn't go to Scarborough,' she said, and out it all came: his journalist friend, the Princess Makarova, Chomsky.

'Dear God,' the Earl said again. 'The man's demented.' He thought for a moment. 'Or else in love with you, in his own ghastly fashion.'

'I think love,' she said. 'Love I do not want.'

'Indeed not. Hence his attack on you. Well, he's been adequately punished for that. Are you saying by the way that you are not Natalya Krilova?'

'Natalya Krilova no longer exists,' said Natasha.

Literally – or metaphorically? the Earl wondered.

'What I am saying is that Natasha Tyrrwhitt is who I am,' Natasha said.

'My kinswoman?' said the Earl and smiled, and then the smile vanished. His kinswoman was crying, tears flowing unchecked.

'I was so happy,' Natasha said. 'Not at first. At first it was merely interesting to watch those three funny men—' *Oliver?* the Earl wondered. *Funny?* '—and I had Greenhalgh of course, which was like being young again.'

Almost he said, 'But you are young,' then checked himself in time. To have survived what she had survived meant that her youth was over long ago. Daisy had seen her scars, and they at least were real.

'Then Michael came,' said Natasha, 'and I fell in love. I did not think I would do that ever again, but I did.'

'Did he fall in love with you?'

'Oh yes,' she said. 'He told me. It was exactly the same.'

'He came to London to see you?'

'Of course,' she said. 'I am a Tyrrwhitt like you. In matters of love I do not like to be kept waiting.' Then the sobs began: the only ugly sounds he had ever heard her make, which made them even more heart-rending.

The Earl produced his handkerchief, put it into her hand and embraced her as he might have embraced a much younger Natasha who had just fallen off her pony and it *hurt*, and muttered words that were meaningless, but soothing. There there, and hush now, and never mind. He has done this before, thought Natasha. He has done it many times, but even so the sobs eased at last.

'Now what's all this about?' said the Earl.

'It's Michael,' said Natasha. 'If Oliver persists in telling these stories he might leave me.'

'Can't you shut Oliver up?'

'I could kill him,' said Natasha, 'but then I might get caught and I'd lose Michael anyway.' To the end of his days the Earl was never quite sure whether she meant it or not.

'Michael wouldn't leave you,' he said. 'From all I've seen and

249

heard, he isn't that sort. All the same it would be embarrassing to you both, if Oliver started telling such lies.'

Lies, she thought. I'm winning.

'Embarrassing to Matthew, too. And to me, damnit. Better let me shut him up,' said the Earl.

'Can you do that?'

The Earl smiled. It was a smile that reminded her of Dimitri when he was contemplating a just reprisal.

'Oh yes,' he said. 'I can do it.' He poured more wine. 'Clean your face, child. You have a duty to be pretty when you're with the head of the family.'

She took cologne from her handbag, and used his handkerchief to remove the tearstains, then repaired her lipstick.

'In Paris,' the Earl said, 'when you were with Léonide, did my name ever come up?' She nodded. 'The fact that I was something of a ladies' man in St Petersburg?' She nodded again. 'Were any other names mentioned?'

'Three,' said Natasha. 'One of them was the late Natalya Krilova's mother. She said she had to tell me in case you might try it with me.'

'With my own daughter, in fact.'

'If I were your daughter that would make me even more a Tyrrwhitt,' she said, 'but I have no proof that you are my father. Have you?'

'None,' said the Earl. 'I was posted to Vienna very soon afterwards. Would you mind if it were so?'

She shrugged, and the Earl too enjoyed it. 'Being your daughter?' she said. 'Of course not. But you treat me as if I already am.'

'You're good for me,' he said. 'I never thought another human being would be so good for me ever again.'

'Greenhalgh,' she said.

'Daisy?' he said. 'Of course. But then Daisy's part of it, just as Michael is.' He got up and rang the bell. 'Finish your wine,' he said. 'It's time you went home. You know how Matthew frets if dinner's late. The car will bring Oliver back here.'

'Tonight?' she said.

'No time like the present,' said the Earl, and she went to him and kissed his cheek. 'You always smell so nice,' he said.

'Chanel.'

'No. You,' said the Earl. 'On most women it would be merely very good perfume, but with you – once you put it on, it becomes part of Natasha.'

She smiled at him, delighted. He was so good at flattery.

'There was something else I had to tell you,' the Earl said. 'What

250

was it? Oh yes, Natasha, you will oblige me by not stealing anything else until we can arrange to have a chat. There's no time now. Do I have your word?'

'Of course,' she said.

Then Cribb came in to say that the car was waiting.

The priest was appalled. He told her so, late next morning, after Lord Kielder had telephoned. To lose Michael was bearable: no Anglican parson should provide board and lodging for a Roman Catholic for too long, and an illegitimate Roman Catholic at that. To lose Natasha could also be endured: Russian Orthodox, smoking, drinking, upsetting Oliver – though it was very possible that Oliver deserved to be upset – but even so, who would run the house, supervise the cook, if he lost Mrs Greenhalgh?

'Let us ask her,' said Natasha, and rang the bell. Greenhalgh must have been listening, she thought, for she appeared at once without bothering with Molly Parker first.

'Sir?' she said.

Natasha told her the problem. When she had done, the priest began fussing at once. 'I was not consulted. It is a matter of concern, of great concern, to me and my household, but even so I was not told until today.'

'But as I understand it, sir,' said Greenhalgh, 'it was only today that His Lordship made his decision. Unless he said something last night to Mr Oliver?'

'What passed between my son and the Earl is something they neither of them wish to discuss with me. That, though regrettable, is their affair.' He thought of some of the things that Oliver had done in his time and left it at that. 'But to lose you—'

'The way His Lordship explained it, sir,' said Greenhalgh, 'I'm a lady's maid, not a housekeeper, and Miss Natasha's a lady who needs a maid, having had one all her life.'

Camp 19, thought Natasha, but before and after it was true.

'So His Lordship – knowing it would suit us both – well, that was his decision, sir.'

'*But who will keep an eye on the cook?*'

'I went to Newcastle yesterday, sir.'

Tyrrwhitt brightened. 'I know. Steaks, asparagus. Did you get them?'

'Yes, sir. I also went to call on a friend of mine, a Mrs Stobbs. She'll be at liberty quite soon. So this morning I called her on the telephone where she works. She's quite willing to come here as housekeeper.'

'But will she be any good?'

251

'Oh yes, sir,' said Greenhalgh. 'Cook won't be able to call her soul her own. Will that be all, sir?'

'For the moment.'

Greenhalgh sketched a curtsey and left, and the priest turned to Natasha. 'Has it ever occurred to you that you are grossly over-indulged?' he asked.

'Occasionally,' said Natasha. 'I have also been shot, imprisoned, beaten many times. A life of extremes, you may say.'

'Forgive me,' he said. 'I mean that. Please forgive me. I know some of the things that were done to you, honestly I do, and I believe them, but when I look at you as you are now, it is hard to believe they ever happened.'

'How kind you are,' she said.

'No,' said the priest. 'Not kind. Just trying very hard to be honest for once.'

Natasha thought that if he continued to talk like that it might be possible to like him.

When he had gone she played the piano: Chopin, and very loud. It was of course a message to Oliver. Here I am, the *Polonaise Militaire* declared. Come down and face me if you are man enough, and at last he came. She finished the piece and turned to look at him.

'You couldn't beat me on my own,' he said.

'It was a fight, not a duel,' she said. 'All I wanted to do was win.'

'You've won.'

A bribe, she wondered? Or the threat of no more money, no more horses to ride?

'At least you didn't set your boyfriend on me,' said Oliver.

'Boyfriend?'

'An Americanism,' he said. 'You go to the cinema: you know what it means.'

'You mean Michael, I suppose?'

'Well, of course I mean bloody Michael,' said Oliver. 'The well-known blot on the Tyrrwhitt escutcheon, but not to you, it seems. And not to the Earl either.'

Now that was interesting, but best to leave it for now. She still had Lord Kielder's reference to her stealing to think about.

'Did you imagine I would ask him to assault you?' she said. 'I can do that myself.'

'I've told you you've won,' he said, 'but there are limits. Don't go beyond them.'

She shrugged, but it still didn't bother him. If she provided the sickness, she also provided the cure, and bloody painful it was.

'You have not seen a newspaper today?' she asked.

'No.'

She got up and went to the table where the newspapers were spread, took up *The Times* and turned to the obituaries. She offered it to him, then lit a cigarette and fitted it into her holder. This could be amusing.

'"The Princess Makarova",' he read, '"last surviving intimate friend of the late Czarina, died in her palace in Finland . . . Devout Christian . . . Tireless worker for charity . . ."' Oliver said something uncouth.

'That leaves only Vitali Chomsky,' she said.

'Who, as you told me, is unreliable,' said Oliver.

'Completely.'

'So that what Kielder said to me need never have happened?'

No bribe, she thought. Bribes were a weak man's solution, and the Earl was not weak. Do as I tell you, he must have said, or not one penny more will I give you. Even so, best to be sure.

'I take it he threatened you that he'd stop giving you money?' she said.

'You take it correctly.'

'But if you leave me alone you'll still get it . . . so why all this fuss?'

'Because,' said Oliver, 'if that silly old bitch could have managed to have her heart attack a few days earlier I couldn't have threatened you. Kielder would never have known.'

'You would have thought of something else,' she said.

Incredibly, he smiled. 'I'd have tried,' he said.

There was no possibility of liking him, as she might have liked his father, but the smile at least helped her to understand him. He had lost everything, or rather he thought he had, and his one solace was to brood on that fact, and use it as the reason for hurting others. And yet he had not lost so very much when compared with O.B. Watson, and nothing at all when compared with the residents of Camp 19.

'I'll leave you to your practice,' he said, and limped doggedly to the door. Acting, she thought, and doing it very badly. She played a song that the maid Parker was fond of, and sang far too often – *Tiptoe Through the Tulips* – until Oliver slammed the door and she began on Bach instead, but not for long. Maddy phoned. She was in great distress because the Haydon Priors rumour machine had reached her at last, and told her that her best, indeed her only friend was leaving her. Natasha suggested lunch and a cinema in Newcastle, and dinner at the vicarage the next night, and Maddy grew calmer at once.

Next day Michael returned, alone and without fuss, no taxi. Instead he sat at the wheel of the car he had bought in Newcastle: an

American car, a Buick, like the one his father had driven in Australia. She came outside to admire it.

'It's very big,' she said.

'Comfortable seats,' said Michael. 'The Yanks like to be comfortable.'

'And very splendid.'

'Secondhand,' he said, 'but it works all right. Want to try it?'

'I would sooner go to bed with you.'

'That's why I bought it,' he said.

She smiled. 'I see,' she said. 'Our love-nest on wheels.'

'Too right,' he said. 'We can't use your bedroom, not with Oliver just down the passage.'

'We can use yours.' He tried to speak, but she covered his mouth with her hand. 'I like your car very much and I look forward to going for a drive with you, but a car is not the place to make love, not for us. We need a bed. Even a big car is too small.' She looked up into his face. He seemed troubled. 'You're not afraid?'

'Not for me, no,' he said. 'But suppose the others find out? Especially the Earl and Mrs Greenhalgh. They like us so much.'

'They will not be in the least surprised because they know us so well,' said Natasha 'As for the others, we are too clever for them.'

It was all very delightful, though sometimes she had to bite on the sheet to stop herself from yelling. Even so . . .

'It is good to see that you have missed me,' she said.

'How could I not?' He began to stroke her in the way she specially liked. A way that was soothing, relaxing, but with a promise of stimulation to come.

'Oliver has been tiresome,' she said, and his hand stopped. 'No, no. It is all taken care of.'

'You didn't hurt him again?'

'I told the Earl.' The stroking began again, and she sighed. 'It is all too complicated to explain in bed, but I *will* explain it, I promise you – if you will give me a little time.'

'Of course,' he said.

What a darling man he was. 'A little higher, please,' she said, and reached for him in his turn.

As she dressed to go down to Greenhalgh she said, 'There was one other thing. What was it? Oh yes. The Earl says I must stop stealing.'

'*What?*'

'Please don't shout,' said Natasha. 'I didn't shout. I chewed the sheet instead.'

'Kielder accused you of *stealing*?'

'Yes, he did,' said Natasha. 'But that is because I do steal.' She pulled on her dress, turned her back, and he fastened it for her. Deft as ever, she thought. Even when he is overcome with shock. She bent to kiss him in a way that was no help to serious discussion. 'You are angry with me?'

'How can I be?' he said. 'I've done a bit in that line myself.'

'You also are a thief?'

'Too right,' he said, 'and I stole rather more than caviar.' She waited, but it was time for her to go. 'Like you say, we'll keep it for later,' he said. 'But I'll tell you, I promise. You've got a right to know, after all.'

How delightful to have rights in such a man.

24

Mrs Greenhalgh must have watched the cook to some purpose, for asparagus and steaks alike were good, and when she and Maddy went to the drawing room there was Benedictine, as Maddy had hoped there would be. Natasha poured briskly for them both.

'When do you go?' Maddy said.

'To the Hall? I think tomorrow. With Michael.'

'So soon?' said Maddy.

'But it is only a few miles,' said Natasha. 'Not far at all.'

'There's no bus,' said Maddy. 'At least, there is – but the nearest bus stop is miles from the Hall.'

'Michael has bought a car,' Natasha told her.

So he is rich, thought Maddy. A Roman Catholic born out of wedlock – and rich. How lucky I was not to succumb, no matter how much money he has. After all, George isn't exactly poor. Nor am I.

Aloud she said, 'That big American car outside the house – that's Michael's?'

'Splendid, isn't it?' said Natasha. 'And so comfortable.'

The Earl is really going to allow him in, thought Maddy. Poor old Tyrrwhitt felt he'd had to allow him in because of the Earl, but the Earl himself invited him. It didn't make sense, but then the nobility rarely did. Best stick to what one knows.

'I have a piece of news for you,' she said, and Natasha did her best to look puzzled. 'Well, perhaps not news exactly,' Maddy said. 'There is to be no announcement as yet – but there will be.'

'Announcement of what?' said Natasha, willing her friend to get on with it. She wanted to talk about George's wounds before the men came in.

'George and I—' Maddy began, and still Natasha waited. 'We intend to become engaged.' Natasha jumped up and kissed her.

'There should be champagne.'

'No.' For once Maddy was firm. 'Not until the announcement.'

'But why not announce it now?'

'First George must tell his father, and then the Earl,' Maddy said. 'George likes to do things properly. So do I.'

'So you do,' said Natasha, 'but even so it is very exciting. 'Where will you live?'

'Not here,' said Maddy. 'At least not in this house – not while Oliver is here. He was once rather marked in his attentions to me. Perhaps you noticed?'

'So many gentlemen were,' Natasha said.

'Natasha!' Outrage rather than delight, but then she was about to become engaged.

'Remember London,' Natasha said.

Maddy said repressively, 'London was different.' Natasha produced cigarettes, offered one to her, and she took it.

'George does not mind?' Natasha asked.

'Not a bit,' said Maddy. 'He said—' She broke off.

'Oh, do tell me,' said Natasha. 'Please.'

And because she wanted to, because every male eligible or ineligible, wherever Natasha happened to be, became infatuated at once even if she had settled on Michael, Maddy told her.

'He said he loves me because I am pretty and charming, and therefore everything that I do becomes me.'

'George said that?'

'Yes, he did,' said Maddy. She was beginning to sound rather cross, which was not what Natasha had intended at all.

'But that is a wonderful thing to say,' said Natasha. 'Truly wonderful.'

Maddy looked warily at her friend, then decided she meant it. She smiled. 'Just because he's a lawyer doesn't mean he can't be romantic too.'

'No, indeed.' Natasha fitted her cigarette into the holder. 'But he wasn't always a lawyer. He was a soldier too. A hero who fought for his country.'

'I don't know about a hero,' said Maddy. 'But he was certainly wounded. Twice.'

Natasha waited, but that it seemed was it, and if I asked her *where* he was wounded she would as likely as not say Northern France. Not that she thought Maddy had seen the wounds. It was just that she needed to prepare the ground, if only Maddy would be more cooperative. Perhaps it would be better to coax Michael into taking George for a swim, or some game where they took a shower afterwards ... Then the gentlemen came in from their port and she remembered that she was still a little cross with the priest. All that fuss about her darling Greenhalgh.

'I completely forgot to ask you,' she said. 'Did you manage to tell the Earl not to go to Slagsby?' She knew perfectly well that he had not, but the question was as good an irritant as any.

'I had not intended a prohibition,' said Tyrrwhitt. 'How could I? To the head of the family? A suggestion, no more.'

'And did you – suggest?'

'I could not reach him,' said Tyrrwhitt. 'In London his valet seemed to think that he had gone to Brighton, no doubt for the races. I considered that unlikely.'

Not in the least unlikely, and not for the races either.

Oliver pulled out his pipe and tobacco pouch. 'Must we talk about the Earl all the time?' he said.

'No,' said his father. 'Nor must you smoke your pipe in here. There are ladies present.'

Oliver rammed his pipe and pouch back into his pockets, but managed not to snarl. His father's allowance was important to him.

'Perhaps you would care to give us some music, since this is our last opportunity?' said the priest. He did not seem to find the fact overwhelmingly sad, Natasha thought.

'Something jolly,' said George, who was looking at Maddy. Now if ever was the time to try out the erotic potential of Debussy, she thought, but it could not be. The Earl had not yet been consulted. Instead she gave them bits and pieces of Mendelssohn: his *Midsummer Night's Dream* music in a piano arrangement she had found: but not the *Wedding March* –that would be rushing things rather.

When she had done she turned to George. 'Was that jolly enough?' she asked.

'Oh yes,' he said, and looked once more at Maddy. 'By Jove, yes.'

'If you don't mind I think I'll turn in,' said Oliver, and left them.

Pique, Natasha wondered, or did the pain still linger? She hoped it was both.

Michael came up to her. 'What time would you like to go to the Hall tomorrow?' he asked.

'In time for lunch,' she said.

Over lunch the Earl and Michael talked of cattle, and the extraordinary variety of illnesses to which they were prone, but Natasha didn't mind because there were lobsters, and a Pouilly Fuissé as good as any at the Jacquards' house. Even so, in the drawing room afterwards (no brandy, but then she was staying for dinner, too) she brought the conversation round to music.

'Slagsby? Is that what you're after?' the Earl asked. 'You know, Daisy Greenhalgh told me the most extraordinary thing. Matthew actually intended to warn me off going there.'

'He had not intended a prohibition,' said Michael. 'A suggestion, no more.'

The Earl snorted. 'You're quoting, I take it?' Michael nodded, and the Earl snorted again.

'But you did go?' said Natasha.

'Certainly I went,' said the Earl. 'Got that young feller to play for me, what's more. We could have done with you as accompanist, my dear, though whether there's a piano in Slagsby that's in tune I very much doubt. Anyway, he was as good as ever.'

'Will he go to London?'

'Took a bit of coaxing, but that parson – Carrick – and his wife and I got round him at last.'

'He had to be coaxed?' said Natasha. 'To leave *Slagsby*?'

'Think about it,' said the Earl. 'It's all he knows. His home, his work, when he has any, his friends in the band – what he calls his marrers ... even Haydon Priors is foreign parts to him. London might as well be the moons of Jupiter. The poor chap's terrified.'

'And yet he's going?' said Michael.

'Oh yes,' said the Earl, 'because he's also in love, you see. With music. With that cornet of his. He's going all right – as soon as he's had a few elocution lessons.'

'*Elocution?*' It was Michael's turn to be bewildered.

'He may play the trumpet like Gabriel,' said the Earl, 'but he's got the thickest Tyneside accent I ever heard. 'Took *me* all my time to understand him and I grew up here. All the estate workers have it too, but not as strong as his.'

'But where will he get elocution lessons in Slagsby?' said Natasha.

'Carrick and his wife,' said Lord Kielder. 'I'm paying them, of course. By the look of them they need the money, but they'd never take charity.'

Natasha went to him and kissed his cheek. 'Oh, I do like you,' she said, then risked a look at Michael. It seemed he still liked the Earl, too.

'It's time to talk about Debussy,' said Natasha.

'Whatever you say,' said the Earl, and Natasha told him about *La Jeune Fille aux Cheveux de Lin*.

'Don't know if I've ever heard it,' he said. 'You'd better come and play it for me.'

He took them to the music room, where there was a Steinway, a much better piano than the late Mrs Tyrrwhitt's.

'I see what Matthew's getting at,' the Earl said when she had done, 'but it *is* about a pretty girl, after all – and if Michael can stay calm I don't see why Matthew shouldn't. You go on playing it. Not that you need my permission. You said you'd ask me to upset him, no doubt.'

'Because he forbade me,' she said.

The Earl looked at Michael.

'Yes, he did,' Michael said. 'It wasn't very – nice.' He used that last word with an air of triumph: so very English.

'Poor Matthew,' the Earl said. 'The trouble is he means well. They'll probably carve that on his tombstone.' He turned to Natasha. 'What will you do before dinner, child?'

'Rest,' said Natasha. 'It is something the doctor says I must do from time to time.'

'After Camp 19 I should think anybody would,' said the Earl.

He and Michael went riding. The Earl had jodhpurs and boots that fitted him, and together they set out to look at his cattle. He talks about them as if they belonged in a medical ward, thought Walsh, but for the most part they looked well enough. Aberdeen Angus nearly all of them, and a little too sensitive for the Queensland outback, but doing well on the lush grass that was theirs for the taking. They didn't even have to look.

'Your horse all right?' Lord Kielder asked.

'Fine.'

'A bit fresh, I thought.'

'He needs the exercise,' said Walsh. 'Come to that, so do I.'

'Let's gallop a while,' the Earl suggested. 'There are even a few jumps if you don't mind stone walls.'

Someone had given them adjoining bedrooms with a bathroom in between, and she had no doubt that the Earl knew all about it. He would know all about everything that happened in his house. On the other hand he would also know that she was no more capable of having a baby than Michael was. Greenhalgh would have told him.

It was a pretty room, she thought. Yellow with a whisper of pink and furniture of white and gold. And one picture on the wall – a little portrait of a lady by Zoffany. No doubt an ancestor of his, she thought. Pretty, too. Soon she would have to talk to him about this stealing business . . .

Greenhalgh woke her firmly, but without fuss, and she went to her bath. No vast, unflattering robe was needed here to shield her from Oliver's lustful gaze. She wondered if she would miss it.

'You got out the blue?' she said, as Greenhalgh patted her dry.

'Of course, miss. And the sapphires.'

'But how did you get here?' Natasha asked. 'Michael could have come for you, since you didn't want to ride with us.'

'That was on account of the vicar,' said Greenhalgh. 'He wouldn't hold with you and me in the same car, not with Mr Walsh driving.'

And yet the Earl is right, thought Natasha. The priest does mean well. Quite often, anyway.

'But how did you get here?' she said again. 'I'm told the bus stop's miles away.'

Greenhalgh looked shifty. 'Lord Kielder sent his car for me,' she said at last.

'Oh Greenhalgh,' Natasha said, 'you did arrive in style!'

Not even jealous, thought Greenhalgh. Not even miffed because she arrived in a Buick and I came here in a Rolls-Royce. A woman in a million.

When she had finished dressing her Greenhalgh said, 'The best dress you bought, miss. You do look a treat.'

Natasha examined what she saw in the mirror. 'I do, don't I?' she said.

And even that wasn't swank, Greenhalgh acknowledged. Just the acceptance of a pleasant if rather obvious fact.

The Earl was enchanted. 'I knew you'd look good in blue,' he said, 'and by God you look perfect. Not always an easy colour for a brunette, but on you – superb. Wouldn't you say so, Michael?'

'I would indeed,' said Walsh.

'We're the luckiest chaps in Northumberland,' said the Earl, 'but at least we both know it.'

Natasha took a cigarette from her case and he lit it for her. 'Had a bit of a shock this afternoon,' he said, but he was smiling. 'This kinsman of ours is the best horseman I've ever seen.'

'That is because he is a cowboy,' said Natasha.

'Stockman anyway,' said Walsh. 'You don't get much work done if you fall off.'

'I took him to the stables,' said the Earl, who had little time for modesty, 'and showed him what was on offer. He settled on a roan called Rattler, which just about sums him up. He rattles anybody who gives in to him, and my head groom tried to tell him so.'

'The trouble is I only understood about one word in five,' said Walsh.

'Just as well you didn't meet the cornet player,' said the Earl. 'Anyway, it wasn't Michael who needed the warnings: it was Rattler.'

Natasha was delighted. 'Did he try to throw you?' she asked Walsh.

'Tried? I suppose so. Only he wasn't very good at it.' The Earl snorted. 'Well, not compared with the brumbies back home.'

'What are the brumbies?' the Earl asked. 'Sounds like a disease.'

'Sorry,' said 'Walsh. 'They're wild horses. Sometimes Chalky and I muster a few good ones – Chalky's my foreman – and break them in. Now they really *can* be difficult. Rattler wouldn't last two rounds with one of them.'

Natasha relaxed in her chair. She was utterly content. Cribb had already poured champagne and her two favourite men in the world were competing for her smiles. Then Cribb came in again.

'The telephone, my lord,' he announced.

'But it's nearly dinner-time,' the Earl objected. Even so he followed his butler out.

'Were you in danger?' Natasha asked.

'Not from Rattler,' said Walsh. 'He tried it on because he's that sort of horse, but when he found I could cope he just got on with his job.' He waved his hand and Rattler was dismissed. 'You look beautiful tonight, even by your standards. The best I've ever seen you.'

'I thought you liked me best in nothing at all,' she said.

'Who wouldn't?' said Walsh.

'You shall like me best later on,' she promised, and then the Earl came back. He seemed sunk in gloom.

'The most damnable thing,' he said. 'Just as we were enjoying ourselves. We'll be two more for dinner.'

'Persons I know?' Natasha asked.

'I shouldn't think so.' The Earl sounded mildly shocked. 'Charles Tring's an MP – Labour, as it happens, and the other one's his wife. She's my late wife's sister, which is why I have to feed them. They were on their way to Durham University to harangue undergraduates about nationalisation and all that, only their car broke down and they're in the Slagsby pub. I've sent my car to fetch them. It'll be a damn late dinner. They'll stay the night, too, I shouldn't wonder.'

'At least they'll learn about the starving masses,' said Natasha.

'By Jove, yes,' said the Earl. The thought seemed to cheer him enormously.

'This Tring – is he poor?' Natasha asked.

'Shouldn't think so,' said the Earl. 'Winchester and New College. All that. Besides, my wife's family weren't awfully keen on allying their daughters with the poor, no matter how deserving.'

'Charles Tring . . .' said Walsh. 'I read about him in the *Morning Post* the other day. He's just back from a visit to Russia. He and his wife.'

'Oh *lord*,' said the Earl, and the gloom returned, then he brightened again. 'At least they'll leave early tomorrow. The

263

lecture's to take place directly after lunch.' He turned to Natasha. 'I've been meaning to ask you – are you anything of a horsewoman? Because you're going to have to learn if you want to keep up with this feller.' He nodded at Walsh.

'Not hunting foxes,' Natasha said firmly. 'For that I am told there are rules, and I am very bad at rules, but I can sit on a horse without falling off. Only I have no riding – what is the word?'

'Kit. My wife's may fit you,' said the Earl. 'We'll ask Daisy Greenhalgh – that is, if you can manage side-saddle?'

'It's the only way I *can* manage,' said Natasha. For some reason this pleased him.

'We'll ride tomorrow,' he said, 'after those Trings go off on their nationalising spree – if you'd like to, that is?'

'Of course,' said Natasha.

'Suits me,' said Walsh. 'Are we going anywhere in particular?'

'I haven't quite decided,' said the Earl, 'but I think we're going to do something rather malicious – though thoroughly well-deserved.'

25

They were finishing the last of the champagne when Cribb came in to announce Mr and Mrs Tring.

'Our revels now are ended,' murmured the Earl, and went forward to greet them. 'Lucinda, my dear,' he said to the tall thin woman confronting him, and kissed her cheek. It was obvious at once that he and his late wife's sister detested each other.

'And Charles too. Which was it – careless driving? Reckless? Dangerous?' His late wife's brother-in-law it appeared was rather more acceptable.

'Surprised you know about such things,' said Tring.

'Have to,' said his host. 'I'm a magistrate. I fine motorists twice a week.'

'You won't fine me,' Tring told him. 'Something called the big end went. Damn nuisance. Decent of you to put us up.'

'We'll find you an attic somewhere,' Lord Kielder promised him, and Walsh wondered if he meant it. Perhaps it depended on their behaviour at dinner?

'—meet some young relatives of mine,' the Earl was saying. 'Natasha Tyrrwhitt – Clemency's niece, you know. She's popped over from Paris for a while, and this is Michael Walsh. He's from Australia – Queensland. All the same he qualifies as a Tyrrwhitt. What is it you said the Queenslanders were called, Michael?'

'Banana-benders,' said Michael. 'How do you do?'

'How do you do?' said Lucinda Tring. 'What a *very* odd thing to call you.'

'How do you do?' said Natasha.

Lucinda Tring nodded, and said, 'Extremely odd.'

She at least might be for the attics, if not the dungeons, Walsh thought. Aloud he said, 'The other Aussies think we're eccentric, even by Australian standards. The general idea is that before we arrived the Queensland bananas were straight.'

'But that's impossible, surely?' said Lucinda Tring, and the Earl looked happy again.

Dinner was not easy. Lucinda Tring had little taste for wit, and the

Earl had taste for little else at his dinner table. Then there was
Natasha to be explained . . . Michael was easy. He had told her that
Australia was filled with offspring of the best families, sent there
because of unfortunate mishaps with cheque books, or parlourmaids,
or footmen. Michael's father had been one such, after all, except that
his mishaps had been with racehorses. But she – Natasha – the
Countess Natalya Krilova – almost *chère amie* of Léonide Jacquard –
how could anyone explain her? Especially to a clever if literal-minded
lady who obviously considered Russia to be the solution to the
world's problems . . .

Then there is my dress, Natasha thought. She *hates* my dress. I
bought it at Fortnum & Mason and it was made in Paris and she hates
it, because it is frivolous. She wears a day dress and I will overlook
that because she has had no chance to change – but such a dress. Grey
and the hem all wrong and the bodice far too high even for daytime –
and such shoes, such stockings. She is a Serious Person, thought
Natasha, and clothes were not to be taken seriously. Not by her;
which goes to prove that she is not quite so clever as she thinks she is.
Moreover, she does not like the way Cribb keeps filling up my wine
glass.

Michael opened the door of the dining room, and they left the men
to their port. She can't wait, thought Natasha, but she's going to have
to, because Cribb was there with a brandy decanter and glasses.

'Would you like me to pour, Miss Natasha?' he asked.

She smiled at him, because Cribb was very decent about pouring,
but even so said, 'No thank you, Cribb. We'll help ourselves.'

If I don't give her a chance to disapprove soon, she'll burst, she
thought, and went to the decanter.

'Shall I pour one for you?' she asked.

'I thank you no,' said Lucinda Tring, but Natasha took the stopper
out anyway. 'Do I take it that you intend to drink that—'

'Cognac,' said Natasha. 'It is very good cognac.' She poured
generously.

'Is it the custom for ladies in Paris to drink spirits after dinner?'

'The custom?' Natasha considered the question. 'No. That would
not be true. But to certain ladies it is permitted.'

'And you are one of those ladies?'

'Well yes,' said Natasha, 'though I must remind you that we are not
in Paris. We are in Lord Kielder's house, and he also permits me to
drink spirits after dinner.'

To help Lucinda Tring's disapproval she took out her cigarettes
and holder.

Lucinda Tring wished very much to rebuke so young a person for daring to lecture her on matters of protocol, but found it to be impossible. The young person was on unassailable ground.

'It is his business after all,' she conceded at last, then: 'Do you miss the Soviet Union, Miss Tyrrwhitt?'

Natasha began to shrug, then stopped herself in time. After all, Lucinda Tring had behaved well about the cognac. She sipped a little of it instead.

'No,' she said at last. 'Not at all.'

'But surely,' Lucinda Tring said, 'it was your homeland.'

'My homeland was St Petersburg,' Natasha said. 'It does not exist any more.'

'What's in a name?' said Lucinda Tring.

A busy night for Shakespeare, thought Natasha, but what *is* in a name, after all? Natalya Krilova, Natasha Tyrrwhitt ... perhaps Natasha Walsh before long.

'Very true,' she said, 'but I found I preferred Paris.'

'No doubt it was your background,' said Lucinda Tring. 'Brought up as you were, a member of a – forgive me – far too privileged nobility, you find it difficult to understand what the Communist Revolution has done for your country.'

'I find it impossible,' said Natasha.

'Of course.' The Tring person even sounded pleased. 'Coming as you do from a background of wealth and privilege, where every social demand was subordinate to the wishes of your class—'

'Like you, in fact,' said Natasha.

Lucinda Tring stopped. It was as if she had stepped on the end of a rake hidden in long grass, and the handle had shot up and hit her in the eye.

'I hardly think the two of us are analogous,' she said.

'The daughter of a baron, so milord tells me, married to one of those who rule your country. Your car breaks down and another is provided at once, and dinner, and a palace in which to sleep.' But please let it be the attics. 'No danger of your spending a night with the proletariat of Slagsby. No meal at a terrible inn: no bed with bugs.' Lucinda Tring winced. 'And tomorrow you will spend your day with students—'

'Undergraduates,' said Lucinda Tring. 'Students' sounded disreputable.

'—and you will tell each other how disgraceful the world is. But they will still be bourgeois, just as you will remain an aristo.'

Gently Lucinda Tring said, 'But we wish to change all that.'

'Would you be kind enough to explain that to me?' said Natasha.

'Of course,' the other woman said, and out it all came. The greatest good of the greatest number, the nationalisation of the means of production, distribution and exchange, the inevitability of history, the classless society. She had learned it all quite well, Natasha thought, but Léonide said it with more fire. Perhaps it was because she said it in French . . .

'This nationalisation business,' she said at last.

'Yes?' said Lucinda Tring.

'In Russia we already had a means of production, distribution and exchange.'

'Yes, of course,' said Lucinda Tring. 'Every country has. But Comrade Lenin wished to replace it with a system that is far more just, more fair.'

'But not to the shareholders.'

'Of course not. They exploit the masses.'

'Your husband looks like a shareholder,' said Natasha. 'When you have *your* revolution, what will happen to him? To you, for that matter?'

'We will be compensated of course,' said Lucinda Tring, 'but we will no longer have the means to subject others to economic humiliation.'

'And will you live in the same house you live in now?'

Lucinda Tring looked bewildered. 'I expect so,' she said.

'Because your husband is a kind of commissar?'

Lucinda Tring brightened. 'Oh, I begin to understand you,' she said. 'You have been out of the Soviet Union for so long you think nothing has changed since the Tsar's time, but my dear you are quite wrong, believe me. We are just back from there and we saw for ourselves.'

'What did you see?'

'The most marvellous houses for the workers, wonderful hospitals, factories and collective farms far, far more efficient than anything we have here.'

'Did you see any former shareholders?' Natasha asked.

Lucinda Tring looked startled. 'I don't think so,' she said.

'Of course not,' said Natasha. 'They are all dead, or else in Siberia, wishing they were.'

'You really believe that nonsense?' said Lucinda Tring.

'Socialism is a new beginning,' said Natasha. 'The old régime must be done away with. Isn't that what you believe?'

'Yes, but—'

'And there must be no place for bourgeois sentimentality. We have a new world to build. The old world must go. The old values. The old bourgeois. We cannot tolerate them, comrades, because so long as they exist they are a threat to the wonderful new world we are about to create. It is sad, but they must go. There is no other way. No bourgeois sentimentality, comrades. Not for us.'

Lucinda Tring stared at her, horrified. 'Where did you learn such things?' she said.

'The Re-education and Rehabilitation Centre,' said Natasha.

'The what?'

'The place where delinquent children are sent.'

Lucinda Tring looked more horrified than ever. 'You were that? A delinquent child?'

'Certainly,' said Natasha. 'There was a whole band of us. The oldest was fifteen. We robbed people.'

'You are trying to make fun of me,' said Lucinda Tring.

'What would be the point? I was twelve years old and considered pretty, so that I became one of the teasers, the ones who lured some disgusting man into an alley so that the boys could beat him unconscious with clubs and we could take whatever he had.'

'You mean this, don't you?' said Lucinda Tring. Natasha nodded. 'But where did you live? Where did you sleep?'

'In 1918 in St Petersburg one lived where one could. It was usually the gutter.'

'But was there nowhere you could go?'

'The Rehabilitation Centre,' said Natasha. 'We preferred the gutter, but the Centre got most of us anyway.'

'Your parents—'

'I know my mother was murdered,' said Natasha, 'because I saw it happen. My father was sent to Siberia. If he is still alive it would be a greater miracle than the loaves and fishes.' She smiled, then added, 'No bourgeois sentimentality, comrades. Not for us.'

Lucinda Tring winced. Best to end the subject there, talk of clothes or perhaps the ballet, but the older woman couldn't. To her it was all rather like a hollow tooth: you probed it with your tongue even though you knew it would hurt.

'At this Centre,' she said, 'what did they do?'

'They taught us Marxism-Leninism,' said Natasha, 'and beat us when we got it wrong.'

'*Beat you?*'

'We Russians have always been good at beating one another,' Natasha told her. 'The comrade instructors were especially good. It was what they were chosen for, after all.'

'Comrades?' said Lucinda Tring. 'Men?'

'Women too.'

'How utterly ghastly,' said Lucinda Tring.

'So it was,' said Natasha. 'Not quite so bad as the hospital, or perhaps Camp 19. But ghastly would describe it.'

'Are you saying that you know for a fact there are such places?' said Lucinda Tring, and thought: If only the girl would stop looking at me as if I were some sort of mythical beast. A unicorn, perhaps, or a rather ineffective dragon.

'I know all there is to know about Camp 19,' said Natasha, and rose to her feet. 'I can show you the marks if you like.'

Lucinda Tring glanced at the door, and hated herself for doing so. This was not the time for a display of prudishness.

'No, no,' she said. 'I will take your word for it. But surely Comrade Lenin and Comrade Stalin were unaware of this?'

'How could they be?' said Natasha. 'They made the laws that sent me there.'

Then the men came in, and Lucinda Tring did her best to hide her relief.

'How serious you both look,' Charles Tring said.

'We spoke about Russia,' said Natasha. 'I am afraid I bored your wife, rather.'

'Not at all,' said Lucinda Tring, and her husband accepted a cigar from the Earl and began to talk about the Bolshoi Ballet, and how good it was.

'Did you never go, Miss Tyrrwhitt?' he asked.

'Do you know, I have never been to Moscow,' said Natasha. 'The ballet in St Petersburg, certainly. And now of course there is Diaghilev in Paris or London. How fortunate that, like me, he and his dancers got out in time.'

Lucinda Tring thought that she might be starting a headache.

'You gave her a real leathering, by the sound of it,' said Michael.

'I should have used a knout,' said Natasha.

They lay together on her bed, for the moment calm, and content to touch and gossip and be happy. It had not begun like that. Dear Michael had been impatient to possess her, as was right and proper, the moment the dinner party broke up, but she had made him wait until Greenhalgh could be summoned to undress her.

'Can't you do it yourself for once?' he'd asked her.

'Certainly not!' The outrage in her voice was in itself a warning, but he had persisted.

'Me, then?' That was better, but nobody could brush her hair like Greenhalgh. The wait had been good for his ardour after all.

'These useful fools,' she said. 'They are all the same no matter where they come from.' Her voice became a savage imitation of Mrs

Tring's. 'My dear, there cannot possibly be any Camps in the Soviet Union. Comrade Stalin assured me himself.'

Walsh looked startled. It had been a surprisingly accurate imitation. The tribute pleased her and she stroked his face.

'It is only a trick I learned,' she said. 'I told you. But it's a good trick.'

'In Camp 19?' She nodded. 'And now you're here.' He held her gently still. 'I wonder if the Earl really put his in-laws in an attic?'

'Not an attic,' she said, 'but it is not a very nice room. Not like this.'

'How do you know?' he asked her.

'Greenhalgh told me. Shall I do something amusing to you now?'

All in all it had been a busy night: frantically busy, and when he'd left her he'd fallen asleep at once, and promptly began to dream of brother Edgar, which was no help at all.

He breakfasted with the Earl, tranquil once more now that his in-laws had gone. 'Saw 'em off myself,' he said, as if by that act of foresight alone he had prevented them from sneaking back in.

'Do you see them often?' Walsh asked him.

'Good lord, no! Charles is all right in his way, but he talks politics all the time.'

'He's a politician,' said Walsh. 'He's supposed to.'

'Not to me,' said the Earl. 'And anyway, Lucinda's not a politician and she talks even more politics than he does. I expect she harangued poor Natasha all the time we drank port.'

Walsh said carefully, 'If she did, I expect she got every bit as good as she gave. If not better.'

The Earl looked at him then, a look of approval. It was just as Dad had told him. The Earl knew perfectly well that he and Natasha slept together. Approved of it too. If he hadn't he wouldn't be sitting down to breakfast with him – but no one must say so. Not straight out. On the other hand there were extra points for the hint he'd just given.

'Do you know I think you could be right,' Lord Kielder said. 'She wasn't exactly brimful of comradely love when Natasha's name came up earlier. Ten o'clock suit you?'

'I beg your pardon?'

'Our ride,' the Earl reminded him. 'Daisy Greenhalgh is helping Natasha into her habit now. I thought we'd hack as far as Haydon Priors. See how Matthew's coping without you both.'

See how Oliver reacts to me on a horse, thought Walsh. Something malicious is right. Something deserved too, if Rattler and I are up to it.

271

'If you'll excuse me, sir,' he said, 'I think I'll go over to the stables and see what sort of a mood Rattler's in.'

'Of course,' said the Earl, 'but don't tire him too much. I want a bit of frisk left in him when we get to Matthew's.'

He was in the drawing room reading *The Times* when the door opened and thirty years fell away. A woman in a bottle-green riding habit and a topper with a veil came in; the habit cut tight to her figure, the long skirt draped over one arm, a little silver-mounted whip in her free hand.

'Oh my God,' said Kielder.

'Do I look so bad?' But Natasha was smiling: she knew she did not.

'Minx,' said the Earl. 'You look enchanting and you know it.' Another source of pain for Oliver, he thought, and serve him jolly well right.

'Your wife must have been quite small like me,' Natasha said. 'Not tall, like Mrs Tring.'

'My wife was like you in many ways,' said the Earl. 'Lucinda isn't like you at all. Did you biff her last night?'

'Biff?'

'Wallop her – verbally, that's to say.'

'She tried to tell me about how Socialism works, but I know much more about it than she does.'

'Ah,' said Kielder. 'That would explain it.' She waited. 'Lucinda is not stupid, you know.'

'By no means.'

The Earl looked at her closely, but there was no sign of irony.

'It is just that she has invested all her emotional capital in her political beliefs, as you might say. A hundred years ago she would have turned to religion – Methodism, as likely as not – but now she follows blindly where Stalin leads. She would have been much better off with Charles Wesley. She said she tried to explain the Communist philosophy to you.'

'Did she?' said Natasha. 'Perhaps so, but she did it very badly. I helped her get it right.'

'According to her you expressed the obstructive and reactionary views typical of a person of your class and background.'

Suddenly Natasha was furious. 'Person?' she said, her voice a scream. 'I wore that blue dress and the sapphires and she called me a *person*?'

The Earl said gently, 'Lucinda isn't like you at all. I just told you that. And you did rather smash up her toys.'

'Please explain,' said Natasha.

'All those lovely hospitals and factories and collective farms,' said the Earl, 'and you told her they were only there to deceive innocents like her.'

'Useful fools,' said Natasha.

'And then you went on to tell her that things which couldn't possibly exist, *did* exist.'

'The Rehabilitation Centre, the Prison Hospital, Camp 19.'

'Precisely,' said the Earl. 'You even told her that Comrade Stalin knew about them because he made the laws that sent you there.'

She shrugged. Even in the riding habit it was noteworthy, thought the Earl.

'It's the truth,' she said.

'For Lucinda, there is only one truth,' said the Earl. 'The Party and its ultimate triumph. The Dictatorship of the Proletariat.'

'After what I told her? She must be mad,' said Natasha.

Careful now, the Earl told himself. Remember she's got a whip in her hand.

'Let me tell you what she – *implied*,' he said. 'But before I do I want to make it clear that I don't believe a word of it. Do you accept that?'

'Of course,' she said.

'Well then. Lucinda knows that she is right: that Marxism-Leninism will be forever perfect, but she also acknowledges that you, in all sincerity, believe yourself to be right.'

'Such foolishness,' said Natasha. 'Black can not be white.'

'Please listen, Natasha,' he said. 'You believe. She *knows*. Since you truly believe what is manifestly untrue, there can be only one explanation.'

'She said I was mad,' said Natasha, and started yelling again. The Earl thanked God for the sake of his staff that it was in Russian. His memories of the language were fading, but he remembered enough to marvel at the breadth and power of her vocabulary. How could she have learned such words in a palace? But of course she hadn't. These were the words of the Centre, the Hospital, Camp 19 . . .

Natasha stopped at last, more because she had run out of breath than of things to say. Unshed tears made her eyes glitter, and the face that looked at him was hostile, furious.

'I said I didn't believe a word of it,' he said. The fury and hostility faded.

'I am sorry, milord,' she said, and he knew he was forgiven. She called him milord when she wanted to be specially nice to him. 'But surely anyone would be angry to have suffered what I have suffered, only to be told it was all in my imagination, because I was mad. Did she say I should see a doctor?'

'One of these new psychiatrist Johnnies,' said the Earl. 'I told her that you were as sane as I was. From the look on her face she didn't look as if she thought that to be much of a recommendation.'

Natasha giggled, then went to him and kissed his cheek.

'How nice it is to be here without her,' she said. 'Come and show me the horses.'

'Let's just settle this stealing nonsense first,' said the Earl.

26

The riding expedition set off at last. Walsh felt over-dressed for the part – his breeches came from Savile Row, his boots were hand-made – but consoled himself with the thought that he had to dress like that to keep up with the Earl. Natasha looked enchanting. Lord Kielder had supplied her with Sweet Friend, a bay mare, part Arab, who was playful at first but responsive enough when she found that Natasha knew her business. The two of them together looked like a portrait from the previous century, thought the Earl, or at least before the big guns fired their opening salvo in 1914.

They walked and trotted to Haydon Priors, the two gentlemen on either side of the lady, the Earl relaxed, Walsh fretting because Sweet Friend was playful for quite a while, and rather stronger than she looked. At last Natasha settled the matter by putting the mare at a drystone wall. Walsh looked on with his heart in his mouth, but she took it flying, as the Earl had known she would. It was after the jump that Sweet Friend decided to live up to her name.

They were a very small cavalcade, but even so it seemed that every available inhabitant of Haydon Priors turned out to watch. It was very good value after all: first Lord Kielder himself, mounted on his grey, Diplomat, that had come second in the Cheltenham Gold Cup years ago: then his relative who was enormously rich and owned a million acres in Australia; and best of all his other relative the Russian aristocrat, who might yet turn out to be a spy. And just look at that fancy riding habit she was wearing . . .

Oliver knew it wasn't his day. To begin with he'd been sitting in a deck chair in the garden, so that not only could he see them coming but they could see him. He had no chance at all to go away and hide. Nothing for it but to look at them: the Earl still with the same Hanging Judge face he'd shown at the Hall, Natasha luscious as a plum in that devastating habit, and that damned Australian riding Rattler, who was obviously stuffed with oats and full of frisk, and yet Walsh was handling him as if he was the quietest nag in an old lady's stable. The three reined up by the garden fence and looked down on him. In every possible way, thought Oliver.

'Morning, Oliver,' said the Earl. 'We felt like a ride so we thought we'd pop over and see how you're doing.'

Bloody liar, thought Oliver, but he's the one with the money.

Natasha asked solicitously, 'How is your thigh muscle?'

That hurt all right, because suddenly Oliver was certain that the other two not only knew that it wasn't a thigh muscle, but that Natasha had done it. He kept his eyes on Walsh, but the Australian looked no more than sympathetic, mildly concerned.

But then his father appeared, wary as always of Natasha and Walsh, but full of hospitable bustle as he scurried to Kielder.

'Well, Matthew,' said the Earl. 'What do you think of our kinswoman?'

Tyrrwhitt risked one quick look. That habit was cut very tightly indeed. 'Charming,' he said. 'May I offer you refreshment?'

Behind him, the housemaid Molly Parker appeared, and began to polish the door's already gleaming brass. She, too, it seemed was determined to see the show.

'No, no,' said the Earl. 'Mustn't keep you. Just thought we might put Rattler through his paces for you. We could use that meadow behind the vicarage.'

'Please do,' said the vicar. 'Come along, Oliver.'

'It's a bit far,' said Oliver. 'My leg—'

'Nonsense,' said his father. 'The merest stroll. It will do you good.'

Oliver got to his feet. After all, his father was the one with the rest of the money.

What followed was Purgatory. Walsh handled the horse not with contempt exactly, but as if Rattler were a run-of-the-mill sort of animal who could, with a bit of coaxing, be persuaded to turn in an above-average performance now and again. Walk, trot, canter, gallop – whichever it was Rattler did exactly as he was bidden. And then, when Oliver felt that he could take no more, Natasha suddenly yelled aloud, clapped a heel into Sweet Friend, and took off after Walsh.

'What a very wild young lady she is,' said the vicar.

'Russian,' said the Earl, and thought, So were the words she shouted. Just as well that neither Oliver nor his father could understand them. 'Wait for me, my darling,' was what she'd said.

The mare shot to where Walsh was waiting, and together they improvised a sort of musical ride, like an equestrian dance or even flirtation, thought the Earl, as they ended the performance by leaping the meadow's hedge side by side.

'How well they perform together,' said Tyrrwhitt, and the Earl nodded gravely, then looked at Oliver.

Still wearing that Hanging Judge look, Oliver noticed.

When Walsh and Natasha trotted back they found that Maddy too had joined the party.

'I couldn't help seeing,' she was saying, then turned to Natasha. 'Darling, you look lovely.'

'Never mind that,' Natasha said, for her friend was looking *so* happy, even if there was still no ring. 'Lift me down please, Michael,' she said. 'Lift me down at once.'

Walsh dismounted. 'Be a pleasure,' he said, and of course it bloody well would, thought Oliver, to get his hands on that, and not for the first time either. But Natasha made a bee-line for Maddy, and they moved away whispering.

Walsh held the reins of Rattler and Sweet Friend as if they were no more of a problem than a couple of ageing pug dogs, thought Oliver, and he's strong, too. Look at the way he handled her. All the same I've got to talk to him. Can't let Dad see me cut him. His father and the Earl were talking cricket and that's another game I can't play any more. I can't bloody run.

To Walsh he said, 'I used to ride that horse of yours.'

'So Kielder told me,' said Walsh.

So he's Kielder now, is he? thought Oliver. Feet well under the table.

'But he isn't mine,' said Walsh. 'You can have him any time you want.'

'You don't like him?'

'Like him?' Walsh sounded surprised. 'He's all right, I suppose, but I'd prefer something a bit more lively.'

And he means it, thought Oliver. The bastard bloody means it.

'I think Rattler's the liveliest one the Earl's got,' he said.

'I reckon he is,' said Walsh. 'Maybe I'll take a look around and buy something better.'

A low blow, he thought. A very low blow, and on two counts: Number One, kinsman Oliver couldn't handle anything better than Rattler, and Number Two, even if he could, he's broke.

Lunch was bread and cheese, and red wine for her, and for the men, beer; but the cheese was excellent (not least, she thought, because the French are sure no Englishman can make cheese), and the beer of a quality, so Michael told her later, he had not believed possible.

As they ate she said, 'I think you should invite Maddy to dinner, milord.'

'That pretty friend of yours? Excellent idea,' said the Earl.

277

Natasha almost purred. 'Pretty' was exactly what she wanted. 'George too,' she said.

'George?' The Earl's bewilderment for once was genuine.

'Your kinsman,' said Walsh helpfully. 'The vicar's younger son.'

'Oh, *that* George,' said the Earl. 'You think I should? Ask him to dine?'

Pretty widows it seemed were one thing, the second sons of parsons quite another, no matter how closely related.

'But of course,' said Natasha. 'They are about to become engaged.'

The Earl brooded on this. 'Then he's a very lucky feller,' he said at last, 'but why doesn't he just get on with it?'

'Because first he must tell his father,' Natasha said patiently, 'which he will do this evening, and afterwards he must tell you.'

'Head of the family stuff?' Natasha nodded. 'I'll give my permission. You two have my permission already.'

For the first time since he had known her, Natasha blushed.

'Good on yer,' said Walsh.

'I beg your pardon?'

'Idiomatic expression,' Walsh explained. 'Sort of "Jolly well done".'

The Earl relaxed. 'Nothing well done about it,' he said. 'If ever two people ought to be married to each other it's you two.'

'You're sure?' said Natasha. 'After the talk we had?'

The Earl went up to her and kissed her. 'Of course I'm sure,' he said. 'Somebody's going to have to keep you in order, and I rather thing Michael's the one to do it.' He left them.

'But you haven't proposed,' said Natasha.

'Five times,' said Walsh.

'In bed yes,' she said. 'But this is serious.'

He took her hand. 'Darling Natasha,' he said, 'will you marry me?'

The blush stayed in place. She looked bewildered and enchanting.

'Yes, of course,' she said, 'but remember – you asked first.' She brooded for a moment. 'You heard me say we had a talk? It was about my stealing.'

'You want to tell me about it?'

She motioned him to sit. A table and chairs by Hepplewhite, he thought, she in a habit once worn by a countess, old ale and *Beaujolais Villages*, and my bride to be is about to explain why she's a thief.

She did so as if she were reading from a statement to a court. No hesitancies, no evasions. Out it all came. The stores in Newcastle, Harrod's, the *mont de piété* in York.

'Caviar?' he said.

'Twice,' said Natasha. 'It is so expensive here. Quite disgraceful.'

'But how did the Earl find out?'

'At Harrod's he knows some of the directors. They told him, and he paid. Fortnum's too. Harrod's warned them about me, you see. It made me feel quite dreadful.'

'It isn't so bad,' Walsh comforted her.

'No, no, of course it isn't,' she said, 'but I thought I was being so clever, and all the time they *knew*. They knew from the very beginning but they kept quiet because I am the relative of an aristo.'

Walsh willed himself to look serious. 'And the Newcastle stores?'

'I told him,' she said. 'He made me. Tomorrow he will go to see the owner and pay him and explain that I am – unwell. It is so *awful*.'

'Kleptomania?' She nodded. 'But if he says you are unwell—'

'No, no,' said Natasha. 'The shop man will believe him, of course, because he is an Earl. It is just that milord will have to take him out to lunch.'

The shop man, thought Walsh. Quite possibly a millionaire.

'I know you said it doesn't matter,' she fretted, 'but does it?'

'Not if you've stopped.'

'Of course I've stopped,' she said. 'I have you now. Far more exciting than stealing.'

'And anyway,' said Walsh, 'I've stolen far more than you.'

'You have?'

'Fifty thousand pounds,' he said.

She called out in Russian, then kissed him. 'I am marrying a bandit!' she said.

He told her about it, and when he had finished she was no longer awestruck, and he knew it. He knew her so well by now.

'Didn't I steal enough for you?' he asked.

'I'm not sure you stole at all,' she said. 'Not properly. After all, it was your money.'

'Try telling Edgar that,' said Walsh.

She wore the red dress, the Vionnet, at dinner that night, because after all Michael deserved a treat, too. (She had thought very carefully about whether he was a thief or not, and in the end decided that he was. His father had meant the money to go to him, but his brother could still have him sent to prison, and that was what counted.) And anyway, the Earl liked the red dress too, so that everyone was happy, and none of the Earl's relatives by marriage came to call, which made them happier still.

It was wrong of course, thought Natasha. They had behaved disgracefully at the vicarage and in time God would punish them,

279

even though Oliver had behaved much more disgracefully: but until then they would enjoy themselves. Good food, good wine, and when the port arrived she left them to it quite happily. In the music room there was brandy as well as the Steinway, and they never left her alone for very long.

'Cricket match next week,' Lord Kielder said. 'Annual blood-letting. Haydon Priors versus Slagsby and District. The District's mostly Wentworth's pits. Matthew tells me you play?'

'I did at the uni, sir. The University.'

'What did you do?'

'Batted four or five. Bowled a bit. Medium pace.'

'For Melbourne University?' Walsh nodded. 'We could use you if you care to turn out.'

'Well, of course,' said Walsh, 'but I'm hardly a resident, am I?'

'We're allowed visitors,' said the Earl. 'Need 'em, too. Those miners see cricket as an extension of the class war. Don't worry about kit either, we'll find you something.' He topped up his port glass, and passed the decanter to Walsh. 'Try to stay in one piece, by the way. It's the Wentworth Handicap two days afterwards.'

'Do my best,' said Walsh, and left the decanter where it was.

'Wentworth's bringing some people up from London,' said the Earl. 'Cousin of his and her husband. Good-looking filly but in foal, from what they tell me. Bonney, would it be? Bowen? No, Bonner – that's it. Her husband's a guardee.'

Walsh changed his mind and filled his glass, just before Kielder discharged the other barrel.

'Had a phone call from the vicarage earlier,' he said. 'That half-brother of yours is there.'

Somehow Walsh's port stayed in its glass. 'What on earth's he doing there?' he asked.

'Ah,' said the Earl. 'Cribb's doing. Good butler, Cribb. If you ask me, he got the idea that you and—'

'Edgar,' said Walsh.

'Exactly,' said the Earl. 'That you don't get on all that well. Don't ask me where he got it from. As I say, he's a damn good butler. Thought it best to have him aired at Matthew's first. After all, it's become a sort of tradition, wouldn't you say? First Natasha, then you. Why should he be spared? All the same, I'll have to have him here tomorrow.'

'Of course, sir.'

Kielder grunted. A grunt of approval, thought Walsh.

'The only thing is, Natasha and I may not be here when Edgar arrives,' he said.

'Why the devil not?' Approval withdrawn, it seemed, but this was a time to stay calm.

'We're engaged,' said Walsh, 'and she hasn't got a ring.'

'Good lord,' said the Earl. 'No more she has. As a matter of fact, I've been thinking about that.' His hand went to his pocket and came out with a little green shagreen box. 'That any use to you?'

Walsh opened it. Inside was the most amazing ring he had ever seen. Diamonds, sapphires, rubies, emeralds, set to look like an exotic flower bursting into bloom.

'My God,' said Walsh.

'Fabergé,' said the Earl. 'Bought it myself. Not an heirloom. I couldn't let you have an heirloom.'

Walsh wondered what had happened to the recipient.

'I bought it in St Petersburg,' said the Earl, 'then they went and transferred me to Vienna before I could–' He drank more port and changed the subject. 'Just right for Natasha, wouldn't you say?'

'Perfect,' said Walsh. 'Provided you let me pay for it.'

'Well, of course,' said the Earl. 'You can't give your fiancée another man's ring. Let's see this off and hear some music, then you can regularise your position so to speak.'

He finished his port, and so did Walsh. At least my hand didn't shake, he thought.

She was playing Brahms, and stopped as they came in. 'How happy you look,' she said.

My God she's right, thought Walsh. I've just received both barrels and I'm the happiest man alive.

'There's a reason,' said the Earl. 'Michael will tell you because I'm off to bed soon. Anything else we have to do?'

'Maddy,' said Natasha, 'and George. They are about to become engaged – I told you. Only of course George must speak to you first.'

'He's a very correct young man,' said the Earl.

'Well, of course he is,' said Natasha. 'He's a solicitor.'

'He plays cricket too,' said the Earl, and turned to Walsh. 'Wicketkeeper. Useful bat, too – on his day.'

Walsh thought how easy it was to stumble on a cricket-field.

'I see what you mean, sir,' he said, and earned another approving grunt.

'Better have them to dinner tomorrow,' Lord Kielder decided. 'I haven't much time to arrange a team.' He went to kiss her cheek, 'Goodnight, child,' he said.

'Please,' said Natasha. 'You promise you will say you approve?'

'Must have a wicket-keeper,' said the Earl.

When he had gone Walsh said, 'I have something for you. At least I think I have.'

'A present? But when—?'

'Please let me tell it,' said Walsh, and did so. When he had done he said, 'If you'd sooner choose your own I don't mind, but I doubt if you'll find one like this.' He opened the box and she gasped aloud.

'*Fabergé!*'

'He bought it in St Petersburg, apparently.'

'And sold it to you?'

'Only if you'll wear it,' said Walsh.

He could have bought it for the woman I call *Maman*, she thought, and now he wants it to come to me.

She went to Walsh and held out her hand. 'Of course I shall wear it,' she said.

EDGAR

27

His father would have been absolutely at home here, Edgar thought, and his mother would have adored it. Mother had adored everything that came from England, and certain areas of Melbourne; the rest of Australia she had despised. He often wondered what his mother would have made of his ambition to govern the place, and yet he had loved her . . .

The parson passed the port to him, and he filled up his glass. That the parson was at ease with him, even liked him, he was quite certain, and he thought he knew why. To begin with there was the voice, the carefully preserved Charterhouse and Oxford voice, and the fact that he knew how to pass the port. All that. He belonged. Not like brother Michael. Every time his name came up the parson winced as if he still bore the marks.

'An unfortunate contretemps,' the parson was saying. 'I can't think how he came to do it. Cribb of all people.'

'Cribb?' Edgar queried.

'Our kinsman's butler. Usually a *most* dependable man.'

'At least it gave me the opportunity to meet you all,' said Edgar.

'You're most kind,' said the parson.

Edgar looked at the parson's sons. The younger one – George was it? – looked as if it were Christmas and he'd got all the best presents, but the other one, Oliver, just sat there and brooded. Not so much a secret sorrow as a secret hate. He'd injured himself too in rather a mysterious way and wanted to talk about it, but his father wouldn't let him.

'He rode over this morning. Not Cribb, of course. Our kinsman. He brought two more of our relatives with him.'

'So I heard,' said George. 'Natasha and Michael. It seems Michael's a clipping rider.'

Oliver's brooding intensified.

'Are you acquainted with Mr Walsh?' the parson asked.

'We've met,' said Edgar carefully. 'My father knew him quite well. But of course he would be an excellent horseman. He's a stockman, after all.'

'Are you close relatives?' Oliver asked.

'Not particularly,' said Edgar, and thought: And that's no lie. I've only met him twice in my entire life. It was still long enough for him to do what he did, though, which is why I'm here.

'Funny to think of a Tyrrwhitt called Walsh,' said Oliver.

His father said, 'That will do,' automatically, like a response in church.

'And he's a Roman Catholic,' said Oliver.

Drunk, of course, thought Edgar. Too drunk to guard his tongue. There might be something worth learning if the parson doesn't pack him off to bed.

'If it comes to that, Natasha's Russian Orthodox,' said George.

The parson sighed. Such exotic faiths were to be deplored, it seemed. 'If I may ask—' he said.

'Church of England,' said Edgar. 'Baptised *and* confirmed.' The parson's smile was like sunshine after rain.

'She never went to that church of hers,' said Oliver.

'How could she?' said George. 'The nearest one's in Paris.'

'So she *said*.' Oliver's voice was a sneer.

He doesn't much care for brother Michael, thought Edgar, but he really hates the girl. Why, I wonder? Because Oliver wants her and brother Michael's got her?

His father said, 'This is neither the time nor place for you to make yourself disagreeable.'

Oliver turned to Edgar. 'Is that what I'm doing?' he asked. 'Making myself disagreeable?'

'I scarcely know you well enough to judge,' said Edgar, and George chuckled, but his father did not.

'Verily thou art answered,' he said. 'I advise you to be silent for a while. It is all very unfortunate.'

'No doubt your son is in pain,' Edgar said. 'It can have a trying effect on the temper.'

'Christian fortitude,' said the parson. 'Prayer.' There was no doubt he considered Oliver deficient in both.

'Natasha is rather a lively person, I gather,' said Edgar.

'Rather,' said George who, it seemed, approved of liveliness. His father, it seemed, did not. He scowled at his younger son, who beamed on him in return. Not just the best presents, thought Edgar. *All* the presents.

'Her life has been an eventful one,' said the parson, and spoke of palaces and the Conservatoire, of the gutter and the Rehabilitation Centre and Camp 19.

'Good God,' said Edgar. 'And she survived all that.' And

then, because the parson was there, 'Please excuse me. I do apologise.'

'Not at all,' said the parson. 'The goodness of God may well be the reason why she is here.'

And there's one for you, thought Edgar. He's turned the other cheek on you.

'Eventful just about sums it up,' he said. Oliver snorted.

George said hastily, 'Maddy thinks the world of her.'

'Maddy?' said Edgar. Another Cribb?

'She's the lady to whom I'm about to become engaged.' Not another Cribb. 'Madeleine Cantripp. She and Natasha are very good friends.'

'Mrs Cantripp is a widow,' the parson began.

'Quite a merry one these days,' said Oliver, and his father turned on him.

'Go to bed, sir,' he said. 'At once.'

Oliver finished his port and left the room. He was staggering just a little, Edgar noticed, but was he not limping also?

'Really,' said the parson, 'I can't apologise enough.'

'Then please don't try,' said Edgar. 'I'm not the one involved, after all, though I admit he didn't show much concern for his brother's feelings.'

'He never does,' said George. 'Not when he's like that, but I'll be out of his way soon enough.' And still he was smiling.

'Mrs Cantripp – Maddy,' said the vicar, 'has an establishment here in Haydon Priors, and George proposes to live there after they're married.'

'After the honeymoon,' said George, happier than ever.

'Her first husband was killed in France during the War,' the parson said. 'He was an officer in a distinguished regiment.'

'Well, so was I an officer in a distinguished regiment,' said George. '*And* I was wounded. Twice.' He chuckled then, which Edgar found almost as bewildering as the look on the parson's face. A blend of horror, bewilderment and fury were about as close as he could get.

There was something about George that his father didn't like – something he considered shameful, even – and yet if shame there had to be, surely Oliver was the one to provide the cause? There was resentment, too, but the reason for that was more obvious. The parson was angry because George was going to leave him alone with Oliver: a little selfish perhaps, but perfectly understandable ...

'Cricket,' the parson was saying, 'and a race-meeting. You have timed your visit to Haydon Priors admirably.'

'Just good luck,' said Edgar. 'Who's playing cricket?'

'Something of a needle match,' said the parson. 'Haydon Priors against our close neighbours Slagsby.'

'Like Dingley Dell and Muggleton,' said Edgar, then wished he hadn't. The whole point of Dickens's description was the ineptitude of the players.

'Precisely,' said the parson, who couldn't have looked at *Pickwick Papers* in decades.

'And the racing?'

'Our most important meeting,' said the parson, 'and our most important race. The Wentworth Handicap. Lord 'Wentworth himself will be there, which argues that our kinsman may well attend.'

'I'm taking Maddy,' said George – and that, it seemed, was all that mattered. Whether Lord Kielder attended or not was of no importance whatsoever.

Altogether a boring evening, Edgar thought as he prepared for sleep, even by bourgeois Brisbane standards, and even more so after Oliver had been sent to bed. That relentless smile of George's was a bit hard to take, especially when he thought of what he had to do next day, and after the second glass of port the parson's conversation became more and more like a sermon: village rivalry, beer tents, the evils of gambling . . . Wearily he climbed into his bed, which had been brother Michael's not all that long ago . . .

Stop that, he thought. Save it for tomorrow. Think about something nice instead. The voyage, for instance. That had been pleasant. Useful, too. That chap Bonner – ADC to the Governor of Singapore – and related to the Australian Governor General. That could turn out to be very useful indeed. Mad about that wife of his too, which wasn't surprising. She was a very pretty woman, even though she was pregnant. Bonner fussed over her like an old hen with one chick, and she just let him get on with it. Calm as you like. Serene, you might say. Funny how a pregnant woman could be serene when she knew what was coming . . .

The visit to Australia House had been a good idea, too. They'd been very pleased to see him. Well of course they had. Rich man, prospective candidate, probable MHR, just what they wanted. But there was rather more to it than that. A couple of chaps who could be as useful to him as he could to them. And a pretty young woman accompanying her husband to Canberra at the same time as he would be there. To the victor the spoils, all that. The cricket sounded like a bore, but he always liked a good race-meeting. Not that he might stay long enough to see either . . .

NATASHA AND MICHAEL

28

'But it is such a little thing to ask,' Natasha pouted.

'Not little at all,' said Walsh.

She sighed. It was very irritating. She had done even more than usual for him – it was their engagement, after all – and he had responded in kind. Nothing wrong there. And when they rested she had still taken care to show off her body to its best advantage, and that too had pleased him, until she had made this simple request and he had refused her.

'One look is all it needs,' she said.

'Well of course it is,' said Walsh, 'but how am I going to get it? I can't just walk in on George and tell him to drop his strides, now can I?'

'Strides?' she said.

'Trousers.'

'Strides. Trousers. *Pantalon*,' said Natasha. 'I like strides best. There is a sort of poetry—' She sat up in the bed. 'But not now . . . You are clever. Cunning too, sometimes. You could do it so easily . . . Such a little thing.'

'Not little at all,' Walsh said again, and suddenly she grabbed him, taking care not to hurt. 'Mistaking me for Oliver?' said Walsh.

'I could never do that,' she said, 'not even when you are as selfish and disobliging as you are now. But listen to me, *mon cher*. This, too, is a little thing' – she flicked it disdainfully – 'and I will not make it a big thing until you promise me you will do what I ask.'

'I'd better go to my bed then,' said Walsh.

'I think you must,' she said, still holding him, and then: 'Oh my God. We are quarrelling.'

'We ought to be good at it,' he said. 'The Irish can quarrel like Russians once they start. Only—'

'Only what, *chéri*?'

'I don't think I could stand it,' he said.

'I also,' said Natasha. 'But if you will not do it—' She looked at him, appalled at what she was driven to do.

Don't say you will, don't give in, Walsh told himself. Once you

291

give in you're doomed. Make a deal and hope she'll accept, because if she won't you really will have to go back to your own bed.

'Let's forget about it being or not being such a little thing,' he said. 'Let's just say it's tricky.'

'Very well.' But she still held him. She'd told him he wasn't Oliver, but all the same, he'd better be careful.

'Now, suppose I promise I'll try?. Really work at it, give you my word on it. Will that be enough for you? Because it's all I've got.'

All this to get a look at George's backside, he thought. But if I don't, that same backside could cost me my marriage.

'I accept,' she said. 'Of course I accept.' Her grip on him altered. 'I am tired of this little thing,' she said. 'Let us make something big.'

When he did go back to his own bed she got out of hers to stare at herself in the dressing-table mirror, long and hard.

'I just wanted to see what an idiot looks like,' she told her image. 'Now I know.'

She went back to bed then, lit a cigarette, and stared at the ceiling. Why had she done it? Anybody else in the world would ask her that, even darling Greenhalgh, but only she, Natasha, knew. Because everything had to be done now, this minute: because there was so little time. Or perhaps there was lots of time. She couldn't be sure and so everything must be now. Even darling Michael. But perhaps somewhere inside him he knew too, which was why he had been so good; a goodness she did not deserve. Suddenly she remembered the Rehabilitation Centre, and a beating she had received from an instructor who even there was famous for her beatings. At least she had paid in advance for her stupidity. All the same, she thought, to risk Michael's love like that . . .

Oh please God, do not let him grow tired of me.

She began to weep.

'Bit of business with George,' said the Earl. 'Won't be long, I promise. Take Mrs Cantripp into the music room, Natasha. I've no doubt Michael will be glad of a word with Edgar. We'll talk in the study, George.'

Ruthlessly the Earl herded them into their places, like a blue-heeler who knew his business, thought Walsh, until he and Edgar were alone in the hall. Up to the start line, fix bayonets, wait for the whistle.

Edgar said, 'I've come to apologise.'

If that's his idea of a joke I'll flatten him, thought Walsh.

'I mean it,' said Edgar. 'I'm sorry.'

Walsh looked at him. It seemed that he meant it.

'But I robbed you,' said Walsh. It's just not making sense, he thought.

'That's one for the philosophers,' said Edgar, 'but you only took back what was yours. I know that. I read the other will before I burnt it. How can what you did be robbery?'

'But—' said Walsh. 'But—' For once the words weren't there.

'You mean why?' said Edgar. 'It's a fair question. Because I was greedy. Rich though I was, I wanted to be richer. And because—'

'Go on,' said Walsh.

'It was all so quick,' said Edgar. 'You, your mother, what Dad had done – and I had no idea. That was the worst of it. Not knowing you existed. It drove me crazy – and so I cheated you.'

'What changed your mind?'

'I found some diaries of Dad's,' Edgar said. 'He'd hidden them, but not very well. I think he knew I'd find them one day. He wrote it all down.'

'About me?' said Walsh.

'About both of us.' Edgar offered his hand. 'Shake?'

Walsh took it. A good grip, he thought. Not like a politician's at all. More like a stockman's.

'Having a brother was hard enough to take in,' Walsh said, 'but having a brother like you, well . . . Nobody knows except Natasha, by the way, and she won't talk.'

'No worries,' said Edgar, and grinned.

In the music room Cribb was pouring champagne, and Natasha and Mrs Cantripp were drinking it. Cribb and Maddy, thought Edgar, as English as pound notes. Then Michael led him over to Natasha.

'Edgar,' he said, 'let me introduce my fiancée, Natasha.'

Lucky, lucky Michael, thought Edgar, but if what Dad wrote is right then maybe he deserves her. 'Delighted to meet you,' he said.

Her eyes moved from him to Michael. Both men were relaxed, at ease. It is all right, she thought. I know it is.

'I also,' she said, and offered her hand.

'And this is Madeleine Cantripp,' said Michael.

'But not for long,' said Natasha.

Another very pretty woman, Edgar thought, as fair as Natasha was dark. 'Mrs Cantripp,' he said.

'Oh, please call me Maddy,' she said. 'Everybody does.'

Natasha moved to join her: she in blue, Maddy in pink. Side by side they enhanced each other to the point where he envied George, too.

Cribb brought more champagne, and as he did so the Earl and George came in.

'Fizz, eh?' the Earl said. 'What a good idea.' As if Cribb had just thought of it. Then he went to the fair woman.

'George has just told me,' he said. 'He's a very lucky feller.' Maddy blushed, as the Earl turned to George. 'Got a ring for her?'

George produced a little leather box and took out a diamond flanked by sapphires.

It's lovely, thought Natasha, but it isn't Fabergé. Not that I deserve Fabergé; I deserve to be beaten. She went to the piano to play. Mendelssohn again: this time the *Wedding March*.

The Earl turned to Edgar. 'Do you play cricket, by any chance? I know your – er – kinsman does.'

'Well, yes,' said Edgar.

'Any good?' said Kielder 'Rude of me and all that, but I've got to get a team from somewhere.'

'Dingley Dell versus Muggleton,' said Edgar. 'The parson told me. I played for Oxford – got a blue.'

'Muggleton won't know what's hit them, 'said the Earl. 'George is playing too.'

Still glowing, thought Edgar. Still living in a Heaven built to his own design.

'Wicket-keeper,' said George. 'Do you bowl?'

'I try,' said Edgar. Natasha was playing something familiar, something he should be able to name and yet couldn't. It sounded like Bach, and yet it wasn't, and then it was like Chopin, but the tune remained the same, and then it was Strauss. *Waltzing Matilda*, theme and variations. Just for the two of us.

His brother came up to him, and Edgar nodded towards Natasha. 'Dad would have loved this,' he said.

'Too right,' said his brother.

After dinner the men stayed to drink port of course, and George opened the door for them, still smiling, but that was all right because she had something she simply had to say to Maddy, and because this seemed to be her time for being an idiot, she simply said it, without even thinking.

'You and George are doing it,' she said.

Maddy neither screamed, had hysterics, nor upset the coffee pot. Instead she smiled, rather like George. 'How on earth did you know?' she asked.

'Partly it was you,' said Natasha, 'but mostly it was George looking at you. You have given him another reason to love you.'

294

'He's given me one too,' said Maddy, and sipped her Benedictine. 'The most extraordinary thing. Darling, do watch the door – if you want to hear about it, that is.'

'I *must* hear about it,' said Natasha, and watched the door and lit a cigarette and prepared to listen.

'It was last Thursday,' said Maddy. 'I'd invited George round for tea – just Earl Grey and bikkies because it was the maid's half-day, but we had to talk about the reception and things – and then at the last moment cook's sister from Sunderland rang up to say that their mother was ill and she was to go home at once . . . I was wearing that yellow dress you helped me choose.'

The yellow dress I made you buy, thought Natasha, because it made you even prettier, but I shall not say so because you are my friend.

'So when George came round I just happened to mention that the servants were out and before we knew where we were, we were doing it.'

'Not with the yellow dress on?' said Natasha. It really was a pretty dress.

'Of course not,' said Maddy. 'It would only have got in the way.'

'Is he—' Natasha bit off the question.

'Good in bed?' said Maddy. 'I've no idea. First time it was the sofa, second time that bearskin rug.'

'Oh darling, how marvellous for you!' And Natasha embraced her.

'Well, it was,' said Maddy. 'I didn't know it *could* be marvellous. I literally had no idea. I'd no idea it could take so long, either. Not that I minded.' She sipped her Benedictine once more. 'That rug, for instance. It was off a bear Francis – my first husband – shot in the Himalayas. It scratched rather, and do you know I never even noticed? I hope I don't come out in a rash.'

'Of course not,' said Natasha.

'Cook's mother got better,' said Maddy, 'and I'm glad for Cook – of course I am – but all the same we had heaps more chances when she was away, and there was only the maid to play hide and seek with.' She sighed. 'You know, in a small house servants can be a dreadful nuisance.' She smiled at Natasha then: a smile of pure affection. 'But how could you know? You've never lived in a small house in your life.'

You are so wrong, darling Maddy, thought Natasha, but I shall not tell you so. This is your night, and to ask you about George's bottom is impossible.

'George and Maddy are doing it,' said Natasha.

295

'Well, so are we,' said Walsh.

'Yes, but for them it is difficult because the servants must not see.'

'Of course they mustn't,' said Walsh. 'Next thing you know they'd be selling tickets.'

Natasha giggled. 'Maddy likes it,' she said.

'So do I like it,' said Walsh. 'I hope you like it, too.'

'You know I do,' said Natasha. 'But you did not ask whether George likes it.'

'He likes it all right,' said Walsh. 'Look at his face if you don't believe me.' She moved from his arms. 'What's wrong, *ma chère*?' he asked.

'George,' she said.

Oh my God, he thought. Not again.

'I behaved very badly about George,' she said. 'It was stupid and wilful and I knew it was, even as I was saying it. But there is a reason – at least I think there is. It's hard to explain.'

'I don't want you to explain,' he said. 'I don't want to talk about it at all.'

'But—'

He interrupted her. He almost never interrupted her. 'I want you to come close to me and kiss me, and talk about something else.'

She moved into him, and her lips were as cool and sweet as ever as she stroked the puckered scar of his wound.

'I am glad you are friends with your brother,' she said. 'He is a most remarkable man.'

'All of that,' said Walsh.

'Last night—' she began, and he interrupted her again.

'Not George,' he said.

'Of course not George. But you were so ardent – even for you. Was it because you thought you might have to run away from Edgar?'

'It crossed my mind,' he admitted, 'but only for a little while. How can I run away if you're not running with me?'

'For that you deserve something amusing,' said Natasha.

'Not too amusing,' said Walsh. 'Not just this once. I've got a cricket match tomorrow.'

The match was one for the book, no question. Edgar and he drove over in the Buick, taking borrowed whites from the Earl, who seemed to have an unending supply of spare clothes: enough to set up in business as a theatrical costumier. They discussed the game as they drove. The trouble was that they had no idea, none at all, what the opposition would be like. All they could do was the obvious, and being Australians that meant going flat out to win.

'This cricket,' said Natasha. 'Michael did his best to explain it to me, but I do not understand.'

'Not a lot of females do, miss,' said Greenhalgh. 'Not even English ones.'

'A game that lasts all day,' said Natasha.

'Some last three days,' said Greenhalgh. 'Some even longer.'

Natasha said something in Russian, then spread butter and marmalade on her toast.

'Very likely, miss,' said Greenhalgh, then added: 'Mr George is playing too.'

'George and Maddy are doing it,' said Natasha, and bit into her toast.

Greenhalgh looked disapproving. '*Pas devant les domestiques,*' she said. Natasha remembered what Michael had said about the servants, and smiled.

'Of course not,' said Natasha. 'I would not dream of telling the servants. I tell *you*. Aren't you interested?'

'Oh yes, miss,' said Greenhalgh. 'I always enjoy a bit of gossip. Thank you.'

'Where did you learn to speak French, darling Greenhalgh?' Natasha asked.

'All employers say it sooner or later,' said Greenhalgh. 'They think we're too stupid to find out what it means.'

Natasha yawned and stretched, and got out of bed. 'Pick me out a cricket dress,' she said.

They were practising at the nets when the Slagsby team and their supporters arrived in two battered charabancs. Both brothers were medium-pace bowlers, and middle-order batsmen, just like their father, but Walsh knew at once that Edgar was the better of the two. All the same, he thought, he'd give Slagsby a game, if that amusing thing had left him enough strength . . .

Then the Slagsby team marched from their charabancs to the nets, led by Carrick, the village curate. Some wore whites, some grey flannels, a couple were in trousers of blue serge, but they all looked formidable. Carrick strode at their head like a Gothic chieftain leading a march on Ancient Rome.

Edgar said easily, 'I almost forgot to mention it. Cribb told me at breakfast that that parson of theirs was going to play for Yorkshire, only he got religion instead.'

'Really?' said Walsh. Carrick came up from a twenty-yard run and knocked out the middle stump with the easy skill of a dentist pulling a tooth. 'Looks like we've got our work cut out then,' said Walsh, as calmly as he could.

'Let's hope we win the toss,' Edgar said . 'The pitch ought to ease a bit by the second innings.'

If only amusing things weren't so amusing, thought Walsh.

They did win the toss, and put Slagsby in, and after two overs Slagsby had scored five for two wickets: one for Edgar and one for Walsh. Then Carrick came in at Number Three and carved them up as if they'd been children on the beach, bowling with a tennis ball at low tide ... When he'd made his fifty, their captain – an earnest if insecure chartered surveyor – took Michael off and tried an off-spinner instead. His first ball went for six ... It was Edgar who got him, or perhaps it was the assembled might of the Tyrrwhitts. Edgar tried a short one, Carrick swung and mistimed for once, George behind the wicket got his hand to it, and Walsh took it at first slip as their captain appealed rather nervously, his voice drowned by the yells of Walsh and Edgar. The umpire signalled out, but Carrick was looking at the sky, reproachfully, thought Walsh, as if he were saying: 'How could You do that to me, Your servant, and in front of folk from Slagsby too?' Then at last he walked off, their captain brought Walsh back on, and he and Edgar skittled Slagsby's tail. A hundred and twenty-two all out, and seventy of them to Carrick. As they walked off Walsh said, 'No wonder Yorkshire wanted him.'

Natasha's cricket dress was by Worth – a summer suit of cream silk and a hat big enough to keep off the sun. The brothers joined her in the refreshment tent.

'Who is winning?' she asked.

'Early days,' said Edgar, and bit into a cucumber sandwich.

'It isn't us,' said Walsh.

'Not unless their parson is struck by lightning,' said Edgar.

Walsh looked out at a cloudless sky. 'Prayer's about all there's left.'

'But I liked him,' said Natasha. 'He worked so hard for the bootless children.'

Edgar looked puzzled. 'Shoeless,' Walsh explained, and to Natasha: 'Certainly you like him. He's a very nice man. He's also very good at playing cricket.'

'Better than you?'

'Better than Edgar even,' said Walsh, and she looked bewildered. How could anyone be better at sport than her darling Michael? Then their captain came to collect them and the rest of the team. They moved, thought Walsh, like men very close to the front line, the rumble of the guns already audible.

'Good luck,' said the Earl, and reached for another sandwich.

'All right for some,' said Edgar.

The chartered surveyor decreed that Edgar bat at Number Three and Walsh at Number Four, demoting himself more modestly – and wisely – to Number Seven.

'Haig was just the same,' said Walsh. 'Always made sure the Aussies took a bashing.'

Carrick clean-bowled their opener first ball, and Edgar walked out to the crease in his place as Walsh looked on, already padded up. He wouldn't have long to wait for his share of the bombardment, he thought, nor did he. Walsh joined his brother when Haydon Priors were two for two. If the pitch had eased a bit nobody had told Carrick, he thought: the ball came at him like a bullet. He and Edgar had only one choice and they knew it. Hold out against Carrick as best they could and slaughter the bowler at the other end. The trouble was that holding out against Carrick was a painful business. When he pitched one short your ribs knew all about it. Still, Australia's honour was at stake, and Edgar was taking a bashing, too.

Carrick finally got him when he'd made twenty-three. He walked off, doing his best not to limp, and left Edgar to it. Edgar really was amazing, he thought. Even when Carrick hit him he gave no sign of pain. Edgar would go a long way in politics.

The pavilion boasted what it called a shower: a length of pipe and a circle of perforated tin. Even so the trickle of water was soothing. At one point his captain came in to ask if Carrick was really as fast as he looked. Walsh told him he was and his captain looked more insecure than ever, but at least he told Walsh where the arnica was kept. Cautiously Walsh dried himself, then looked out of the window, just in time to see Edgar hook Carrick for four: the high point of the day. Soon afterwards their captain came and went and George took his place.

Walsh was applying the arnica when George returned. Clean-bowled for ten, raw meat for Carrick's lion. He looked at Walsh, blissfully dabbing by the washbasin.

'My God,' he said, 'he certainly didn't like you.'

'I bet Edgar's worse,' said Walsh, and George winced, unsmiling for once, then began to loosen his belt.

He's going to do it, thought Walsh. *I'm going to see.*

Still dabbing he said, 'What's the score?'

'A hundred and ten for nine,' said George, and took off his shirt. Carrick must be tiring.

'You got your share,' said Walsh.

'I must be mad,' said George. 'Save me some of that arnica, will you?' He took off the rest of his clothes and got under the shower, and Walsh saw what there was to see, left George the arnica and put on his clothes.

When he went outside Haydon Priors were a hundred and eighteen, and Edgar had lost the strike. Their Number Eleven faced Carrick, who bowled at him as if he were opening the innings. Number Eleven swung his bat as if it were a shovel, the ball went for four, and again Carrick looked up to his God in reproach, then clean-bowled Number Eleven next ball. The game was a tie. Haydon Priors had met and held one giant and ten manic pigmies. Even then Edgar strolled off as if he felt no pain at all. A cabinet minister at least, thought Walsh, as Edgar came up to him.

'Fifty-one not out,' he said. 'Seventy-four between us. Advance, Australia Fair. Still, that last boundary from the Pom came in handy. He told me he had his eyes shut when he made the stroke.'

'What on earth for?' said Walsh.

'He was praying.'

'Go in and shower,' said Walsh. 'There's still some arnica left. I reckon you'll need it.'

'I reckon I will,' said Edgar. 'But we did all right, didn't we?'

'Especially you,' said Walsh, and went to find Natasha.

She was in the refreshment tent with the Earl and another white-haired man almost as brown as Walsh himself.

'This is Major Carr-Gore,' said Natasha. '*Chéri*, he has invented the most delightful drink.'

All three of them held tumblers containing ice and lemon, and a colourless liquid that fizzed gently.

'Not invented,' said the Major. 'Brought it back from India. It's called gin and tonic. Let me make you one.'

'Please,' said Walsh, and sat down cautiously.

'You're hurt,' said Natasha.

'Just a flesh wound.'

'I do not understand this cricket,' she said. 'If that terrible priest is allowed to hit you with the ball, why did you not hit him with the bat?'

'Against the rules,' said the Earl.

'Such rules are foolish,' said Natasha, 'but you were very brave, and so was your—'

'Kinsman,' said the Earl.

29

Next day Walsh and Edgar drove to Newcastle to hire racing clothes. The Earl's theatrical costumier's business had failed them for once. Both men moved rather cautiously, and the news that Carrick had been carried shoulder high round Slagsby if anything increased their pain, especially when Cribb explained that it was because of the damage Carrick had done to the toffs.

Walsh was indignant. 'How can I possibly be a toff?' he said. 'I'm an Australian.'

'You should have told him before the game,' said Edgar. 'Anyway, I'm Australian too. On the other hand I did go to Charterhouse.'

Natasha and Greenhalgh talked of weddings: first Maddy's, then Natasha's own.

'I expect Mr George's father will marry them,' said Greenhalgh, and Natasha nodded, 'but who will give Mrs Cantripp away?'

'She wants Michael to do it,' said Natasha.

'Even though he wasn't an officer?' said Greenhalgh, and Natasha giggled.

'Even then,' said Natasha. 'The thing is that Michael will soon be my husband and he owns quite a bit of Australia and that is enough. Also his brother seems very English, and for some reason that also helps. She says she can't be married in white.'

'Well, of course she can't,' agreed Greenhalgh.

'Because she and George are doing it? But Michael and you and I are the only ones who know.'

'Because she's a widow, miss,' said Greenhalgh.

'I forgot,' said Natasha, then added proudly: 'She doesn't look at all like a widow, does she? Though she did when I first met her.'

And whose doing was that? thought Greenhalgh, equally proud.

'Soon be lunch-time, miss,' she said. 'Would you like some champagne?'

'If you will have some too,' said Natasha.

'Thank you, miss,' Greenhalgh said. 'I'll use the toothglass in the bathroom. We can't go upsetting Cribb. Not that you won't upset him anyway if you don't put your dressing gown on. I don't know how they did things in Russia, but in England a lady doesn't receive the butler in her knickers.'

Once again Natasha put out her tongue at her, and looked about twelve years old, but even so she submitted to the dressing gown. Not that it made all that much difference.

When Cribb had left them and the champagne was poured, Greenhalgh said, 'And where will you be married, miss?'

'In Paris. In the Russian Orthodox Church there. It will be tre-men-dous-ly grand. Michael will hate it,' she added smugly.

'Will the Earl give you away?'

'I haven't asked him yet,' said Natasha.

'He'd be heart-broken if you ask anyone else, miss.'

'Then I shall ask him at lunch,' said Natasha. 'You I am asking now.'

'Me, miss?'

'How can I become married if you are not there to dress me?'

'Oh thank you, miss,' said Greenhalgh.

'Besides,' said Natasha, 'it might not be safe to let the Earl run around Paris on his own,' and Greenhalgh giggled, and Natasha too, then suddenly she was sad. 'Oh Greenhalgh,' she wailed, 'I shall miss you so very much.'

'Me too, miss,' Greenhalgh said, 'but it won't be for ever, will it?'

'I mustn't cry because I do not have time to make up again,' said Natasha, 'so I shall pray instead.'

'Me too, miss,' Greenhalgh said again, then added, 'But I shall look forward to the wedding.'

'Three weddings,' corrected Natasha, 'because Michael wishes to be married in a Catholic church and the law in France says that we must also be married by a *fonctionnaire*.'

'Would that be like a registry office, miss?'

'I expect so,' said Natasha vaguely. 'It will be very boring compared with the other two. But at least it means we shall have three wedding feasts. And you shall be at all three – and you will look lovely, I know you will.'

'I wish I could persuade the demon parson to emigrate,' said Edgar. 'He could play for Queensland.'

'Give it a go,' said Walsh. 'I'd feel safer if he was on our side.' Cautiously he changed gear.

'You still feeling his souvenirs?' said Edgar. 'Me too. You know, it's funny.'

'I could do with a laugh,' said Walsh. 'If it doesn't hurt, that is.'

'Funny peculiar,' said Edgar. 'I can say this because we're half-brothers and I feel as if I'd known you for years.'

'Me too,' said Walsh.

'All the same when you get right down to it there are some who would say that you robbed me, and I certainly robbed you. And yesterday we were both punished for it. And by a parson, at that. As I say, funny.'

'Worth thinking about, certainly,' said Walsh. 'Maybe tomorrow. —If I'm not aching quite so much.'

'There's another thing,' said Edgar. Walsh waited. 'Back in Brisbane I said I didn't want people to know you were my brother. I was wrong.'

'No,' said Walsh. 'You weren't. We get along together, and that's fine, and Natasha likes you, and so does the Earl. But if you're going into politics they're the only ones who'll know we're related. That doesn't mean we can't be mates.'

'Thanks,' said Edgar.

'And just to prove it you can be best man at my weddings.'

'Weddings?' said Edgar. 'How many are you having?'

'Three.'

'Strewth,' said Edgar.

They were almost in Haydon Priors when they saw him: just past the station, in a narrow, winding country lane, dairy cattle grazing on one side, wheat almost ready for cutting on the other. He lay on his back on a strip of grass beneath the fence that held in the cattle, and he too looked part of the landscape, thought Walsh. Neat country suit, regimental tie: but lying on his back was a dead giveaway. Walsh braked, and his bruises reminded him that there is a price for everything. Oliver was singing, to the tune of Dvorak's *Humoresque*.

> *'Passengers will please refrain*
> *From urinating while the train*
> *Is standing at the station as they do.*
> *Navvies working underneath*
> *Will get it in the eyes and teeth*
> *And they don't like it any more than you.'*

'Drunk as Chloe,' said Walsh, and moved to put the car in gear.

'No, wait,' said Edgar. 'I've just thought of something. He could be useful.'

'Oliver?' said Walsh. '*Useful?*'

'Didn't you say he used to be some kind of spy?'

'More like a secret policeman, according to Natasha. He was in the Black and Tans.'

'Good at it?'

'Above average, she reckoned, and she would know. She was on the receiving end for long enough.'

'Then I could use him,' said Edgar. 'In politics it's always useful to have somebody who can find out secrets, and Queensland's a bit short of spies.'

He'll finish up as Prime Minister, thought Walsh. What he's after is nasty, no question, but it's too late now. He'd have to do a lot worse than that before I stopped liking him.

'So what do you want to do?' asked Walsh. 'Get him home before the traps get him for Drunk and Disorderly?'

'Drunk and Incapable more likely,' said Edgar, 'but that's the general idea. That way he'll owe us a favour.'

'You,' said Walsh. 'He doesn't owe me a thing, and I want to keep it like that.'

Oliver bellowed on.

> '*"Stay," cried the porter,*
> *Withhold your water . . .*'

They picked him up and crammed him into the car, then set off for the vicarage.

George was walking down the path as they got there. Summer suit, rose in his button-hole, the faintest whiff of eau de Cologne.

'I was just off to see Maddy,' he said, then looked at his brother and ceased to smile. Doing it would have to wait a while. But at least Oliver had passed out on the way: the housemaid's blushes would be spared. Somehow they got him up the stairs, while the parson stood on the landing and keened about the ingratitude of children as if he'd taken lessons from King Lear. A bit hard on George, thought Walsh, then Oliver came to and started to struggle, until he hit his head on a stair. Edgar was holding his head . . .

When they came down, Edgar went up to the parson, now babbling his apologies. It seemed he'd reached the 'foolish, fond old man' stage, thought Walsh, but who could blame him? Oliver was enough to drive anybody crazy, except Edgar, perhaps. He and George walked out into the sunshine.

'Give you a lift?' said Walsh.

'No thanks,' said George. 'It's only a stroll. I'm very grateful to you.' He adjusted his tie. 'You know, Maddy and I have been thinking – it isn't always a good thing for a family to live on top of one another. It might be a good idea for us to sell up here and move to Newcastle.' When he went off he was smiling again.

Edgar came out at last looking – not jaunty exactly, he could never look jaunty – but briskly pleased with himself.

'The parson agrees with me,' he said. 'A change of air would be good for Oliver.'

'He could hardly get a bigger change than Australia,' said Walsh. 'Did you tell him you wanted him as a spy?'

'Private secretary,' said Edgar. 'He's a public school man, damn it.' He thought for a moment then added: 'It's the same thing, after all.'

'You really think he can talk Oliver into it?'

'Oh yes,' said Edgar. 'The parson's had enough.'

A good day for racing. Everyone was agreed on that, including Cribb, whose opinion in such matters was so valued by the Earl that he took him with him, though that may have been because there was a picnic hamper: the Earl was far from happy with the local catering. Natasha argued that if the Earl could have his butler she should have her maid, but was foiled by Greenhalgh herself, who had already arranged to spend the day with her friend Mrs Stobbs, the vicarage's new house-keeper. When they got to the course Cribb gave his judgment: the going was firm.

'What you wanted, isn't it?' said Kielder.

Natasha smiled at him. He had agreed to give her away *and* take Greenhalgh to Paris. 'Brillig, milord,' she said.

For once the Earl was startled. 'I beg your pardon?' he said.

'In the Wentworth Handicap. I can say no more than that, but I must find Greenhalgh and tell her.' She set off into the crowd as Walsh helped Cribb unload the hamper.

'Good Lord,' said Edgar. 'There's Margaret Bonner.'

Somehow Walsh managed to retain his grip on the hamper and lower it to the ground. 'What was that?' he said.

'The fair girl – the one who's so very pregnant – I met her on the boat coming over. The dark chap with her is her husband.'

'So I should hope,' said Walsh.

'Tom Bonner,' said the Earl. 'I was at school with his father. They're with Wentworth's party. Might as well say hello. He always brings decent champagne, and he's left his mother behind for once.'

Nothing else for it, thought Walsh. He could hardly run away. There was nowhere to run to, and even if there were, Natasha would find him. They walked over to the Wentworth party, three tall men in grey morning coats and grey toppers. Margaret Bonner watched them, then turned to smile at her husband, anxiously hovering. 'I'm all right,' she said. 'Honestly.'

Her voice was lower-pitched than he remembered. He wondered if she would laugh . . .

The introductions were interminable; Wentworth and a girlfriend and old school chums and their girlfriends, then his cousin Margaret and her Captain at last.

'How do you do?' she said, her voice vague and with just a hint of boredom. Far too many names to remember, the voice said. How tiresome. Every pretty woman was an actress when she had to be, Walsh thought. It took him all his time not to gape like some galah from the bush. She smiled past him.

'Edgar,' she said. 'How nice.' Case dismissed, he wondered, or judgment deferred?

He went to help the Earl drink Wentworth's champagne. He seemed to have brought a whole vintage. Good stuff, too: the Earl was right. Not that he didn't need it.

The Earl was eyeing Margaret warily. 'She looks pretty well on to me,' he said. 'Awkward if she dropped her foal in the owners' enclosure.'

'Too right,' said Walsh, and meant it. He was watching Natasha come to him, with George and Maddy in tow. They were moving far too slowly towards the champagne.

'They arrived late,' Natasha said. 'They were—'

'Unavoidably detained,' said Maddy.

And that would be the truth, thought Walsh. With Cook and the maid given the day off for the races, why shouldn't they be detained? He wished – oh, how he wished! – that he and Natasha could have been detained all day. Natasha went to her host.

'Or perhaps it is just that they are shy,' she said. 'But Bobby Wentworth did say I could invite who I like. Didn't you, Bobby?'

'Yes of course,' said Wentworth. 'You're all jolly welcome. Do help yourselves.'

'Such a generous man,' said Natasha, and did so.

'Oh I say,' said Wentworth. His girlfriend bridled at that, then noticed the ring on Natasha's finger and relaxed. When Edgar came up she relaxed even more. They had met at a dinner in Australia House, and he was devastatingly handsome.

'George says you are sending Oliver to Australia,' Natasha said to Edgar.

'Not sending exactly,' said Edgar. 'Not in leg-irons on a convict ship.'

'He is to work for you?'

'Private secretary,' said Edgar.

'But not to Stony Creek,' said Natasha. Edgar looked puzzled.

'That's my property,' said Walsh on cue. 'It's near Toowombah.'

'His ranch,' said Natasha, 'where he is a cowboy.'

'Oh,' said Wentworth's girlfriend. 'So you're Australian too.'

'He can even speak it,' said Natasha.

'But you're not.' Wentworth's girlfriend was one who believed in making things clear.

'I will be when we are married,' said Natasha. 'For the moment I am English because my *Maman* was English, and before that I was Russian.'

Poor girl, thought Walsh. Things aren't clear at all. Things are bewildering, in fact. Then the first race began and things were clear once more. Her horse came fifth.

Walsh spent most of the afternoon trying to hide the fact that he was afraid, which was nonsense. He'd met Margaret before he knew that Natasha even existed: just like her and Dimitri. But Dimitri was dead, and Margaret was about to give birth, and Natasha was both perceptive and clever, and barren. So being afraid wasn't nonsense at all. He was afraid because he might lose her, and not just the golden girl stuff. He could lose *her*, and he wasn't all that sure that he could bear it. Suddenly clouds began to gather, which suited his mood perfectly, then thunder softly rumbled, like a drumroll before the National Anthem. It might be a cliché, he thought, but by God it's apt.

In the end he had to speak to the cause of all this fear because there was no help for it. Her husband, like Natasha, had gone to place a bet, she dropped her handbag, there was no one else near and Margaret Bonner was much too pregnant to pick it up herself. He had to do it for her.

'Thank you,' she said.

'You're welcome.'

Before he could move away she said, 'The baby. It's yours.' He waited. 'Just as well you look so like my husband.' Still he said nothing. 'Are you angry?'

'No, of course not,' he said, 'but like you told me, it's over.'

'Worried about your new lady?'

'We'll be married soon.'

'She'll be a bit of a shock for the outback.'

'They'll just have to get used to it,' said Walsh.

'Will she back Brillig too?'

'I expect so,' said Walsh, and before she could object: 'Wentworth told her to.'

307

'Wentworth?'

'He's another bloke who wanted to marry her.'

'One sees why, of course,' Margaret said. 'She's gorgeous. Oddly enough, so is Tom these days. In a way. You did my marriage a lot of good, Mr Walsh. Believe it or not. I wish you very happy.'

Natasha walked back with Tom Bonner, who was telling her at length what a tricky business it was moving his wife around in her condition. You should have tried it in Camp 19, she thought, but that was unfair. She rather liked Margaret Bonner. Then she saw Michael talking to her and knew beyond doubt that they had once been lovers. She risked a glance at Bonner, who was still babbling away about nursing homes and ambulances and obstetricians, all there when they were wanted, one hoped. It was obvious that he didn't suspect a thing, but then men were hopeless at knowing beyond doubt. The next question was obvious. Was Margaret's baby Michael's baby too, despite all the ambulances and obstetricians and nursing homes? The only way to find out was to ask him, and that she could make him tell she had no doubt, she knew him so well, but if the answer was yes, could she bear it? Probably not, she thought, because Margaret Bonner would have given him the one thing she could never give. Better, far better, not to ask. Never mind that she had told him about Dimitri: this was different. This was about a baby. She would just have to make do with all those grown-up black orphans in Stony Creek.

'When do you go back to Singapore?' she asked.

'Soon as the little beggar makes his appearance – or hers,' said Bonner. 'Margaret will come out when they're both fit to travel.'

'I wish you and your family happiness,' said Natasha, then Michael came to her and they went to join Edgar and the Earl to eat from the hamper. Maddy and George joined them too, which was good. She needed a crowd, though even in this dreadful blend of bewilderment and despair she did not need Oliver.

But at least Michael did not know about the bewilderment and despair, let alone why she had them.

'Next race is the Wentworth Handicap,' Lord Kielder said. 'Everybody got their money on?'

'Backed it ages ago,' said Edgar. 'For everybody. The odds are bound to shorten.'

The Earl nodded his approval. There was no doubt that the boy was a Tyrrwhitt, just like his father, though one hoped without his father's tendency to lose.

'Brillig is down to even money,' said Natasha. 'Edgar got five to one.' The ideal brother-in-law, it seemed.

Brillig obliged by a length, which was close enough to make her clutch Walsh's arm in despair. From the look on his face Walsh should have been clutching hers.

What the devil's the matter with the feller? the Earl wondered. He's just won a packet. By God, if he's been playing fast and loose with my niece or daughter or whatever she is. But it wasn't that. He could see it wasn't. He still adored her, so how to explain the gloom? But young lovers were like that. Even he could still remember. Either *aux anges* or in the depths.

Thunder rumbled again, then the first rain began, and Cribb produced umbrellas as a conjurer might produce rabbits, and Wentworth's Rolls-Royce made its way across the grass to where Bonner could urge his wife into it as the soft, fat raindrops fell.

No ambulance, thought Natasha, but a Rolls-Royce is so much better – if they got to the nursing home in time.

'I was damn nearly right,' said the Earl. 'She nearly did slip her foal here.'

'Just as well she didn't,' said Walsh. The raindrops burst against his umbrella. 'We could do with some of this in Queensland.'

The Earl was looking at Wentworth. 'Better offer him a lift,' he said. 'First time in his life the poor chap's been deprived of his Rolls-Royce.'

'Do him good,' said Edgar.

'Teach him how the other half live,' said Walsh, but Wentworth's despair, thought Natasha, is nothing like so terrible as mine.

'The vicar's going to buy a dog,' said Greenhalgh. 'What with Mr Oliver off to Australia and Mr George off to Newcastle, he reckons a dog would be company. He's looking forward to it.'

'In Australia they have dogs called blue heelers,' said Natasha. 'I hope it isn't one of them. It would tear the priest to pieces.'

But she wasn't smiling. Greenhalgh held her dress, and Natasha stepped into it.

'I forgot to say thank you, miss,' Greenhalgh said. 'For Brillig. I made twenty quid.'

'You deserve much more,' said Natasha, but still no smile. Get on with it, Greenhalgh. You love her like a daughter.

'What's wrong, miss?' she said, and Natasha looked at her.

'Oh, Greenhalgh,' she said, and burst into tears, and Greenhalgh scooped her up and held her because there was no doubt in miss's mind that her world was ending.

At last, as the tears stopped streaming and the sobs grew quiet, Greenhalgh said, 'Where's your vodka, miss?'

Natasha told her and Greenhalgh poured, then found her cigarettes and lit one for her.

'I must look awful,' said Natasha.

'Not to me, miss,' said Greenhalgh. 'You just tell me.'

Natasha told her, and Greenhalgh listened, and when she had done there was no nonsense about guesswork and thinking the worst and how could you possibly know. Instead she said, 'You could be right, miss, but like you say, if you ask you're finished.'

'I know,' said Natasha.

'It wasn't as if he even knew you.'

'You are telling me I am a fool,' said Natasha, 'and you are right, but she is giving him a *baby*.'

'You mean she can and you can't – if you're right, that is.' Natasha winced. Darling Greenhalgh, you can hurt too, thought Natasha. 'But have you ever thought,' said Greenhalgh, 'that Mr Michael mightn't want that baby?'

'How could he not?'

'Mr Michael's a proper man,' said Greenhalgh, 'but he's a decent man, too. And from what you tell me, Captain Bonner's quite sure the baby's his. Now I'm not saying Mr Michael wouldn't say no to a bit of how's your father with Mrs Bonner, but that doesn't mean he'd want to make Captain Bonner a what'sit.'

'Cuckold,' said Natasha.

'I dare say, miss. And if you're right – and I'm not saying you're not – that could explain why Mr Michael's been so miserable, too.'

Natasha looked at this idea, turned it over in her hands. It was flawless. 'Greenhalgh, I adore you,' she said.

'That's as may be,' said Greenhalgh, 'but you'd better go and wash your face. Putting it right by dinner-time won't be easy.'

When she came back, Greenhalgh went to work at once. 'Would you like a bit of good news for a change?' she asked.

'Oh yes please.'

Back to being fifteen, Greenhalgh thought. Not that she ever had been fifteen. Twelve when she saw her mother shot in front of her, and from there on she'd joined the grown-ups.

'Me and His Lordship's been talking,' she said.

'You're not coming to Paris?' Natasha seemed ready to weep again.

'Of course we are,' said Greenhalgh. 'Don't be silly. We said we would, and anyway we want to come.'

Natasha remembered a phrase of George's. 'A bit of oo-la-la,' she said.

'The thing is this,' Greenhalgh went on, 'we fancy a bit of travelling, and so we thought, why not Australia? What do you say to that?'

310

'I cannot embrace you again,' said Natasha, 'but would you kiss me, please? Wherever the make-up will not spoil?'

In the drawing room Walsh helped himself to whisky, then looked at the siphon and decided against it.

'You're going it a bit tonight, aren't you?' said Edgar.

'A bit.'

Suddenly Edgar looked horrified. 'My God, you and Natasha haven't quarrelled?'

'No,' said Walsh, 'If we quarrel I'm finished.'

We may be half-brothers, Edgar thought, but it's too early to share that. You mean it. Walsh changed the subject. 'Did any of us Tyrrwhitts ever do a perish?' he asked.

'Disappear presumed dead, you mean?' Walsh nodded. 'Only Dad. And he only did a perish in England. Once he got to Australia he was fine. Michael, what is this?'

'Blowed if I know,' said Walsh. 'The only thing I do know is this is far too much whisky on top of Wentworth's champagne.' He put down his glass.

Over dinner Natasha was happy, and went out of her way to show it: flirting with the Earl, demanding details of Edgar's love-life, and all the time smiling at Walsh in a way that said: 'We're together. You know we are.'

She even left them to their port without a struggle. They would not leave her alone for long, and while she was, she would make a start on Chopin, the étude known as *Tristesse*. She found that she couldn't. It reeked of misery as a church reeks of incense. When it came to wallowing in it, she thought, the Poles can give the Russians a game any day, except that after her talk with Greenhalgh she did not want to be miserable. Couldn't, in fact. She turned to the *Valse Brillante* instead. Darling Greenhalgh. How could she exist without her? It was wonderful that she would not have to, especially if things went wrong . . .

The Earl finished talking of his plans, and Greenhalgh's. 'So it amounts to this,' he said. 'Daisy and I have decided to stay together, which means I'll be happy. And I hope to God so will she. We thought we might take a cruise. See the world.' He topped up his glass, and pushed the decanter to Edgar, then added: 'You chaps may think it a bit strange my telling you all this—'

'Honoured, sir,' said Edgar.

The Earl grunted. If I were Daisy I'd say that's as maybe, he thought, but instead he continued: 'The thing is, I know Daisy will tell Natasha. She's probably done so already if the way she was behaving at dinner's any sign, and if Natasha knows, so will Michael, and I've no doubt you will too.'

Walsh raised his glass. 'All the very best, sir,' he said.

Edgar raised his. 'Home on the pig's back,' he said.

'Not sure I follow you,' said the Earl.

'He's talking Australian,' said Walsh. 'I didn't think he could, after Charterhouse and Oxford.'

'He bats like an Australian,' said the Earl. 'You both do.'

Edgar was intrigued. 'How do Australians bat?'

'It's a combination of technique, hate, rage and bloody-mindedness,' Lord Kielder said. He smiled. 'Rather like a Yorkshireman, in fact. Thank God you've got it, the pair of you. If you hadn't that scourge of the bourgeoisie from Slagsby would have slaughtered us.'

'Edgar wants to take him to Queensland,' said Walsh.

'Best place for him,' said the Earl.

'Which reminds me,' said Edgar. 'I hope you and Mrs Greenhalgh will be visiting Australia on your travels?'

'Certainly,' said the Earl, and turned to Walsh. 'We'd rather like to stay with you for a while, if we shan't be in the way.'

'Long as you like,' said Walsh, and then it hit him. Natasha's fears, suspicions, worries, all so rigorously suppressed – the only one who could cope with them was Greenhalgh, and he roared out his relief. 'Oh you beauty,' he said. 'You bloody beauty.'

'I say, steady on Michael,' said the Earl.

'No, no, sir,' said Edgar. 'My brother's talking Australian, too. He's telling you what a wonderful chap you are. Rather excitable, my brother, as I'm sure you'll agree, but he's a bonzer feller.'

When he went to her room she wore nothing but a cigarette in a jade holder and a ring by Fabergé.

'You're late,' she said, but she was smiling.

'Brought you a present,' said Walsh; and handed her two sheets of writing paper. She stared at them, uncomprehending.

'Full face and profile, as you might say,' he said, and she gave a soft gurgle of delighted laughter.

'It's his bottom,' she said. 'It's George's bottom! But how—'

'It was at the cricket match,' said Walsh. 'Your idea, really, only it was more good luck than anything. See if he took a shower, you said. Well, he did.'

'And you didn't tell me?'

312

'Telling's no good,' said Walsh. 'What's needed was a diagram, but after the bashing I took from that parson it had to wait.'

'My English governess had a word,' said Natasha. 'Serendipity. It means—'

'Discovery by happy accident,' said Walsh. 'Bull's-eye.'

'Come to bed at once,' she said. 'You look far too relaxed.'

He came into bed and embraced her. 'I've been drinking all day,' he said. 'That's why I'm relaxed. Bloody fool.'

'Sometimes it is good to drink,' said Natasha. 'For a change. Touch me, please.' He touched her. 'We made a lot of money on Brillig, didn't we?'

'Five hundred quid. Edgar said all the bookies were crying. But that's not the best news. The Earl told us—'

'Greenhalgh,' she said. 'Australia. It's wonderful, *mon cher.*'

'Too right,' said Walsh. Still enjoying his touch, she looked again at the drawings.

'Like dimples,' she said. 'Enormous dimples. How big were they really?'

'Size of a carty, say,' said Walsh. 'Like a florin, the top pair, that is. The others were more like deeners. What the Poms call shillings.'

'How splendid for Maddy,' she said, and threw the drawings away, edging closer to him. 'Greenhalgh told me a story today,' she said. 'Would you like to hear it?'

He almost said, 'What, now?' That's how big a nong he was, but he caught himself in time. 'Yes, please,' he said.

'Only you mustn't interrupt,' said Natasha.

'Whatever you say.'

'Well,' said Natasha, 'once upon a time, years ago, Greenhalgh's husband knew a man who had an *affaire* with a married woman, and as a result she had a child ... I did not say you could stop.' The touching resumed. 'But before the child was born he met his true love, who could not give him a child, not because she didn't want one, but because God had decided she couldn't – and oh dear me, how sad and upset and worried Greenhalgh's husband's friend was. Isn't that a sad story?' We will know very soon, she thought. Only a Russian would risk her happiness on such an obvious lie, but all the same she had to know. If she could still make him want her—

'That depends,' said Walsh.

'Ah,' said Natasha. 'A little more *brio*, please.' His hand moved upwards, and she cried out very softly. 'Depends on what?'

'Whether his true love stayed with him or not,' said Walsh. Her hand reached out for him.

'Yes, yes,' said Natasha. 'She did, she did.'

313

'And whether the poor idiot realised that the past was over and the present was all that counted.'

'That too,' said Natasha. 'Oh yes,' and did something amusing. He responded splendidly.

So it would be all right, she thought, as she drew him to her. Whatever time they had together would be beautiful. According to the French doctor she had six more months: the English doctor had said that it could be years. It would be interesting to find out which one was right.